*Also by Jeff Gomez*

Our Noise

# Geniuses of Crack

## A NOVEL

## Jeff Gomez

SCRIBNER PAPERBACK FICTION
PUBLISHED BY SIMON & SCHUSTER

SCRIBNER PAPERBACK FICTION
Simon & Schuster Inc.
Rockefeller Center
1230 Avenue of the Americas
New York, NY 10020

Designed by Brooke Zimmer
Text set in New Caledonia
Manufactured in the United States of America

1   3   5   7   9   10   8   6   4   2

Library of Congress Cataloging-in-Publication Data

Gomez, Jeff
Geniuses of crack: a novel/Jeff Gomez
p.    cm.
I. Title.
PS3557.O456G46          1997
813'.54—dc21          97–17703
CIP

ISBN 0-684-83194-5

*For my father*

*There's a special kind of magic in California—black.*
—Mike Ryan

# Verse

**In the year 1993, Mark, Steve, and Gary were in a band.**
Being in a band in late-twentieth-century America was kind of like being in trouble—it seemed that *everyone* had been in it at one time or another. Friends of friends taught themselves some chords, learned how to sing (kind of), and jumped on stages in clubs that were managed by a friend of the original friend or a friend that knew the band in the first place. Guys dated girls who played guitar in a band, and when they went to see her play her first show, her old boyfriend, the one that played drums but now played bass, would inevitably be sitting at the bar knocking back beers with his own band, and the new boyfriends all hated it. Girls dated guys who were in bands with their old girlfriends, and even though the guys swore there were no remaining sparks, that it was all just because of the music, the new girlfriends all hated it.

Housemates practiced in the kitchen or garage twice a week; neighbors in cheap housing in university towns borrowed guitar strings and picks as if they were sugar and flour; little brothers asked big brothers to help them figure out barre chords for punk songs or else the mumbled lyrics to early R.E.M., back when R.E.M. meant something and the older brother still liked them, back when everyone *wasn't* in a band, like in the nineties.

Mark, Steve, and Gary's band was called Bottlecap, an innocuous and fitting name for late-twentieth-century America, when mundane monikers were not only accepted but expected.

They were from the small town of Kitty, Virginia. They had put out one album and a few singles on a local independent record label, which was actually just a friend with some cash, too much time on his hands, and a big living room floor good for the folding over and over of Xeroxed paper to pose as seven-inch sleeves. They toured the East Coast and some of the Midwest twice, were written up from time to time in the local zines. Then Bottlecap caught the attention of larger alternative newspapers, and then the nationally distributed and glossy pages of more-popular music magazines. College radio stations actually began to play their records and not just use them as coasters for whatever was the cheapest beer on sale that week. Beer always seemed to be on sale in college towns.

Kids began to show up at their shows, and Mark, the singer, was always amazed to see his words on the lips of the drunken youth in the crowd, chanting along the lyrics he'd scrawled on the back of a napkin and now was repeating a few months later at one in the morning, behind a barrage of Gary's bass playing and Steve's frenetic drum pounding: *"The people who think I'm shit are starting to outnumber those who don't . . ."* It was only when he heard someone else sing them that he realized how truly stupid his lyrics were.

Gary couldn't believe the way girls would talk to him before and after shows, introducing themselves and offering to buy him a drink and requesting perhaps a moment of his time later in the evening, alone. This was the main reason he got in a band in the first place, but after years of lugging his bass cabinet in and out of clubs, of the only conversation being sneers from the other bands or a grudgingly offered "You guys weren't as bad I thought you'd be," women now came up, wanting to meet him. And it was all because he played bass for Bottlecap.

Steve was just happy that people were showing up, happy to be able to take out aggression on his drum skins twice weekly during practices and every once in a while during a show. He figured it was cheaper than therapy.

Like everyone else in town, Steve had a brother who had also been in a band. His older sibling, Phil, formed some sort of group every year or so that would play a few shows, record some sort of a tape on a four-track, and then break up. Phil spent most of his time in between bands bitching about the members of his old band and looking forward to the members of his new one. In small towns like Kitty, there just wasn't much else to do.

But by the time Steve met Gary, who had already met Mark, the three of them knew they wanted more out of a band than to just waste time. In 1993, being in a band had suddenly become a career move.

Two years after forming Bottlecap, Mark, Steve, and Gary were flying out to Los Angeles in order to sign a lucrative contract and record their major-label debut. It would have seemed a heady sequence of events for participants in most generations, at most times in most centuries, whether they were heading off to apprentice with a master glassblower in Florence in the late seventeenth century or to study printing under Gutenberg himself in the mid-fifteenth, but remember that this was the last decade in the twentieth century in America, when kids might find $20 on the ground but then complain about having to bend over to pick it up.

**"*Fuck.*" Gary groans, bending over in his seat.**

Steve, sitting next to him, his face pressed up against the window and warmed a pleasantly barbecued pink, stirs out of sleep.

"Huh?" His arms rise out of the swaddling of baby blue covers tattooed with AMERICAN AIRLINES AMERICAN AIRLINES AMERICAN AIRLINES. "What?"

"There's a twenty-dollar bill"—Gary madly motions with his combination fork and spoon, which he is, as they are preparing to land, for some reason still holding on to—"right *there*. But I can't reach it."

Steve looks to his right and sees the skyline of Los Angeles beginning to come into view through the cottony clouds. Instead of the gridiron design of Virginian farmland—with only a road or two every mile separating the fields of bright green dotted with brown in the form of herds of cows or else mud— southern California is stacked full of life: cars, buildings, freeways, people crammed into every square inch. To Steve's left, Gary is still fiddling with some object at his feet, obviously out of reach.

"Where?"

"Down *there*," Gary says quietly, not wanting to wake up the man sitting in front of him, from whose wallet the bill had to have dropped. "But I can't *reach* it."

Steve leans over to examine the situation. Gary's crown of longish black hair is in his face, his bright red tongue clenched between the cold purple lips of his struggle, his pale skin raised with goose bumps.

"Just . . . can't . . . quite . . ."

Steve sighs, squirming in his seat, wondering how much longer it's going to be before they land.

"I'm going to go see what Mark's up to."

A little shorter than Gary's five feet eight, Steve easily slides through the space between Gary's probing legs and the back of the chair in front of him, easing his way into the aisle. Halfway down the plane, Mark is seated on the aisle, in the middle of three sections of the plane, next to an older couple. Although Steve was sitting twenty feet away and was wearing headphones half the time, he could still hear them fighting. Now they're going on about something else, an argument about who is going to pick them up at the airport.

Steve nudges Mark, who's cowering with his eyes closed, trying to pretend he's somewhere else, that he's already arrived.

"Hey, it's me."

Mark comes to life, revealing bloodshot eyes limned with dark circles and sagging pools of purple flesh, the result of the last couple of days spent in Kitty, of leaving his girlfriend and his hometown, doubting he'd ever return to either.

"What's up?" He wipes a tuft of sandy brown hair out of his face. Amber-colored gunk has gathered below the corners of his watering eyes, and he scoops it up with the tip of his finger and wipes it on the back of the tray tucked neatly in the full upright position in front of him.

"How are you doing?" Steve asks.

Mark looks at Steve, then glances at the couple next to him.

"Tired," he finally says.

Steve looks down the aisle to where Gary, now with his sneaker off, is poking a stained white sock, an inch and a half of cotton extending past the end of his toe, into the gap between the floor and the seat bottom, which doubles as a flotation device.

"Yeah, me too."

"We landing soon?"

"Take a right, check it out."

Mark looks past Steve to hopefully see land instead of sky, but the couple seated near the window who have been kissing the entire flight, makes him feel bad for leaving Laura the day before.

He and Laura had dated for four years, beginning in their junior year of high school. In a small town like Kitty, couples tended to stay together longer than they did in the bigger towns (or so the citizens of small towns had been led to believe) simply because the opportunity for change was usually too scarce to be exploited. Mark and Laura grew comfortable with each other over the years, and if her minor imperfections and his glaring ones didn't smooth away over time, they at least became easier to deal with, until finally each lover could just tune out the other's more annoying aspects, as if disagreeable moods were a program on television they could ignore until a better one came along. But when the band got the chance to come to Los Angeles, Mark shed every aspect of his former existence, including Laura.

Mark sees the city now getting closer by the second, signs becoming visible (mostly fast food restaurants, billboards, and strip malls) and cars and people rapidly rising to the realm of actual size.

"Cool."

"Yeah, cool."

A stewardess stumbles down the aisle and grabs Steve by the shoulder.

"Sir, we're landing, you *have* to get back to your seat."

"But I was—"

"Now!"

The NO SMOKING and FASTEN YOUR SEAT BELTS signs posted in the ceiling continue to flash on and off every few seconds, the way they've been doing for the past ten minutes.

"Alright, alright"—Steve begins to head back to his seat—"don't push."

Gary's still trying to get at the bill, which recedes farther and farther every time he pokes at it.

"So . . . fucking . . . close . . ."

Steve scoots by him and sits down, choosing to look out the window rather than at his struggling friend. The plane is now coming over the crest of a hill, behind which is Dodger Stadium, a sports arena surrounded by a crown of palm trees, the large black video screen dormant. It is October, but L.A. did not make the play-offs.

The plane whooshes over downtown Los Angeles on its way to the airport, a few more towns away on the coast. The gaggle of taller buildings sprouts out from the rest like mushrooms in short grass, a cluster of shimmering glass and shining metal among a field of trafficking commerce and big business. The morning sun hits the tallest one, the First Interstate Bank building, and the sun shoots out from it as if from the staff of Ra showing where to dig in the life-sized map of the city below, and Steve thinks of how bitchin' the pyramids must have looked whenever it was that they existed.

"Hey, hey, look, look." Gary quickly turns to Steve, barely able to contain his excitement.

"What?"

Gary cups the folded-in-half bill in his hand, his face beginning to blush.

Before turning back to the glimmering vista of the city below, Steve pets the currency in Gary's twitching fist and says, "You rule."

The bright California sun pierces Mark's face. In a fluid motion he reaches into one of his bags and dons his sunglasses like a cowboy draws his gun in a shoot-out. He looks back at the crowded terminal behind him, the electronic doors constantly swishing back and forth, swallowing people and throwing them up just as quickly. He runs a hand across his heated brow, rotates his shoulders in his warm flannel shirt, and thinks, *Why in the fuck did I wear this? I'm in goddamn California.* Looking around, he finally sees Gary and Steve, both of them struggling with their luggage.

Mark pats down his faded green-and-red plaid shirt for his

cigarettes. He smoked half the pack at the bar in Charlotte, sipping on watered-down drinks even though it was only noon, trying to use the liquor to douse the flames of his fears about the big trip, the deal, and the entire shape of his life, which seemed, at this very moment, to be in a sharp arc. He smells his fingers, licking with his nose for the last traces of nicotine that he tried to wash off in the airplane's bathroom as the captain repeatedly blinked the NO SMOKING sign. There was a large placard above the teensy stainless steel sink that reiterated the FAA laws and warned of the dire consequences of breaking them.

The airport is crowded, smoggy, crawling with traffic, deafening with the roar of jet engines above and cars all around, nothing like the small, one-terminal airport of the hometown he left only a day before.

"What now?" Gary whines, pulling up an overstuffed garment bag and straddling it like a mechanical bull.

"I guess we, I don't know, take a cab?" Steve replies, tugging a bag of cymbals that he refused to check into baggage. The circular lids of vinyl and leather straps look like a pizza warmer and kick up gum wrappers and receipts as they drag against the ground. "Mark, do *you* know where this place is?"

Mark sighs. They had been over this six times since they left Kitty the day before: twice on the flight to Charlotte, three times at Gary's friend's who lived in Mt. Holly, where they spent their last night in the South, and once more at the Fly By Night Cafe in the main terminal of the Charlotte airport, earlier in the morning. Like George explaining the rabbits yet again to Lenny, Mark digs in his heels and explains.

"All Henry said was to take the ten o'clock American Airlines flight into Los Angeles." Mark shrugs his shoulders. "He said he'd take it from there."

*You're doing the right thing,* Henry James reassured him over the phone when Mark agreed to fly out to California. *We're going to make you big stars.*

The words still echo in his head with the resonance of a timpani drum. Mark also can't help thinking, *Big losers. Big frauds.*

*Big disappointments.* All through the flight his knees kept knocking together like a set of clackers. He kept wondering if he'd made the right decision, if it was a wise choice to go ahead and sign with Subterfuge Records, a label he had never heard of. Should he have just stayed back in Kitty and taken that safe, reliable job his father had pulled strings for him to get? Even now, as he was wondering if they had done the right thing, he was also wondering if it was too late to escape.

Steve and Gary, on the other hand, had acted like children on the flight to California, throwing peanuts across the aisle, pinching the stewardesses' asses. "You're the leader, Mark," Steve said when they were first approached to sign to the label; "the decision is ultimately yours," although he and Gary were against it. Now that the agonizing part was over and Mark was trying to live with his decision, Steve and Gary were living it up. Bottlecap's rhythm section already had plans for their portions of the generous advance: back rent and taxes, a new car, pay off the old car, and so forth. Mark resented the fact that to them this was just the beginning of a great adventure. He kept worrying it all might be a big mistake.

"Will you get a load of that?" Steve jumps off the warm concrete sidewalk and points to a black limousine parked a few feet away. In front of the limo is a Hispanic driver, dressed in a uniform complete with black cap and shiny leather gloves. He's holding a sign that reads BOTLECAP.

"Can you believe that shit?" Gary yells.

"That's . . . us," Mark slowly says, carefully looking over the crudely written cardboard message, "even though it's misspelled."

Steve heaves his cymbal bag over his shoulder and brushes past Mark on the way to the limousine.

"Cheer up," he says, "it could have read 'Bottle*crap*.'"

Steve and Gary push each other out of the way to be the first inside the limo, while Mark sighs and begins gathering up the pieces of luggage that they have left behind. The driver intervenes as Mark's trying to get the trunk open to put in his bag.

"No, sir, please, allow me." He wrestles the luggage out of Mark's hand.

"That's okay, I don't want you to have to do it . . ."

"Please, sir." He finally peels the black bag out of Mark's grip. "It's my job."

Mark relents and joins his friends in the limo, where Steve's already on the car phone.

"Yeah, could you please give me Teri Hatcher's home phone number?"

Gary's rummaging through the tiny refrigerator set into the interior. "Look at this shit!"

"What do you mean, it's unlisted?" Steve slams down the phone.

"What?"

"All they stocked in this thing is soda pop. Where's the hundred-dollar bottle of champagne? And where's the hot blond who's supposed to give us a blow job while we snort cocaine off her tits, like in *Wall Street*?"

"Yeah!"

Gary and Steve's hands meet for a high five.

"Did Charlie Sheen snort the cocaine off her tits?" Steve asks a few seconds later.

"In real life, probably," Gary says.

"Will you guys please stop it?" Mark explodes. "You're both acting like a couple of three-year-olds! I mean, what are we, the goddamned Replacements? Now calm down before you blow this whole deal!"

"Well, excuse me," Gary says snidely, slamming shut the refrigerator door.

"Yeah, sorry. We didn't know we were such an embarrassment to you."

The car sinks every few seconds as the trunk fills with their luggage.

"You're not, really. It's just, I guess I'm just really nervous about all this. It's making me edgy. The money, the expectations. I'm sorry. I'll try and loosen up." Mark leans back into the plush seat. "This *is* pretty nice."

"You fucking bet it is. So relax and enjoy it." Steve puts his feet on the portable television. "We've earned it, baby."

"Well." Mark laughs. "I wouldn't say *that*. I mean, the worst thing that's happened to us is we all bounced a few checks. Your dad bought you your drums"—he points to Steve—"and don't think I don't know about your 'allowance.'" He points to Gary, who swiftly takes his feet off the television.

The driver slams the trunk shut and slips in behind the wheel. He fires up the engine and slowly pulls away from the curb, carefully negotiating the tide of cars.

The area outside the airport is made up of mostly expensive hotels and strip joints. The Sheraton Inn next to the Seventh Veil. Right beside a Carl's Jr. burger place is a club with a huge purple-and-yellow sign that reads ALL NUDE NUDE NUDE 24 HOURS A DAY! The limo climbs onto the 405 Freeway, heading north toward Hollywood.

Feeling paranoid, Mark taps on the glass separating the large backseat from the driver's compartment. A tinted window between the front and back seats suddenly descends with a buzz.

"Uh, where are you taking us?"

"The Mondrian Hotel," the driver blankly says.

"Hey, do you know if that hotel has a pool, because I was thinking of—"

"All I know," the driver's voice booms, "is that I'm supposed to take you to the Mondrian Hotel."

There's a moment of silence as the driver eases his way onto Interstate 10, the off ramp veering to the right, downtown now straight ahead, the Hollywood sign to the left, barely visible through the thick haze of smog.

"Hey." Steve props his arm on the partition. "I read in a book that people are afraid to merge on the freeways in Los Angeles. Is that true?"

By way of an answer the dark window slowly inches its way back up.

The limo exits at Robertson, lazily cruising down the off ramp as the drivers in small cars like early-model Hondas and Toyotas try to peer through the tinted glass to see who's inside, while those driving Mercedeses and BMWs are either on cellular phone or too bored to care. Steve and Gary crane their heads out of the windows, sipping from imaginary champagne flutes, joking, elbowing each other, spilling phantom streams of Dom Pérignon on the intersection of Robertson and Venice.

The limo begins climbing steeply, pausing at Sunset Boulevard before turning right. After a few more blocks, the glass window separating the front seat and backseat descends again as the driver turns right into a short, circular driveway.

"The Mondrian Hotel," he says plainly.

Gary, Steve, and Mark get out of the car and stand awkwardly at the curb.

"You're registered in suites five-oh-six, and five-oh-seven." The driver yawns. "I'll see that your luggage is brought up immediately."

Gary says in a Thurston Howell voice, his back teeth clenched and his jaw straight and stiff as a coat hanger: "See that you do."

Mark moves to the rear of the limo and again tries to help with the luggage and is again batted away by the driver. Mark pats down his pockets for some cash for a tip but then remembers his wallet is in a duffel bag he noticed was tossed first into the trunk with everything else on top.

"Oh, I know this place," Steve says, walking toward the entrance, squinting as he glances at the profile of the tall, multicolored building shining in the sun.

"Maybe you saw it in a museum," Gary sarcastically says, tapping the limo driver on the shoulder and taking from him his black bass case covered in stickers.

He turns to Gary but can't see his face, just an array of bright colors, purple, red, orange, his pupils shrunken. "Ah, I'm blind."

"That's what you get for staring at the sun." Mark laughs, taking his eyes off the bellhop currently mangling his guitar case and a backpack filled with books and magazines.

"How should I know? I'm from Virginia. We don't have this

kind of sun there," Steve whines, pointing to the sky. "These rays are like fallout, like Chernobyl."

"You've got to get a pair of these . . ." Mark waves his recovered sunglasses in front of Steve's still-dazed and confused face.

"What are you talking about? This is Los Angeles . . . I thought they'd issue them to me upon arrival, for my own protection."

"Will you two come on?" Gary calls out, standing underneath the awning that leads into the lobby. "Let's go check out our rooms!"

As Gary and Steve scramble up the driveway, being honked at by a yellow cab as it pulls away from the curb, Mark repeats a line of Steve's from a few seconds before.

"How should I know? I'm from Virginia," he mumbles, following after his band mates. "I have a feeling you're going to be saying that a lot."

Steve keeps jumping on the bed, the same way he did when he first switched from crib to mattress at the age of two, while Gary raids the minibar.

"Whoa, check out this fridge!" Gary yells from across the room, at the open door of a small refrigerator the size designed for college dorm rooms. Inside are various cans of soda, liquor, and snacks like candy bars and packets of nuts.

"Awesome," Steve shouts as he crosses the room and pulls out a mini bottle of vodka.

Before Mark can slap it out of his hand, Steve has already twisted the cap and swallowed half of the contents.

"What are you doing?"

"No, Mark, what are *you* doing?"

"Yeah!" Gary backs Steve up.

"Come on, guys, take it easy." He points to the fridge. "You think this stuff is going to be free?"

"Aw, it's just a little bottle," Steve protests, "it can't cost *that* much."

Mark picks up the small glass vial from the floor and shoves the bottle with the large blue block lettering into the faces of Gary and Steve.

"This is Absolut, not Winn Dixie brand. I bet even a *small* bottle like this costs five bucks. Or at least that's what this fancy-shmancy hotel is going to charge us." Mark moves closer and pokes at their pockets with the still-wet rim of the bottle, leaving alcoholic circles on Steve's faded jeans and Gary's khaki chinos. "You got five bucks? How about you?"

"Hey, look." Gary slaps at Mark's hand, sending the bottle to the ground for the second time. "I don't have five bucks *now*. But check with me tomorrow after you meet with Henry. You heard the voice mail he left us. 'Mark, stop by the office tomorrow for a chat,'" Gary recites from the message that had been waiting for them at the Mondrian. "'Make sure to enjoy your stay.' You see? Even *he* wants us to have a good time." Gary hops onto one of the beds and leans back, wiping some gum from the sole of his beat-up sneakers, then places them on the expensive Mikata bedspread. "We'll be on easy street."

Mark shakes his head, unbelieving, while Steve moves toward Gary in a show of solidarity.

"I agree with Gary, Mark." He sits down, sinking into the soft mattress. "You're being *way* too uptight about this."

"Yeah, man," Gary continues to double-time Mark and his worries. "First of all, you were a total wreck all last night *and* this morning. You talked for years about how you couldn't wait to get out of our bogusly small hometown, and then, as soon as you do, you're homesick for it."

Mark flinches.

"I'm not homesick for it. It's just . . . I didn't like lying to Laura that way, saying we were leaving yesterday when we were actually spending the night with your friends in North Carolina."

"Oh, *I* see. You can lie to her about screwing some chick on tour a few months ago, but heaven for*bid* you fib about your itinerary."

Mark stares into the floor as Gary and Steve high-five each other.

"But, you guys"—Mark sinks into a soft black leather chair next to the minibar—"we can't get carried away with this."

Steve, who isn't listening, grabs the laminated room-service menu from a drawer.

"'Carried away'?" Gary says as Steve orders up a lobster dinner in the background. "Who's getting carried away?"

In the morning, Mark climbs into a rental car he finds waiting for him in the driveway, a burgundy Plymouth Acclaim, trying to remember the directions the concierge gave him the day before when Mark gave him the address Henry James had left on the hotel's voice mail.

Once on the road the car feels like it's gliding on a cloud. Power steering and brakes, automatic transmission, air conditioning blowing in his face like a storm, the radio blaring. Mark feels that if he takes his hands off the wheel the car will steer by itself and neatly deliver him to his destination.

Sunset Boulevard winds first past tattoo parlors and strip joints, then a succession of swank-looking eateries with names like the Roxbury Cafe and Chin Chin. A little farther down are a few strip malls replete with the coolest two-storey McDonald's Mark has even seen and a Rafallo's Pizza. After a few more blocks the restaurants get nicer, then worse, then better again, the street more like a stock price than a road, constantly changing, up and down.

"Ooh, there's Tower Records," Mark says out loud, as if this will prevent him from getting lost. "The guy mentioned that, I think." The record store is a one-storey yellow-and-red bunker, stretching back from the street as guys in yellow windbreakers direct traffic in the parking lot. Mark tries to spot the addresses on the businesses around him, but he can't get a clear view from the cars passing on either side of him.

The road takes a deep dive and curves to the left, and by the number of amazingly huge houses with neatly manicured lawns it's obvious to Mark that he's now in Beverly Hills. Palm trees line the road like towering streetlights, fronds dancing in the midday breeze. There are wide sidewalks and a grass-covered island that separates the two lanes of traffic.

"Wait a second. I think I've gone too far."

He turns into a side street and makes a left, heading back up Sunset. Coming east to west he sees the number 9750 in large black letters on the side of a white-and-blue building. A golden placard above the address reads *Pacific Media Arts International,* and underneath this, *A Division of the Kobiyashi Entertainment Group.* Mark cruises through a yellow light and parks on the street, slipping into a space left vacant by a white BMW, which speedily pulls away from the curb.

"May I help you, sir?" a receptionist sitting behind the front desk asks him as soon as he enters the air-conditioned lobby. With his faded red T-shirt and jeans, Mark doesn't look like your average guest.

"I'm here for a meeting?"

"Sir?" The woman replies, lifting up the phone and about to call security.

"Uh, Henry James?" Mark says, unsure of it all himself. "My name's Mark, uh, Pellion."

"Oh, yes," she says, relieved. She dials. "Have a seat."

Mark sits down in the bustling lobby as the receptionist answers the phone and receives messengers and food deliveries from the Thai restaurant around the corner. Sometimes she is signing with one hand and operating the large switchboard with the other. Mark is duly impressed.

From the half dozen people wandering in and out of the lobby, a lanky man approaches. He seems about Mark's age.

"Are you Pellion? From Bottlecap?"

Mark looks up from the issue of *Billboard* he's glancing at. At first he thinks the man talking to him is from the Thai place, wondering where to drop off the food, eager for a tip.

"Uh, yeah, but I don't—"

"Don't what? You're here for Henry, right?"

"Oh, yeah."

"I'm Hanes, let's go."

He hastily gets up as the man, who he can now see has shabbily arranged blond hair and sagging jeans over which hangs a long black sweatshirt, is already halfway down the hall before Mark can catch up.

"Uh, are *you* also in A&R?" Mark asks, trying to make polite conversation and forcing his voice forward as Hanes leads him through the labyrinthine hallways.

Hanes barely slackens his pace as he looks back, points to a spot on his sweatshirt where his breakfast burrito from that morning has dried and crusted, and says, "I'm not exactly executive material . . . Not yet, at least. I work in the mail room but I help out from time to time as needed." As he expertly takes a corner, making sure to show off the employee lounge with its three vending machines and patio, his reddened eyes focus on Mark's own bloodshot ones. "But don't you worry about *me*. I've got a few tricks up my sleeve."

After a few more twists and turns, Mark is led into a large open room with cubicles sectioned off into work spaces in the center, while offices line the perimeter, glass windows with mini blinds looking into the center section, and tinted windows looking over the traffic currently jammed on Sunset Boulevard.

"Here you are," Hanes says before clearing out a black plastic scoop marked HENRY JAMES, tucking the bundle of mail under his arm, and heading back the way they came. Mark absent-mindedly pulls a five out of his pocket and turns to hand it to the man, but he's already gone.

As Mark watches Hanes fold into the traffic of the office, he sees Henry approach. The A&R man walks quickly down the hallway, followed by a number of subordinates, each trying to get his opinion on something. Signature on a check, approval on artwork, and so forth. Henry nonchalantly gives his okay with a nod, dashes off his signature with a flick of the wrist, indicates that a question bores him by rolling his eyes. It will have to wait until later. He is so much more in his element than when they had met a few weeks ago back in Virginia that Mark barely recognizes him. Confidence has changed his face the way that fatigue had lowered it before.

Bottlecap had just finished coming off a disastrous four-month tour that was only supposed to last two months but that doubled in length only as their misfortunes seemed to quadruple. Clubs canceled at the last minute, other clubs that had been scheduled months in advance suddenly hadn't heard of them. The van broke down, then their gear fucked up. Money once literally flew out the window after a vandal had shattered the passenger-side window and Steve had put the dinner money on the dashboard, only to watch as the wind carried it into the night. It was only through the gracious hospitality of a small number of fans who gave their cold floors and warm food to Mark, Steve, and Gary that Bottlecap managed to survive. The trip proved to the trio that they wanted more out of their musical careers than survival. So when Henry James, a scout for Subterfuge Records, showed up a few days later and began offering large amounts of cash, promises of recording a record in a professional studio, releasing a CD with national distribution, and producing a video, the boys jumped at the chance. Or rather, Mark had jumped while the other two looked the other way, complaining about all the jumping going on just so they could bitch about it later. It would have all seemed to be happening too fast for Mark if he hadn't already been waiting for years.

Henry stood a few inches under six feet tall. It was hard to tell for sure exactly how many under because most of his shoes seemed to have large blocklike heels to remedy however short he was. His hair was brown-blond, cut short and sitting in awkward layers around his head, as if he were growing out a Caesar haircut. His eyes were deep blue and penetrating, looking like the glow of two rockets that propelled the streamlined spaceship of his face. He seemed too good-looking to be just a record executive, a fact that seemed to occur to Henry as often as to those around him.

Back in Kitty, Steve had called him "the math teacher" simply because he was wearing a blazer in a small club in Virginia at the tail end of the summer, where any male wearing a shirt with buttons would have been considered overdressed. Henry had

indeed looked stiff that night, something—the A&R man con-
fessed to Mark later, over dinner—that was due to the fact that
he had been on the road for nearly as long as they had; he had
been crisscrossing the country looking for a new band to sign to
the label.

"You, Mark, are it," he said as he leaned across the table of
the Chinese restaurant, a small dragon carved out of wood the
only thing between them. They had grown that close. "Bottlecap
is *the* band."

Mark had heard that A&R men were always these young, hip
guys whose come-on to eager bands was that they were *one of
them,* regular dudes, when they were really slick company types,
wolves in sheep's clothing. But Henry looked as if he'd be
uncomfortable in any clothing other than his own, which he had
specially made for him by a tailor in Brentwood. This made
Mark feel that even if he was being somehow cheated, at least
he wasn't being tricked.

"Any trouble finding it?" Henry James asks as he scoots by
Mark and into his office. Mark follows.

"Yeah, actually."

"Good, good. Come in."

On the wall are posters for bands Mark has never heard of
but who must be some of Henry James's other discoveries. A
sepia-tinged photo of four guys dressed in vaguely cowboy
getups says RANK AND FILE above their Stetsoned heads.
Each band member looks off into the far distance, past the eye
of the camera, as if stoned.

"They're playing at the Palomino tonight," Henry says as he
steps behind his desk, clearing away a pile of promotional CDs,
faxes, and interoffice correspondence as he does so. "Say the
word and I'll put you on the guest list."

Another poster is of four girls, one posing with a stand-up
bass, the others sitting in old elementary-school-style desks.
Three of them are pretty, while the singer is heavyset, butch.
Below the quartet the word WHISTLEBAIT is spelled out in a
thick font.

"How are they doing?"

"Actually, we just dropped them. The only reason they ever got signed in the first place is because of their parents. Rich types. Knew lots of people. Warhol, stuff like that. 'Course, now he's dead." Henry pulls a tack out of the lower left corner of the poster, the lip curling up instantly, as if it hadn't been up for long. "Never liked them anyway."

"Henry," Mark says lightly, "how come the sign in the lobby and outside the building said 'Pacific Media Arts International' and not 'Subterfuge'?"

"Subterfuge is actually a newly created subsidiary of our parent company, Pacific Media. Pacific deals mostly in old catalog material, a few pop groups, 'best of' collections from artists you've probably never heard of, and sound tracks for films which never make it into theaters. We were bought last year by a Japanese concern"—Henry coughs into his hands—"and as part of that, uh, expansion, we're creating new divisions, trying to cross over into that alternative market."

Mark bristles at the word *alternative*.

"Let's just say that our new bosses discovered that there's an awful lot of kids out there with fifteen bucks just eating a hole in their worn-out Levi's."

Mark self-consciously looks down to his own worn-out Levi's.

"So, how are you liking the Mondrian?"

"Fine, fine. Steve and Gary are having the time of their lives. Which reminds me, shouldn't I have brought them?"

Henry makes a *phffft* sound.

"Mark, like I said in my message. This little meeting is just to get further acquainted. As an A&R man I don't have the jurisdiction to draw up a contract. That has to be done by a lawyer."

"Are you saying I need a lawyer?"

"Nah." Henry waves the comment aside. "We've got a firm we're really friendly with and we'll let them sort out all the little details. In the meantime I *do* need to get your John Hancock on this little baby."

Henry James pulls out of a manila folder a legal-sized piece of paper covered front and back with small writing.

"What's this?"

"This is a letter of intent, or deal memo, as it's sometimes called. It's no big deal, it just says that Bottlecap will sign with Subterfuge Records, a division of Pacific Media Arts, once the contracts are drawn up."

"But this isn't the actual contract?" Mark scans the preprinted form where Henry has written in a few dollar amounts and percentages, the numbers they had agreed on when he visited Mark in Virginia the week before. He signs it quickly.

"No, not at all. Like I said, this is just a little informal thing that the boys upstairs like to have in their filing cabinets. After all, we flew you out here, right? We're putting you up at the Mondrian, right? Say, how do you like that place?"

"You just asked me that."

"And what'd you say?"

"I said it was fine."

"Anyway, don't get used to it. The Mondrian, that is. We'll be moving you out after the weekend. Subterfuge has a house in Hollywood, right near the studio, where we put up acts during the recording. I'll have Hanes give you the directions." Henry makes some notes on a legal pad and Mark notices he's right-handed and not a lefty, like he is. This makes him jumpy, and he's tempted to think the deal, this trip, his future is already doomed. "After that you guys'll head to the studio and meet Kenneth Kelly. He'll be producing the record, and when you meet him he'll show you around and lay down the schedule for the recording."

Mark's making so many mental notes he's running out of space even though they always said the large map of the brain would go forever untapped. Everyone's except Mark's, which is currently busting at the seams.

*Kenneth What? Studio, schedule? What day is this?*

"Oh, uh, okay."

"Good. Now, do you have any questions?"

"Yeah." He tries to cover his malnourished white, saggy flesh showing through a rip in his jeans. "When will we get that, uh, money? You know, the guys were asking."

Henry leans back. *The same old questions.*

"Well, we'll have to process some paperwork first. But it shouldn't be too long. A few weeks, tops. I'll have Hanes deliver the checks as soon as they arrive." Henry looks to a Post-it note sitting beside a legal pad on which he's scribbled a few topics he wanted to cover for Mark's initial meeting. MONDRIAN. ADVANCE. NO SINGLE. Like an actor trying not to be seen reading cue cards, he says, "Oh, I listened to your tape . . . and I have a few reservations."

Mark can see, to the side of the pile of paperwork that Henry kept referring to, the tape he'd just mentioned. It was something Bottlecap had recorded before heading out on their last tour. It was all of the songs they'd written during the past year, all of the songs they intended to put on the record they were going to record for their friend's label once they got back on their feet after the hellish trip. Now that fortunes had changed considerably, Mark's mind had not. Those eleven songs were still the only ones he wanted on his major-label debut.

"Reservations?"

"Thoughts, really. I mean, I like this stuff, I like it a lot." He laughs. "I wouldn't be signing you if I didn't, right? But the problem is . . . I don't . . . well . . ."

"Well, what?"

"I just don't hear a single. Nothing is sticking out as being commercially viable, not immediately at least. A single song isn't rising to the surface. I'm speaking tunewise, of course."

"I always thought 'Parisian Broke' was a strong song, or else 'I Like This Frown.' The crowds always seem to react strongly to that one."

"No, no. One's too slow and the other's too long." Henry James leans across the table and touches Mark's elbow with the exposed tip of a ballpoint pen, leaving a star-in-the-sky dot of black on his soft white expanse of skin. "I know all about the old jokes like 'A&R stands for "Arguments and Recriminations,"' but that's not the way I want it to be. I'm on *your* side. But, we have *got* to get you heard on the radio. And that means a hit single, and a hit single is the engine that pulls the train. Of course, sometimes running a song up the charts is like pissing in the wind . . . it feels great but it doesn't accomplish much. However, you guys have got to get some exposure. And I don't know how else to do it."

Mark just sits there. He cannot think of anything to say.

"Look, I've got a meeting to get to. I hate to cut this short, but promise me you'll consider what I've said?"

Mark excuses himself from the table, his stomach queasy. He stumbles through the maze of offices before finding himself again in the lobby.

"Good luck," an attractive, auburn-haired receptionist, different than the hour before, calls out to Mark as he slides into the already moving revolving doors.

"Yeah," he calls back, only half interested, "whatever."

He notices there's a parking ticket tucked underneath one of the windshield wipers of the rental car, rolls his shoulders, and takes it from underneath the long, black eyelash of plastic, rips it into quarters. He passes back by the Roxy and the Whiskey Au Go Go. He semireads the names on both marquees, doesn't recognize any of the bands, then tries to imagine Bottlecap sandwiched in with the others but just can't. He searches for a decent radio station on the stereo but gives up after hearing the same Whitney Houston song on no less than three different stations at the same time. Some crap about how she'll always love you.

A valet rushes out to park the car just as he pulls into the driveway of the Mondrian. He rides up the elevator in a sort of trance.

"So?" Gary rushes him at the door. "Is it official?"

"Yeah, I guess so." Mark stumbles into the room. "What's that smell?"

"Oh, we ordered room service," Gary says casually, as if a week ago he wasn't trying to total grocery prices in his head so he wouldn't be stuck at the checkout line without enough money to pay and have to put things back, which was what happened every time anyway.

"Again?"

"Yeah. So, what? Is it official?"

"Like I told Tweedledee a second ago, yes." Mark plops down on the bed. He looks over to the table, which is filled with trays with two plates, each with a round bone and strips of fat, the shell of a baked potato, and two salad bowls, both empty except for three cherry tomatoes in one and half a dozen carrot slices in the other. Lying next to the empty plates are eight beer bottles. Heineken. "Geez, guys, no filet mignon? I'm sorry you had to settle for rib eye. Will you *ever* forgive me? And imported beer is the *most* expensive thing they had? Couldn't they find some German guy to come up here and brew it for you fresh? I hate the idea of you two having to drink it out of the bottles. It's so . . . so . . . Philistine."

"Okay, okay," Gary admits, "we went a little overboard. But who cares? You said so yourself, the record company's picking up the tab for all of this. Why not live it up a little?"

"A little?" Mark asks, watching as Gary drains four drops from every beer bottle in order to get one good sip and Steve soaks up the last of the steak sauce with the rump of a sourdough roll.

"What's with you, man?" Steve asks with his mouth full, using all of his saliva to soften the crusty bread.

"Yeah," Gary adds. "Why aren't you enjoying any of this?"

"Why is everyone, you guys included, acting like we just won the lottery? That some anonymous guy in a bad tuxedo just gave us a million dollars and doesn't expect anything in return? That's not the way it is." He kicks at the expensive carpet that lies under him. "Don't you guys see that? You know, when I was leaving the offices, the receptionist called out, 'Good luck,' in this ominous tone, as if they were keeping all the bands who *didn't* have good luck in the basement or something. It's like, this company doesn't want to be our friend. We're just a cash source to them."

Gary walks over to Mark, begins patting him on the back. "Talk about solipsism! I've heard of people thinking they were the center of the universe, but you're like some fucking black hole that's trying to suck everything else down with it."

"All I'm saying," Mark says calmly, "is that we're going to have to *earn* this money."

"And we will," Gary returns, as if swatting back a tennis ball.

"But what if we don't?"

Gary stares blankly into Mark's long, drawn-out exclamation point of a face.

"This is what we've been waiting for," Steve says, sitting down cross-legged on his own bed. "Why are we all fighting about it?"

"But that's just it." Mark gets up. "It's *not* what we've been waiting for. We didn't call this guy and tell him to come see us. We didn't record a demo tape and then shop it all over the country. We just wanted to make music, and none of *this*"—he casts a disdainful glance around the room—"was a part of it. Until now."

"You're saying you don't like *this*?"

"Maybe I do," Mark says, adding softly, "maybe that's what scares me."

"Don't be scared of success. Embrace it. Fuck, man, we're going to have this town by the balls. Hell"—he motions toward the window overlooking the entire city—"we *already* do."

"But that's just it. We *don't*. Driving home I saw so many people just crowded onto the streets and so many clubs with so many bands inside, and man, that's happening all over the country. And I just wonder if we'll make it, because if not . . ."

"If not, what?" Steve ominously asks.

"Well," Mark says, "could you go back to your shit job for five bucks an hour after staying in a place like this and eating stuff like that?" He points at the trays of food that, even empty, smell delicious. "Can you imagine even going back to Kitty? I can't."

"You're being a defeatist, Mark. So many bands never reach this stage, never even get *this* far, and you're just sitting there knocking it, being Mr. Minus."

"Negative," Steve says, "you mean Mr. Negative."

"Yeah," Gary continues, "Negative. I just think you're purposely looking on the bad side just because you're afraid of the good."

"No, it's not . . . it's just, I don't know. I was in the office with James and I signed that piece of paper and, man, it was just *so* anticlimactic. Like I'd been thinking about it for so long that once it finally arrived it was no big deal. Maybe that's what's really scaring me, not the fact that we'll just be some one-hit wonder, if we're that lucky, but just that I'm not really feeling anything. To be honest, I'm not even really scared. I'm really just not *any*thing."

"Jesus, man, nothing's going to make you happy. First you get a great chick like Laura and then you dump her. Now you get this major chance that most people would kill their mothers for, and you're just sitting there like it's just another day."

Mark swivels in the chair and turns to the window, looking out onto the city that was a stranger not more than twenty-four hours ago but already feels like a monkey on his back. In the background he can hear one of the guys slap the other and say, "Can you believe this guy?" Mark can't believe it, either.

"Okay, okay," he says. "I'll try and enjoy all this."

"Good," Steve says, sighing, "because I'd hate to have to go back to Kitty now, looking like losers. Especially after I . . ." His words quickly fade.

Mark, still consumed in his own thoughts, takes a second to react.

"Especially after you what?"

Gary, an ally only moments before, retreats to the opposite side of the room, sits on the bed, and absentmindedly plays with the address tag on the handle of his suitcase.

Steve remains silent.

"Come on, Mr. Drummer, not after *what*?"

"Well," he backs into a wall, "not after I told everyone. You know, where we were going and all."

"Jesus!" Mark explodes. "You told *every*one? Hopefully by 'everyone' you mean your very small and uninfluential circle of miscreant friends from the comic book shop and *not* idiotic loudmouths like Jim, Stoner, and Dave."

"Well, sort of. You see, I didn't tell Dave, since you insisted. But yeah, I told Stoner and Jim."

"Why?" Mark's voice rises. "Why?"

"Because I was proud, okay? Because I was excited. Aren't you?"

"No, frankly, I'm not." Mark, beginning to feel shaky again, crosses the room and sits in the black leather chair. "I'm fucking scared shitless."

Gary leans forward. "But why? This is what you've always wanted."

"I know, I know," Mark says quickly, as if trying to convince himself. "It's just . . . the fuckup potential is growing so large now. I mean, Henry's already talking to some U.K. labels for a licensing deal, trying to get us a slot on some big tour as opening act and maybe a second stage gig on Lollapalooza this summer . . . I don't know. It's all going too fast. It's out of control and we haven't even started making the album."

"Hey, do you guys know something?" Steve asks. "This just occurred to me last night, just as I was falling to sleep. I can't remember my boss's last name. Isn't that great? Jack . . . Jack . . . Jack . . ." He keeps snapping his fingers but the name won't come. "Since we were out on tour and came out here, my mind's a complete blank. And I like it that way. Well, you know what I mean. I just feel like we've left those shackles behind us, cast them off forever. Why go back to them? Why even consider it?"

There's silence for a few seconds as Steve's words soak in.

"Decker," Gary says, repeating, "Decker. Jack Decker."

"But, guys, look," Mark says, breaking his stare on the second hand of a clock on the wall that keeps going around and around. "We're talking failure on a global scale now. Do you comprehend what I'm talking about? Imagine walking down a sidewalk in Kitty and tripping on a crack and falling head over heels. Well, no harm done, right? Worst thing that happens is a few kids playing street hockey or an old lady mowing her lawn will see, and maybe she'll invite you inside for a glass of milk and poppy-seed cake and you'll actually come out of it all ahead. But now imagine tripping and falling and having the entire world watch, having your tumble beamed all over the world, live, via satellite. Even the astronauts orbiting the earth at who knows how many miles per hour will see. Can you even *fathom* that?"

Steve turns to Gary.

"What's poppy-seed cake?"

"You guys! Listen to me." Mark lets out a heavy sigh. "They're making up the contracts right now, as we speak. Once we sign them there's no backing out. You sure this is what you want?"

"I'm sure," Gary says.

"I'm sure," Steve agrees.

"We're both sure," Gary says again.

"Okay, then." Mark throws up the words. He sees his bass player cross the room and approach him.

"Come on, man, don't be depressed." Mark feels Gary's hand massaging his shoulder. "We just ordered more food!"

**One day, in practice, when Bottlecap had been together**
almost three months, Gary looked at Mark, then to Steve, then
to the floor, where their incubatory set list was held down with
about an inch and a half of silver duct tape. Mark thought something was wrong, that something had thrown Gary off, or he
wanted to stop the song and start over. Gary kept looking
around but kept playing, so Mark and Steve did too. After the
song was over Mark asked him what had been the problem.

"Nothing," Gary said in a combination of shrugging it off and
pouting.

"What do you mean, 'nothing'? Then how come you look all
pissed off?"

"It's just . . ."

"What?"

"The set list."

"What about it?" Steve asked.

"It's just . . . I'm sick of doing the same seven songs in the
same order. *Every* time we practice," Gary said, leaning up
against his rig.

Mark looked over at Steve.

"Yeah, I am too, sort of." Steve leaned forward on his drums,
an elbow on each tom-tom and his face cradled in his hands.

Mark stared back at them.

"Jesus, guys, all we *have* is seven songs. I mean, come on,
we're a new band. We don't have fifteen years of material to fall

back on, okay? And it's not just that . . . we've got a good order for our songs." He tried to stare both of them down. "And it works."

But Mark's staring them down did not.

"It's like," he tried to explain further, "you've only got a few pieces of furniture in a room. No matter how you rearrange it, it's still going to be the same old pieces of furniture."

"Yeah, but even a little bit of rearranging is a change," Gary said, putting down his bass, signaling that the practice was over even though they still had a nonrefundable prepaid half hour to go. This was a week before they would get their little practice shed in the woods, where they could play whenever they wanted to, for as long as they wanted to, even though various girlfriends and the six-packs of beer either Steve or Gary would bring usually kept a practice to about two and a half hours.

Mark watched as Steve followed suit, tearing down his drums, looking sort of pissed off as well. With his toe Mark kicked out the three-inch cables connecting his various pedals, beginning to see their point. *Even a little switching of the order would bring some variety to the practice sessions, and maybe we could even switch off picking the order. One day Steve could pick it, the next day Gary, and then me. It'll make us feel like equal members, even though I'm the one who got us all together, wrote the songs, and picked out the name.* But Mark didn't want to tell them any of this. He wanted to stick to his guns. His plan was for Bottlecap to become machine-gun tight even if it meant boring the other two, even alienating them to an extent. He knew they wouldn't flat out quit, because they'd already come too far, were just a few weeks from playing their first show. All of them had played with various bands in town long enough to know that the rapport they'd developed was not only distinct but rare. So they did what Mark said, and it was just another brick in the foundation of Mark becoming leader of the band, a direction he was consciously steering himself toward anyway.

"So, uh, how long should it take?"

Mark looked up, startled, thinking Steve and Gary had

already left. Steve was standing in the doorway, his leather case of drumsticks under his arm and a half-empty bottle of Rolling Rock in his hand.

"Huh?" Mark placed his guitar back in the case, snapped the two-inch leather strap over the neck to keep it from slipping, closed the faded silver lid, one of the hinges creaking. "How long should *what* take?"

"For that guy, what's-his-name, at the club. The Scene."

"Todd? The owner? Yeah, so"—Mark squatted on a bent knee, packing his distortion and overdrive pedals into an old suitcase covered with band stickers—"what about him?"

"Well, how long's it going to take? For him to get back to us? About playing?"

"Oh, *that.*"

Steve was referring to a crude demo tape they had cut the week before using a four-track tape recorder belonging to Jim, a former boyfriend of Mark's current girlfriend, Laura. About a month ago, and against Gary's wishes, Mark had decided that Bottlecap was ready to play live. They had a half-hour set, most of the necessary confidence, and enough chops to get them through a weekday night at the Scene, sandwiched between three or four other bands in the same situation. The only problem was that Kitty was such a small town that the Scene was the only place to play, and Todd, the owner, knew this. It was a fact he used to lord over the small musical community in town. If Todd didn't like you, you didn't play. Period. Mark had met him only twice, once to ask if Bottlecap could play, when he was gruffly told he needed a tape, and again to give Todd the tape he'd grumbled about days before. On neither occasion did Mark come away with the sensation that he was well liked.

"Uh, any day now, I hope."

"Yeah, well"—Gary switched his bass case from his right hand to the left hand—"let me know when you do. Okay?"

"Uh, sure."

"So, you guys want to get a beer?" Steve suggested, taking the last drag of the one in his hand and tossing it into the trash.

Mark was startled. A few minutes ago he was sure they were pissed at him, and now they were being friendly. He wasn't quite sure what to think. This was the biggest problem he had being in a band, not dropping picks or his guitar falling easily out of tune but the separation of friendship and personal matters when it came to band politics and the music. It was pretty much the same dynamic used with roommates or lovers, acknowledgment that the relationship was built on friendship but that there was also business to get done. How could you get as mad as you wanted at your dorm mate when she ate the last of your cream cheese, knowing that after you finished shouting at her she would be spending the next semester with you, like it or not? Or how did a lover broach the subject of morning breath without endangering the mood of that day's lunch and dinner? The answer was, of course, delicately and with maturity; but the members of Bottle-cap were barely in their twenties and the only balance they were concerned with was the scale of alcohol and sex.

"So, Pellion, you coming for that beer, or what?"

"Oh, no. Can't." He finished loading up his gear and carried it out to his car as Steve held the door open for him. "It's my and Laura's one-year anniversary tonight. She's going to *try* and cook. Wish me luck."

That night she had attempted to make veal scallopini and he couldn't taste the veal and wasn't sure what scallopini was, so he didn't know whether he was tasting it or not. But they consumed two bottles of good red wine and the bread was fresh and garlicky, and afterwards they laughed, smoked too many cigarettes, and reminisced how they met twelve months before.

When they finally made it to the bed, drunk but not too drunk, Laura slyly led Mark's hand to the underside of his pillow, where he found a pair of silk boxers and a Monet card in which she had written, "Happy Anniversary. I'll always love you."

Of course, the second that Mark, Steve, and Gary began to be successful, Mark forgot all about this night and many others just like it.

●   ●   ●

A week and a half after Mark had delivered the tape, Todd called him back. Bottlecap would be playing at the Scene along with four other bands that Thursday. Mark didn't know if he should be happy or scared.

A few days away from the show, each of the band members was mixed with equal amounts of excitement and fear. At one point, just two days exactly before they were to take the rickety stage of the Scene and belt out their opening number, "Playing Hackeysack with the Punks," Mark could no longer tell the difference between giddy expectation and no-holds-barred fright. And yet, just as Tolstoy said that "every unhappy family is unhappy in its own way," so was it that no member of Bottlecap was anticipating gigging in the same way.

Steve was frightened of the technical difficulties that could arise—breaking a drumstick halfway through a song, or the little metal chains under his snare drum staying loose when he pulled the lever to tighten them, causing the drum to sound embarrassingly hollow. Steve was afraid he would forget his patterns to all of the songs. His brother Phil (who didn't help matters by closing his throat and making choking noises) prophesied that, on Thursday night, Steve wouldn't remember the order of the shout *one-two-three-four!* that led into almost half of their songs.

Gary also was nervous. He was afraid of the way the crowd might receive the band and its music. He was afraid that, after working their asses off in the hot rehearsal space all summer, they would get onstage, perform their set, and then only hear a faint cough, the clinking of a few glasses, even the minuscule sound of the back of a match colliding with a scratchy stretch of cardboard in response. Gary had his own confidence in their songs, yet there was a creeping, nagging doubt. *Are any of these songs good? Would I buy these songs if I hadn't been involved with them from the beginning? If I saw my band playing on a stage, would I watch, throw beer bottles, or place a quarter on the console of the cigarette-burn-strewn Galaga video game in the corner and wait my turn with my back to the stage?*

For Mark, the horror was different from Gary and Steve's anxiety. It wasn't stage fright, or that people might hate the songs. He just didn't want it to be anticlimactic. He didn't want to shrug his shoulders and say to himself, *Is that all there is?*

Mark had wanted to be in a band for so long now that he couldn't remember when it ever began. He couldn't begin to calculate the hours spent after school staring at the cardboard album covers of his favorite bands. Then there were afternoons when he and his friends gathered in the old field on the outskirts of town, elbows slung over the handlebars of their Jag, Mongoose, and Redline BMX bicycles as they talked about the band they were going to form. They doled out the instruments among them, Mark, even then, deciding on guitar. The guy who showed up to the meeting last was stuck with bass, since no one was ever sure exactly what a bass player did. In the videos the bass players were always in the background, and that one in the Rolling Stones barely moved, but every band had one, so Mark's band would have one, too. Mark can't remember those friends' names, but he remembers the planned names of the groups they came up with. When junior high came and they were scattered to different classes, the one who was supposed to play drums was bused to a different school entirely, the band dissolved before it could even form.

Mark got turned on to music again in high school through Jim's radio show during lunch at Kitty High and picked up a guitar and taught himself how to play it. Now, even though he was about to make his debut onstage with his group, formed only a few months before, it was the culmination of a dream planted in his head for over half his life. The closest he'd come so far was when he borrowed Phil's drum set and he and a few friends mimed to Scorpions' "Blackout" at a school talent show in the sixth grade. Mark remembers that the event took place in the cafetorium (budget cuts demanded the auditorium and the cafeteria be merged, and the former cafeteria was then divided up into new classrooms) and before the show he broke a girl's lipstick in the library because he'd never seen one up close.

During the song, which seemed woefully low in volume, not blasting like they'd hoped, he had barely raised his head. The one time he looked over the gold-glittered Gretsch bass drum he saw his mother and father in the front row trying desperately to look proud.

Mark just wanted to make sure his relationship with playing live was a long-term love affair and not a conquest. He was afraid that once he faced down the fear, he'd never feel the itch again, because the challenge would be gone. Yeah, he knew he'd done it, so why would he have to do it again?

The night Bottlecap were to make their debut at the Scene, the plan was to get in a few hours of practice, load up the instruments in Mark's father's van, and then head over to the club. They were scheduled to go on at midnight, so they were meeting at nine to have enough time. Mark arrived at the practice space a few minutes after nine and was, as usual, the first one to arrive. Ten minutes later Steve rolled up in his green Volvo.

"Hey, did you hear?" he began, in a mock-excited voice. "Gary's car broke down! He's stuck up in Richmond! We're going to have to call off the show."

"Huh?" Mark said, feeling crushed but also a tad relieved. "What?"

"Ahh, just kidding." Steve pulled the bag of drumsticks out of his car and jabbed Mark in the ribs with it. "Anyway, sorry I'm late."

"Yeah, real funny."

Gary showed up a few minutes later and they set up and began to play. They started off with the songs they usually screwed up on, "I've Been Talking to Stephen Hawking" and "I Like This Frown." For some reason or other, during "Stephen Hawking," Gary came out of the first chorus too slowly and it threw the others off, and Steve was always struggling with the drum part of the verses in "I Like This Frown." They played each song twice again and, surprisingly, nailed them each time.

"Okay, cool," Mark said, wiping some sweat from his forehead and checking his watch. "It's ten o'clock. Let's run through the set real quick."

Ten minutes later, halfway through their third song, "Ham on Wry, Hold the Malaise," Steve froze.

"What is it?" Mark turned around. Steve was sitting on his throne, drumsticks placed across the snare drum, his left hand clutching his right shoulder.

"My neck," he said weakly. "Can't . . . move . . ."

"Come on, stop kidding," Mark said, tired of his jokes.

"I'm *not* kidding, Pellion. This is that old pinched nerve I got when I worked as a box boy at the grocery store three summers ago. I told you, it comes and goes, remember?"

"Seriously?" Gary asked, lighting up a cigarette and leaning against his Mesa Boogie cabinet.

"I'm serious, you assholes." Steve fell to the floor and began rolling around, his hand now tentatively kneading the back of his neck.

Mark looked to Gary, who spit out a mouthful of smoke, rolled his shoulders in a don't-ask-me fashion, and flipped the yellow STAND BY switch on his amp, the low-end hum crackling out and then off.

"Well, what do we do?" Mark said to anyone who would listen, only no one was. Steve lay on the floor, dead, his eyes closed. Gary was playing with a large plastic case shaped like Darth Vader's head, in which he used to carry *Star Wars* action figures, which now stored his bass tuner, spare set of strings, strap, picks, and cords. "I mean, Steve, can you play?"

"I don't know," Steve croaked, barely lifting his head off the ground. "I'd like to cancel, but . . ."

"But nothing. I had to *beg* Todd for this spot, and if we fuck up tonight he may never give us another shot." Mark took off his guitar and went to where Steve was lying prostrate on the smelly practice-space floor. "Look, everyone knows it's going to be our first show. No one's expecting us to be good. We just need to make sure the people buy some beer and then make sure they don't throw it at us. Okay? Can you do that much, at least?"

Steve sort of rolled over, like a cockroach stranded on its back.

"Yeah"—he tried again—"but I won't be able to carry anything."

"That's okay. Me and Gary will do it, okay?"

Gary, finally noticing other people in the room, looked up.

"What? I'm not carrying *his* drums. The last time I helped with the drums the ride cymbal fell on my toes and—"

"Gary, shut the fuck up and grab something, okay?"

He tossed Darth Vader to the side and, grumbling, got up.

Gary and Mark loaded their stuff in first, beginning with the amps and then the guitar cases. Mark wedged his suitcase filled with gear into the space between the wheel well and Gary's bass case, hoping the amps on casters wouldn't roll backward and crunch the guitars.

Back in the rehearsal room, Steve was now sitting upright in a chair, his right shoulder sort of hunched, but his elbows resting on his knees. In his hands he held a *Penthouse* magazine, his eyes earnestly scanning the pages.

"Feeling better?" Mark asked as he slung a golf-club bag filled with Steve's cymbal stands over his own beginning-to-ache shoulder.

"Getting there," Steve nonchalantly replied.

A half hour later they were loaded up and ready to head across town to the club. As Mark hopped in the driver's side, with Steve limping to the passenger seat, they noticed Gary retreating to his own car, parked to the side of Steve's.

"You going to, uh, follow us there?" Mark asked, hope in his voice.

"Actually," Gary began, hesitating, "I've got to go pick up a friend's girlfriend."

"Which friend?"—his eyes tried to find Gary's in the scarce moonlight—"and which girlfriend?"

"Uh, you know, that guy John?"

"The one in Juvy?" Steve asked, rotating his shoulder over and over, wincing in pain.

"Yeah, that's him," Gary called back. "His girlfriend wanted to come to the show and I'm going to go pick her up."

"But doesn't she live up in Mechanicsville?" Mark asked.

"On the outskirts, I guess, but don't worry. I'll be there in plenty of time. By the way, do you know if they're going to be carding tonight?"

"Why?" Steve managed to laugh, despite the agony. "How old is she?"

"Never mind, just make sure her name is on the guest list." Gary hopped in his car and sped off. "Samantha!"

Mark watched as the taillights faded into the night.

"Uh," he said quietly, "we don't *have* a guest list."

Once at the Scene, Mark scrambled to the liquor store next door and bought a travel-sized bottle of Tylenol for Steve. Steve chugged half a beer and ate about four tablets, continuing to knead his neck and upper arm. Since he was busy in his physical therapy and Gary was off playing chauffeur, Mark was the only one left to unload the van. He began with the drums, unceremoniously dropping them on a little patio to the side of the raised stage, where the second-to-last band of the night was preparing to go on.

"Hey, watch it!" Steve called out from the bar, clutching a half-empty Corona. A girl was giving him a back rub. "I just bought that kick pedal."

The inside of the club was warm and muggy, more so than usual, it seemed. This fact, coupled with Mark's own nervousness and the strenuous workout he was getting from unloading the equipment, made him start to feel hot and damp. He brushed his dark blue sleeve against his glistening forehead and was horrified when it came back streaked with moisture.

*No,* he begged his body, *don't get me all sweaty before I even go on.*

Mark struggled, as usual, with his Twin Reverb amp, the power cord and vibrato/reverb foot pedal falling out of the open back and onto the gravel-covered alley behind the Scene. He picked the whole thing up, one of the casters falling out of its place and lost temporarily in the rock-strewn ground and dimly lit surroundings. Mark walked through the door to the side of the bar from the van to the stage half a dozen times, Steve's shouts to be careful with his equipment alternating with Todd's yelling at him to hurry up.

Once Bottlecap was loaded in, Mark had a chance to relax, drink a beer, and watch the band now onstage. But it felt weird; how many times had he leaned against this bar, waiting for a band to go on or enjoying one of them playing? He tried to rationalize that this night was no different, only it was. Instead of turning to Laura and saying, "Let's go home early, I'm tired," he was in the next band to go on. He turned and looked around the club he'd been going to for almost three years, which suddenly looked different to him. He was already no longer part of the audience, though he'd yet to play a single note.

The pressure was getting to him and Mark went into the bathroom off the main entranceway. Stickers of other bands were everywhere, over the mirrors, on the cracking tiles, toilet seat, and even pipes that looked near bursting, trails of rust-colored water leaking out of the tired seams. And where there weren't stickers, there lay the fuzzy residue and ghostly outlines of stickers from years ago, worn off naturally or picked away by a jealous thumbnail. Mark took a quick piss, his fifth of the night, and headed back out to the bar.

"So, where's Gary?" Steve crawled to Mark's side.

"Huh?" He was shaken out of various worrisome thoughts. "What?"

"Gary." Steve pointed to his watch. "This band just said they've only got a few more songs and *we* are without a bass player."

Mark quickly consulted the large Miller Genuine Draft clock hanging above the bar. Steve was right; it was eleven-forty-five, close to show time, and Gary was nowhere in sight.

"What was that girl's name?"

"What?" Steve shouted.

"That girl!" He shouted back. "Should we call her?"

Steve looked perplexed.

"What girl?"

Mark waved him off and ran outside, stopping on the way to take another piss. He dropped his jeans, the heavy belt he was wearing sending the worn-through Levi's straight to the ground, but his shriveled-up penis just lay there, half sucked into his body as if he'd been swimming. He could feel the slightly warm burning sensation in his bladder, only nothing would come.

Outside, Todd was standing behind a small podium counting money, mostly $5 bills, the price of admission for the night.

"You ready to go on, Pellion?" His head bobbed as he spoke, not letting up the counting inside his brain.

"Oh, yeah," Mark said, trying to sound confident.

Down the sidewalk came half a dozen young kids. They were sort of stumbling, probably a little bit drunk or stoned or a combination of the two.

"Hey, who's playing tonight?" asked one of the guys, his arm around the waist of a good-looking girl. Behind them were two more couples.

"Varsity Donkey Kong," Todd said gruffly, "from North Carolina."

"Oh, thanks," the young kid said, and the group kept moving down the sidewalk.

When they were safely out of hearing range, Mark turned to Todd.

"Why didn't you tell them about us?" he asked. "Why didn't you say, 'A hot new local band, Bottlecap'?"

This time Todd stopped counting. He lay the wad of cash on the wooden stand before him and looked deep into Mark's eyes.

"Because you're not hot *or* new. You're just two guys who can probably barely play their instruments and have too much time on your hands, so you sit around and write songs while Daddy helps pay the rent."

The worse thing was, Todd was right. Almost.

"Actually, there's *three* of us."

"But I only saw you and the hunchback."

"Yeah, well." Mark glanced down at his watch again. Inside the club he could hear the lead singer scream out, "Thank you, good night, Esporia!" Off by one town. "There's supposed to be one more."

"Look, Pellion, I don't care if it's just you *solo*, but get up there and play. It's getting late. Curfew's coming and I want to sell some alcohol."

Mark ran back inside the club. Steve was trying to drag his bass drum from the patio as the band loading off the stage stared at him queerly. Mark ran to help Steve but felt the gnawing below his stomach to take yet another piss. He knew this was impossible since he'd relieved himself already a dozen times that night. He ignored the feeling and began to help Steve load the equipment onto the stage.

When there were only a few pieces remaining, Mark felt some assistance come from the left.

"Need a hand there, partner?"

He looked up. Gary was carrying his preamp in his right hand and a gig bag over his shoulder.

"Y-y-you're lucky I'm too nervous to be pissed," Mark managed to get out. Even though the stage was much smaller than the floor of their rehearsal space, they were still able to construct a semifaithful re-creation of the way they set up at the practice, Gary to the left while Mark took the right, and Steve in the center behind them.

"Mike?" Steve said, his eyes just a slit as he continued to wince in pain. "What about microphones?"

"Oh, yeah."

Mark noticed there were three mike stands branching up from heavy circular bases placed around the stage, but at the top of the crab-claw neck, no microphones were inserted. Mark ran to the bar, where Todd, his confidence in Bottlecap completely evaporated, had given up the door and figured he'd try and push the mixed drinks, since it was already a quarter after twelve and he was lucky to have the dozen or so people milling around the bar. After all, it was just a Thursday.

"Mikes," Mark shouted out, "microphones."

Todd, cleaning a beer mug, didn't even look up.

"Talk to the soundman." He pointed with a suds-covered hand to a wire-mesh cage.

Mark zigzagged through a few customers, who looked familiar, and tapped on the painted black fencing with his sweaty palm.

"Hello?"

A shadow emerged from the darkness, a row of red and green lights from the mixing console the only illumination in the thin space.

"Yeah?" A hiccup.

"Hey, I'm in the next band and we need three mikes."

The shadow disappeared for a second but then reemerged with the three microphones in his hands. He exited the cage and Mark followed him to the stage.

"I hope you brought your own soundman," the guy said. He was short, about five five, with sandy brown hair, tousled, his eyes glazed over and his lips wet.

"Why?" Mark cautiously asked.

"Because I'm . . . drunk," the soundman slurred.

*Great,* Mark thought to himself, *fucking great.*

"Look," he told the guy, "just make sure my vocals are turned way up and that the others are just midrange, okay? We've got our levels set, so just make sure the vocals are up high."

Mark jumped up on the stage as the soundman snapped the mikes into the necks of the stands and then connected the eight-pin plugs, which led back into a mixer hooked up to the club's PA. He noticed there were no monitors set up onstage, though he could have sworn seeing them in place for a band who played earlier. Stepping in front of his mike stand, he adjusted it a little, and it reminded him that it was the first thing a stand-up comedian did when taking the stage. Some comedians could even make that funny, but Mark, as he fumbled with the goddamn stand, it not wanting to work for some reason, hoped people weren't laughing at him. He left it where it was, a few inches too tall, but that was okay.

"Hello, we're, uh, Bottlecap," Mark said into the microphone, which gave out a deafening hiss of feedback. The soundman just raised a small plastic glass and gave him the thumbs-up signal.

"Now?" Gary asked. Mark looked over, noticing Gary's pants legs waving back and forth. Either there was a breeze or the bass player was shaking.

"Now."

Steve raised his drumsticks like a crucifix, beat them against each other in the center four times, and they burst into their first song. When it came time for the lyrics, Mark approached the microphone, raised himself on the balls of his feet, and began to sing. He could barely hear himself.

During his guitar solo in the fourth song, "I Hate the Way You Act, But You Look Okay," Mark's mind wandered. He thought about Laura, how it sucked that her family was out of town and that she was missing the first ever Bottlecap show. He thought about the large pizza he'd had earlier in the evening and how people said that dairy was bad for the throat and that he was beginning to believe them. As his fingers played hopscotch up and down the neck, he looked out on the dozen kids scattered about the Scene. The lights shining down on the stage precluded him from making eye contact. He could clearly see feet but things got fuzzy around the chest, and by the time he looked toward where a head would be there was just a pool of black. It made it easier and he didn't have to use the advice that his mother had given him the day before that he'd heard hundreds of times in his life, *Just look over everyone's head and stare at the back of the room.* Before corralling his thoughts he marveled how easy it was for him to lose them. This level of uncaring about the performance he was giving made him feel like he really was cut out to be in a band.

However, in the next song, something happened that made him feel the opposite way. During the second chorus Mark only sang his *ba-ba-ba*s once and then stopped playing altogether, his arm outstretched in a grand motion, his guitar reverberating the last glorious note. He then looked over at Gary and Steve, who were still beating and strumming out the tune, and remembered, *Oh, yeah, we play the second chorus twice.* Mark scrambled, unsure how much effort to devote to worrying about how many noticed him fuck up and how much to finding his way back into the song. He played a few haphazard chords but couldn't find his place. Just as he figured out what he should be playing, the song was over. Then Gary's guitar strap broke, his bass falling to the floor, where it landed with a thud.

"Mark, can I borrow your duct tape?"

Mark scrambled to his sticker-covered suitcase, fishing out the roll of thick, silver tape from the packs of guitar strings, most missing the high E string, the one he seemed to break most often. He tossed the tape to Gary, who bent over and began repairing his strap. Mark stared into the audience, shadowy heads still visible even though most should have left by now. He knew he would have.

In the awkward silence he felt he should say something, provide some clever banter that he'd witnessed so often at shows. "I wrote this next song while I was . . ." or else, "How you all doin' tonight?" Stuff like that. At the very least he could have inquired as to the crowd's readiness to rock. But nothing was coming to him.

Now Mark, for the second time in the evening, began to sweat. He wiped it away, feeling bad that both times it was because he was nervous, not because he was giving a mind-blowing performance.

"Ready?" Mark asked hopefully. "Please say yes."

"No." Gary retrieved the pick from where he'd shoved it underneath the pick guard almost five minutes before. "But let's go anyway."

Just after the first few bars of "Bad Skin Day" and already more than halfway into their set, the lights in the club flickered off. Mark, who was trying to pluck out arpeggio, his fevered eyes alternating from the precise picking of his right hand to the placement of barre chords along the neck with his left, looked up quickly and instantly lost his place in the song. He could see lights on in the back of the bar, Todd's imposing frame a silhouette in the glare of a DRINK BUD neon sign, so Mark could tell that Kitty hadn't been hit with a blackout. Then the lights flashed on, but in a light purple, then faded out, returning a few seconds later a misty foam green. *Misty?* thought Mark quickly. *But how . . .*

From behind Gary's booted right ankle came an audible hiss, then a stream of smoke, cold and musty, wafting out onto the floor. Todd, thinking the show was lacking, was trying to give it some oomph with dry ice and a light show. Mark kept losing his place in the fog, the clay dots set into the rosewood neck of his Fender Jaguar barely visible. Gary choked once or twice and tried to scoot out of the path of the smoke, only to bump into one of Steve's crash cymbals, knocking it over. When some customer ordered a vodka tonic Todd abandoned the set of light switches and the dial set just above the cash register and switched on the normal stage lights. They popped on in the last wrong note of the song.

The soundman then cut through the crowd, which at this point meant asking two people to step aside, and approached the stage.

"I hate to tell you this"—he released a balloon of alcohol-soaked breath—"but you've got one more song."

Mark glanced down at the set list: two more songs to go.

As the soundman crawled back to the cage, Mark turned to Gary and Steve.

"Pixies cover," Gary said quickly.

"'Birthday Ache,'" replied Mark.

"No, let's do the Pixies cover," Gary said again. "Besides, we always fuck up on 'Birthday Ache.'"

"Yeah, but . . . it's a better closing song. 'Cactus' is too slow."

Steve, looking pained, said, "Let's just play *some*thing."

"The Beatles song?"

"Look, why don't we play that other Pixies song"—Gary thought he was compromising—"the one in Spanish?"

"Gary"—Mark wipes the sweat from his forehead—"*which* Pixies song in Spanish?"

From the floor a cough punctuated Bottlecap's quibbling over which song to play.

"Alright, fuck it." Mark turned away from Gary to what remained of the audience. "'Cactus' it is."

Mark stood waiting for Gary to play, thinking, *Yeah, he likes this song because* he *starts it. Goddamn egomaniac.*

Mark missed his cue for his first line, and even when the words came, he was grasping at them. He wasn't used to playing "Cactus" as the last song. He usually took it easy on his voice, saving it to lose during the last screeched chorus of "Birthday Ache," letting the lines *"This hurts so bad that I can hardly speak, it sure is going to be a fucked-up birthday week"* burn the back of his throat. But tonight there was no reason to save his voice, and yet, the more he felt compelled to act "into it," the more the words to the song escaped him. He closed his eyes to the yellow lights of the club, seeing patterns against his eyelids, and tried to imagine looking at the lyrics Gary had written out for him two weeks ago and brought to practice, the title decorated with a cactus or two, stars and moon above, and dots for grains of sand below. But the lyrics weren't coming.

Mark struggled for the words, which seemed to come a split second after he needed them, and this of course slowed the song down considerably. Was it his imagination, or was the version on *Surfer Rosa* twelve minutes long, or did it just *seem* to him to be lasting that long?

The last out-of-tune chord had yet to dissipate into the empty club before Gary turned quickly and violently toward Mark.

"Why in the fuck did you play that song so goddamn slow?" His strap snapped again and sent the instrument falling to the ground, a menacing hum emanating from his amp.

"Well, where in the fuck were you till five minutes to twelve?" Mark shot back, bending over and flipping the off switch of his amp, the four tubes fading from a warm and hazy powdered blue to nothing.

"Shut up," Steve said, limply rising, one of his drumsticks broken in half and hanging like a broken leg, by just a few minor strands of wood ligament up the side, "both of you."

As they began to tear down their respective gear, Mark was disappointed, had to take yet another piss, and was still a little nervous, though the reason for being so had already passed. The soundman approached the stage and began disconnecting the mikes. His eyes caught Mark's in the house lights that had been switched on seconds before by a pissed-off Todd.

"That was . . . that was . . ." The soundman slurred his words, his eyes slit and his face flushed red. "Painful."

**On the morning of the big day, Mark wakes up before**
either Steve or Gary.

He marches into their room fully dressed, his hair still wet
from a shower, and dried white patches of toothpaste at each
corner of his mouth. He sees Gary buried beneath the covers,
his body a fake-looking lump, while Steve lies in the fetal position, a rotting teddy bear clutched tightly under his arm. Mark
chuckles, having seen the bear many, many times before. He
had noticed it earlier when Steve unpacked, its tattered ear
sticking out from the pillowcase in which Steve shoved it for
traveling. Mark wonders if Steve has some sort of umbilical
attachment to that specific bear or if he just needs something to
hold on to.

It was weird, but Steve *did* sleep with the bear just to hold on
to something—not that he was using it as a substitute for a girl
(at two feet long the bear was still three feet short of anything
he'd consider), but Steve would be lying if he insisted the way
he held the object close to him was too far off from being with a
female. Not that he would ever try anything remotely sexual
with the bear; it wasn't like that. The beige shag of its skin was
bunched together and almost rough from years alone in a corner
of Steve's abandoned apartment, or stuffed in a backpack when
he had the courage to bring it along on tour, fearing recrimination from his band mates the entire time.

But if Steve had always liked the bear, a cozy artifact of his childhood, he now felt that he needed the stuffed animal more than ever.

Over the past few nights he had jerked himself awake and wondered where he was, disoriented by the sight of the messy room in the Mondrian Hotel and the unfamiliar Los Angeles skyline. Out of instinct he turned to his right, accustomed to do so from their last tour, when his regular sleeping area was hugging the left side of the Ford van, the protruding wheel well fitting snugly behind his bent knees in an inanimate spoon position, to look for Gary, who slept a few feet higher on a constructed ledge above the stacked guitar and drum cases. Whenever he did this at the Mondrian he met only the wall, which freaked him out further until he raised himself, sometimes shaking, onto his hands and knees and looked in the other direction, to where Gary slept across the room. Seeing his old friend allayed his fears momentarily, but in seconds the strange terrain engulfed him again, and he thought, *Where in the hell are Gary and I?*

The weekend and first couple days in L.A. had been fun, and with only a week in Kitty since their exhausting tour, Steve felt that not only did he deserve the time off, but without it he and the others just might crack and quit the band right then and there. Yet now he was still tense. As he and Gary tentatively took in the sights (Mark keeping to himself and packing his bags for the move), Steve couldn't help but let the pressure of the upcoming weeks nag at him. Going to sleep on their last night in the hotel, Steve clutched on to his bear tighter than he had in a long time.

"Come on, you guys, wake up!" Mark kicks the foot of each bed. "We've got to move into the new place and be in the studio by noon!"

Even though Steve is stirring to life, pushing his bear into its pillowcase hiding place, it is Gary who speaks, his voice coming from a motionless mound under the covers.

"What do you mean, 'move in'?" His voice is muffled, still tired. "We're not going to need the Starving Students here. It's a couple of suitcases and a guitar or two."

"Yeah, but"—Mark tensely pats down his jeans pocket, producing a scrap of paper with the address Henry had provided for him on Monday—"I'm not sure where this place is. I'm just trying to leave enough time, that's all."

Steve scratches at his belly, yawns, and pads across the room to the bathroom.

"Now come on, Gary, Steve got off *his* ass . . . now it's your turn."

"No fair." Gary raises himself like a zombie, from the waist with his arms outstretched. "His ass is smaller than mine."

"Ha ha," Mark says as he begins to go around the room, picking up various T-shirts, socks, and pairs of jeans from the floor, stuffing them into Steve's Lands' End garment bag, regardless of who the items belong to. A trail of Gary's clothes from the night before—a long-sleeve T-shirt, baby blue boxers still inside khaki chinos, and like some Hiroshima silhouette blasted onto a wall, phantom gray sweat socks sticking out of each pants leg with the form of Gary's foot still apparent—leads Mark to the center of the room, where he spots the courtesy bar. The door of the off-white dorm-room-sized refrigerator is open, and leaning in, Mark can hear the engine chugging away, the way it has been all night.

"Whoa, Gary, I think you're losing your touch." Mark points to the nearly vacant insides of the refrigerator. "You actually left half a pack of Trident and a pepperoni stick behind. I thought you had a scorched-earth policy when it came to free grub."

Grinning, Gary gets out of bed and walks to where Mark is standing, and pulls out the two remaining items from the fridge. He unpeels the pepperoni stick and immediately bites off half, then unravels a few rectangular strips of the spearmint gum and tosses them into his mouth as well.

Mark and Gary stand there for a second until the sound of the showerhead rearing into action breaks the silence in the room. The constant hissing of sheets of water slamming against the tiled walls becomes varied, staccato, the water meeting with resistance, hitting Steve's body on its way down the drain. Mark looks plainly at Gary.

"Did you know he's still sleeping with the bear?"

Gary finishes chewing before answering.

"He doesn't know *I* know, but yeah."

"Look, there's Fairfax," Steve says from the backseat, pointing his arm into the front.

"I see it, I see it. But now what?" Gary calls out, annoyed.

"Quick, Steve, read the directions," Mark says, glancing around the generally nondescript intersection, which consists of a Thrifty's drugstore, a Mobil gas station, a Crown Books, and a delicatessen on the far side. "Which way do we go?"

"At Fairfax . . ." He points to the green street sign hung from a pole, dotted with buckshot. "Take a right."

Gary's view, for a second trained on a Kentucky Fried Chicken with a Blockbuster Video just beyond and a Bank of America across the street, switches to the sloping hill of Fairfax.

Before them lies Los Angeles, the Hollywood sign visible in the rearview mirror, while in front Fairfax cuts neatly through the city, cleanly slicing it in two. The liquor stores, tattoo parlors, strip bars, and nightclubs of Sunset give way to apartment houses that look like motels built in the fifties or sixties, apartments with cheap iron railings circling empty kidney-shaped swimming pools.

"Okay, what next?"

"Two blocks. Turn left. From there we're looking for Sierra Bonita."

Gary stalls the car at Sierra Bonita, and just as Mark's wondering how he manages this, since the rental's an automatic and also brand new, Gary restarts the car, ignores the honking behind him, and peels out through the intersection under a traffic light changing quickly from yellow to red.

"This the right street?" Steve asks.

"I think so"—Mark keeps looking at the crudely drawn map in his hand to the houses lining the street—"but there's no goddamn numbers. . . . They must have all been stolen in the big riot."

"That wasn't in Hollywood, it was in South Central," Steve chides.

"Well, then, it was during the riot before that one."

Mark continues to scan the facades of the buildings, not seeing any of the tin cutouts hanging on the steel-gated entryways.

"Geez," Gary wonders, "what are these people afraid of?"

"Is that night stalker guy still on the loose?" Steve asks from the backseat, his elbows propped on Gary and Mark's headrest.

"No," says Mark, still scanning, trying to concentrate.

"Remember that Intellivision game Night Stalker? Man, I used to hate that system, with that little disk as a joystick and those pointy, skinny cartridges. But then again, they had that voice module thing, and that B-17 Bomber game wasn't too bad. Hey, remember that TV commercial with some guy doing that cheesy Winston Churchill impression and—"

"Will you please shut the fuck up?"

"Easy," Gary says, noticing some numbers sandblasted into a set of stone steps leading to a courtyard with buildings on each side. "Hey, what's that?"

Mark glances out the window, then to the paper in his hand.

"Let's see, eight-twenty-and-a-half to eight-twenty-two. Yeah, we're sandwiched in there somewhere . . . pull over and park."

Gary notices the dozens of cars stationed next to the sidewalk. He stops for a second, trying to find a space, but the street is full except for a few gaps where driveways empty out onto the street or a four-feet expanse of blank curb turns out to be either painted red or else too close to a fire hydrant.

"Why don't you guys hop out? I'll park on the next block and meet you."

"Sure, sure," Mark and Steve respond, getting out of the car and retrieving a load of baggage before Gary drives away.

"Nice, huh?" Steve says hopefully from the sidewalk.

Mark looks up and down the block, which despite the parked congestion, is relatively quiet. Sounds of the city, the wavelike whooshing of constant traffic and the wailing of the occasional siren, are not far off but seem at least somewhat absorbed by the large palm trees lining the street.

"So far so good . . . but let's not count our chickens before, well, you know."

Mark and Steve trudge up the set of steps, dragging their heavy luggage into the courtyard. On either side of the cracked cement walkway is a large building housing two units; thick wooden doors at the far end of each face each other, set in beneath arched entryways.

Perpendicular to the two larger buildings is a separate apartment, now vacant; and a red-and-white cardboard FOR RENT sign stapled to a wooden stake is driven into the slightly overgrown grass. To the left, round stones form a path to a jumble of large olive plastic trash cans with hinged lids, while an identical trail on the right ends at a small shack filled with a washer, dryer, and an industrial-sized sink.

"Let's see, eight-twenty-one-and-a-half . . . it's over this way."

Mark drags his luggage on the sidewalk, glancing behind at the white chalk scratches he's engraving in the cement. He pushes the scribbled directions into his pocket and fishes out the keys that Hanes had delivered to them the day before at the hotel.

"Now *that's* a big door." Steve recites a line from *Tron,* not that anyone notices.

"Yeah, nice." Mark examines the thick door, which creaks as he opens it, the front crisscrossed with black metal strips, and a cubby-hole covered in wire mesh with a tiny hinged door set at about eye level.

Steve leads the way in, dropping his large black garment bag just inside the door.

"Whoa, look at all this space!" he shouts out while twirling around Marlo Thomas–style in the middle of the living room. "With furniture, too."

Mark drags his heavy bag next to Steve's, trying not to scratch the darkly stained hardwood floors even though he does.

"And check out the ceiling." Steve points to his head as he falls onto a white couch that is anchored on either side with oak end tables, on top of one a lamp with a black base, on the other coffee-table art books on Caravaggio and Tintoretto. Mark looks up and sees half a dozen wooden beams running the length of the room, stained dark brown to match the floor.

The living room empties into a dining room with a modern table with a glass top and black metallic legs, six painted black wooden chairs around it. Mark wanders through the swinging door of the dining room, which leads into the kitchen. The counters are tiled and a large white refrigerator with an ice-cube and water dispenser laid into the door sits opposite a gleaming sink and faucet, which Mark is willing to bet is stainless steel.

Back in the living room Steve is lying on the couch, sorting through four remote controls, trying to deduce which correspond with the stereo, television, cable box, and VCR set around the room.

"How's it look out here?" Mark asks, reentering the living room.

"Great. This couch is ultracomfy, and I think"—Steve keeps pointing various remotes at the television, trying to get it to turn on—"we've got cable. Only, *shit,* I can't get this fucking thing to work. There's a stereo over there, but no turntable."

"Well, you know what they say about beggars being choosers."

"Who's a beggar?" Steve asks as the TV suddenly pops to life; only, snow fills the screen and white noise pours out of the stereo speakers. "We're on a major label now. I don't choose, I expect."

Mark just rolls his eyes and sits down in one of the armchairs next to the couch.

The surroundings are making Mark uneasy. First at the hotel and now here. And all this before he'd placed a foot inside the recording studio. Already he was feeling the pressure. It is mounting behind his eyes, pushing his brain against its cell of a skull.

Steve turns and sees Gary carrying a bag in each hand and another slung over a shoulder, drooping under the weight.

"Hey, Gary, I just figured out the cable box. Look, we've even got HBO!"

"Come on, Steve, go get your other bags." Mark rubs his eyes, trying to calm down. "I don't want to be late for the studio."

"Yeah, yeah."

Steve gets up, only to be quickly replaced by Gary, who drops his bags and stretches out.

"Man, I had to park two blocks over," he shouts out to Steve, who mopes out of the apartment. Turning to Mark, he says, "Parking on this street is going to be a bitch."

A second later Mark responds.

"What?"

"A bitch," Gary reaches for one of the remote controls.

"Who?"

Steve saunters down the street, the keys jangling in his hand, beating back and forth against his callused and blistered fingers, which still haven't recovered from Bottlecap's tour that ended only two weeks ago. The neighborhood, casual, semiquiet, if not slightly upscale from the one he lived in back in Kitty, soothes him. On parked cars he spots stickers of bands he recognizes and even likes or has played with.

The street, like his battered bear, makes him comfortable, feel less homesick. This street could just as easily exist in his Virginian hometown three thousand miles away, sans palm trees and the expensive cars that occasionally cruise by.

He gets out his remaining two bags and even unselfishly fishes out Mark's blue duffel bag that's filled with scores of CDs. Slamming the trunk closed, Steve jerks his head around when he spots a beautiful blond drive by in a convertible Corvette, catching just a glimpse of her as he swears she winks at him.

As he trudges back to the apartment, Mark's bag, which he's looped around his neck, digs uncomfortably into his back, the harsh right angles of the thirty or forty jewel boxes poking him through the canvas.

"Need some help there, kid?"

Steve looks up and sees at the top of the steps a tall black-haired guy, his unshaven beard perhaps just a few days old but already wiry. He's wearing black pants, a white T-shirt (tucked in), and motorcycle boots. For a second Steve laughs to himself and compares the differences between California and Virginia. *Back home his shirt would be untucked, he'd be wearing sneakers, or if he was wearing motorcycle boots he'd actually ride one.*

"A hand? Yeah, I guess." Steve lets out a gasp and hands one of his bags to the stranger. "We had to park over on Fountain and . . . man"—he regains his breath slowly—"it's a long walk."

"Parking's tough around here sometimes," he says as he follows Steve to the apartment. "And make sure you watch it Thursdays."

"What's on Thursdays?" Steve gravely asks.

"Street-cleaning day," the guy says, just as serious.

"There you are." Mark meets them at the door. "Why in the fuck haven't you . . . oh, hey."

"Hey."

"Hey, Mark."

"So, who's this?"

"Actually"—Steve turns, puzzled—"I don't know."

"Sam," the stranger finally offers. "I guess you're my new neighbors."

"Yeah, I, uh, guess," Mark says plainly before retreating, taking only his duffel bag from around Steve's neck.

"Oh, that was Mark." He offers his hand. "And I'm Steve. Nice to meet you."

Sam steps back a bit, as if measuring Steve against something invisible.

"So, you're the next big thing?"

"Excuse me?"

"Well"—Sam daintily laughs—"Pacific Media owns this place, right?"

"Uh, yeah," Steve answers, too confused to be impressed. "How did you know?"

"Well, it used to be sort of a safe house where the vice presidents could bring their mistresses, sort of like Jack Lemmon's place in that film . . ." His words trail off, his memory obviously escaping him.

"*Missing?*"

"No."

"*The China Syndrome?*" Steve again suggests.

"Jesus, kid, you're way off. No, wait." Sam's body convulses quickly, as if he'd received some sort of shock. "*The Apartment!* Duh. Anyway, then Pacific started to have their acts stay here when they recorded their records. Must be close to some studio and cheaper than a hotel. Some publicity guy lived here years ago, so it's all rent controlled, but probably not legal."

"How do *you* know all this?"

"I have a, uh, friend who works there," Sam says with a shady undertone, as if caught and he didn't want to divulge information. "But you're the newest, the *next*. Yeah, every few months or so you types check into this place"—Sam casts his eyes over the Spanish-style building—"thinking you're going to be stars. But when you leave, things have changed."

"What are we, test pilots?"

Mark opens the door then quickly slams it shut, a not too subtle hint for Steve to get moving.

"Well, I'll see you," Sam says, turning around and heading to the apartment directly across from theirs.

"Okay," Steve says as something distracts him, a noise from above, and he looks up to see a jet streaking across the sky, an already disappearing vapor trail behind.

"According to the address it should be around here somewhere."

Mark keeps glancing from the paper in his hand to the buildings rushing by on the street, little tin numbers nailed above the doorways flashing by even though Gary is traveling barely above twenty miles per hour. Even the old people are honking at him.

"What's the place called again?" Steve asks from the backseat, leaning forward with both elbows propped on a headrest.

"Star-something Studio-and-something. It says the cross

street is . . . wait." Mark's arm shoots forward like a thunderbolt. "There it is."

Gary spots the silver words STARMAKER STUDIOS AND SOUND hanging above a long wall of dull gray stucco, a fenced-off parking lot to the right-hand side.

"Wow, I wonder if there's anyone else cool recording here, you know?"

Gary pulls into the lot, trying to ignore Steve while Mark's noticing the three BMWs and two Mercedeses parked alongside their rental car.

"Like when Chuck D was recording next door to Sonic Youth and he came in for a little part on 'Kool Thing.' Or when Bruce Springsteen sang on Lou Reed's *Street Hassle* and—"

Gary pulls the rental car into a spot and, still not used to the power brakes, jolts the car to a stop.

"If you don't shut up, *I'm* going to street hassle you."

The three make their way to the front of the building, the never-ending traffic on Sunset drowning out the crackling sound of their sneakers on the trash blown underfoot from a warm Santa Ana breeze. Mark holds the door open for the other two.

"B-b-b-bottlecap," Steve nervously says to a red-haired male receptionist wearing a telephone headset and sitting on a bar stool behind what looks more like a podium than a desk, a platform raised high off the ground.

"Studio two E. They're expecting you."

Gary is already heading down the corridor stretched out in front of them when the receptionist fake-coughs into his hand and points a pencil in the opposite direction.

"Oh, yeah, forgot. Thanks."

At the end of the hallway stands a large door that reads 2E. Gary, deciding to be brave, leads the way and opens the door, crossing through quickly. He is just as quickly met with yet another door, but not before smashing his face against its inset glass of a small window.

"Jesus, buddy, you okay?"

The second door opens and Bottlecap pours into the room, Steve in the middle, Mark taking up the rear, and Gary at the front, rubbing his nose.

"Sure, I'm, uh, fine."

The man who opened the door sort of laughs and turns to a bearded man sitting behind a large mixing console, who does not laugh.

"My name's Kenneth. I'm the producer on this little project. This is Paul, the engineer. You boys must be Bottlecap." He offers his outstretched hand to all three at once.

*This little project. You boys must be Bottlecap.* Mark hears these words repeat in his head as Steve introduces himself as the drummer.

"And I'm the bass player," Gary says, whipping his hand feverishly back and forth as it clenches the producer's hand, as if to convey confidence to Kenneth, who looks to be slightly more than ten years older than even Mark, the oldest member of the group at twenty-four.

"Yes, nice to meet you. Nice . . . handshake." He releases himself from Gary's grasp, turning to the last member of the group. "So, you must be Mark. I've been listening to your tape and I have a lot of ideas. A lot."

Mark examines the man, taller than he is as well as older, and Mark's not sure of which to be more suspicious. He figures you can't really control your height or your age, but the degree that you used either as a weapon against others was key.

"Oh, wow, I'd like to hear them," Mark lies. "Your ideas, I mean." He doesn't give a shit about what this old guy's got to say about his music. It had been hard enough the other day when Henry James had said he hadn't heard a single in Bottlecap's repertoire. Mark wanted to suggest that he try listening again.

"This your first time in a professional studio?"

Kenneth says this as Gary and Steve, looking around, keep bumping into each other like two baseball players who lose a pop fly in the sun.

"No, I mean yes." Steve doesn't want to seem too stupid too

soon. After all, there was plenty of time for that later. "I mean, we recorded stuff back home. But nothing like this."

Kenneth just laughs, his thin chest barely moving but his head bobbing up and down, not much sound coming out.

"Hell, take a look around. Get acquainted. After all, we're going to be here for a while."

To the right of the second door leading off the hallway sits a brown couch, a little beat up and dusty. Gary sits in it briefly and then finds it hard to get up, his head slung back toward the wall and his ass feeling as if it were suspended just inches above the ground. A few feet in front, lying perpendicular to the couch, is the twenty-four-track mixing board. Mark approaches this slowly, in awe, as Kenneth and Paul step outside for a moment to discuss something. The device is at least ten feet long, the face four feet wide, covered in dials the way a head is covered in hair. Each track has its own set of knobs and a fader, each track a space possible for recording a voice or instrument.

At the far end of the console sits a large jumble of patched cords sticking out of what looks like an old telephone switchboard; the top says AUTOMATED PROCESSES, INC., and centered underneath in smaller writing is *Melville, New York*.

Two large speakers sit atop the mixing console, with two more even larger speakers set into the wall above a set of double glass sliding doors that leads to three different rooms.

"Mark, check this out."

He turns and sees Gary behind him, to the left, standing before the twenty-four-track recorder.

The machine is slightly larger than a washing machine, twenty-four rectangular windows vertically sprouting up from the main body. Behind each window is a VU meter, all of which currently lie sleeping on their side. Each window is numbered consecutively from one to twenty-four, a green READY light to the left and red RECORD on the right. On top sit two large reels; one is full with tape, the other is not. The thick, two-inch tape is colored a rich brown, looking like milk chocolate before it has a chance to solidify. The tape is fed through a series of rollers until it passes through the tape heads, respooled onto the empty reel.

"Pretty cool, huh?"

"Yeah," Mark says, impressed but not wanting to show it. "I guess."

"Hey, guys," Steve calls out from the series of rooms behind the glass doors. "Come here!"

Gary leads the way through the glass doors and then two more sets, which lead into dark closet-sized cubbyholes, before finding Steve in the largest room. The doors make a swishing sound whenever they're opened or closed, excess bits of gray carpeting tacked on their fronts and backs scuffing against the ground like a bit of jean caught underfoot. In the corner of the room a set of black drums is stacked, one on top of the other.

"I guess this is where I'll be spending most of *my* time." Steve says this as if examining an apartment.

"Either in here"—Gary laughs—"or on the couch."

Through the series of open doors they hear Kenneth and Paul reenter the studio, laughing at something. At least, Paul shrugs his hunched shoulders and Kenneth's chest moves up and down, but still not much sound comes out.

Steve, Mark, and Gary walk back into the studio and stand before the producer and engineer, as if for inspection.

"Uh, where's your gear?" Kenneth asks, nervously sizing up each band member as if examining his aura. Each has his hands in his pockets, two of Steve's fingers slipping out a hole in his jeans and back through another hole just a few inches below the first.

"All I brought were my cymbals," he begins, since Gary and Mark are just staring at the walls which are covered in thick, crisscrossed foam wedges that remind him of the interiors of those large yellow vans where they used to test his hearing, "and I saw that stacked up Tama set, so I guess *I'm* okay."

Steve sighs and looks at Gary and Mark.

"We brought our gear. At least, our guitars. Uh, that guy,

what's-his-name, he was going to stop by the hotel and pick them up."

"Who?" Kenneth turns to Paul, who gives a sort of hunch of the shoulders, and from this small gesture Kenneth somehow learns the answer. "Oh yeah, Hanes."

Just then the door at the back of the control booth flies open, Hanes appearing with Mark's electric guitar case in one hand, Gary's bass in the other, and Mark's acoustic guitar stuck underneath his left underarm.

"Hey, you didn't need to bring the acoustic. I'm just going to take that right back to the apartment."

Hanes, dripping with sweat, replies, "Thanks for telling me. If anyone cares, I totally bashed my finger on the way in here. It's turning all purple."

"Hey"—Steve nudges Gary—"wouldn't that be a great name for the record? *It's Turning All Purple*, huh?"

"An e.p. maybe"—Gary turns to Steve as Hanes drops off the guitars and heads back out to his compact car for the rest of the gear the band brought from Virginia—"because then you could put *the* in front of it. You know? Like, 'The It's Turning All Purple e.p.' What do you think, Mark?"

"I think," Kenneth interrupts, "that *we* should get started."

"That's a stupid name for an e.p.," Steve whispers.

"Sshhh."

"Okay," Mark says, "what's first?"

Kenneth sits down in a chair, resting an elbow on the tape remote, a large black machine on wheels used to operate the tape recorder.

"Well"—Kenneth smiles weakly—"I thought we'd spend the first couple of weeks in preproduction. Sort of playing the songs over and over and seeing what works and what doesn't. Making decisions on how they sound, and a rough order of where you want to put them on the record. You know, sort of a plan of attack. During this we'll lay down the work track for each song and then go back one by one, instrument by instrument, and lay down the final version."

Steve and Gary just look at each other. Mark stares at the ground for a second before looking up, seeing that Kenneth is waiting for something.

"When do we start?" Mark asks uneasily.

"Right now."

Paul tears a piece of paper from a gummed pad sitting on a shelf underneath the mixing board. The sheet looks like a calendar and is divided into twenty-four numbered sections; in each box is to be written the input recorded on the corresponding numbered track. Mark didn't know much about big-time recording, but he knew enough to know that you started with the drums, then recorded the bass, then the guitar, ending with the vocals. Any overdubs needing to be done came last.

At the top of the sheet lay spaces for the start time, date, song title, artist, client, producer, and engineer. Kenneth nods to Paul, who grabs a black felt pen from the desk before him as he glances at his digital wristwatch, marking *12:43* in large, inky numbers.

**Mark realizes it's been a slow two weeks when, reaching** into the top drawer of the dresser, he sees that a full ten days after he last did laundry, every single pair of his "nice" boxers has still not been worn. These consist of four pairs of underwear that he had splurged on, each a plaid or paisley pattern, and each in a color that complemented a certain group of clothes that Mark was prone to wear as an outfit. He saved them either for an important event (like their last show at the Scene, back in Kitty, when Henry James had been present) or for dates when he thought it would be somebody else's hands undoing his zipper and discovering what lay underneath. But now, ten days have passed since that first weekend in Los Angeles, when, on the Sunday before they moved into the house, he had sent all of his laundry down to the basement of the Mondrian, which had returned it later in the day, the pants on wire hangers with cardboard dowels and his shirts pressed, folded, and each in an off-white box with the hotel's logo, and he still had yet to wear even one pair of his nice boxers.

"I've got to get out and do something," he mumbles as he reaches for yet another of the Wal-Mart brand boxers, the ones with the generic prints that boringly looked like electronic circuitry, the cotton paper-thin from years of use and the elastic band barely effective anymore, now just sort of a spent rubber band that slacked whenever not additionally held up with a belt. At public urinals he had to watch that his underwear did not fall down completely.

"*We've* got to get out and do something." He amends his earlier thought to include the whole band, the fraying of whose nerves he had witnessed just as his own were beginning to come apart at the seams. Their first two weeks in the studio were over and the only thing they had accomplished was laying down most of the drum tracks and a few of Gary's bass lines. This left Mark sitting for hours in the engineering booth, watching his band mates in the other rooms sweating under the glaring lights, which Steve wanted turned down but Gary up, in order to see the fret board of his guitar, for the placement of his fingers upon the strings. How he could not find them in the dark now, even though he had done so for months while on tour and upon barely lit stages, with smoke in the air and trails of beer whizzing past them in the air every twenty minutes, amazed Mark. But Gary's confidence had been eaten away by the treatment he saw Kenneth give to Steve—his insistence on a click track and Steve's insistence that it was not necessary, which, ultimately, it wasn't, even though it would have saved time. Time that meant money, which came out of Bottlecap's pocket anyway, but Mark looked at it as an investment, Steve's pride worth more than a grand saved on studio time. After almost two weeks of ten-hour sessions in the studio, Mark was running out of things to read, things to think about, while Gary spent countless minutes tuning up in the next room, the glare of bright lights on his tuner making it hard for him to see the little row of red lights with the sole green one in the middle that told you when you were exactly in tune. Mark wasn't exactly relishing the day when Kenneth stood there and ate up his guitar lines the way he had done with Gary. His hand thoughtfully on his chin for the duration, once Gary was finished—when he looked up, placed his pick in the corner of his mouth, and wiped the sweat from his face— Kenneth would say, "Uh . . . no."

"Got to just get *out,* have some fun. After all, we're in Los Angeles, right?"

From the drawer below the one filled with socks and underwear he pulls out an old dark blue T-shirt and tosses it on his body, slipping into a pair of jeans that lay crumpled on the floor.

Mark heads downstairs, passing Gary, who's watching television from the couch. Cartoons.

"Hey."

"Hey."

Mark wanders into the kitchen, puts two slices of white bread in the toaster, fills up a glass with orange juice, and begins to hunt for the cereal, which is not perched atop the refrigerator like it should be, when he is hit with a sudden memory of Laura. Maybe it was the morning, the smell of the bread already toasting brown, that made him think of mornings they spent together, making simple little breakfasts of cereal with fruit and juice, maybe an English muffin or a bagel with cream cheese as an added treat. And then they'd relax, read the *Kitty Courier,* and around noon or even one o'clock (depending on when they woke up), they would decide how they were to spend the rest of the day. It was weird because, except for the handful of tours Bottlecap had done, and her trip two years ago to Europe for a month and a half, not a day in the past four years had gone by without him at least momentarily seeing Laura. In the early days it might have been for coffee or just a quick dinner before he went to band practice or she spent time with her friends or studied. Then, as they became closer and spent practically all their time together, they would wake up and go to bed with each other but might spend the entire day alone or with others, working toward individual goals. But now, it'd been almost two weeks since he'd even seen or heard from her. It was weird. And it hurt.

He had slept with her the night before they had left Kitty, and then slept with someone else the next day, at a party at Gary's old college buddy's in Mt. Holly. He had lied to Laura that day, saying they were flying straight to California, not thinking she'd understand the slight detour they were taking in their trip out West, and since it was most likely the end, not really caring enough to explain it as the final good-bye it probably was. So, drunk on both the keg that was located outside at the top of the stairs of the apartment building where they were staying (early October and it was already cold out; you could see your breath between every sip of beer that was as cold as the night) and the fact that they were headed to L.A. to make their first real record, Mark met some girl whose face is now shadowy to him and her name even murkier, and he fucked her the way he'd fucked Laura for years, and the way, he figured—burping right after, drifting off to sleep, not caring whether she came or not—he'd fuck many others before he died, perhaps at the hand of one of them, or perhaps his own, tired of so many years of this useless fucking.

But now it had been almost two weeks since he'd slept with anyone. It didn't sound like a long time and yet already it seemed to change something within him. He no longer felt sexual. He no longer felt connected to a vital area of life, of human experience, to something that countless millions were participating in just as Mark's toast was turning black and he was starting yet another day. But after just a short while out of the race, Mark felt like he could no longer reenter it simply by jumping in and resuming his gallop the way he had done before. He had been too long with one woman. He had let the glue harden and now he fears he'll never be free.

She had called the night before. Gary and Steve had taken the car to pick up Chinese food and a couple of six-packs. Mark picked up the phone on the first ring, something he rarely did, only because he thought it was one of the guys, lost, needing the number to the restaurant even though small children could find the busy intersection of Sunset and La Brea.

"Mark?"

The voice instantly shocked him. It simultaneously was an answered prayer and a punishment because he'd been thinking of her for the past couple of weeks, but knew he couldn't speak to her.

"He*llo?*" Her voice pleaded, knowing Mark was there. The silence sounded like him just as much as his gravelly voice. She sniffed, trying to hold back a tear. Laura's reluctant sob sounded like her. "Please? Mark . . ."

Just as a smell will make one taste food, so did hearing the voice put a picture in his mind, which helped, since he had thrown away every photo of her the day he left Kitty. He could envision her sitting in the large black chair in her living room, the one they had picked out together at an estate sale outside of town. The thing was too big for either the trunk or the backseat, so Mark strapped it onto the roof of her Galaxie 500, the entire way home holding the reins of the twine that crisscrossed the piece of furniture as if it were a giant being held captive. The remembrance made him smile, but it did not make him talk.

Laura put down the phone first, leaving Mark without an appetite and the phone in his hands. Gary and Steve arrived soon after, laughing, dumping the alcohol and three large brown bags of food onto the table. Mark hated that they were always laughing, hated that nothing got under their skin the way that misery seemed to live underneath his. Mark barked at his band mates, saying the food was shit, that neither of them would know good food if it bit them, at which Steve made a joke. Something about food biting *him.* Mark didn't laugh, continued looking miserable, a pose the boys had recently grown used to.

He wanders back into the kitchen to check on the toast. He peers into the two slits stuffed with bread, trying to gauge their doneness. He loses the surface of the pieces in the glare of the glowing red wires that surround the bread. He can't tell what's actually brown, black, or just shadow created by the glowing pink heat. Turning quickly to the sink he knocks over the glass of orange juice he filled up only a minute before, sending it to the ground, where it lands with a smash, an orange juice imprint on the ground that looks like a Day-Glo grenade blast.

"Smooth move, Ex-Lax," Gary calls out from the other room.

Mark, in a daze, goes to the pantry to retrieve the mop and dustpan he spotted in there the other day, and in doing so trips over the cord to the microwave. He slips and almost falls in a corner of the slippery juice, evenly flattening a chunk of the broken glass with his heel, lucky not to cut himself in the process.

*Fuck*, he thinks, *what's wrong with me?*

He always made the joke that, like the recovering alcoholic

whose hand shakes without the drink, his own hand trembles when deprived of regular sex—and yet the comparison was, to a certain degree, true. Already he was losing the physical connections, the familiarity of his body and how it worked. When actively with a lover he felt his muscles and senses primed, hyperaware of his relationship with the physical world; even with his guitar-deadened fingertips he could apply his hands to the various nerves of life and caress, stroke, or smooth out any conclusion he wanted. But now he felt he was losing that edge, losing that touch within himself that he had used to touch other people, and it was making him trip over cords, knock over glasses, and be clumsy.

"Uh, I think something's burning." Gary appears in the doorway.

"Huh?"

Mark looks up and sees smoke rising from the two vents in the toaster.

"Shit."

He rushes over and pops up the bread, which has been turned into slates of charcoal.

"Just not your morning, I guess," Gary says, cackling as he walks back into the living room. Mark follows.

"Hey, why don't we go out tonight?" He sits down in one of the armchairs while Gary lies outstretched on the couch, three of the four remotes in front of him. "You know, let off a little steam. We've all been working hard and I think we deserve it."

"That's a good idea."

"You think Steve'll go for it?"

Gary answers but keeps his eyes trained on one of the remotes.

"Why wouldn't he? He's been itching to get out, especially after a week of Kenneth bugging him about keeping time and using a click track and all that shit."

"Cool." Mark rises out of his chair. "When he wakes up, why don't you ask him? I'm going out for a while."

"Where are you going?"

"I don't know . . . I'm bored. I spotted a cool vintage-guitar store on La Cienega. I'm going to check it out."

"Okay," Gary calls out as Mark heads upstairs for a shower, "but don't spend *all* your savings. We still haven't got our money yet!"

"Just a matter of time." Mark's voice disappears into the second storey of the house. "A matter of . . . time."

Steve's in the bathroom shaving, an expanse of foamy cream covering his chin. For a second he ponders leaving his beard intact, growing that goatee the way he'd been threatening to for years, when the phone rings. He wanders into the hallway, where he's met by Gary, who's buttoning up a shirt, also staring down the hall to the phone, set into a nook in the wall.

"Who would call for us here?" Steve asks.

"I don't know. Do your parents know you're here?"

"Sure," he replies. "California, but not *here.*"

The phone continues to ring.

"Maybe it's the record company people," Gary suggests.

"Well, if it is, *I* don't want to talk to them. They give me the creeps."

Meanwhile: *ring-ring-ring.*

"Then again, maybe it's Mark. Maybe he got knifed at that guitar store and he needs our help."

"Why would he need *our* help?" Steve notices that Gary's one button off for the length of the shirt. "He would need an ambulance, not us."

Finally, Gary nervously picks up the phone and says, "Hello?" as if he's not sure what the word means.

"Hey, is this Gary?" the female voice asks.

"Uh, yeah. But who's this?" Gary scratches his head. The name of the girl's voice is on the tip of his tongue, only he can't quite place it.

"This is Laura."

Gary cups his hand over the mouthpiece and stares at Steve.

"*Shit!*" Gary whispers as forcibly as he can to be heard by Steve but not Laura. "It's *Laura.*"

"Again?"

"Hello? Gary?"

"Oh, sorry." He turns back to the phone. "So, er, what's up?"

"Nothing much here. How about there?"

"Same old thing, I guess."

"What do you mean, 'same old thing'? Since when has hanging out in a fancy hotel and then getting your own house, rent free, in a cool city like L.A. been the 'same old thing'?"

Gary covers the mouthpiece again. "She's too fast for me!"

"Look, Gary, is Mark there? I need to talk to him."

"Hang on, let me check. Steve, is Mark here?"

"He's out right now, Gary, you *know* that. He told you himself that—"

Gary tries to cover up the phone so Laura doesn't hear, but he's pretty sure she did.

"Oh, look, uh, forget it." Her voice is shaky on the other line, not confident or bright the way it was just moments before. "Just tell him I said hi. I've got to go."

Gary slams down the receiver.

"You fucking dumb shit!"

"What?" Steve innocently asks.

"When I asked you where Mark was, I didn't want the truth!"

"Then why didn't you say that?" Steve grabs his wallet off an end table.

"With her on the phone? I was tossing you the ball to come up with some excuse. Like he's out buying *her* flowers. I thought you'd be smart enough to pick up on it, but I guess I was wrong, again."

"Well, how did she even know we were here? Like that's my fault, too?"

"Actually, it probably is." Gary sighs and looks down at his shirt, which is hopelessly askew. He looks as if two photos of separate people were taped together in the middle and the seam didn't match. "You just *had* to call up the boys back at DISContent and rub their noses in our good fortune."

"So?"

"So"—Gary picks up a pair of green pants lying in the hallway and begins putting them on—"so you know that Jim, who also happens to manage DISContent, never lost the hots for Laura ever since they dated back in high school. I bet he waited about, oh, two seconds after Mark was gone before heading over to Laura's place with a bouquet of flowers and a handful of promotional CDs."

"But"—Steve's confused—"aren't Mark and Laura broken up? Like he should care that she's with Jim or she should care that he's here fucking some starlet. What's the big deal?"

"That's true"—Gary tries to decide on untucked or tucked—"but that doesn't mean it still doesn't hurt."

"I mean, relationships these days are just like playing musical chairs. The music stops and you move on to the next. I'd think we were all used to it. Who's got time for guilt?"

"Still, it's fucked up the way Mark handled it." Gary looks into the mirror, checking out his clothes. His eyes look tired. The strain Mark was talking about earlier in the day is easily apparent. "Fucked up," he says.

Steve, growing impatient with his roommate, stamps his feet and keeps glancing at his watch as Gary combs his hair for the fourth and fifth time.

"Speaking of fucked up, when will we be?"

Steve shouts into Gary's ear, trying to be heard above the loud blues rock of the bar band of the Roxbury.

"I keep melding here and there!"

"What?" Gary pulls a $10 bill out of his wallet. "What have you been drinking?"

"Whiskey sour," he shouts back, "but that's not what I was saying!"

Gary shoves his way to the bar, edging between a tall Chinese male with a ponytail and a blond female with a satin bustier and too much makeup. Almost every person in the bar is dressed in black, as if trying to hide, just disappear against the city's black mood. The truth was the reverse; everyone just wanted to be noticed. Most of the crowd frowned at the dim lighting in the club; it wasn't light enough to be seen.

"Two whiskey sours!" Gary shouts out, managing to draw the attention of the busy bartender.

In this, the bottom floor of the triple-tiered club, the room is a long terra-cotta rectangle, the bluesy band at the opposite end of the entrance. *The Hundred Dollar Band,* reads the bass drum, almost obscured by two guitarists and a bassist, each trying to look *and* play like Stevie Ray Vaughan.

The bartender delivers the drinks and Gary puts down his $10 bill, checking out the crowd as he waits for his change.

"What?" Gary screams, seeing that the bartender is trying to tell him something through a series of ornate gestures.

"TWELVE dollars!" the bartender says.

*Twelve?* Gary's thinking. *American dollars? Why, back in Kitty we could buy three rounds for twelve dollars.* Trying not to act like a total hick, he fishes two more singles out of his Velcro-fastened wallet.

He adds the two bills to the other, frowning at the ten and adding apologetically, "Sorry, thought it was a fifty."

The bartender half smiles, takes the cash, doesn't expect a tip, which Gary doesn't leave anyway, and before beginning on someone else's drinks makes a mental note to ignore Gary the next time around. Gary carries the drinks to the far corner of the room, where Steve managed to get a table. On the dance floor upstairs Mark has been dancing with a girl he met at the bar in the first five minutes of their arrival. He made it look too easy. Steve and Gary have been waiting for their turn. Only an hour had gone by now and they are getting progressively more drunk, which seems to turn away the females and not attract them, not that they thought it would.

Gary sets down the drinks in the only area of blank space left, and Steve sort of nods in an oblique thank-you motion that Gary, after four years of friendship, understands.

"So," Gary says as he reaches across the table for Steve's pack of Marlboro reds, "what were you saying?"

Now the music's not so loud and the sound waves are absorbed into the crowd, creating a background of sound, not an all-encompassing blanket.

"I was saying that I keep melding here and there. You know, Kitty and Los Angeles." Steve reaches for the cigarettes himself and pulls one out, rips a match from the shiny golden match-book lying in the center of a clear glass ashtray, and lights it. "Like this guy standing in line on the way in. I could have sworn he works at the Eckerds across from Moore's Mall, but obviously that's impossible."

"I know what you mean." Gary takes a drag off his cigarette, taps some ash onto the floor, and sips on his drink, which is at least powerful if not exactly worth $6. "It's like, when we got lost in the Hollywood hills looking for a place to park tonight, some of those quiet little streets could be one of those little back-road side streets back in Kitty, and for a second it's like . . . we haven't gone anywhere, really. But then, two lefts and a right and here we are in Los Angeles, the fucking Sunset Strip, a totally different world. It's too weird."

"I know, that's what I thought the other day," Steve agrees.

"I hear you," Gary adds, even though he barely does.

Off to their right is a large window that runs the length of the club. Outside, the crowd waits behind purple velvet ropes, let in only a few at a time. Behind them mostly Mexicans, wearing little red jackets, valet-park the cars pulling into the lot. A few photographers lurk on the sidewalk, hoping to get a shot of somebody famous going into the club. Beyond this, cars rush down Sunset Boulevard, fast in both directions, as if there is action and danger each way.

"Finish your drink," Gary shouts, "and let's go find Mark."

"What?"

Gary snubs out his cigarette, getting up.

*"Find Mark!"*

Steve, still clutching his drink, sucking on the ice cubes, follows Gary as he cuts across the room and heads up a flight of stairs. The middle level of the club is a restaurant, but closed down for the night. Large booths with elaborate place settings line the wall, with tables scattered throughout the floor. Gary hiccups as he wonders how much a meal in this room would cost, but then gives up, knowing that it would be too expensive for his blood. At least, it would have been in his old life, a month ago. But still, he wasn't sure he liked this place. They wouldn't even have come if Henry James hadn't mentioned it when Mark called for a suggestion, and Hanes rushed over with three guest passes, snorting as he handed them over.

The top of the stairs empties into a large room with two more bars, a few booths, and tables, but most of the room is devoted to a dance floor. A DJ, set in the far corner, is spinning bad seventies music, only now it's considered good. This is the driving force behind Generation X culture: irony. Whatever used to be bad, trashy, or tasteless is now good. *Charlie's Angels,* the Bee Gees, bell-bottoms, Abba, platform shoes, *Three's Company, The Brady Bunch,* you name it. Gen Xers may not be able to spell *irony,* but they sure as hell know what it is.

"Hey!" Mark calls out as he approaches them, a girl stuck to his side. "I'm getting a ride home tonight"—he patronizingly pats Gary and Steve on the shoulders—"so don't worry about me."

"Goddamn lucky bastard," Gary mumbles.

"What?" Steve shouts out.

Gary recoils at Steve's thunderous word.

"I said, let's get *another drink!*"

Steve nods in agreement and makes his way to the bar. He orders another round of whiskey sours, doles out the $12, and tries to add up how much money he's spent already tonight, but then balks halfway through as the number rapidly approaches triple digits. He marvels at how quickly money disappears in this town, how in the span of just a few hours he had squandered away what half of his friends paid for rent back in Virginia.

He carries the drinks to where Gary is hugging a wall, still biting his bottom lip after watching Mark exit the bar with his arm around the attractive girl, her ass swinging back and forth and Gary's head following as if hypnotized. Angrily, he clutches the drink in his hand, splashing a little of the sweet and sticky liquor onto his fist as he does so.

"No offense," he screams into Steve's ear after smoking half a cigarette and downing most of the drink. "But I'm tired of looking at your ugly face."

Steve just smiles, drunk, fishes out a smoke from his pack, which is already beginning to thin out, and he'll be needing a new one soon, more money down the drain.

"Why would that offend me?"

"Let's fucking mingle, man." Gary pokes Steve in the ribs and makes his way onto the dance floor. "Okay?"

"You go get 'em, killer. I'll finish my drink."

Steve watches as Gary wades into the good-looking crowd, sidles up against a few girls who just as quickly slide away, in time to the beat, and it's so subtle you really can't tell it's a rejection even though it is. Steve marvels at the way couples dance these days, just sort of in orbit around each other, and you can't tell who is with who since it appears as if everyone is flying solo on the dance floor. Close dancing in the mid-1990s means an absurd bump and grind where usually the male hovers close to and runs his hands over an undulating female, who jerks her head from side to side in posed rapture, and, Steve guesses, Patrick Swayze should be blamed for this.

On the dance floor Gary struggles for control over his half-drunk feet, which have not danced in quite some time, perhaps even years. The melody of the song blaring throughout the room is muffled, but the pulsating bass ripples through the floor, and right now he's just trying to make his tiny steps in circles coincide with the pounding of the beat. Turning left with unusual flair, his right hip out and his hand in the air almost as if he were doing the Charleston, he bumps into somebody. He turns around, murmurs, "Sorry," although it is hopelessly lost in the music, and then notices that the person he ran into is a girl, a young girl. An attractive girl. As she moves a few steps away, her head down and long brown hair cascading over her shoulders, oblivious to Gary, he follows.

"Hey," he shouts, unable to think of anything else to say.

At first she doesn't notice him.

"Hey."

The second time she does notice him, but pretends like she doesn't.

"What's your name?"

"Astrid," she says, finally looking up but not missing a step, "with a *d*."

"Asterisk?" Gary laughs. "What in the fuck kind of fake name is that?"

"Huh?" she shouts, trying to hear him over the driving beat.

"I mean, what do you do?"

"I'm dancing. What's it look like?"

"No." Gary shakes his head, again trying to keep with the beat, making himself look like he's having convulsions. "I asked, uh . . ." He watches as Astrid slows down her pace for a second, really trying to listen. Gary sees how attractive she really is and he decides to save time and money and just give up now. "Nothing. Bye."

Gary turns away, each step in time with the song. After two more verses and another chorus, he's reached the bar, where Steve is sitting talking with a tall blond.

"How are you doing?" Gary shouts, jerking his head toward the girl.

"Fine, thanks." He grins. "Her name's Marcella."

"Marcella?" Gary laughs, ordering a drink, patting down his pockets for his cigarettes.

"She said I've got half a brain but a quarter of a soul," Steve tries to shout as she smiles. The girl on his side leans over and kisses him on the cheek. "She's getting married tomorrow."

Gary is delivered his drink and he fishes another six bucks out of his pockets. His wallet was filled at the beginning of the evening, and after dinner, parking, a few drinks here and there, it's almost gone.

Steve leans over and screams, "How are *you* doing?"

"Bad." Gary takes a hit off the drink just delivered to him. All the whiskey seems to be floating at the top and the first sip tastes like gasoline. Gary chokes it down, then gulps a few sips in order to mask the bitter taste with some sour mix. He's growing desperate for a cigarette, something to take the edge off the alcohol. "I just met a really hot chick . . . but she was way out of my league."

"What?"

"A girl! *Her name was Asterisk!* Can you believe that shit?"

"You're drinking what?" Steve says, putting his arm around Marcella.

"No—" Gary begins, but before he can finish, a cigarette appears in his mouth and then is quickly lit. He turns to his right, to see from whence the answered prayer came, only to find the aforementioned Astrid shoving a shiny Zippo lighter into a sleek black purse.

"Meet my friend," Marcella leans down and shouts into Gary's ear. He looks down and sees an arm appear around his waist.

"I think"—Gary startles at her touch—"I already have."

# 5

**Waking up, Mark can tell by the way the small Banana**
Yoshimoto book is bulging that his cash is still folded inside and
that, contrary to his paranoia, he has not been robbed.

The girl he brought home the night before opened her eyes
earlier than Mark even dared, sometime around seven, and he
only faintly registered her presence as she sneaked out of the
bed and into the bathroom, where he heard the faucet turn on,
then off, and the toilet flush once.

Instead of joining her at the kitchen table and asking whether
she prefers a three-egg vegetable omelette to French toast
made with thick bread he'd baked the previous day, he rolled
over, folded the pillow around his head like a taco shell, doing
his best to drown out the sound of the strange woman searching
for her underwear in the living room.

He'd had the money, $200 in cash, stuffed in his wallet the
day before in anticipation of buying some new musical equipment, but unexpectedly, nothing in the guitar shop caught his
eye the way so many things usually seem to, and he had to bring
the cash home. He felt uneasy having that much money in the
house and scoured for suitable hiding places; only, every location he selected seemed far too obvious, and even the most out-
of-the-way spot, a crevice in the splintering plaster above a
doorway, seemed so outrageously perfect that Mark was positive
would-be crooks would be drawn there as if by a divining rod.
So he settled on the book that he recently purchased, a new

hardcover with a photo of an attractive Asian girl on the pink cover, which was sitting atop a pile of magazines in the corner of the room, where the girl from the night before seemed to linger for a few minutes before escaping completely.

He grabs the book and examines the cover again, still unsure if the woman in the photo is the author, since there's another photo of an Asian girl on the author's first book, but it's a different person.

"Whoever she is," Mark says, his voice cracking from the layers of phlegm that have settled there overnight, "she's cute."

He opens the pristine cover and the pages easily separate to the spot with the folded cash. He picks up the small bundle of money, tossing it from hand to hand.

*It's really not a lot,* Mark says to himself, reflecting how foolish he had been to worry, as if he had a briefcase overstuffed with $100 bills lying around. *I probably shouldn't have been so suspicious.*

Mark sighs and tosses the book back onto the floor, which is strewn with debris though he cleaned it the day before. The wreckage, all of it from last night, lies in clumps like land mines all over the ground. In one corner are a dozen CDs separated from their covers, shiny jewel boxes with their hinged flaps open, some cracked from the airplane ride from Kitty, their corresponding shiny discs either lying on the floor, laser-etched sides up, already collecting dust and hair, or stamped into the tight tendril catch of the wrong CD case. Near the bathroom door lie most of his clothes and two gray socks curled into balls, which Mark expertly peeled from his feet with the opposite toe while he and the girl began to fuck on the bed.

He cannot, at first, find his underwear, the patterned pair of boxers that not only perfectly matched his shirt and pants, but also had a thin slate thread running throughout the plaid pattern that matched his socks. After five minutes of searching he still cannot find them. He grins, thinking that perhaps in a Milan Kundera–esque moment his boxers have been snatched as some sort of prize, a move in a game where the next would be his and he would, of course, dashingly play his own hand, the strange girl waiting with an ache between her legs for him to do so. But, from the corner of his eye, he spots the underwear, folded in half and lying over one of his shoes, and even though it ruins his theory, he's still not sure he's *not* in some sort of game.

As he emerges from the fog of the night before, clouds still in his lungs from too many cigarettes, the nagging suspicion that he might not have worn a condom joins the already confirmed fact that he's all alone.

Downstairs Gary clutches his pounding head. His temples feel like a bubbling crust, like at any moment the hot insides will burst out and ooze down his face, creating steam as it hits the cool morning air.

"Mark, do you feel as bad as I do?"

Mark sits down next to Gary at the kitchen table, spotting Steve passed out on the couch in the living room. Even though Mark's not suffering from a hangover, he says, "Yeah, man, I feel bad, too."

"Fuck," Gary sort of mumbles.

Mark stares at Gary, his face shrouded in a chalky pallor. Seeing Gary like this lightens Mark's own dark mood.

"Man," he chuckles as Gary gargles though there's nothing in his mouth, spit bubbles forming around his dry, cracked lips, "what did you two *do* last night after I left?"

"Oh, went out, got shit faced, struck out with a couple of chicks. At least, *I* struck out. Steve did okay, for a while. Er, anything else? Oh yeah, I got a tattoo and, uh, we got another parking ticket even though I could have *sworn* all the signs said it was okay to park there."

"Wait a second." Mark raises his hand to stop Gary from talking. "You got a tat*too?*"

Gary deflates a little, sinking into his chair, his entire body shrinking a few inches.

"See?" He holds his now-marked-forever biceps up for Mark to see.

Mark squints to read the black-already-turning-dark-blue squiggly writing.

*"There is no one what will take care of you?"* He says the phrase out loud. "Uh, what the fuck does that mean?"

Despite his throbbing headache Gary gets up and begins pacing back and forth.

"I don't know, really." He brings his fingers to his rubbery jaw and cheeks before pulling back his hands and seeing that the black ink from the *L.A. Weekly* he'd been reading has been transferred to his face. "It's the name of this record I used to listen to back in Kitty. And you know, it's this quiet country record that some of the guys from Slint played on, and, well . . . you know how much I like Slint, so . . ." He walks a few more steps before returning to the table. "Don't blame me, blame Slint."

Mark ruffles the grayish pages of the newspaper, shaking his head from side to side. "Don't blame me, blame Slint. How many times have I heard *that* before?"

"Anyway, just using the simple law of averages, I know your night *had* to have been better than ours. How did you do with that cute little number you left with?"

"Uh . . . well . . ." Mark hesitates.

"Were those her little feet I heard pitter-pattering around the house this morning?"

"Yeah, yeah." He relents. "That was her. She spent the night. We screwed. Big deal. Drop it, okay?"

"Drop what?" Steve says groggily, entering from the living room.

Gary turns and answers since Mark has shoved the newspaper aside and crossed his arms, staring at the floor.

"Mark wants me to drop the fact that he brought home some gorgeous chick while all I brought home was a fucking tattoo and all *you* brought home were the memories of a peck on the cheek from that chick *you* were working on."

"Hey, she's going to be married today." Steve tries to defend himself as he wipes the sleep that has hastily gathered around his eyes during the paltry hour and a half of slumber. "In fact"—

he glances around the room, seeing the green LED display from the microwave glowing in the half-lit room—"she's probably saying 'I do' right now."

"Or maybe *you're* on her mind," Gary says sarcastically, "and instead she'll say, 'Can I think about this a second?'"

"Ha, ha." Steve slaps Gary on the back of his head on his way to the kitchen, where with a bottle of Vittel water he quickly washes down four Extra Strength Tylenol.

Steve stares at the kitchen, trying to figure out what food his quasinauseous stomach won't immediately reject. He begins digging through his bruised memory file, trying to remember the ragged events of the night before. A subtle face comes to mind, but it turns out to be the bartender of the Roxbury. Another face appears, but it's of a girl standing in line at the tattoo parlor, trying to pick the coolest skull from a book to have tattooed on her buttock while Gary himself vacillated between the title of the Palace Brothers' record and the line to one of his favorite David Bowie songs, "Think of us as fatherless scum."

Steve and the engaged girl danced around the floor as Donna Summer looked for hot stuff, his hands wrapped around her waist and clutching at her small ass. His eyes were trained on hers, locked, as they drunkenly made figure eights around the floor, lights blinking on and off above their heads, bumping into other dancers but not caring. During a slower song they gravitated to a corner and kissed, his tongue lapping up the sweat dripping off her nose as it circled her lips on its way into her mouth. Now he grabs a bowl from the cupboard and a box of Raisin Bran from the pantry, and maybe he's being stupid, but he really is wondering if the girl will go through with the wedding after the dances and kisses they shared just hours ago.

"What are you guys talking about?" Steve asks as he sets down his bowl, spoon, and a half-gallon carton of milk on the table.

"We're talking about how Marky Mark here got lucky with this hot little number and—"

Mark reaches out and slaps Gary.

"Ouch! What'd I say?"

"Just drop it," Mark says, lowering his face to the table and covering the back of his head with his hands. The quick puffs of breath warm the cold spot of the table that chilled his cheek seconds before.

"Mark, what's wrong?" Steve struggles with the milk container, finally pulling so hard that both corners of the cardboard carton give way and the container looks like a room with the ceiling blown off.

"It's just . . ."

"What?" Gary asks.

"It's just . . . I'm not sure if I used a rubber or not."

"What do you mean, you're not sure?"

Suddenly Mark raises his head, the blood flowing into his brain and causing his vision to momentarily become blurred.

"I mean, I was really drunk and I don't remember putting one on or taking one off. I barely remember fucking her."

"Okay, okay, this is simple." Gary leans forward, glad to be able to concentrate on something other than his bombarding hangover. "Did you see a condom wrapper on the floor?"

"Or in the trash?" Steve asks, trying to pour the milk; only, a three-inch sheet of milk begins to douse the table, so he stops.

"No, no," Mark mumbles. "I checked everywhere, in the bathroom, under the bed."

Gary looks at Steve, and then to Mark.

"You think she took it with her? Like, in some sort of futuristic way to trap you? You know, go to some scientist and have herself implanted with your child?"

"Oh, give me a break." Mark slaps the tabletop. "This is the nineties. Chicks don't like to be called chicks anymore. Half the time it's *us* who have to trap *them,* what with their careers and all. Try and remember, this *is* Los Angeles." There's silence in the room for a second as Mark stares into the tabletop, contemplating his own existence, which may have been, in the last twenty-four hours, cut woefully short. "I even . . ."

"You even what?"

"No, I can't . . ." Mark pauses.

"Come on, you can tell us."

Mark stares intently into the top of the table, his own image lost as his gaze blurs out of focus.

"I even tried to smell my dick."

After a second Steve asks, "For what?"

"To see if it smelled like latex, you moron. I was hoping there'd still be a trace." Mark shakes out of his trance. "Because I remembered that Laura would always beg off giving me a blow job the morning after we'd have sex because she said my cock still tasted like a Hefty bag."

Steve plucks a sugar-coated raisin from his bowl and pops it into his mouth. "Maybe she just used that as an excuse."

Gary reaches across the table and smacks Steve upside the head. The dried fruit in Steve's mouth shoots from between his lips and skitters across the floor as if it were a liberated tooth.

Mark is flooded with embarrassment and can't believe he actually admitted to Steve and Gary what he had done. His sides and back are still sore from his attempt to gain the closest proximity to his groin. As bizarre as the attempt was, it was not the first time in his life he had tried it. He had, years before, while in the dirty throes of puberty, tried to give himself a blow job.

"Boy, talk about scoring." Steve sucks on the tongue of his spoon. "It looks like *you* got fucked *twice*."

"What am I going to do?" Mark asks, panic in his voice. "If this chick was willing to fuck me after just a few hours, then she could have any disease in the book. She could even have . . ." His lips don't even want to form the word. His teeth don't want to separate to let it through. His brain refuses to even *think* of it while his mind tries to forget what it means. AIDS. "I never would have worried about this back in Virginia, where, I think, the swingers are finally starting to come down with the clap. I used to think it was a disadvantage that the junior high schoolers were just *now* getting into Def Leppard and wearing those insipid sleeveless British-flag T-shirts, ten years out of style, but now I miss it because here, man, AIDS, I mean, well, *you know*, the chances are *real*."

"Don't kid yourself, Mark. It's real back there, too. It's real *every*where now." Gary flips down a corner of the *L.A. Weekly* and Mark can read the upside-down ad now facing him. ADULT VIDEO BLOWOUT. *Hundreds of titles to choose from.* HOT HOT HOT. "For the last three years I made it a personal rule never to fuck a chick without wearing a rubber. Even when I was shit-faced drunk I managed to comply."

"Usually I do," Mark whines, "but this time . . . I don't know . . . I . . . I mean we, no wait, I guess it was just me. I got swept up in the moment. But now . . . I'm starting to panic."

"Well, then, get yourself checked out. It's either that or else wait a couple of years and see if you get any dark blotches all over your skin. Personally, I'd opt for the latter."

"The what? The blotches one?"

"Huh? Oh, no. Then the former."

"The skin thing?"

"Get tested!" Steve finally shouts.

Mark tries to come up with reasons why not to go, figuring not knowing is better than knowing for sure.

"I-I-I-I wouldn't even know where to go."

Steve sighs and grabs the newspaper from Gary's hand. He flips through it for a few seconds before coming to an ad he saw the other day. He rips the page out of the paper and sticks the torn sheaf into Mark's face.

NORTON MEDICAL CLINIC. THE SAFEST SEX IS HIV TESTING. BLOOD TEST FOR AIDS $45. NEXT DAY RESULTS.

**From the booth in the recording studio Mark calls the** 800 number in the ad and is amazed when a human voice and not a recording answers his call.

"Uh, hello?" he says, caught off guard.

"Norton Clinical Labs, how may I help you?"

Mark squirms in Kenneth's chair, swiveling away from the large window that looks into the studio. Steve is yelling at Gary from the back room and Gary is tuning his bass, winding his thin fingers around the large gold tuning pegs, ignoring Steve.

"Oh, yeah, er, I was calling about one of those"—Mark shuts his eyes and finally says, embarrassed—"tests."

"An *AIDS* test, sir?" the female voice replies.

"Yes," Mark tries to say authoritatively. "An AIDS test. That's right."

"When would you like to schedule one, sir?"

*Schedule?*

Mark had thought he would call and only receive recorded information. He had no idea he'd have to talk with a human being, much less a human being who would try to pin him down to specifics.

"Er, uh . . . ," he stumbles, even though there really was no other reason to call except to make an appointment. He had already decided to be tested, and all other pertinent information about the test was in the ad: price, location, hours available.

"Sir?" The operator ventures into the silence, the sound of

Steve's forehead beating against the glass only barely audible. "Are you *there?*"

As he hears the operator on the other end of the line begin humming to herself, bored, probably filing her nails, thinking about her lunch plans or the date she had the night before, he speaks up.

"Today. Later to*day.*"

"Four o'clock?"

"Yes, that will be fine."

The operator takes his name, phone number, and other facts, and he hangs up the phone. Resting the receiver back in the cradle, he looks into the studio and sees Steve poking at Gary's bass and Gary sitting on Steve's drumming throne, annoyingly wailing on the kick drum. He sighs and, turning around, sees Kenneth, who has just entered the room, his arms crossed and a fake Italian loafer tapping the way Gary's foot is smashing into the metal contraption hooked up to the bass drum in the next room.

"Are those two still bickering? Jesus, it's almost noon and we still haven't put anything down on tape."

Mark vacates Kenneth's chair and heads into the studio.

"Mark, Gary won't even *listen* to one of my songs." Steve drops Gary's bass to the ground and runs up to Mark the second he enters the room. "Won't even give it a chance."

Mark says, "Gary, is this true?"

Gary taps his fingers on a China cymbal, a low hiss like constantly shattering glass emanating from the hubcap-shaped object.

"Yeah, I guess," Gary admits, "but what are we, the Eagles? Fucking Gene*sis?* I mean, who ever heard of a *drummer* who wrote songs? And on a *bass* for God's sakes."

"What about Sebadoh!" Steve shouts, rushing for his kit.

Gary just yawns, twisting back and forth on the cushioned seat.

"Sebadoh, shmebadoh," he says flatly.

"Will you guys just cool it?"

"Okay, Steve, why don't we try *again*, to lay down the drums for 'I've Been Talking to Stephen Hawking'?" The producer's voice booms from the talk-back mike, flooding the room.

Mark wearily moves to exit and sees that Gary is eyeing Steve with an I-wish-you-would-just-die sneer, to which Steve is responding with an outstretched arm, his fist clenched and a whitewashed drumstick sticking out between his fingers, two on either side, flipping Gary off.

Back in the booth Paul punches in a few numbers on the tape remote, the twenty-four-track recorder rewinding as Kenneth fiddles with a few knobs on the mixing console. Gary and Mark sit down on the couch behind them.

Steve, inside the drum room, waiting for his cue, is sniffing. He inhales deeply and smells the clean odor of wood. He can't tell if it's coming from the Tama drum set (which looks brand new; the only gray slicks on the bleached white drumheads are Steve's own from the past couple of weeks) or the half dozen planks of whitewashed pine that the drum set is sitting upon, the rest of the room, walls and ceiling included, covered with carpet.

He squirms uneasily on his seat, waiting to begin, his nostrils still twitching, and he fears that again tonight he'll toss and turn in bed, unable to get the aroma out of his head, the same way the week before the incessant *tick-tick-tick* of the click track was tattooed onto his brain after hearing it through the headphones day after day.

Steve twists at the waist to stretch out his back, which is feeling tense after the days of recording and the ensuing anxiety, but he does so gently, not wanting to disturb the carefully placed microphones around the set and room that Paul and some guy who they had hired to come in and tune the drums had spent an entire day arranging, at the end of which they declared the sound to be "punchy" yet "warm." Six microphones with yellow cables poke their way around the set. Two more microphones are stationed around the room, one on a large boom mike stand and positioned above the entire set, while another, a boxy,

1950s-crooner-looking microphone with a shiny steel grating, stands four feet away from the set.

"You ready?" Kenneth's voice fills the room even though Steve cannot see anyone.

His back begins to hurt again, and that smell of the wood fills his nose. He rubs his tired eyes and grabs for the headphones resting on the floor tom.

"Yeah."

Steve begins to play to the music filtering through his headphones. All he can hear is Mark's temporary guitar track, and he finds it hard to keep the beat without the rhythm of Gary's bass chugging alongside him. He tries it once, only to be cut off by Kenneth, who says he's alternately slowing down and then speeding up. On the fourth take he drops the sticks in frustration, the music skidding to a stop a few seconds after.

"Steve." Kenneth's voice, with a little bit of static, fills the room. "What's wrong?"

"I just can't get the feel of the song. It sounds weird. Uh, can you turn up the bass in the mix?"

Paul looks to Kenneth, who stares through the glass doors to where Steve is beginning to sweat.

"Oh, you wanted that recorded?"

Worried hands tentatively clutch the steering wheel, fingers nervously tapping the semisoft deep purple plastic.

Mark turns right onto Melrose from La Brea, following the directions the woman had given him, hearing her deep voice in his head, "Make a right, on the left-hand side, a few blocks down, second floor . . ."

His eyes dart from the road in front of him, various automobiles swerving in and out of the lanes, to the numerous storefronts, trying to read the numbers. Lining the street is a dilapidated park filled mostly with winos and a couple of brave kids avoiding the winos, a few cheap liquor stores, a thrift store and a Baskin-Robbins with a corner parking lot that is riddled with potholes. This length of Melrose is bleak and untrendy, unlike the ten or fifteen blocks that begin just a few streets west of Highland and stretch to just past Fairfax. This fact doesn't stop smarmy landlords who own run-down duplexes built in the forties from overcharging rent to overzealous youth who are willing to shell out big bucks due to the cachet the address still affords, even if they were a few blocks away from the action. "Just off of Melrose," prospective tenants would hear themselves saying to their friends as they tried not to notice the peeling plaster, the cockroaches darting in and out of the cracked floorboards, and the landlord in the corner twirling a set of rusted keys on a paper clip and reciting over and over, "Twelve hundred dollars a month . . . plus deposit . . . twelve hundred dollars a month . . ." The renovation that had begun to creep up La Brea like a vine from Wilshire on up, thanks most exclusively to the numerous American Rag stores, the Living Room Cafe, and a few restaurants and bars, had yet to seep sideways into Melrose and the few blocks that Mark's bloodshot eyes were now combing.

"Aha," he shouts out to the empty interior of the car, "there it is."

He slams on the brakes and turns on his blinker, intent on making a left onto the side street. A few cars behind him zoom out of his way, into the right-hand lane, while others bottleneck in his wake and begin honking repeatedly. Mark, already confused, looks up and sees a sign attached to the traffic light. NO LEFT TURNS BETWEEN 4:00 P.M. AND 7:00 P.M. He quickly glances at the green digital clock in the dash. Four-oh-seven.

"Oops," he says as the light turns yellow, and hunching in the cushioned seat, meekly makes a left turn, leaving Melrose and a chorus of honking and shouting behind him.

He cruises alongside a parking meter and quickly gets out, trying to distance himself from the spectacle that occurred seconds before, avoiding the gaze of the drivers now stranded behind the red light, who will now be late thanks to him.

He shuffles along Melrose, passing a coffeehouse called the Cinema Cafe, where, peering inside, he spots the usual small tables and mismatched furniture, chessboards, and cluttered ashtrays. The door to a small back room is half open and a dozen people of varying ages sit on metal folding chairs and look up at a homemade screen painted onto the wall while a sixteen-millimeter projector shoots a fuzzy black-and-white image onto the concrete surface, yellow subtitles trailing the bottom and only barely readable.

MELROSE CANTINA, a neon sign screams in gaudy red-and-blue, audibly crackling as Mark finally spots the address, 7204½, which is a side entrance with a staircase leading to the second floor.

At the top of the stairs he finds a shallow lobby set at odd angles, as if the entire floor were at one time a huge open space that was later sectioned off with room dividers forming triangle-shaped rooms. The sitting area consists of a few cheap metal chairs with plastic coverings, a small table strewn with a few magazines, *Time, Newsweek, Cosmopolitan,* all a few weeks old, and the routine doctor's office receptionist behind the frosted sliding-glass window. On the wall are large colored reproductions of the same ad he saw in the *L.A. Weekly,* one done all in red, another in blue, pasted onto cardboard and hung by nails in the middle of otherwise bare walls.

"Uh, my name's, er . . . Mark," he says nervously to the receptionist, pausing for a second, wondering if he should give a fake name. "I made an appointment."

The woman, a girl, really, who can't be much older than Mark, hands him a few multicolored forms attached to a rigid wooden clipboard along with a ballpoint pen. She yawns into a small, tanned hand that fits in well with the rest of her dark skin and jet black hair.

"Fill this out," she says without interest, jerking a painted thumbnail to the row of chairs.

Mark walks across the room and takes a seat. He quickly fills out the form, carbon copies reproducing the information in triplicate on different-colored paper, the first white, the second goldenrod, the final a tissue-papery pink.

He delivers a tiny fake cough to get the receptionist's attention, who's on the phone and complaining about her schedule to someone on the other end.

"Uh, all done . . ."

She looks up and, somewhat pissed off, turns to the phone and says, "I'll call you later," in an offhand tone before reaching under the uncluttered white desk and hitting a button, which releases the lock on the door leading from the lobby into the office. Mark drops off the form, shrugs, and enters the room.

From the inside looking out, the lobby looks even more pitiful than before, and he only imagines how many times this young girl must watch some poor guy or girl as they sit, waiting either for their results or to get tested, squirming in their uncomfortable chairs.

"If you'll hop up over here, please."

He turns and sees the young girl standing next to a medical table, the kind covered with the wide racing stripe of meatpacking paper, bent in the middle like a Y with one of the branches sliced off.

"Oh, in *here?*" Mark asks, uneasily sliding onto the table. He was hoping for an office where a stately old man who reeked of respect and reminded him of his departed grandfather, sans the embarrassment factor, would appear from behind an X-ray-riddled light board and tell him everything was going to be a-okay.

"Yes, right here," the girl says with a nervous laugh.

*Please don't be another psycho.* She shakes her head, getting a hypodermic needle, a small vial, and a rubber hose out of a drawer. *Please, not three in one day.*

"Would you mind taking off your jacket?" she says, clamping her tongue between her teeth for a second. "And also, uh, rolling up your sleeve?"

Mark tries to fake-laugh, as if he's being impudent on purpose. He rolls up the white cotton sleeve to around the middle of his biceps, his pale arm laid bare before the girl and the searing lights in the ceiling. The girl taps at the small expanse of flesh on the opposite side of his elbow, where his forearm and upper arm meet in a small, crescent playing field of skin. After a few tries a squiggly, greenish-blue vein floats to the surface the way a nipple awakens when it is caressed or lightly bitten.

"Okay, now," the girl is saying, readying the needle in her right hand, "this isn't going to hurt a bit."

*You?* Mark's thinking. *You're going to perform the surgery? Well, no, it's not surgery, but I worked at the mall for a summer and they didn't even let me use the credit card machine, and I'm going to let* you *draw my blood?*

"Something wrong?"

"No, no," Mark squeaks out.

"Look, if it's the pain you're afraid of, I can assure you it's really nothing. I've done this *hundreds* of times, and no one's ever passed out or anything."

"Hundreds?"

The girl fakes a smile.

"Okay, *dozens,* but really, nothing bad has ever happened." She pats his clenched fist as if consoling a child who was not getting candy. "Trust me."

The needle hovers above his arm for a second or two before the girl slowly lowers it in. At first it just pinches, the poked skin becoming taut, not quite giving way, and for a moment Mark fears the needle isn't sharp enough, but then the skin breaks and bounces up, taking the steel into his vein.

It seems odd to notice this about the girl while she's drawing blood from his arm, but just above her left eye is a small patch of dark black hair, emanating from a phantom mole, which, he guesses, has been covered up with an excess amount of base makeup. Instead of a dark splotch on her face there's a pale white one, and it still looks freaky. He glances down at his arm, forgetting for a second what's happening, and, startled, jerks his body.

"Steady now," she says, reaching up and holding on to his arm with her free hand.

He feels like the needle's being driven into his bone and he shifts his arm, only to watch the syringe stay exactly in place, the little line of silver metal twisting his vein around it like yarn on a knitting needle.

"Just a bit more."

The liquid being sucked into the empty cylinder, the black plunger backing up, creating a vacuum and making space for the cargo, is deeper than red, almost bluish green, and nothing like any blood Mark has seen in the movies.

From the other room the phone rings and the girl looks over her shoulder impatiently. Three rings later she removes the needle from Mark's arm in one swift move and for an instant Mark guesses how all those lovers must have felt when he jumped off them only moments after sex.

"Here"—the girl grabs a cotton ball from a jar and places it over Mark's already bruising exit wound—"put this there."

As soon as Mark grabs hold of the ball of cotton the girl jumps up and runs across the room and answers the phone.

"Look, Jerry, I can't talk right now. Yes, I *know* you're sorry." Mark can hear her trying to whisper. "I know. I *know.* Call me in five minutes, okay? Okay, bye."

The phone crashes into its cradle and the girl marches back toward Mark, stopping at a counter to grab from a plastic dispenser a stretch of tape that has adhesive on one side and dental floss crisscross on the other. She lays this over the cotton ball horizontally, the ends lapping each other and forming a tourniquetlike bandage around Mark's arm.

"How long do I keep this on for?"

"A couple of days at least."

Mark folds the sleeve down over his elbow and scoops up the jacket underneath his other arm.

"So, I, uh, guess that's it?"

"Not quite." She moves back to the desk and picks up a receipt pad and begins filling it out. "That'll be forty-five dollars. Please."

"Yeah," he says, embarrassed, "sorry."

He fishes two twenties and a five out of his wallet and as he's leaving he contemplates throwing in the three singles left as a macabre tip, but decides against it.

"See you tomorrow?" he says.

"Can't wait."

Noticing something about Mark as he crosses the room from the living room to the kitchen, Steve asks, "What's that bulge on your elbow?"

"Huh?" Mark replies nervously, opening cabinet doors and then shutting them, trying to create a diversion. "Bulge?"

"Yeah"—Steve rises out of the chair and follows Mark to the refrigerator, where he's staring at its sole contents: a head of rotting lettuce, an empty Rafallo's Pizza box, half a jar of Miracle Whip, a milk container with about two sips left, and half a lemon—"*that* bulge."

Mark hides one arm behind the door of the refrigerator, moving the other behind his back.

"Quit clowning around and show me."

Mark finally stops waving his hands about the room and, giving in, rolls up his sleeve, exposing his arm with its cotton ball and bandage barely covering a half-dollar-sized bruise.

"So, you went and got tested, eh?"

"Yeah." Mark shrugs.

"You worried? About the results, I mean?"

"God, I don't know."

"Like, what would you do, I mean . . . *if* . . ."

"Look, Steve, don't even *say* that."

"Yeah, but . . . *if so* . . . how would you do it? You know . . . how would you do what needed to be done?"

Mark decides to concede Steve's grim scenario and philosophically rubs his chin, formulating an answer.

"I think I'd do it with . . . a gun. Right to the head. No wait"—he reconsiders—"that's too messy. And you guys would *never* clean it up. Maybe I'd hang myself, or else drive the rental car off a cliff, into the ocean. Yeah! Or maybe—"

"No, you idiot. I meant, how would you call all the girls? You know, the ones who you might have infected?"

"Huh?"

"Forget it." He moves on. "So, how was it?"

"Okay, I guess, but, man, that was the first time I've ever had blood taken, and that needle scared the shit out of me." Mark's voice rises with enthusiasm. "You know, seeing that thing go right into your arm and suck the blood out. Yuckola."

"I know what you mean." Steve laughs as he hops onto the counter next to the sink full of dishes. "I always feel bad for junkies whenever the blood drive comes around and I'm sitting in the gym at the YMCA drinking my orange juice and staring down at that hole in my arm."

"Yeah," Mark says, "poor Royal Trux."

Steve laughs a little and begins humming, *"Junkie nurse, my junkie nurse . . ."*

Mark starts cracking up and he pats Steve on the back as the two of them head into the living room.

Gary comes out of the bathroom a second later and steps in front of the refrigerator, whose door is still wide open, the large white machine's engines feverishly kicking in to create cold air as a stale room-temperature odor smacks him in the face.

"Hey, who ate half my lemon?"


Mark parks on the opposite side of the street from where he parked the day before, not even looking up at the three rectangular metal signs on the dark brown telephone pole that outline the street's parking policy.

He gets out of the car and inserts the key in the door to lock it, then turns to leave, the keys dangling in the wind, slapping into the side of the auto with an almost tinkling sound.

"Oh, yeah," he mumbles, wiping the sweat from his palms onto the back of his jeans before reaching for the key ring.

Earlier in the day he had to call and set up a time to request his results, using the code name, M411, that the receptionist had issued to him the day before as he was leaving the building. Kenneth was pissed at Mark for cutting short the session a second day in a row. He warned that Henry James would hear all about it, and asked who was it exactly who had flown the three of them out here, were giving them advances, and supplying them with a fully furnished home in which to live. Mark just gave Kenneth a *Well, duh* look and marched out of the room, jittery hands clutching at the doorknob leading out of the studio.

This time there's a person waiting in the lobby, whose presence only accentuates the dreariness of the oddly shaped room. For a second the man, slightly older than Mark, looks away, tries to seem interested in the magazine he's reading. Mark tries to smile, to reassure both himself and the visitor, who, without the blood-dabbed cotton ball on his bare arm, is either waiting to be tested or waiting for someone who is, whose fate may also be his.

"Hi, uh, *M four eleven,* here for my results," he whispers through the bivalved window to a receptionist, a different girl from the day before.

"Just a moment please," she says in a deadpan, rising from her chair.

Mark peers through the open space and can see the dangling legs of a person sitting on the table, but he can't tell if it's a male or female because the tattered jean leg and industrial hiking boots, these days, could belong to either sex.

"Here you go, Mr. Pellion," the girl says, handing Mark a piece of paper, dispensing with the smoke screen of his ridiculous code name.

"Thanks," he blurts out, grabbing the sheet from her hand and quickly scanning the two-color form riddled with dot matrix printing. Blue sections with headings like LIPIDS, ENZYMES, HEMATOLOGY, SEROLOGY give way to pink boxes where results are printed under subheadings that read *Globulin, % Saturation,* and *CHOL/HDL Ratio,* all unreadable to Mark, whose red eyes are searching for the simple plus/minus symbols he learned back in grade school, when such dangers as he was encountering now never existed.

At the bottom the cheap computer printout reads HIV ANTBY BY EIA . . . NEGATIVE.

Mark jumps a few feet and yelps, unable to control himself. The receptionist and the man waiting in the lobby stare at him but he doesn't care. He hops down the staircase taking three or four steps at a time.

After a few blocks of zigzagging in and out of the crowd, some of which he dances through and jogs with his hands in the air like a triumphant Rocky, Mark comes upon a record store called Bleecker Bob's Records. He decides to go in and see if they have any of his band's singles. The owner of his old label, Dave, had always promised him he was getting distributed all over the country, but Mark never quite believed him. Now was his chance to prove it.

The store is long and thin, bins of vinyl to the right, while CDs lie in rows of glass cases on the left. Lining the walls are posters, calendars, and rare records. Behind the cash register is a line of bootleg videos as well as a few rock and roll books, and in the very back of the store a weathered woman with bright orange hair sells T-shirts, stickers, and patches. Mark looks around but can't find the seven-inch-singles bin. He looks around for some help, but the only other people in the store, a couple and a girl, are customers. Finally a big burly guy with a shock of red hair emerges from a room in the back eating a hamburger. He sets it down at the cash register, takes off the record that was playing, and puts on another.

"Uh, excuse me," Mark says politely, approaching the counter, "do you have—"

Before he can finish, the large man behind the counter cuts him off and bellows in a Cockney accent, "No 'e don't, an' piss off!" He picks up the hamburger and marches down the hallway, disappearing again into the back room.

Somewhat stunned, Mark exits the store, finding himself back in the middle of sidewalk traffic.

"Don't worry about that," says the girl who was inside the store a few seconds ago. "They're like that all the time." She glances back at the store. "This is a new location. It used to be on the other side of the street, about five more blocks down, but it's still the same store. Overpriced imports, promo copies on sale at regular price, and *lousy* service."

Mark looks into the girl's hazel eyes, not saying a word. Her shoulder-length hair is pulled back, her tan, somewhat wide face is healthy, sporting a grin with deep dimples. She's wearing faded jeans, cowboy boots, a tight white T-shirt, and a thick black leather belt.

"My name's Mark," he says just as she's turning to walk away.

"Oh, mine's Corinne. Nice to, uh, meet you."

*Quick,* Mark's mind is racing, *think of something funny to say.* "So, uh, I mean, er . . . so, you come here, I mean, *shop* here, often?"

While Corinne grins, thinks Mark's fumbling is somewhat cute, and begins to formulate an answer, he's making a mental note to strangle himself when he gets home.

"Um, yeah, I guess so. I mean, it's such a hassle getting in and out of the Beverly Center just for one or two items, and the parking at Aron's is a disaster. I was just at the Soap Plant and thought I'd walk down and see if they had anything new, so . . ."

"Yeah, yeah," Mark's agreeing, nodding his head, trying to find a suitable place for his hands: in front of his chest looks too tense; right hand in his pocket with the other elbow locked against his hip, fingers splayed against his left temple, looks too contemplative and, he figures, fake; both hands in pockets suggests oafishness; and with both hands hanging at his sides he feels bare, naked. "Yes, oh yes, *I completely* agree."

Despite Mark's continued fumbling, Corinne actually laughs. His shyness seems real, not an act he's putting on just because he thinks it's the way to get her to like him. She thinks that the way he's mincing around nimbly on his feet, nervously shifting his weight, and after a few minutes of conversation still doesn't know what to do with his hands is not only genuine, but cute.

"Well," she says slyly, waiting for him to make the next move, although it is visibly painful for him to do, "I should be going."

"Wait." Mark maneuvers his way through the crowd, trying to keep up with Corinne, who is easily slipping in and out of the passersby. "Could we go out sometime?"

Corinne stops, grins, and just as she's about to answer in the affirmative, something catches her eye and derails her comment.

"Hey, what's that on your arm?"

"Hmmm?" Mark asks, glancing down to the left side of his body, where the short sleeve of his blue T-shirt falls just above the thin strips of gauzy tape and the ball of cotton, ill-shaped from the shower that morning.

"I, uh, gave blood . . ."

Corinne laughs a little.

"I can *see* that."

"I mean, at the Red Cross. Yeah, the Red Cross." Mark grins at coming up with an excuse. Feeling cocky, he decides to push it. "You know, one of those blood drives. I figure, I got it, they need it, so why not?"

Corinne smiles and moves down the sidewalk with Mark following.

"I know what you mean. I give blood all the time." She stops and turns, examining his face. "So, which one did you go to?"

"What?"

"Which Red Cross?"

Mark racks his brain, trying to come up with an answer. When she sees he's stumbling, she helps him out.

"The one in Hollywood or over on the West Side?"

"Oh, Hollywood," he says quickly, as if it were apparent all the time. "Hollywood, yes. Didn't I say Hollywood?"

"Uh, no."

"So, how about that date?"

They pause on Melrose for a second, crowds of people passing them by like the opportunity Corinne imagines Mark just may be.

"Sure," she sighs, adding, "Why not?" as she fishes around in her purse for a pen and a scrap of paper.

"Here, write it on this," Mark offers, shoving his folded-into-fourths AIDS test printout toward her left hand, which is already clutching a red pen streaked with black mascara.

Mark smiles as the girl scribbles her number and name below the words PEDIATRIC REFERENCE RANGES, which is printed in light gray type, some of the pink and blue from the other side seeping through.

# Chorus

# 7

**Climbing out of the shower, Mark catches a look in the** mirror at two hairy trails leading down from his hairline past the base of his neck. Angling wildly, twisting at the waist, he finds it impossible to get a better look at the back of his head in the mirror above the sink in the bathroom. He wraps a dark blue towel around his midsection and sets out to search through the many still-unexplored drawers of the house for a second mirror to augment the first, the way hairdressers always gave him a handheld mirror and then turned him around in the chair. The first time this happened Mark was amazed that he could see the entire back of him in the long mirror on the hairdresser's wall that he'd been casually staring into for the past fifteen minutes, praying she wouldn't cut the top too short, like the last one did, some kid from the beauty college who, thanks to the pineapple effect of Mark's haircut, eventually flunked out. Sitting there that first time, seeing what appeared to be the reverse image of him in one mirror with the help of another, two seemingly disparate worlds joined only by Mark's eyes, he had been freaked out. Years before, a teacher had explained to his science class that the atmosphere was so dense on the planet Venus that if you were walking on a beach, you could see the back of you walking in front of you. But while the other students thought that the fun fact was interesting, nothing extraordinary, and certainly not as cool as what any kid could see at the movies, Mark alone was truly intrigued by the idea. He never forgot this, and years later this concept would pop into his head whenever he tailgated a car that was the exact same model, year, and color as his own brown Toyota Tercel, half expecting to see his own stare reflected in the rearview mirror of the identical vehicle in front of him; but the first time he felt he might be on Venus, not that it happened too often, mind you, was the first time he examined the back of himself while looking forward, maybe ten years ago now.

"You, uh, got a mirror?" Mark, dripping onto the floor, asks Gary, who's sitting on the couch watching TV.

"Hmmm?" Gary says at first, not looking up. "No . . . the only one I know about is in the bathroom. Well, there's a full-length one in my room, but it's set into the door." He finally glances at Mark, whose hair is slowly drying, his bangs curling up into reeferlike dreads. "Jesus, man, what's the emergency?"

"No emergency," Mark says, trying to sound nonchalant as he walks away, holding the towel above his waist in the back, where it has come loose and his ass is exposed to the room. "Just need a mirror . . . is all."

Mark returns to the bathroom and, he's convinced, his fuzzy neck is actually making a scraping sound like fat thighs rubbing together sheathed in corduroy. Forced to innovate, he grabs a CD from his room and marches back into the bathroom, his head hot with an idea. Sitting on the sink with his back to the medicine chest, he holds the CD by the hole in the center, gazing at the reflective side, trying to catch the back of his head in the mirror behind him. At first he thinks it might work and, excited, he grabs the blue disposable razor and brings it to the back of his neck.

Just before the first swipe he realizes it might not work. His reflection is too grainy, clouded even, for him to be precise. The back of his neck is only half visible anyway due to the disc's paltry, five-inch circumference (not to mention the hole in the middle). In a last desperate attempt he shimmies up even farther on the sink, the nose of the faucet poking into the half-moons of his rear, dribbling a slight but constant flow of warm water onto the underside of his leg. This time he holds the CD close to his face and squints, trying to get as exact a view as possible. He brings the razor to his neck with his right hand, crossing over his shoulder to shave the left side of his neck, but once it slides slowly into view and he tries to place it against his skin, he loses all control. He tries to plant the razor squarely along the lines of his shoulders, in an upside-down *T*, and just rake upward, and finally finagles the blades outward to accommodate the rising angle of his hairline as it disappears behind his ears, but the razor's reaction is the opposite of what his hands tell it to do.

He tries twice, three times, and still his dexterity fails him. Both hands begin shaking and he makes only a few crude swipes side to side before slamming the razor on the top of the toilet.

"Damn," he shouts out, craning to see the thickish line of hair still trailing to the root of his back, only now there's a small section slightly cut away. "I can't stop now or it'll be obvious that I *tried* to trim this."

He readies the razor again and encounters the same problem. He tries to trick his brain by moving his hand in the opposite direction he desires, thus fooling both the mirror and his mind, but somewhere along the line the trick's been played on him because the razor still does not move in the direction he expects it. He slaps his bare kneecap out of frustration.

A few houses away, across the courtyard, Mark hears loud voices, crowd noises, and sound effects coming from someone's TV. Before starting in again on his neck, he sits for a moment, sliding open the bathroom window slightly, the voices coming in clearer than before.

"I don't know you . . . I don't like you"—he hears some piece of clothing hit the floor in the film—"and as of right now, I'm all over you."

This line is followed by a gut-sickening *slap,* which Mark knows means someone's been punched in the movie. Crowd noise now drowns out some girl yelling at someone, and Mark closes the window.

"Ha," he says, passing the blades underneath the faucet, rinsing out the long hairs that the razor's not designed to handle,

*"Encino Man."* He brings the disposable again to his neck and makes his first protracted pass, the skinny, sharpened silver cleanly slicing away his stubble like soft trees in a forest. At the bottom of his hairline Mark means to curve to the left, but in his mirror move his wrist angles to the right, sending the metal into his skin. "Hell of a way to spend a, *ouch,* Saturday night."

"Hey, what's going on in here?" Steve asks as he enters, knocking on the door once already inside.

"Uh . . . nothing, go away."

Mark dabs at the red trail of blood oozing down his neck.

"Wait a second," Steve asks, beginning to laugh, "were you shaving your neck?"

Mark doesn't respond and instead grabs at a piece of tissue.

"Hey, Gary, come in and see this!" Steve shouts to the other room.

"Steve . . . no . . . ," Mark protests.

"See what?" Gary calls back.

"Look, just leave me alone, okay? Yes, if you *must* know, I was shaving my neck. Is that a crime? I've got a date and it was just looking sort of unruly and I didn't need a whole haircut and I wasn't about to go to some foo-foo place in Beverly Hills and have them charge me forty bucks just to trim my fucking neck."

"So, your solution was to maim yourself with a disposable razor, saving forty dollars but looking like an idiot, guaranteeing that the girl you were trying to impress in the first place will never talk to you again?"

Mark turns away from Steve and back to the mirror. Despite the flakes of already dried blood and the glowing red cut mingling with his hairline, his neck does look better.

"I'm not so sure about that." He again picks up the razor and CD and turns around, his back facing the medicine chest.

"So, I guess since the clean bill of health, the girl from the other night is going to get a *repeat* performance?" Steve cackles.

"No, actually. This is a different girl."

"Different girl?" Steve cries out in a mixture of horror and jealousy. "Who? What? When?"

"What is this, a freshman journalism class? I met her the other day."

"What other day? You mean Tuesday?"

Mark tries to replay the week in his head, searching for an answer just to make Steve disappear.

"Uh, yeah, Tuesday."

Steve starts laughing, unclenching his arms, which are wrapped around his chest, long enough to slap his leg with his right hand.

"Am I to understand that you picked up a girl at an AIDS test? Oh, this is classy. And I thought that Gary's pickup line of 'I bet you have a nice little pussy' was bad." Steve stops in a moment of reflection. "Of course, maybe that works because he says it in a French accent."

"I didn't pick her up at the actual test. I met her the day I got the results."

"Yeah, big difference. Instead of being an asshole you're now just a prick."

Mark ignores him and turns again to the mirror.

"Hey, is that one of mine?" Steve asks as he turns to exit the cramped bathroom, referring to the silver disc in Mark's hand that is dripping water and covered in short black hairs and some blood here and there. It's actually one of the few CDs Steve brought from Kitty.

"Uh, no."


Mark smells at the air before knocking on Corinne's door, trying to sniff out any traces of the jojoba hand lotion he slathered on his red-hot and freshly sheared neck in an attempt to both cool down the burning sensation and wash away the pink tint of the scraped skin. He smells again but can only detect the faint scent of flowers in the air, which he's pretty sure is not coming from him. Just as he's raising his hand to his mouth, to try and test his breath, the door flies open.

"Oh," Corinne says, looking somewhat confused. "I, uh, thought I heard something out here."

Mark scrambles for an excuse.

"Oh, yeah, I got here a second ago and just wanted to make sure this was the right address."

Slowly both of their heads rotate, locking eyes on the center of her door, where tarnished but still recognizable tin letters exclaim 620¼.

"I mean . . . ," Mark begins, his face flushing and his neck now feeling on fire.

"Don't worry about it." Corinne grabs his damp hand and pulls him in. "Feel free to look around while I get us something to drink."

The apartment's sparsely furnished with shiny black chairs, table, and couch. There's a sleek stereo in the corner, sporting only a CD and cassette player. Mark walks through the black-and-white-tiled kitchen, then a breakfast nook that has a marble-topped table and two black bar stools situated around it. In the background Mark hears "Anything, Anything" by Dramarama on the radio as a DJ with an English accent cuts in, "It's another Flashback Weekend on KROQ, the Rock of the Nineties."

"This is really nice, how much is your rent?" Mark shouts out as he examines a space set into the wall where a sleek black combination phone/answering machine rests beneath a small Dubuffet print clipped from *Interview* magazine. "Three hundred? Three fifty?"

Corinne laughs in the kitchen as she pours the contents of a Canadian Glacier bottle into two wine glasses.

"I'm glad I ran into you." She meets Mark in the hall and hands him the glass. For a second Mark thinks it might be vodka and so sips at it carefully. "Try eight fifty."

"A month!"

"Yeah, but don't forget, it's in a decent neighborhood, has hardwood floors, *and* parking."

Corinne completes the tour through the back of the apartment, through the bedroom, spacious hall closet with a built-in vanity mirror, and a small backyard with a dead lawn that all eight tenants use as a parking lot. They retreat to the living room.

Mark sits on the couch and at first it feels nice. But then he becomes anxious, mired in a minor anxiety attack, and instead of feeling free, he feels lost. Where in the fuck is he? Who in the hell is this girl? Where, exactly, has he parked the damn rental car? Mark's feeling as if he's swum out too far in an effort to escape, the beach no longer in reach, and he needs somebody to save him.

"So, what would you like to do tonight?" he blurts out.

"Oh, okay," Corinne says, somewhat shocked, as if Mark had clumsily driven off the road to Getting to Know Each Other and plowed right into the oncoming traffic of the First Date Expressway. "I thought we could order in some food and just talk. There's a great Chinese place that delivers, okay? And later a friend of mine is going to be giving a poetry reading at Beyond Baroque books out in Venice, if you feel like going."

Mark nods, even though he can't stand poetry read aloud, especially by the poets themselves.

"You know," she says, "I think I even have some sake in the fridge."

"Sake would be nice," Mark says with a grin, thinking, *Sake in the refrigerator is Chablis.* He's glad to see she's not perfect.

Corinne consults a menu, sitting on the edge of her couch, and picks up the black phone and orders. As she racks up item after item, Mark checks for his wallet.

"It'll be about forty-five minutes," she states, looking over at Mark just as he whips his hand out of what looks like his underwear.

"Uh, so, what do you do?"

"I'm a PA," she says with a slight laugh. *Jesus, this guy's not wasting any time, is he? Starting right in on the old boring stuff.*

"PA?" Mark frowns. "Like, in a club? I don't get it."

"God," she turns to him, "you really are green, aren't you? 'PA' stands for 'production assistant.' I work for a motion picture production company. I started out as a receptionist but worked my way up—or, at least, sideways."

"Oh, really?" Mark says, cheerfully trying to make it seem like he knows what she's talking about. "So, production assistant, it's a neat title, but what do you do?"

"A little of everything. 'Gofer' would be a better way of explaining it, but 'PA' sounds better." Corinne laughs. "You know, office stuff, Xeroxing scripts, answering the phone. When we're making a movie it's more fun because I'll spend some time on the set. But in between it's just boring office work."

After twenty minutes Mark relaxes enough to stop asking stupid questions. Then Corinne asks Mark some questions, about his past, the band, how the recording is going. She's genuinely interested because she's never met anyone like him. The people she'd met in the past who had moved to California from somewhere else all wanted to be movie stars or directors and all they wanted from Corinne was jobs. She was tired of dating men from the entertainment industry who would describe the inevitable gaps in their relationships as a "hiatus" and felt an almost pathological need to be seen at the right films, the trendiest restaurants, and the most expensive clubs. Mark, underdressed, semicoarse in manner, but cute, was a welcome change for Corinne.

When the food arrives Mark jumps up to answer the door. He pays for the meal and tries to show off by tipping the driver a $5 bill, which the driver is expecting and which Corinne doesn't see.

As she scoops onto his plate, white surrounded by a thick border of black, bits of chow mein, sweet and sour pork, kung pao chicken, and vegetable fried rice, Mark stares at her, trying not to do so obviously.

She's wearing a gray cotton full-length dress that clings to her shapely body, the material drooping around the left shoulder, where a black satin bra strap can be seen.

"Hot mustard?"

Mark hesitates, not wanting to say the wrong thing, seemingly unable to come up with the right thing, and so he sort of gargles, spit in the back of his mouth bubbling up.

Mark keeps trying to stare at her without being noticed, sneaking glances at her breasts when she shows him how to tear open the silvery package of plum sauce without dousing the room or covering yourself with gelatinous shrapnel. When Corinne gets up to get more napkins and her panty line is right on Mark's eye level, he tears into a packet of soy sauce and sprays her tablecloth with dozens of pinhead-sized black-ink dots.

Mark is noticing all the small things about her, like Corinne's manicure and painted nails, her shiny earrings (*Are those real diamonds?*), her subtle dash of makeup so well hidden that at first he wasn't sure she was wearing any at all, and the light trace of her scent, a perfume so well chosen and complementary that one had to be close to detect it.

"More sake?" Corinne asks, calling from the kitchen.

"Uh . . . no thanks." He brings his hand to the tabletop and wipes at the soy sauce, only smearing it all into even-more-conspicuous black streaks.

"I wonder what your friends are doing tonight," Corinne says, noticing the little wet spots on the beige tablecloth, already thickening as they soak into the fabric, turning brown.

Mark quickly reaches for a napkin and covers as much space as he can.

"Friends?" he asks. "What friends?"

"Your friends, uh, Steve and, don't tell me, Gary, right? Aren't those their names? You know, your *band?*"

At first Mark doesn't place the names. "Oh"—his eyebrows shoot up in recognition—"them."

"Yeah, *them.*" Corinne laughs. "Geez, you tour the country with them, fly all this way, spend so much time together, and you can't even remember their names?"

"Yeah well, anyway"—Mark doesn't even try to defend himself—"I'm sure they're having fun tonight. After all, they certainly don't need *me* to have a good time."

Gary's thumb is sore from the remote control.

"Goddamn," he shouts, dropping the small black plastic rectangle to the couch as he tries to dial in HBO. "Why don't they make that up-and-down channel button a little smaller, so I can get an even *bigger* blister, you know?"

"Huh?" Steve pokes his head out of a magazine he'd bought at the airport a few weeks ago.

"This fucking remote!" Gary scrambles for it in the soft cushions of the couch, desperate to change the channel from the religious program now playing.

"Oh," Steve says, lackluster, "yeah."

"Hey look, *Encino Man*."

Steve sets aside the magazine for a second.

They watch the screen as a couple dozen kids party in tuxedos and evening gowns around a makeshift pool represented by a muddy hole in the ground. Among them is a defrosted caveman with, as we've discovered in the course of an hour and a half, a heart of gold.

"Happy ending," Gary sneers.

"Typical," Steve replies.

"You know, for years I kicked myself for not having cable back in Kitty, but what's the point?"

Steve looks at the TV screen, on which Gary is changing channels every few seconds.

"Like I'm supposed to be sad I'm missing all of this?" Gary runs through about forty channels in just about as many seconds, old reruns, infomercials, sports coverage of esoteric events (wood chopping, cheerleading competition), B-movies, cooking shows in half a dozen languages but strangely the same cuisine. "Back in Kitty I had a dozen channels and there wasn't much worth watching. Here we've got, like, three or four dozen, and there's *still* nothing worth watching. Cable, *sheesh*, what a joke."

Steve just sits there, feeling numb. He disagrees with Gary but doesn't have the energy even to start the argument.

"People think crappy stations like TBS or USA actually have their own programming? Like they're *missing* something? Hell"—Gary picks up a copy of a TV guide that comes as a supplement to the Sunday *Los Angeles Times*—"all they're going to miss is *Can't Buy Me Love* at eight o'clock."

Steve perks up.

*"Can't Buy Me Love?"*

Gary tosses the *TV Times* onto the coffee table a few feet away.

"That's what I said."

"Want to order a pizza?"

Gary sits up quickly, checking his watch.

"Yeah, we've got half an hour. Better hurry."

Gary runs into the kitchen, where he swears he saw a drawer filled with takeout and delivery menus. He's rifling through cabinets, while Steve rummages through the credenza lining the wall behind the couch, looking for a phone book. Somebody rings the doorbell and Steve looks up suspiciously.

"You expecting anybody?"

"Who would I be expecting?" Steve can hear cupboard doors open and then slam shut. "Just answer the door and let's order this pizza. We're losing valuable time!"

Steve gives up the hunt as he sees Gary has found a clear green plastic business card that says *Damiano's New York Style Pizzeria. We deliver!* The doorbell rings again and Steve moves to answer it.

"Hey kid, what's up?" Sam says as he stands in the doorway, wearing the same clothes as when Steve met him two weeks ago.

Gary sort of groans when he sees who it is, but Steve invites Sam in, since Sam and Steve have hung out a couple of times since Bottlecap moved in. Mark and Gary didn't like him much but Steve thought, if nothing else, he was a welcome change from Gary and Mark, who he is forced to hang around with every second of the day. Sam has driven him to a few requisite Los Angeles landmarks like Carney's up on Sunset, Norms down on La Cienega, the Chateau Marmont on Sunset, where John Belushi died, and he promised to take him up to the Hollywood sign one of these days. Sam said he was an actor even though Steve has not heard of him working on an acting job, or any jobs for that matter. He always seemed to be hanging around the front porch of his apartment, smoking cigarettes, drinking a beer, starting conversations with the tenants of the complex, who, unlike Sam, had somewhere to go and someplace to be. He was always asking about the recording: how was it going, was everyone in the band getting along? Steve thought the strange questions were not only odd, but a little out of line. But then again, what did he know? He was from Virginia.

Gary interrupts Steve and Sam's conversation concerning an attractive girl who lives across the courtyard with her boyfriend.

"Uh, 'scuse me, guys, but, Steve, what kind of toppings do you want?"

"Ooh." Sam picks up the scent even though the food hasn't even been ordered. "Pizza?"

"Uh, yeah," Gary says reluctantly, kicking himself for not calling Steve into the kitchen and asking him in private.

Steve turns to Sam, then to Gary, an idiotic grin on his face and the lightbulb above his head almost visible.

"Hey, I've got an idea. Why doesn't Sam join us?"

"It's a Saturday night, Steve. I'm sure Sam has more important things to do than sit around and watch *Can't Buy Me Love* with a couple of guys like us."

"No way! Patrick *Dempsey*! He sort of went downhill with crap like *Loverboy* and *In the Mood,* but his ensemble work in *Coupe De Ville* was sensational and, man, that scene with Jennifer Connelly in her underwear in *Some Girls.*" Sam is shaking his hand, loose at the wrist, back and forth. "Whew!"

"So you'll join us?"

"Sure." Sam crosses the room and sits down on the couch where Gary was sitting before. He raises his dirty motorcycle boots and sets them on the coffee table, crusts of dried mud flaking off. "Make mine a sausage."

"Yeah, sausage for me, too!"

Gary warily retreats back into the kitchen, picking up the beige wall phone next to the refrigerator and grumbling under his breath. He orders a large sausage for Steve and Sam and, feeling crowded out, a small pepperoni for himself.

"Hey, kid, you got anything to drink?"

"Oh, good thinking." Steve's eyes open wide. "Hey, G got anything to drink?"

Gary is just finishing reconfirming the address and order with the restaurant when Steve shouts out to him. He plugs his exposed ear with his thumb, pressing the phone hard against his other ear.

"Wait a second, did you say *South* Sierra Bonita, or North?" The line goes dead, but already depressed, Gary figures the food will get to them sooner or later. "Huh? Something to drink? Oh, shit, let me check."

In the fridge there's about half a glass worth of orange juice, a few drops of nonfat milk, an opened can of soda, and an entire container of nondairy creamer that Gary's never seen before.

"Uh, no, we're out!" Gary makes for the phone again. "I'll call them back and see if they can deliver some pop or something."

Just as the number begins ringing, the line goes *click, click,* and then nothing. Gary swings around to see what's happened and he finds Sam's bony finger in the phone cradle, holding down the tongue and making it say *ahhh.*

"Tell you what," Sam says, "why don't Steve and I go get a six-pack or two of beer? There's a liquor store right around the corner. Beer really goes better with pizza than soda, don't you think?"

From the other room Steve pipes up, "I think so!"

"S-s-sure," Gary says, still clutching the phone.

"It's just around the corner." Sam walks briskly ahead of Steve, who has to jog to keep up, his untied shoelaces getting caught underfoot. At the top of the street they turn left, the liquor store on the next corner.

As they skirt the building, Sam gets in close to the wall, peering over a large vinyl banner promoting Coors Light that uses a girl in a bikini and a race car to do so.

"What are you doing?"

"Just making sure the place isn't being robbed. That we're not walking into something we don't want to be walking into."

Steve gulps as they turn to enter the garishly lit liquor store.

"After all," Sam continues, "this *is* Los Angeles."

He winds his way through aisles of overpriced, already expired foodstuffs, the $6 box of corn flakes, the $3 loaf of bread, and past the coolers filled with eggs, cheese, and milk, all priced two bucks higher than their grocery store counterparts.

"Beer, beer," Sam mumbles underneath his breath.

"It's quiet in here," Steve says, noticing the only other presence in the store besides themselves is a small black-and-white TV set hung in the corner of the room. "*Too* quiet."

"What is this, *Repo Man?*" Sam chuckles, grabbing two six-packs of imported beer. "Come on, let's go."

Hanging over the cash register is a sign painted on a thin metallic sheet that reads NO CREDIT PLEASE DON'T ASK.

"Hello?" Sam calls out, shaking one of the six-packs, the bottles of beer knocking together in the cardboard holder.

From the back room comes a very straight-looking older man, thin, about forty, with rectangular glasses and a crew cut. He glances at Steve and Sam quickly, sizing them up.

"Will this be all?"

"Yes, please," Steve says politely.

"Hey," Sam says, "I saw all those movie trucks the past couple of days parked around the block. Were they filming in here?"

"No," the man says blandly, "but they didn't hesitate to ruin my business for two days." His thin fingers punch at the ancient cash register, the total popping up on flash-card-like numbers in the window of the slot-machine-shaped device. "The beer is twelve fifty, and it's two dollars for the news."

Steve laughs weakly at the man's joke and pulls at the bag of beer (which tears instantly, so he has to carry it from the bottom), while Sam just glares as if terribly insulted. Once outside he turns quickly to Steve, a shocked expression on his face.

"Could you believe that guy?"

"Huh?" Steve asks. "Oh, yeah, a real geek. Why, back in Virginia we'd call him a—"

"No, no, it's what he said." Sam waves his hands in the cool night air. "That comment."

Steve doesn't really see the point.

"It was a dumb little joke. So what?"

"So what? That guy works in a liquor store in Los Angeles. The odds of him getting shot by some teenage wacko are so high that I don't think he's got the, shall we say, margin of error to talk to me like that."

They round the corner, now off Sunset, sheathed by the cool shadow of an enormous palm tree, its huge fronds audibly shifting back and forth twenty feet above.

"It's like, once he was sure we weren't going to blow him away, he got cocky. And that just pisses me off."

"Ahh, don't worry about it." Steve smiles in the darkness, feeling the cool bottles through the bag and on his forearm. He anticipates the sudsy taste of the beer.

"No, I *am* going to worry about it."

Sam stops on the sidewalk. Steve keeps going for a few steps before noticing that Sam is still on the curb and has not begun to cross the street with him. He looks back and sees his neighbor, little wisps of wet grass clinging to the soaked toes of his black boots, his face drenched in shadows, half his body doused in a queer yellow light from the street lamps half a block down.

"So, what are you going to do?" Steve calls out, trying to laugh, but getting a chill down his spine.

Sam smiles and lifts up the front tail of his white T-shirt. Despite the darkness Steve can see the butt of a small pistol, the pearl handle against Sam's stomach and the slate black metal of the trigger and the nose where it disappears into his pants pressed against his flesh.

"I'm going to go back in there," Sam says, reaching for the weapon as he turns back toward the direction of the liquor store, "to teach him some manners."


As Mark and Corinne drive out to Venice on Interstate 10, Mark sinks deeper into the comfortable seat, the wind from the sunroof tossing his hair around as he begins to unwind.

"Isn't this nice?" Corinne says loudly, combatting the wild rushing of air.

"Yes . . . very," Mark replies as he stares out the window, watching the exits go by: La Cienega, Olympic West, Sepulveda.

Mark's amazed by how nonchalantly Corinne weaves in and out of the dense traffic. She's wearing a pair of Ray-Ban sunglasses, a Depeche Mode song is on the radio, and she holds the steering wheel between her knees as she reaches into the backseat for her purse, returning with a small tube of lip gloss.

"You like Depeche Mode?" she asks.

"Um, no," Mark says, slightly afraid to be honest.

"Good, me neither, but there's nothing good on NPR right now."

After a few more minutes of driving, the sun now swallowed completely by the shimmering horizon and the rushing breeze a tad cooler than before, Corinne haphazardly switches lanes.

"I just thought of something."

"What?" Mark asks, clutching the door.

"What do you say we ditch the poetry reading? I just started to imagine all those supposedly deep people sitting around that old musty church and I just don't think I could handle that tonight."

"Okay. What should we do, then?"

"Hey!" Corinne shouts. "Do you want to go to Palm Springs? I know this great hotel in Rancho Mirage that overlooks the entire city. It's really pretty and it'll be a nice drive, you know. You'll get to see some actual desert."

Mark nods in agreement, thinking, *Why not?*

Corinne maneuvers her white Jetta off the freeway, loops under the overpass, and gets back on the Interstate, now heading east.

On the drive through the desert they pass through half a dozen cities that Corinne describes as stuck in an identity crisis because "they're not exactly the Valley, but fall just shy of Orange County, so they can't decide whether to be stupid or racist." The towns roll by every fifteen minutes or so, each with the requisite glaring neon visible from the freeway: Burger King, McDonald's, Wendy's, Taco Bell, Kmart. Mark checks the names of the exits to make sure they're not all the same town, figuring he and Corinne might have stumbled onto one of the inner circles of hell, a never-ending loop of strip malls, department stores, and fast food restaurants. Replace Kmart with Wal-Mart and Carl's Jr. with Hardee's, plant a few trees, and it would look like Virginia. Mark suddenly gets depressed; it's as if he hasn't gone anywhere.

"Can you feel it getting warmer? We're getting closer." Corinne begins playing tour guide. "Off to the left, see the big dinosaurs from *Pee-Wee's Big Adventure*? Remember? When he watched the sunrise with that French waitress?" She points to a small diner and a gargantuan parking lot where two hollow dinosaurs stand about three storeys tall. "But in real life they're not lit up as much."

Fifteen minutes later Corinne exits the freeway and turns onto a dirt road.

"Have you ever seen these?" she asks, bringing the car to a stop.

Littering the landscape like wild weeds in a field are hundreds of sleek, modern windmills, tall as telephone poles, with three blades circling at the end like a propeller on a plane. The alternate rotation of the windmills' blades makes the hill look like the uneven surface of an ebbing ocean. Moonlight glints off the horde of brilliant silver machines.

"Yeah, yeah," Mark says, jumping out of the car. "They're beautiful, but what do they do?"

"I don't know," Corinne says, surprised, as if she'd never thought of it before. "I guess it's some sort of energy thing."

Twenty minutes later (and after Corinne has stopped and asked for directions at a gas station) they find their way to Rancho Mirage, steadily climbing a long hill to the hotel. It seems to get a degree warmer every few inches until, when the car finally levels out and enters a huge circular parking lot, it feels like ninety degrees. Not bad for October. Corinne pulls up to the lobby entrance as two young men in white shorts and polo shirts descend upon the car, opening both of the doors.

"Good evening, sir!"

"Any luggage, ma'am?"

"No." She laughs. "Not tonight."

The huge lobby features a marble floor and ornate columns leading up to the tiled ceiling. Thick rugs rise almost an inch off the ground, upon which stand thick granite tables adorned with large and colorful floral arrangements. Off to the right is the registration desk, and to the left is a bank of elevators leading up to forty floors of rooms.

"Well, where's this bar you were telling me about?" Mark nudges Corinne as a man in a suit behind the registration desk eyes them.

"I haven't been here in a while," she pleads, "but I think it's straight ahead."

To look more official Mark grabs Corinne's hand, but she just chuckles and pushes it away. At the end of the hall the marble gives way to hardwood floors, and the bar and accompanying dance floor feel more like the interior of a cozy lodge than a palace. Tucked away in the far corner are a trio of older men in tuxedos playing a stand-up bass, guitar (tiny amp, no distortion box, Mark notices), and a drum kit. They're producing gentle, danceable melodies for about half a dozen couples, most of them older, one or two newlyweds, and a few embarrassed boys dancing with their proud mothers. Lining one wall is a row of tall, gangly girls too shy to ask the boys hugging the opposite wall to talk.

Mark and Corinne take a seat at the deep mahogany bar.

"What'll it be?"

"Vodka martini, on the rocks. Stoli. Double."

"Make it two." Corinne examines him. "That's a pretty stiff drink."

"After the past couple of days"—he swings around on the bar stool, facing the room of sluggish dancers—"I need it."

The bartender sets down both of the drinks, each in a short glass with two green olives skewered on a black plastic sword.

"That'll be sixteen fifty, please."

Mark pulls out two tens and drops them to the bar.

"Let's go outside." Corinne stirs her drink and then eats the garnish, placing the swizzle stick on a stack of cocktail napkins. "You've got to see this killer view."

They sneak out a side door, walk through the pool area (Corinne stopping for a moment to slip a toe into the glowing blue water), and pull up two chaise longues from a group skirting the pool, turning them the opposite direction, overlooking Palm Springs. The city shines with cars no bigger than pinheads, while a stream of white and red lights enters and exits at opposite ends of the town.

"This is really . . ." Corinne pauses as she simultaneously takes a sip of her drink and tries to follow a pair of tiny red lights out of town. "This is really nice."

"What, your drink?"

"Sure, Mark, the drink is fine." She laughs as she turns on her side, resting her face on her hands, the vinyl bands of the chair eating into the back of her hand. "But I meant that *this* is nice. You. Me. The night."

"You sound surprised."

"I guess I am. Not that I didn't think you were a nice guy and all. I mean, I went out with you, right? But . . . this."

"This what?"

"This feeling."

"*What* feeling?"

"This warm feeling I've got"—she puts a hand to her chest—"right here."

"Oh, so it *is* the drink."

"Very funny. It's just, I'll tell you my sordid romantic past some other time, but suffice to say, I haven't felt this relaxed in a long time." She drains the last of her alcohol. "It probably didn't sound like it, but that was a compliment. How about another drink?"

"Yeah. Another martini. And could you make sure they put it in a tall glass this time? Shaken, not stirred. I'm feeling like James Bond tonight. Great, thanks."

"I meant how about *we* get another drink."

"Oh." Mark grins. "Sorry."

She rises off of her chair and offers a hand to help him get up. He grabs her hand and hangs on to it even after he's on his feet. They retrace their steps to the lobby, comically swinging their joined hands like a couple of third-graders. Just outside the large oak door they hear the band and stop for a moment, watching the shadows of the middle-aged dancers on the drapes.

"Come here," Mark whispers, pulling Corinne toward him.

They dance for a few slow songs.

"Whew, I'm getting dizzy." Corinne pulls away for a second, taking her hand from around Mark's waist and applying it to her forehead.

"I don't think chugging that drink helped very much."

"I think you're right."

She peers through the large door, looking in at the dancing couples and shy boys and girls. The room has thinned out considerably from before.

Mark stands behind Corinne with his arms around her slender waist, hips swiveling slowly to the lazy beat rapped out by the drummer, who's now using wire brushes. One of the dancing couples retreats, leaving an older man and woman flying solo on the parquet floor.

The man is guiding them around in graceful turns, a figure eight and even a dip. He's wearing a spotless tuxedo that clings to his trim frame like paint. At over sixty, he's still dashing. The woman, almost a full foot shorter than her companion's six feet plus, has a full head of gray hair that's swept off her shoulders, wound tightly in a bun, and held in place with an ivory comb. She's looking adoringly into his eyes.

"Anniversary," whispers Mark, nibbling on Corinne's ear. "Fiftieth."

"Nah," she replies, "twenty-five." She reaches for his hands and pulls them like a belt, tighter. "They had full lives before they met each other. It's better that way."

He kisses the top of her head, more a sentimental act than a pleasure-seeking principle, because Mark tastes only a dry tuft of hair and Corinne feels an odd, wet sensation on the top of her head. She looks up with a smile, the limitless sky beaming overhead. A shooting star? Probably not.

"Want to stay the night?" Corinne asks.

"Oh, uh." Mark's stunned, slightly scared. "How much would it cost?"

"Forget the cost." She twists in his grasp to face him. "Credit cards, remember? Plastic? It's a known fact that scientists invented plastics, and thus credit cards, for situations exactly like this."

Mark weighs the decision in his head for a moment before answering.

"Sure."

He positions his other arm at the base of her back, bringing their clasped hands up. Corinne leans her head on his shoulder as he guides them in shuffling circles to the drowsy beat of the band.

"You're very handsome," Corinne says quietly.

Mark spins her away from his body like a yo-yo, letting her float for a few seconds before reeling her back in.

"I know."

"So the nigger says . . ." Sam continues with his off-color racist joke while Gary stares, horrified, and even Steve, usually Sam's supporter, looks to the floor in disgust. "Don't you know that milk chocolate melts in your mouth, and not in your hands?"

At first there's just silence, the only sound in the room above the music playing in the background the folding paper sound Steve's dry skin makes when his face crinkles up in amazement.

"Uh, yeah, *real* funny," Gary says.

Sam, oblivious, breaks into laughter, clutching his sides with hands still greasy from the pizza, his fingertips leaving tomato sauce dots on his white T-shirt.

"Uh, excuse me for a second." Gary rises. "I'm going to get another beer. Anybody want one?"

Sam, still laughing, shakes his head while Steve grunts and watches as Gary retreats to the kitchen. As soon as he's sure his roommate is out of earshot he turns quickly to their guest.

"I can't believe you did that earlier."

"What?" Sam leans back with an innocent look on his face, grabbing a pack of cigarettes from his back pocket, the outline of the gun apparent. "Go back in for some smokes?"

Steve leans forward, then looks to the kitchen to make sure Gary is still out of hearing range.

"I can't believe you acted like you were going to rob that place."

Sam chuckles, popping a cigarette into his thin mouth, which is even thinner as he talks and clenches the cigarette at the same time.

"Hey, I'm an actor. I can't help it if I'm so damn good."

"Yeah, acting like you're going to blow some guy's head off." Steve finds his voice shaking, the fear he felt an hour ago on the sidewalk coming back to him. "That's real good."

"Will you quit crying?" Sam waves off both Steve and his admonitions.

"Who's crying? *I'm* not crying."

"You know what I mean, kid. Just don't get all bent out of shape about it."

Steve sinks lower in the chair, feeling the coiled springs tight against his ass and the wooden foundation just below that. He's still pissed off at what Sam did, but he's also miffed that it's bugging him so much, that perhaps Sam is right to rib him. Steve, in a small way, wishes he was more like Sam, ready to roll with life's punches, occasionally swinging first in a sort of preemptive strike. He wonders where it was in life he became so safe, staid, downright priggish. Steve figures that, like most things, it began in childhood, most likely stemming from being held underneath the thumb of his older brother for too many years after the decampment of their father.

"It's not like I was scared or anything," Steve says in a whisper. Gary is still fumbling in the cupboard in the kitchen, noisily looking for something. Steve shifts his weight, the chair giving slightly as he turns to Sam.

"Yes, you were," his guest says with a devilish smile.

"N-n-no, I wasn't," Steve replies with as much conviction as you can while stuttering, which seems about as assured as proclaiming one's innocence while simultaneously blushing.

But Sam was right. Steve had been scared. And why shouldn't he have been? After all, armed robbery led just as often to death as it did to making it out the door with a couple hundred dollars stuffed inside either your underwear or a greasy brown paper bag. But it wasn't the prospect of stealing and everything that could go awry that turned Steve's insides into jelly, because Sam didn't mention robbing the place, only that he was going to teach the man "a lesson," though Steve imagined this entailed a fate worse than demanding the contents of the cash register and then running like hell. It was the sight of the gun that sent chills down his already shivering spine. Just seeing it set his nerves on edge, never mind that the thing was tucked safely behind Sam's leather belt with the marijuana belt buckle. What scared him so much was the possibility, the unfulfilled future, that the gun represented. It was the polar opposite in emotion, but identical in dynamic, to seeing a piece of woman's lingerie on the floor; without the body to fill out its shape, the thing seemed only half real, but the implied reality, just knowing what this thing could do, was always enough to make his cock do a half twist in his pants.

"I don't know, kid, you may not be as cool as I thought."

"What do you mean?" Steve juts out his chest and sucks in his stomach, conscious of how much of his skin is folding over his belt. "I'm cool."

Sam grins, leans forward, also cognizant of the fact that Gary is out of the room but may still be able to hear them. It strikes Steve as odd that Sam, an actor who, it seems, is always seeking an audience, would care.

"The way you shook out there, on the sidewalk . . . that wasn't too . . . cool."

Steve swallows quickly. "But there was a breeze and . . . I had on short sleeves. Besides, since when is it cool to get shot in the chest by an edgy liquor store owner during an aborted robbery attempt?"

"Huh?" Sam says as he laughs.

"I asked, since when is it cool to get shot in the chest over forty or sixty dollars?"

"Since when?" Sam bounces up and down, chuckling wildly. "Since about six months ago!"

**Quincy O'Connor had reached her limit. It was now** halfway through the lunch with Corinne on the Monday after her date with Mark, and Corinne had yet to spill the beans. She had acquiesced on a few points of the evening, relating her impetuous U-turn on the 10 and that she had indeed followed Peter's advice on what to wear (Peter was a thirty-five-year-old married man with impeccable taste to whom everyone in the office went for fashion tips), but Corinne was holding out. And it was the topic in which Quincy was most interested.

"So it didn't happen? Or did it? I'm confused."

"Well, let's just say we slept together, in the classical sense."

"Wait a second," Quincy, Corinne's friend and coworker, says, pausing before she takes a bite of corn bread. "You guys stayed the night, but you didn't fuck?"

"No," Corinne says in a hushed voice, hoping Quincy will adopt the same volume. She looks around to see if anyone else in the restaurant heard her friend's loud remark. "I mean, yes, we stayed the night, but no, we didn't *have sex.*"

"But why not?" Quincy dips the corn bread into a large bowl of red vegetable soup. "You wanted to, didn't you? I mean, that's why you spent the night?"

"I don't know what I wanted." Corinne thinks back to Saturday night, as the bellhop led her and Mark down a hallway to their room. She kept wondering if it was all a mistake, and he kept wondering if he had enough money for a tip. "I mean, I *think* I wanted it. The sex, I mean. But it's still too soon. After Tim."

"Tim," Quincy says, her mouth still full of food. After every motion of her jaw up and down she says, "Tim, Tim, Tim," the way Corinne had repeated the name over and over in the past few months. "When are you going to get over Tim?"

Again Corinne glances around the Soup Plantation, *Tim* being a popular name, and she fears some guy will think she's interested in him.

"I *am* over him. I just can't forget him. There's a difference."

"Yeah, in the voltage, maybe. I just don't see why you're not getting on with your life."

"I am. I mean, I'm trying. That's why the date with Mark was still a success. Even if things didn't, uh, work out . . . sexually speaking."

"Work out?" Quincy's pale ears perk up, becoming infused with blood, a sort of gossip erection. "What do you mean?"

"Well, the no-sex thing isn't because we didn't try."

"Was it his fault? It was his fault, right?"

"Of course it was his fault!" Now it is Corinne's turn to raise her voice, assuring everyone in the restaurant that she can still cut it, womanwise. "But *fault* is sort of a harsh word. So he couldn't get it up. Is that such a big deal? Or rather, couldn't *keep* it up."

Quincy can't stop shaking her head. A mouthful of soup is ready to go down her throat, but her continuing laughter just may send it out the way it came.

"Actually, I'm glad. It would have been too much, too soon. Anyway, it allowed me to receive a handful of sex credits without actually going through with the deed."

"What do you mean?"

"Well, you know, we got right up to the precipice. And I would have, even if I knew in my heart it wasn't right. I was saying all the usual things." Corinne hangs her head in embarrassment.

"Like what?"

"You know, stuff like, 'I want you inside me. Oh, this feels so good.' And panting when we were just kissing. I had the old familiar 'Ooh, you're so deep' standing by, but"—she pops the last of her lunch into her mouth and says matter-of-factly, "it turns out I didn't need it."

Quincy's attention is broken when Elliott, a messenger in their office she's had a crush on all summer, sits down three tables away.

Outside the restaurant Corinne and Quincy walk the three and a half blocks down Wilshire to their building. Despite the encroaching autumn, the day is still bright, their cheeks warmed by the sun and the stroll a good way to begin hollowing out their now-full stomachs.

"I know what you meant back there," Quincy says, trying to catch up to Corinne as a family brushes her out of the way, crowding her off the sidewalk and onto a skinny strip of grass.

"Which part?" Corinne turns and laughs as she sees Quincy jump to avoid a small splotch of mud before stepping back onto the sectioned concrete. They had known each other ever since elementary school, and their talks then consisted of the number of ways they could contort their Barbie and Ken dolls and the best tips on operating a lightbulb oven, but now Corinne could see in her old friend's face that a nugget of knowledge was about to be imported pertaining to the area of sex. It sometimes shocked Corinne how far they had come.

"About when, you know, a guy just *can't*."

Corinne smiles, keeping quiet, waiting for Quincy to elaborate.

"It's like, for a few minutes afterward they're just silent. You know they just want to disappear."

"And then what do they want?"

"They want us to climb all over them and tell them it's okay. That the night's going to be just as fun without it. The sex, I mean. As if that's not why we crawled into bed, naked, with them in the first place."

"Oh yeah?" Corinne laughs. "And *then* what do they want?"

"A second chance."

Corinne just laughs but after a few seconds she notices Quincy is staring at her. She wants more, but of what, Corinne doesn't know.

"Yeah, so?"

"Well, are you going to give it to him?"

"To who?"

"Mark, that's who. Are you going to give him a second chance?"

Corinne hadn't really thought about this yet. When Mark decamped late Sunday they had left the situation with the proverbial 'I'll call you,' and in the minutes after he left and she searched her apartment for her cigarettes, she really didn't bother to think if he meant it.

Across the street a bright yellow school bus passes the La Brea Tar Pits, full of kids who shout out to cars passing by, waving hands and arms out the window. Corinne notices the driver is wearing a Walkman, oblivious to the chaos behind him, and she looks carefully for that long rectangular mirror above the windshield that the bus driver uses to scope out any illegal activity, but she can't see it. She figures maybe they've done away with that mirror. Maybe the rules have changed since she was a child.

"It would seem sort of cruel not to. I mean, to give Mark just that one chance."

"You're right. He's probably in training right now. Doing push-ups and slathering his body with vitamin E."

They both laugh as they pause for a light at Spaulding, across the street from the Los Angeles County Museum of Art. They can see the long line of steps set at a gentle slope as it leads back to a box office, and beyond that the large buildings holding various exhibits. On the right, following the rise and fall of the stairs, a three-foot aqueduct of cascading water splashes against a marble wall inlaid with the names of individuals and corporations who have heavily contributed to the museum. Off to the left of the entrance stands a violinist swaying back and forth, his eyes closed, in his own world, while at his feet lies his instrument's open case, collecting a few dollar bills, but mostly just change.

"Yeah." Corinne watches the traffic going by, doesn't notice that the light has changed. "I'll give him another chance. I mean, I guess he's giving me one, too."

"But when?" Quincy laughs.

Corinne is startled at her friend's unrelenting questions. She fears Quincy may want to be on hand for her and Mark's next date, a witness to the rematch.

"He's coming over to watch a movie." Corinne glances to the sky in order to avoid Quincy's glare. "Tonight."

The brilliant blue afternoon air is being quickly replaced by dark, menacing clouds that lumber slowly, pregnant with water. Corinne hopes this is not some sort of sign.

It just wasn't fair. Gary was from Virginia, just like Mark; was in a band; was new to California and so needed a helping hand, needed an attractive woman to show him around. But while Mark is over at Corinne's, which was where he'd spent most of the weekend, Gary is at the house, doing the laundry.

But then again, everything seemed to come easy to Mark. From the very beginning. From before they even met (junior high), Mark's life contained tints of upper-class wealth—summer vacations at a rotating selection of expensive locales. When he was ten they bought a boat, not content with the offerings they were forced to rent in Cape Cod or the Gulf of Mexico. During high school these stories only intensified in scope and dollar amount, only now Gary was somewhere in the background, either left completely out of Mark's family summer trips or sometimes invited along. He could never figure out which hurt his feelings more, but whenever he came home from one of these glittering vacations, his own existence seemed shabby by comparison. He was mad at his family simply for being themselves. He hated the fact that he was not rich like Mark.

After high school, Mark's parents offered to send him to college anywhere in the country, all expenses paid, and Mark decided not to go (Gary thought this the height of arrogance), preferring to stay in Virginia, close to his girlfriend and the band he had recently formed. As soon as he moved out of the house his parents moved to Tiger Bay, an exclusive section of town.

Mark knew his parents were considered rich by Kitty standards but that they had only an inkling of the wealth accumulated by older, more gentrified Eastern and Southern families. The truth was that Mark himself felt a little uncomfortable cavorting with the dandified sons and daughters of oil and cotton magnates at the fancy resorts his parents dragged him to while he was growing up. He preferred to be back home, where he could show off his wealth to those who had none. Though he always complained about it, ranting about what phonies his mom and dad were, Gary and Steve always took this to be a sham. They believed Mark was proud of his parents' relative wealth. He felt that he deserved it.

Now that Bottlecap had their record deal and were on the cusp of making some real money, it looked as if Mark again had saved himself from financial obscurity, though this was just as much an illusion as was his constant humble shuffling back in high school. For Gary and Steve, California meant everything. They knew that this was their one shot. They were painfully aware that the only things left for them in their small hometown were jobs they had quit, apartments they'd vacated, and friendships they'd brutally dissolved; the two would be lucky to get any one of the three things back. But they knew Mark would land on his feet, as always. His father would be there with a handshake palmed with cash and a well-paying job somewhere, under someone who owed him a favor. To Gary, it just wasn't fair.

He reaches into the pile of multicolored clothes that form a small hill on his floor. T-shirts, jeans, underwear, socks—it seems as if every article of clothing he had brought was now dirty and in need of washing. He can smell a rotten odor coming up from the pile as if the mound were made of garbage and not cotton, denim, and a few metal and plastic buttons.

"Jesus." Gary yanks his head out of the way of the scent wafting into his face. He had always been squeamish about bodily scents, his own or others'. He once broke up with a girl, left her standing on the doorstep on New Year's Eve (a night that ceremonially peaked at midnight was over that year at half past nine), just because she had bad breath.

"Where's Mark?"

Gary turns and sees Steve standing in the doorway.

"Guess."

"Katherine's?"

"*Corinne's,* and I think you'd better get to know the name."

"Hey, you doin' laundry?"

"No, I'm flying to Mars and this is my spaceship."

"Oh, well, do you want to do mine, too?"

"No!"

Steve sulks down the hallway, mumbling afterwards, "Geez, sorry. Just asking."

Gary goes back to pulling out articles of clothing. He searches the pants pockets for spare change and folded-up pieces of paper in the back or keys in the front. He had once ruined an entire load of laundry because he'd thrown a batch of clothes into the dryer with a tube of Vaseline Lip Therapy tucked into a shirt pocket. The clothes came out covered with gelatinous streaks that did not come off, no matter how hard he tried. At the time, they were all the clothes he had, and so he was forced to wear them, playing off the gobs and dots as if they were some new style, as if he wanted them there. No one believed him.

He also had a mild fetish about his shirts. He hated sending a buttoned-up shirt through the laundry, sleeves rolled to the elbow. A garment such as this did not get clean, Gary felt, and would have to be washed again, and washing it again only doubled his chances for some Chapstick or gum to destroy the thing completely. He became very stressed over laundry.

The laundry finally sorted, he takes the wicker basket that was in the corner of his room and that he figured was a hamper, though no clothes had been deposited there yet, and goes downstairs. He finds the bundle too heavy to carry out from his body, so he rests the thing on his chest as he takes the steps slowly, one by one, wisps of the wicker cut at an angle sticking him in his exposed white gut leaking out between shirt and jeans.

Once outside, Gary looks up to the sky and sees black clouds that appear heavy with rain. Since he'd arrived in Los Angeles, the skies had been almost permanently clear, the temperature bathwater warm; he was beginning to think weather did not exist in California.

As he heads toward the rear of the complex where a small laundry room is set up in a drafty shack, he sees a girl sitting on a small stone wall, smoking a cigarette.

She has light red hair, which is pulled back, and is wearing a navy blue sweater that is too large for her; the cuffs are drawn down over her fists, except on her right hand, where two very white fingers clutch at a skinny brown cigarette. She is wearing a long skirt that goes well past her knees; underneath are dark brown tights that end in black shoes with thick soles. It's the first time Gary has seen a female in California wear anything warm. Seeing this makes him warm. As he approaches, she looks up and small red lips curl into a smile and pink cheeks (the chill bringing out their color) bunch into hemispheres on her otherwise flat face. He thinks she is beautiful.

"Laundry, eh?" she says.

Rather than make a smart-ass remark the way he had done minutes earlier with Steve, he puts on a bright, wide smile, hoping his teeth show in the darkness.

"Yeah." He laughs, unsure how to counter her own comment. *Laundry, yeah. You know it. Just doin' the old laundry. Can't let it pile up, you know.* None of this sounds good, so he passes her, entering the brightly lit laundry room. He quickly shoves a bundle of clothes into the washer (colors and whites together, something he usually considered a sin), pours in a large dollop of detergent, and sets the machine's dials without looking.

*Get a hold of yourself, Gary.* He finds himself out of breath, as if his heart has been turned to ice. He can still see the look on the girl's face, her smile like the sun he has stared into. He can see her curved mouth as a neon sign against the night shade of the back of his eyes. *Just go back out there and say hi.*

"You know, the thing about laundry is . . ." Gary finds himself standing on the stone pathway, talking to no one. The girl is gone. All that remains of her presence is a small pile of spent cigarettes, stamped onto the cement ground. "Damn."

Steve looks up and sees his friend sit down on the couch, his face white, his shoulders slumped.

"Jesus, man, you okay? You look like like my brother used to look like whenever his Little League team had to forfeit a game."

"That's what I feel like." He puts his feet on the coffee table and his head in his hands. The TV in the background is a noisy, gross distraction.

"What happened out there?"

"I met this girl. Or rather, I *saw* her."

"Yeah, so? Was she hot?"

"Yes, very."

"What'd you say?"

"Nothing. That's the problem. I passed her on the way into the laundry room, said hi, got totally freaked, and when I came out she was gone."

"Ooh," says Steve, a hand on his heart and wailing as if he had chest pains. "Story of your life."

"I know. But this sucks. I mean, I'm *still* thinking about her. It's crazy."

"Well, then do something about it."

"Like what?"

"I don't know." Already bored, he turns toward the TV, to someone else's drama.

Gary knows he's being irrational, that all he'd gotten was a glimpse of the girl, shared a word or two, or maybe it was just a grunt. Now he can't even remember. Five minutes later and everything is sketchy, everything except her face.

"I can live without her," he says, though Steve is not listening. "It won't kill me."

Trudging up the stairs in search for quarters for the dryer, he repeats the sentiment. "I'll live."

Gary figured the worst kind of pain was the kind you could live with, because that's often what one did. Lived with it.


Mark feels like he's in high school as he and Corinne lie together on the couch and kiss with the news on. It reminds him of being seventeen, of having girls over and kissing them on the sofa while his parents slept two rooms away, the sound of the TV drowning out either moans or the clinking of teeth armed with braces.

Every few minutes he gives up the bottom half of his mouth and Corinne sucks it in, nibbling at first and then running her tongue over the soft lip. It feels like a cat tongue, dotted with coarse hairs, running over his smooth flesh. It makes him laugh because it tickles and also because it turns on the attractive girl sitting on the couch with him, news blaring in the background.

"What?" she asks, pulling away as she loses her grasp of his tongue now that his face is curled into a grin.

"It's nothing," he says, trying to hide the fact that he's worried about fucking her later. What if it happens again? "The noise . . . broke my concentration."

Corinne looks at him skeptically, retreating momentarily to her side of the couch. A burst of lightning, followed seconds later by thunder, erupts outside and Mark trains his eyes out the fogged-up window.

As he stares out onto the gray, stained pavement, he sees trees waving back and forth, branches slapping against the window. The street is littered with mangled palm fronds, the large Q-Tip-like trees bending at their textured shafts.

"You call *this* rain?" Mark uses the dangling cigarette in his left hand as a pointer, aiming it at the damp window sill.

"Yeah," Corinne blankly replies, "what do *you* call it?"

"Back home"—Mark pauses to take a sip of white wine from

the fluted glass with a blue stem sitting beside the couch—"we'd call this mist. I mean, look at it, it's barely coming down and yet . . ." Now he points to the TV's flashing images of haggard weathermen broadcasting from various locations around southern California: the L.A. reservoir, mud slides in the Hollywood hills, Pacific Coast Highway temporarily closed, flooding in Sherman Oaks, power lines down in Encino, cable out in La Habra, an elderly lady swept away in Pasadena while hiking in the arroyo. "You get two or three inches and it's chaos out there. All the TV stations we've seen so far have been using this as their lead story, like it's the end of the world or something."

"It's the end of some worlds." Corinne lifts her foot off the burgundy ottoman, aiming it toward the screen, now filled with a live shot of an old man's living room in Santa Monica, water up to his knees, papers, clothes, and photos floating on the dirty brown surface.

"All I'm saying is that this isn't even a heavy downpour. Why, back home—"

Corinne breaks out in laughter.

"'Back home. Back home.' Milk this huckster-in-the-big-city routine a little more, why don't you?"

"What do you mean?"

"Oh, come off it, Mark. Every two seconds you're pointing out some Los Angeles anachronism. Like, I realize that parking may not be the biggest problem back in Virginia, but do you have to stare at a parking meter like it's an alien being? And complaining to the manager of the Cineplex Odeon Theaters about the seven fifty ticket fees? Or to shout out at the top of your lungs, 'Eight dollars for a goddamn hamburger?' at lunch the other day. That was a bit over the top."

"But eight *bucks!* That didn't even include fries, just *salad,* and then it was served on some wheat-germ bun. I mean, come on!"

"But still, don't you think you're pushing it a little? Or do you really hate L.A. that much?"

"I don't hate L.A. at all." Mark squirms on the couch.

"Although it *is* hard to respect a city whose main cultural export includes crap like *Gremlins 2*. And all the mindless trends that always seem to sprout up, like, what's with all these different types of water you sell out here?"

"What do you mean?" Corinne says, laughing, even though she knows what he's talking about. In her own fridge is a square bottle of Vittel, a quart of Canadian Glacier, three mini bottles of Perrier, a four-pack of San Pelligrino, and a squirt-top of Evian.

"You know *exactly* what I mean. Two aisles devoted *just* to water in that store you took me to the other day."

"Gelson's. Yeah, so?"

"So? So, two aisles makes up some of the entire stores in Kitty. Out here it's like, La Dolce Vitamin. It's crazy." He pauses for a second, concentrating on the rain outside, which seems to have intensified. "It's just . . . maybe I miss Kitty more than I thought. It's funny"—he reaches for his wine, takes a sip—"but all the time I was there, I thought Kitty was just this hick, one-horse town, but now that I'm seeing it at a distance . . ."

"It's what?"

"Well, it's *still* a hick, one-horse town, but the thing is, that just doesn't seem so bad. I miss the quiet Sundays, just sitting around, or getting into shows for two bucks' cover charge and not fifteen, like they were charging at the Roxbury the other night. I miss the Scene. I miss the Capital Cinema. I guess I just miss it, that's all." He takes another sip, emptying the glass. The wine is cool and sweet going down. Corinne had bought it at Trader Joe's on her way home from work. The price attracted her to it in the first place, then the bottle caught her eye: black, sleek, slightly frosted glass. It hinted at mystery and a good time guaranteed for all. She bought it, brought it home, and they ordered Thai food. The chardonnay she had chosen was acidy and too fruity to be considered a fine wine, but still, she had paid with a $10 bill and received change, and Mark now had a nice buzz on, so neither is complaining. Mark continues, "The greenness of it, you know? How the sides of the highways looked like a forest. Out here it's just weeds, dried, wiry brush.

No wonder we see you guys have all those fires in the summer. What's the matter, don't you water your plants?"

Corinne laughs and then reaches out and rubs the back of his neck. It's an odd moment because, despite the attempt the other night, Corinne has yet to show a simple emotion such as outward caring, tenderness, affection. Even Corinne is surprised by the small gesture that, so far, means more to Mark than anything she's done. He looks back at her and smiles, then bends at the waist, putting his head into her lap.

Without a word she begins caressing his hair, her hands against his tired scalp weaving back and forth. The experience creates a warm sensation all over his skull and puts out the fires of a wine-induced headache that had formed a few minutes before.

"What are you thinking about?" Corinne's now making circles on his temples with her right index finger.

"Nothing," he answers, shutting his eyes tight.

"It can't be nothing."

"Okay. You're right." A commercial explodes onto the screen, a used car salesman shouting at almost double the volume of the show they were just watching. "I was thinking about the other night."

"At the hotel?"

"Yes."

"Don't worry about it, Mark. It's no big deal."

"Not to you, it's not."

"It's not." She turns his face so he's staring right up at her. She thinks this is an intensely emotional moment until she realizes he's looking right up her nose. "In any event, it's not like it was a one-time shot. We'll try again."

Mark takes this to mean *right now* instead of the vague future Corinne was implying. He reaches up and pulls her head down to his. They begin kissing and Mark turns her over so that she's lying on top of him. After he rolls over and his elbow brushes against the remote control, shutting the television set off, they move into the bedroom.

They kiss as they stand near the bed, the room dark and the

rain quieter than before. Mist drifts down into various pockets of the city like luck: some had it, some did not. Teetering on one foot, Corinne begins to lose her balance and rather than break free, push Mark away, and plant both feet firmly on the ground the way her mother had been begging her for years to do, she falls to the bed and takes him with her.

"Traffic light's still out."

Steve enters the dining room, where Gary is sitting, attentively staring at a piece of gray card-stock paper. He holds the sheet with his left hand, desperately trying to cut a straight line with his right. He squints, trying to see clearly; he tries to keep his cutting hand rock steady but the concentration only makes his hand wobble more. He has never been good at this. All of his life his mother and his various Valentines had received homemade cards with flaring edges, odd curves in their lines that, when they were placed upon a nightstand, would cause them to fall right over. His mother found the refrigerator was the best place for these gifts, held in place with a magnet, while the girls mostly hid them in shoe boxes along with the other Valentines they'd received from boys over the years. He could not draw straight, could not cut straight, and very often he found he could not walk straight. The straight line did not seem to be something Gary could create. It often made getting between points difficult. He was always taking the long way home.

He places the pieces of card stock on the table. He places on top of it a piece of white linen paper, just as inaccurately cut. Gary folds both, going over the crease repeatedly with the back of his thumbnail. Reopening the makeshift card, he applies rubber cement between the light cardboard and the heavy paper. He sets it aside to dry, going to work on cutting a small print of a beautiful painting by Pissarro, which he had found as part of a set of Impressionist postcards. He trims the excess border so it will fit on his card, letting the laminated scraps fall to the floor. He had found all of the materials in the drawer of a pinewood credenza that lines the hallway opposite the staircase. He had discovered a number of art cards, differing grades of stationery paper, small note cards with corresponding envelopes, some old ribbon, a roll of tape, rubber cement, and a large pair of scissors. Gary guessed that at one time or another a female had occupied the house. Guys weren't supposed to keep such things on hand.

"I said, the traffic light's still out."

"What?" Gary sets down the scissors. He is unable to cut straight while concentrating, and distraction only makes him butcher the object worse. "What traffic light?"

"The one on the corner." Steve pulls up a chair and sits down. "It's blinking red. Has been doing that for the last hour."

"Yeah, well, the lights went out for a second. Big deal."

Shortly after Gary reentered the house from piling his clothes into the washer, stunned by the appearance of the beautiful, mysterious smoking girl, it had started to rain. Lightly at first, making the two Virginians feel slightly at home, glad to see California was not immune to the tragedies that befell the rest of the country. They had also heard about earthquakes, and more than slightly hoped one would occur during their stay. But then the rain intensified, coming down in thick black sheets, and Steve got spooked while Gary got angry. He wanted to go back out there and find the girl. He swore to himself that he would say something this time. Peering out from the small window set into the door, Gary saw, through the shimmering blanket that was wetting where she had sat, that she was not there. He grinned. She was smart, knew when to stay inside. This made him love her all the more. Beauty *and* brains.

A half hour later the lights went out. First only as a flicker, the way a candle would dip and duck if disturbed by wind; the lights in the house dimmed, regained full force, then were extinguished, returning seconds later. The TV crackled like a fireplace, going from picture to static to black and back again. It was so quick that Steve did not lose his place in the Movie of the Week he was watching. A minute later the electricity was cut again. This time it lasted almost ten minutes. The boys scurried around the house in search of candles. They took the box of matches from the kitchen that they used to light the old gas stove, and marched around the house, one match at a time, holding the small toothpick sticks like torches, as if they were villagers searching out Frankenstein.

"Ouch, I burned my fucking hand," Steve said more than once as the flame exhausted its wooden fuel and tried to make the leap to skin. Gary sighed, amazed that his friend hadn't learned from the last three times this happened.

By the time they found a number of candles in a linen closet on the second storey, the lights popped back on, then off again, then on, this time staying on. Somewhere in this darkness Gary got the bright idea for the note.

"But if the electricity's back on . . ." Steve's sentence is punctuated with a burst of thunder, causing him to halt. Gary doesn't even notice, thinks instead that something is wrong with Steve. "Then why aren't the traffic lights working? I mean, they're on, but why aren't they working?"

"They're working, they're working." Gary picks up the card to make sure the rubber cement is drying evenly, without leaving brown blotches. "They're just not working *right,* that's all. Give the city some time to get out here. After all, I bet power was knocked out to half the city. It'll take some time to get things back up again."

Steve gets up quickly, points to the window.

"You call *this* rain?"

"I *called* it rain, yeah. Earlier." He looks to the window Steve's now staring out of, trying to see above the trees to the traffic light on the corner. See if it's working or not. "But it's stopped."

"So what? Fuck the rain. Did you notice it was a full moon tonight?"

"Steve, you're getting paranoid."

"I'm not paranoid. I just don't like full moons. They're creepy."

Gary, not waiting for Steve to leave him alone, decides to finish his card before the rain starts up again. He'd been waiting for his chance all night, and now that it had finally arrived he wasn't about to let it be ruined by his chattering roommate. Gary places three dots of cement on the front of the card, then quickly mashes down the postcard. He bends over, sticking his face into the table (the smell from the glue reminding him of when he was young and would get high on anything), trying to straighten out the print before the glue hardens. Of course, it is crooked.

"Jesus, Steve, you distracted me. What'd you say?"

"I said the full moon . . . it makes people do things they normally don't do. Speaking of, what are *you* doing?"

"Something I normally don't do."

"What?"

"Making a card to give to a girl."

"See?" Steve shouts, turning back to the window. "I was right. Goddamn fucking full moon."

"Steve, will you leave me alone? For five seconds? Please?"

"Okay, okay." He marches into the next room.

Free of distractions, Gary takes a black pen and begins to write on the inside of the card. *To the cute redhead I saw smoking a cigarette . . .*

In the other room Steve lights his own cigarette, his hands shaking as he does so. What he was afraid of was not the rain, thunder, or full moon, but the effects these had on the citizens of Los Angeles. He had watched the intersection of Sierra Bonita and Sunset for nearly half an hour, standing underneath one of the blinking lights as cars rushed blindly through the intersection. Cars had to fight their way to turn either left or right and were honked at when they did so. Tires peeled out on the wet pavement, a dozen accidents narrowly avoided. Pedestrians had to sprint through the crosswalk. The sound of shouted curses almost drowned out the thunder that was causing the curses. This set Steve's nerves on edge, adding to the disorientation he had experienced the past few weeks. He did not know what the citizens of this city were made of, and was terrified to find out.

"Where you going?"

Gary is halfway to the door when Steve's question stops him.

"To give the note to the girl."

"How do you know where she lives?"

"I don't, but I figure if she had one cigarette out there tonight, she's bound to have another."

He quickly departs and just as quickly returns.

"There. Now, to wait."

"You wait," Steve says, clicking off the TV. "I'm tired. I'm going to bed."

"Fine. Go."

Gary retreats to the dining room to clean up his scraps of paper from the table, then into the kitchen to begin on the dishes from last week. An hour later he hears a dainty knock on the door.

"Shit."

He makes her knock twice, just to make sure he's not hearing things.

Gary walks slowly to the door, takes a deep breath, and swings it open.

"You Gary?"

A tall guy, about Gary's age, is standing wearing a brown corduroy jacket and blue jeans. His face is unshaven, black hair combed back, a slightly pissed-off look on his face. Because of the puffy coat Gary can't tell how big he is, only he's afraid most of the lumps are flesh.

"Yeah, I'm Gary."

"Great. Well, I'm the boyfriend of the cute redhead."

**"You're no one in this town till you've seen** The Piano.**"**

Corinne folds the Calendar section of the *Los Angeles Times* across her bare legs, her black miniskirt riding high on her thighs, and she lifts the paper quickly, making sure she's not leaving black ink on her kneecaps.

"What?" Mark asks, flipping through the comics.

"I said, you're no one in this town till you've seen *The Piano*. I mean, just try to go to lunch these days without being able to pontificate on the sad state of mute Ada and her little daughter."

"So, you've seen it?"

"No, actually. That's why I'm tearing apart the Calendar section. I've got to see it soon unless I want to be left out of yet another conversation and look dumb."

"But you just said something about Ada and her daughter, so I thought . . ."

"No, no, no." She crumples up a Target circular and tosses it at him from across the room. "I just gleaned that much from reading a few reviews. A touch of Siskel here, some Ebert there, a hint of Peter Travers I picked up from a *Rolling Stone* that was lying around the office." She grabs from the center a pullout marked L.A. HEALTH WATCH '93 and drops it to the ground. "Plus, I saw the uncensored version of *Bad Lieutenant,* so I figure that full frontal nudity of Harvey Keitel is pretty much universally applicable. Like, I was at Citrus with some friends from Carolco the other day and *of course* someone brought up *The*

*Piano.* I just took a slice of my cilantro-and-barbecued-chicken pizza and said, 'Well, *I* think Harvey Keitel needs to do some push-ups or something."

"And?"

"It worked like a charm." Corinne's still proud of the moment, even three days later. "But I can't keep risking it like that." Her eyes zero in on an ad that shows a lone piano sitting deep in the sand on a bare beach, waves lapping perilously close while two figures clothed in black sit on the piano's bench, one an adult and the other a child. Both are female. "Aha. There's a six o'clock show at the Beverly Center. Want to go?"

"The *Beverage* Center?" Mark mangles the word. "We had one of those in the cafeteria back at the community college in Kitty."

"No, you cute little Neanderthal. The *Beverly* Center. It's a mall. Didn't you have those back in Virginia?"

Now Mark's only half listening. Instead he's scouring through the funny pages, trying to find anything that's actually funny. On the back page is something called *Magic 3D.* There's a six-inch-by-three-inch amalgamation of swirling colors, pinpoints of shade, and a somewhat discernable pattern. Mark follows the directions, only nothing happens. He tries it again, holding the paper close to his nose, looking at the blurry image, then slowly moving it away, trying to hold his gaze, only his eyes water quickly and he blinks. He tries it again, even slower than before, but it still looks like just a bunch of ink spots. Besides, an unfunny Marmaduke cartoon keeps distracting him.

"What is this, a Rorschach test for three-year-olds?"

"Oh, give me that." Corinne tears it out of his hands, quickly puts the paper close to her face, just as quickly draws it away, and then announces, "A pig smelling flowers." She tosses the crumpled section to the hardwood floor.

"You just read that at the bottom."

"Do you want to see the movie or don't you?"

"Sure, sure."

"I don't know, though." Corinne takes a cigarette out of a

fresh pack. "With my luck I'd probably run into Brandi and her crew."

"Who's Brandi?" Mark asks.

"Oh, she's an old friend from high school who I seem to run into all over town. I've been avoiding her for the past couple of weeks."

"Why?"

"Well, we sort of liked the same guy."

"Who won?"

"Neither of us."

"Sounds like a great bunch of friends you've got."

"Yeah, well." Corinne yawns, despairing that over half of her Sunday is already gone. "What's that old phrase about picking your nose and not your friends?"

Mark laughs.

"I think it's 'You can pick your nose, but you can't pick your relatives.' Your friends, you can pick." He gets up off the floor and joins her at the kitchen table, squeezing her exposed knees before sitting down. "So if you don't like them, why hang around them?"

"It's just not that easy."

"Why not?"

"I went to school with Brandi. All of *her* friends are *my* friends. The whole little"—Corinne cups her hands to symbolize the union—"group, I guess. It's so cliquish, but unless I move away, there's nothing I can do. Even Quincy, from work, she's a part of it, so there's no escaping it."

"But still, I don't see how you just can't avoid them. It's not like back in Kitty, where if you cut off a guy in the street and called him an asshole you could pretty much guarantee standing behind him at the grocery store a few days later. Los Angeles is so huge."

"Yeah, it's a big city"—her voice is filled with near exasperation—"but our peer group is so small. It's like, there's thousands of places to go but there's only half a dozen that *I* go. That sounds weird, but that's the way it is. It's really not *that* big a town."

Corinne thinks back to the inescapable gang, how she's always running into them everywhere, and how Tim, her ex-boyfriend, a part of that gang, used to always pop into her life after she'd tried so hard to shove him out. How he always looked good, was smiling, while she herself felt cracked inside, the makeup on her face thicker than usual. She liked to think it was a mask, that no one could see what lay underneath, even though friends pulled her aside and asked what was wrong. After Brandi slept with Tim shortly after the breakup, she always winked at Corinne, as if they were now somehow connected, which Corinne supposed they were, but she didn't like to go out on a Friday or Saturday night, or even a Tuesday, and have to be reminded of the fact over and over again.

But that was weeks ago. It'd been almost two months since Tim had left for Arizona on a shoot, and now that Brandi had also been left in his wake she wasn't as cocky and kept their shared past quiet, or as quiet as she could. And now Mark was in the picture, and things were becoming easier to take again.

"Not till six, huh?" Mark scoots over and nibbles on Corinne's neck.

"Yeah," she says, laughing, "six."

"Hmmm." He continues to nibble, stopping every few seconds to talk before returning his lips to her skin. "That's not for a few hours, right? So . . . what should we do till then. Huh?"

The headline on the front page on the floor catches her eyes, something about an insurrection, thousands of dead, hundreds of thousands heading for refugee camps, but the more Mark kisses her, as he takes her in his arms and begins to lead her to the bedroom, the more the news, like an electrical current fighting its way into her brain, fizzles out and disappears altogether.

The animal, a tiger, is in midstride, all four limbs outstretched as if galloping across an African plain. Its tail is curled up along its back, like a *U* on its side. The striped body is light blue, outlined in white, just a dot for an eye and a dash of red stitching for the ferocious, perennially roaring mouth.

"What are you doing?" Steve asks as he walks into the living room and spots Gary sitting on the couch holding a shirt close to his face, a CD on in the background.

"Looking at this new shirt I bought," Gary answers. He holds the insignia up to his face one more time, then lowers it, admiring how the design perfectly complements the porous dark blue cotton fabric.

"Hey, wow," Steve says, amazed, as he circles the couch and gets a better look. "Is that a Le Tigré?"

"You bet," Gary says proudly.

"Where did you get it?"

"A thrift store in Fairfax." He hands over the shirt to his band mate. "Isn't it cool?"

"Cool, *way* cool. I haven't seen one of these in years." He turns the garment over and over in his hands. "And it's in such good condition. It's not like those Fred Perry shirts you'd find every once in a while at the Love Is Christ thrift store back in Kitty that had all those holes in them, were stained, and smelled like a middle-aged tennis pro."

"Or a middle-aged mod." Gary swings his arm in a Pete Townsend–windmill fashion.

"Yeah." Steve laughs. "So, how much did you pay for it?"

Gary takes the shirt back before answering.

"Three bucks," he proudly says.

"Wow, good deal."

"Yeah, and it's all part of this new look I'm cultivating."

"New look?" Steve sort of chuckles. He's been through this before with Gary. When he first met him, years ago, he was going through his black phase. Everything Gary wore was black. Black shoes, socks, shirts, jackets; he even sported a pair of all-black boxers. This lasted until the cruel Southern summer, which routinely ran the mercury over a hundred degrees with humidity almost to match. Sometime around early June Gary showed up to practice wearing a white T-shirt, a pair of beige cutoff shorts, and purple Converse sneakers he'd dyed himself. "Not a word," he said gruffly. "Not a word."

"So"—Steve can barely hold back a laugh—"what is it *this* time?"

"I'm going for a sort of geek chic look. You now, retro early eighties, sort of faux preppy. Like maybe a cross between the before *and* after of Judd Nelson in *Making the Grade*. Oh, check this out." Gary pulls out a digital watch from a paper bag on the floor that reads OUT OF THE CLOSET. "Check out this Pac-Man watch!"

"Whoa!" Steve's eyes light up. "I used to have one of those. Let me see, let me see!"

Gary grudgingly hands over the watch, adding, "Okay, but *be* careful."

Steve delicately takes it in his hands and examines the artifact the same way a religious man admires sacred texts, with a mixture of clinical inspection and awe. The flimsy plastic strap is slightly worn and, Steve notices, missing that little loop to hold the excess amount of strap close to the wrist. The face is spotless, the yellow Pac-Man logo still vibrant. On the liquid crystal screen is a crude approximation of the video game, just a few corners and dead ends, measly compared to the blue electronic labyrinth of the arcade version. Scattered throughout the trail are dots and stars in the four corners, representing the power pellets that turn Pac-Man invincible and permit him to digest any one of the four ghosts floating around the maze. Beneath the screen are four skinny buttons laid out in a North-South-East-West configuration, each one responsible for Pac-Man's movements on the playing field.

"This is great, man," Steve excitedly says as he tries to play the game, only his large hand and blunt fingertips send his man into a corner and he's unable to maneuver him out. "Did they have any of those great *Head to Head* games by Coleco? Or those handheld versions of Donkey Kong and Frogger that looked like little arcade games and had that tiny joystick?"

"No such luck." Gary reaches over and takes the beeping watch out of Steve's hand, quickly strapping it to his wrist before Steve gets any ideas of stealing it for himself. Gary pulls on the

Le Tigré polo shirt, which fits a bit snugly (even though it's a large), bunching around the small of his back and the slight paunch that's developed in the past few weeks of living well after months of the horrendous tour.

"What do you think?"

"I think that if this new look keeps bringing in cool stuff like that Pac-Man watch, then go for it. But, uh, what else is there? How far are you going to take this?"

"Well, for one thing . . . this"—he runs a hand through his black hair and sighs—"will have to go."

"Go? Go where?"

"Away, dumb shit. I need it short and, you know, geeky."

"Wait a second, let me get this straight." Steve sits forward on the couch and tries to get a grasp on the situation. "You're trying to cultivate a look that most people spend their entire lives trying to avoid?"

"Pretty cool, huh?"

"No! I think it's pretty stupid. Why don't you just go all the way and copy that Urkel kid from TV, get some floods, speak in a whiny voice. You know? *He's* pretty geeky. You could be his mentor."

"Prodigy, dick brain, prodigy. He'd be *my* mentor. Anyway, I don't mean be a nerd, just sort of square, but in a cool way. *Damn*"—he snaps his fingers—"if I only had to wear glasses. Man, a pair of horn-rims would go a long way on selling this look."

"Yeah, that's it, Gary, curse nature for giving you good vision. Wow, a back brace would really look cool, too! Or maybe some of those blocky black shoes with the metal bar running up the side, or even—"

"Okay, knock it off. And quit ragging on me, because don't think I haven't noticed that goatee you're *trying* to grow."

"I am not *trying* to grow anything." Steve jumps up from the couch and runs to a mirror in the hallway, examining his face. "It's just I hadn't shaved in a while and I thought it looked cool around the chin area, so I just sort of, uh, left it there." He runs his fingers over the delicate blond whiskers protruding from his upper lip and below. "And it's not a goatee. It's more of a Vandyke."

"What the fuck's a Vandyke?"

"I don't know, but that's what my dad used to call them. Besides, I'm not trying to look like Maynard G. Krebs, I'm going for more of a that-evil-guy-from-*Moonraker* sort of thing."

"Yeah!" Gary says, making the connection. "Drake. No, wait, I *know* who you're talking about. The space shuttle dude. Oh yeah, Drax! Okay, then," he reconsiders, "that's cool."

"And anyway"—Steve returns to the couch—"I'm just sort of giving it a chance. If it comes in, cool; if not, no big deal. After all, the only people to see it during the awkward formative stages are you, Kenneth, and Paul. It's not like Mark's here to see it or anything," he says snippily.

"No shit," Gary quickly agrees. "What's with him lately? He gets this hot Hollywood chick and he forgets all about us *and* the record. Laura calls twice and he ignores it. Kenneth's getting more and more pissed off at the way my bass is sounding, and we're just about ready to record Mark's parts, and he's never around."

"I think he's just on the rebound. Plain and simple."

Gary fishes out a few more items from the thrift store bag on the floor, a paperback of *Portnoy's Complaint* he got for a quarter and a *Battlestar Galactica* pin that reads CYLON PATROL. At the bottom is a receipt.

"You're right. He misses Laura more than he thinks." Gary crumples up the receipt in his hand and tosses it into a wastepaper basket that's skirting the coffee table to the side of the couch. It bounces off the phone, then the answering machine, and trickles into the trash can.

"Rebound."


Corinne tries to make the light at Sunset, but can't. She slams on the brakes and Mark flies forward, his body held in check by the seat belt while his arms and legs flail about. From underneath the seat slide various bits of debris previously hidden: a tube of Revlon mascara, a plastic cup from Del Taco, a couple of pieces of mail, a parking ticket.

"There's a guy around here"—she's sitting high in her seat, leaning over her steering wheel like a little old lady—"and he lives in his car."

Mark, who's been zoning out for the past couple of minutes, pipes up.

"Oh, yeah?" he says, training his eyes on a strange-looking restaurant, Roscoe's Chicken and Waffles. "What kind of car?"

"Mercedes."

"Wouldn't you know it." He sighs. "Fucking bums here live better than whole families back in Virginia."

The light turns green and Corinne instantly steps on the gas.

"Not really. Wait until you see the car."

Mark keeps looking around as they head south down Gower. HOSEP'S CAR CARE. He catches this one out of the corner of his eye as Corinne floors it to make the light at Santa Monica.

"Okay, up here, up here," she starts saying fast.

"Which side?" Mark's twisting his head, searching the street for the car. "Left or right?"

"I don't know. It switches. He must have to move it every couple of days for the street sweeper. Oh, there it is! Right side, next to the yellow Mustang on blocks."

Corinne slows down as they pass, and Mark trains his eyes on the filthy car. Nearly every inch of the interior is filled with garbage: plastic bags, aluminum cans, beer bottles, cardboard boxes. The windows on both sides are brown and caked with dust. The car is indeed a Mercedes, but an out-of-date model from the early seventies; and where once, perhaps, it glowed a brilliant jet black, it was now, thanks to years of neglect, weathered a very dull dark gray. Just as Corinne's own white Jetta hits a bump in the road, the Mercedes now half a block behind them, Mark swears he can see an arm protrude from the pile of trash like the neck of the Loch Ness monster, a white, flabby, mittened hand, pale flesh exposed through the various holes in the red knitted fabric.

"That's really something, eh?" Corinne says, as if the man and the car were an inanimate display at the Ripley's Museum and not a living person. "Sometimes, on the weekends, I'll see him sitting on the curb washing his hair with gutter water, scooping it over his head with one of the hubcaps. Then he'll dry out on the sidewalk. But I tell you, that car still works. Every couple of days it switches sides of the street."

"Maybe he pushes it," Mark says, turning back around in his seat.

"You know, I never thought of that."

The car speeds through the light, turning onto Melrose.

"I bet you haven't."

"What?"

"Nothing."

Corinne hangs a left onto Gardner and cuts down the residential side street, turning right onto Beverly. Instantly Mark can see the gargantuan mall ahead, the shit brown facade curling around an entire city block, pin-striped on both sides with a zigzagging escalator and the red flashing sign for SAM GOODY'S RECORD STORE hung at the top of the curving building.

"That's no mall, that's a space station."

As they get closer Mark spots a Taco Bell on the left-hand side of the street that has a parking attendant in a little red jacket and black bow tie and white dress shirt, scrambling around the tiny lot, trying to coordinate the constantly changing catalog of cars. As a limo waits to enter, its ass hanging out onto the street, blocking oncoming traffic, a flurry of honking from behind makes the man in the coat run faster, as if he were in a Western and an outlaw were shooting bullets at his feet and yelling, "Dance!"

"Ahh, this light's always a bitch," Corinne moans as she accelerates, approaching a green-turning-yellow stoplight at the intersection of Beverly and La Cienega. "Hang on!"

He's thrown against the window as Corinne screeches through the intersection. Mark catches sight of the light turning red as she does so.

"Whew, sorry, but we would have been there for at least five minutes if I hadn't done that."

"Oh, five minutes. Well then I'm *glad* you risked my life."

"Look, buster, it's already a quarter to six. I just don't want to be late."

"Will you relax?" Mark examines his own watch, surprised to see it's actually ten till. "We've got plenty of time."

"You're really not from around here, are you? This is Los Angeles. This is a hot movie. It's Sunday afternoon and this is the goddamn *Beverly* Center. We've got to find parking, we've got to get tickets, and . . . oh, forget it . . ."

Corinne enters the mall, heading up an inclined ramp crowded with cars.

"Welcome to the Beverly Center," screams a woman's recorded voice emanating from a silver speaker in a yellow stand that looks like an intercom for the drive-through at a fast food restaurant. "Please take . . . *the* ticket." A canary-colored stub sprouts out of a thin opening. Corinne slides down her power window and grabs at the ticket, which sticks a little as she pulls. Just as she yanks it out of the opening, the black-and-white striped bar in front of them lifts up from the hinge to the left, allowing them to cruise up the ramp and into the parking garage.

Corinne curls her Volkswagen around the tight curves of the structure, narrowly avoiding the noses of vehicles peeking out from the various parking levels, and hangs a right onto level five, sending a thin rubbery squeak echoing through the air.

"The closer we park to the escalator"—she's pointing to an opening in the far wall where Mark can see people passing back and forth, in and out, and beyond that a billboard, a movie marquee, and then the city—"the less we have to walk." Corinne's ignoring the painted STOP signs that litter the path in front of her every few car lengths, one hand still on the volume dial of the radio (fading out as the signal is blocked by the thick walls of the garage) and both eyes looking for a parking space. Pedestrians jump out of her way like flies about to be swatted.

Corinne finally settles on a space about fifty feet down from the escalator entrance, right at the edge of the garage. Mark gets out of the car and moves to the open ledge, staring at a gigantic Guess Jeans ad that hovers over the corner of La Cienega and Third. Almost an entire city block is looked down upon by a gorgeous young blond lying sprawled out on her back, no shirt on, faded jeans. *Someone to watch over me.* He chuckles.

Corinne and Mark hold hands as they approach the subway-station-like tube of six tiered escalators. A well-dressed man walks frantically in the opposite direction with a cellular phone in his gloved hand, saying over and over, "I'm losing you, I'm losing you."

Deposited at the top and strolling into the mall, Corinne rushes, like she always does, to the window of a pet store that lies to the right of a small photo shop. She coos at a small gray dog in the window rustling around in scraps of shredded newspapers, looking adorable. Mark thinks it just looks hungry.

"You know they don't feed these things, don't you?"

"What?"

"That's why they look so cute. You think it'd lick your hand that way if it had a full belly? He's probably just smelling that chicken you had for lunch on Friday."

"Oh, *you.*"

Mark drags her away by the hand, and after traversing half the length of the mall, Corinne has to guide him to another set of escalators, heading to the top floor, where the movie theater is.

On a large marquee that spans almost fifty feet, *The Piano* is listed alongside five other movies. The building holds eight different theaters, but popular movies like *The Piano* are playing on two screens at once. Corinne, frustratingly, has been to this movie theater many times. It's certainly not her favorite; that would be the Showcase on La Brea, or even the Rialto out in Pasadena or the Nuart in Santa Monica, which was a hell of a drive in traffic, but usually worth it. All of those movie houses held only one theater, and the architecture was in the old style of the lone box office out front and flowing velvet drapes inside with thick red or purple carpeting, harking back to an older, more elegant era of Hollywood and the films it produced. But the Cineplex Odeon, like so many other things in Los Angeles, was a strip-mall equivalent of the real thing.

Mark looks over the bright white marquee, frowning when he sees two words placed over not only the six o'clock showing of *The Piano* but also the rest of the night's showings.

"Sold out?" He turns to Corinne. "What do they mean, sold out?"

Corinne shrugs her shoulders, kicking herself for taking Gower.

"Mark, what do you think it means?"

He continues to stare up at the myriad of movie listings as patrons brush by him, queuing up to buy tickets for one of the other movies.

"But I don't get it. How can *every* showing be sold out? Are Holly Hunter and Sam Neill going to act it out live?"

Corinne shrugs again, this time for a different reason. Now, instead of kicking herself, she'd like to kick Mark.

"Look, let's just"—she's brushed aside by somebody rushing to get their tickets to *Wayne's World 2*—"get out of the way."

They move out of the line of movie traffic just as the crowd surging out of *Dracula* exits the theater, and instead of discussing the finer plot points, the witty subtext, or strong characterizations, most of the audience is trying to remember where they're parked.

"Now what do we do?"

Corinne starts feeling less like a date and more like a cruise director on *The Love Boat,* so she waves her arms toward the Barnes & Noble bookstore next door to the theater.

"Why don't we just look in there for a while? Try and think of something to do while you're browsing."

"Okay, okay," Mark says as he enters the large open mouth of the bookstore. To the right is a long magazine rack, and to the left four cashiers stand with green aprons, waiting to ring up sales. He ventures deep into the store, following the large fiction section as it winds its way over half the space.

Twenty minutes later he feels a hand slide through the space between his arm and hip, reaching down and grabbing his crotch.

"Not now, I'm here with someone."

"Very funny," Corinne says, giving a delicate squeeze.

"Ouch." He turns and gives her a kiss on the cheek. "So, you find anything?"

She produces a paperback copy of *The Devil's Candy* and the newest issue of *Marie Claire* magazine.

"How about you?"

They both turn to the wall of lined-up books as Mark begins to point something out to her, only to be cut off halfway through.

"I was looking for this novel by—"

"Well, well, well . . ." A female's voice purrs behind them.

Mark turns quickly but Corinne hesitates, since she already knows who it is.

"Look at what the cat dragged"—Brandi pauses for second, savoring the moment—"*out.*"

Mark stands there, trying to figure out if this person is making a joke or a mistake while Corinne feigns laughter, fighting the temptation to grab Mark by the sleeve and run.

"Uh heh, heh," Corinne bleats.

"I mean, *really,* it's been *months* since I've seen you—"

"Weeks."

"—out of your apartment and among the living. To what do I owe this special occasion?"

Brandi strides forward, closing the gap between the three of them, and lands closer to Mark than to Corinne. She begins looking him up and down, not even trying to conceal the fact that she's doing so.

"So, have *you* been keeping Corinne under wraps for the past few months?"

"Weeks," Corinne again corrects. "It's only been a few weeks, Brandi, and no, Mark and I only met recently."

"Uh, yeah." Mark tries to think of something to add, but can't.

As Brandi and Corinne exchange small talk, Brandi keeps stealing glances at Mark, while Corinne eyes the exit. Mark examines Corinne's old friend. She's more flamboyant than Corinne, dressed expensively and elaborately in a navy blue pantsuit with brass jewelry, as if for a dinner party and not an evening at the mall. Yet Mark notices that a large percentage of those around him are dressed the same way. It makes him glance down at his weathered Timberland moccasins, faded Levi's, and old button-up shirt, and feel self-conscious. Corinne kept saying she didn't care about what he wore, but Mark still couldn't help feeling that, in her mind, she was taking points off.

Brandi's hair is light brown but streaked with blond highlights that emanate mostly around the temples and run the length of her thick, shoulder-length hair. She's thin, almost too thin, like a waifish model, and Mark can imagine her saying, "I eat and eat but just *can't* gain a pound," just to make other girls jealous, her weight actually a much-sought-after goal and difficult to achieve and maintain.

"So, what were *you* two doing this evening?" Brandi finally tosses an innocuous question Mark's way. "I can't believe you came all the way here just to shop for books."

"We—," Corinne begins, panicked, only to be cut off by Mark.

"We came to see that movie, *The Piano*. You know, that one about the deaf chick? But it was sold out."

Brandi turns quickly to Corinne and says in a mock-hushed tone, "But the other day at Citrus you said . . . Oh well, never mind. The whole gang's here and we're going out for coffee. You've just *got* to come." Brandi jauntily disappears down the aisle, her black leather purse shimmying back and forth.

Corinne turns to Mark with the evil eye.

"Oh, *she* was at the lunch?"

Mark stands at the outer perimeter of a semicircle formed by Brandi, Corinne, Quincy, three males named Charles, Holland, and Jake (each of them similarly dressed, in slacks and dark sports jackets, only Jake, true to his macho-sounding name, wearing a weathered, Hemingwayesque vest). Mark is unsure whether these guys are Quincy and Brandi's dates, or if two of them are actually dating each other, or if they are all just friends. None of them stands too close to another, as if their dreams and failures are a disease that could be caught by mere casual contact. Certainly a girl like Brandi wasn't going to let anyone stand in her way of getting to the top. Mark is standing three bodies away from Corinne, and she's making a cutting motion across her neck, signaling to Mark that she wants to get the hell out of here. He thinks she's just scratching an itch.

"Let's go to Java!" Charles brightly suggests.

The crowd becomes silent. Mark can't understand why. Holland looks awkwardly at Quincy, who's too ashamed to look back. Brandi takes Charles aside, and Mark can hear her whisper into his turning-red ear, "Haven't you heard? Java went out of business *months* ago."

Charles gasps.

"It's now called Insomnia," Brandi continues, "and *no* one goes there. Well," she amends, "no one who's *any*one."

Brandi turns back to the crowd, who still can't believe Charles made such a mistake. Mark is not sure what exactly the mistake was.

"How about the Living Room?" Holland suggests.

"Nah," shoots Jake quickly. "I drove by there today on my way from the Lichtenstein exhibit at LACMA and on my way *to* American Rag to pick up some *new* old jeans, and I saw that they were doing some filming there. Besides, they tore down a wall and expanded it to, like, twice its size, and now that it's so huge, why bother going there?"

"Wait a second," Charles cuts in, "how could you pass the Living Room on the way to American Rag? Why didn't you just go down Wilshire and head north up La Brea?"

"Wilshire was jammed," Jakes says plainly. "I cut through Park La Brea and took Third."

Quincy says, "It's like the Authentic Cafe all over again."

"The poor Living Room."

"I agree," Charles says. "Exactly."

"How about the Pik-Me-Up?" Holland says, glancing down at his shoes.

"What?" Quincy says snidely. "And be sandwiched in there with all those *artists?* Sorry, but I left *my* black turtleneck at home."

The crowd politely half laughs while Mark's still trying to catch up to a joke from five minutes before.

"Ministry?" Charles timidly suggests. "Just north of Melrose?"

"Gone," Brandi says as she fishes around for the parking ticket in her dainty black patent leather Versace handbag. "My God, Charles, where have you *been?*"

"Cafe Mocha?"

"Sitting in a booth for a cup of coffee?" Holland says. "For Norms or Ships, maybe. But café au lait, I think not."

"Well, if it was Ships," someone says, "they'd better put an espresso machine on every table."

"Exactly," Charles replies, beginning to stutter. "J-j-just like the toasters."

The conversation is like speeding traffic, too fast for Mark to keep up.

"Okay, okay." Holland quiets the group with a wave of his immaculately manicured hands. "I've got it. Big and Tall Books."

The group all shrug their shoulders in a why-didn't-I-think-of-that gesture.

"Okay," Quincy says, a filtered Camel dangling from her lips even though she won't be able to light it until she's outside the mall. "Who's driving?"

An hour later Brandi is holding court at a circular table near the entrance of the cafe/bookstore. She's retelling a story that happened three weeks ago at the casting agency she works at, even though half the table has heard it already. This time she's reciting it mainly for the benefit of Corinne, whom she hasn't seen in a while, and for Mark, whom she's trying to impress.

"We're trying to cast this romantic lead, right? So my boss says, 'Get me a Baldwin! Start with Alec and work your way down!'"

The table erupts in laughter while Mark stares at a painting on the wall.

"Did anyone see that the new Wim Wenders film is playing in, like, just one theater in town?" Quincy says, motioning with her arms for people to pay attention to her. "There's just this small little microscopic ad in the *Weekly* for it, and that's *it*."

"Shame," Holland says, repeating, "shame, shame, shame."

"It's like, sure, *My American Friend* is the best work Dennis Hopper will *ever* do." Now it's Jake's turn to speak, and he does so in a stage voice, mock deep, not the same tone Mark heard when he ordered his coffee forty-five minutes ago. "But how do you forgive something like *Until the End of the World?*"

"Yes," Brandi says, taking a drag off a Cartier cigarette, "but it was a good sound track."

"Good sound track," Jake says, his voice even deeper than before, as if he were announcing checkmate, "bad film."

Mark jerks his head, trying to follow the subject, Wim Wenders, and also whoever is speaking, trying to recall the name of the speaker, who he was introduced to just an hour ago.

*Candy? Brenda?* He asks himself as the girl sitting across from him starts talking about narrative form in obtuse film language.

Everyone sitting at the table is completely aware that Mark is lost in the conversation, and is content to let him drift. Corinne stares out the window onto Beverly, watching the traffic go by, wishing she were in one of the cars on their way to someplace else.

She knew her friends wouldn't approve of Mark. Worse than this, they were being condescending, tossing back and forth arcane subjects relevant only to their shared profession along with esoteric subsections of an art they could tell Mark knew nothing about. It was as if they were playing keep-away. Mark gamely tried to join in every once in a while, only to be batted down, but then drawn back in with bathetic effect minutes later.

"So, Mark, do you like Pasolini?"

"I don't know," he began, looking to Corinne for help, but she was not paying attention. "Is that like *tiramisù*?"

Admittedly, compared to Tim, who was both handsome and intelligent, Mark was making a poor showing. Tim had been adored by Corinne's friends, especially by Brandi, who would have renounced all of her goals and become a kept woman if Tim were doing the keeping. What the table did not know was that Tim could be abusive, was a closet alcoholic and a layabout underneath his artistic gloss. Even though whiffs of this behavior permeated their circle of friends, no one chose to believe. Tim was just too handsome to be a jerk. It was years before the spell wore off Corinne and she came to the realization that he was, indeed, an asshole. She always thought of his heart as a black flower that bloomed only indoors and preferably at night. One of the few things in the world that needed darkness to grow. If Corinne's friends could not see that Mark was crude but decent, or at the very least not smart enough to be decidedly wicked, this was not her problem. She neither had the energy to convey this to them nor was convinced they would believe her if she did.

"Well, Wenders's technique has *always* been overly didactic," says the guy sitting next to the girl whose name Mark can't remember. Giving up, Mark tries to think of something to add to the conversation. His mind races back to the couple of times *Wings of Desire* had played at the Capital Cinema back in Kitty. Thinking back, he can't remember if he actually ever saw the film, even though he'd been meaning to for years. Images course through his mind of a dilapidated Berlin, of humans with shoddy wings taped to their backs, hanging out on massive, stained stone sculptures, but he can't be sure if this is actually from the film or from the trailer he saw while waiting to see a different film. He decides not to risk it and keeps his mouth shut.

Mark glances at the five strangers seated around the table and is alarmed to realize that he doesn't recognize one of them. Even with Corinne it is only a surface connection, an incubatory history—he does not yet feel like he *truly* knows her. This makes him feel completely lost. Searching for some sort of anchor, his eyes scan his surroundings, looking for anything familiar that might make him feel safe. The cafe, its snooty denizens, and avant-garde art-covered walls stare coldly back at him. He wants to run for refuge, but he's not sure where, in this place, refuge is exactly found. Hell, he's not even sure where the bathroom is. He feels the urge to vomit, to cry, but he doesn't know if the toilet is in the little hallway back near the counter where he didn't put his change into the carnival-glass vase and received a dirty look from the girl behind the bar, or behind that long thin door that lay immediately to the right as he entered.

"Excuse me." Mark gets up, only Corinne noticing.

As he heads deeper into the cafe the conversation of the table hangs in the air behind him.

"I mean," Brandi continues, "remember when people used to give a damn about Wim Wenders?"

After heading twice into the kitchen and once into a stock-room filled with bundles of napkins and cleaning supplies, he finds the sole bathroom around the corner, the door directly opposite a separate entrance from the parking lot behind the building.

Mark locks the door behind him, nervously fiddling with the primitive nail-and-half-a-hinge catch, his paranoia creating a scene where one of Corinne's friends wanders in in the middle of his taking a dump.

*Calm down, calm down,* he's repeating to himself like a mantra. *Take it easy, take it . . . easy.*

He moves to the sink and wipes down his face with cold water. His slightly shaking fingers find eye sockets that seem deeper than he can ever remember.

"Fuck," he says out loud, "the best time of my life and it feels like I'm . . . dying."

Drips of water run off his nose and onto his shirt, even the front of his pants.

*Great.*

He stabs with handfuls of balled-up tissue paper at his wet clothes, pinpoints of water looking like piss spray. He turns to toss the paper from his hands but can't even find the trash can. This again sets his mind on edge. At least, back in Kitty, if he were freaking out in some situation, he could look up and see places that had surrounded him his entire life, a city that had been with him through everything, summers spent exploring back fields and abandoned farms on his bike, winters spent sliding down icy and sometimes snow-covered hills. He even lost his virginity in an empty lot on the outskirts of town, and it wasn't just that once; there were girls who would swear he lost it there twice. But now, in this strange city, leading a life nothing like the one he had led previously, surrounded not only by unfamiliar surroundings but by faces he had never known, or in the case of Corinne, known intimately and perhaps too much, too soon, he feels lost.

*Gotta pull myself together.* He pats down his hair that's sticking up in clumps from when he nervously ran his fingers through it minutes before. *Gotta stay cool.* He feels his chest and face becoming hot, the beginning of a moist patch underneath his arms.

Mark gives himself a final look in the mirror and concludes he looks like shit, but he decides to leave the bathroom anyway. What else can he do? He's afraid if he stays in any longer everyone at the table will think he has the runs and will shrink away from him the rest of the night. More so, that is. Upon exiting he bumps into a surferish-looking guy who rushes into the restroom just as Mark stumbles out.

"What's your prob, dude?" the guy says, knocking into Mark's shoulder. Mark doesn't notice and, oblivious, heads back to the table near the front of the cafe. Corinne, sitting near the large window facing the sidewalk, catches Mark's glance as he approaches the table. Her eyebrows scrunch up and her lips become tightly pursed, wondering what's wrong. He tries to shrug it off, comically rolling his shoulders, muttering an inaudible *Heh-heh* under his breath as he sits down. The conversation has not strayed far from where he left it.

"So Trev says, 'Let's go see *Faraway, So Close*,' and *I* say . . ." Brandi stalls before delivering the punch line, holding the table's attention. "'Why don't *you* go far away and *I'll* stay so close.'"

Mark feigns a laugh and puts his hand on Corinne's knee. She notices that his fingers are cold and wet.

"What number clip do you use?"

Gary, too busy admiring his Pac-Man digital watch, doesn't even hear the young woman standing behind him with an industrial-sized shaver in her hand, to her left a tray of plastic accessories of varying sizes.

"Huh?" he finally says, shaken out of a daze. "What?"

"I asked you what number clip you use. You know, clip?" She waves an electric trimmer in front of his face. "It determines how short to cut your hair? Only I can't tell on yours because it's so uneven."

Gary turns his head to each side, looking at his hair in the mirror. "It's been a while since I've gotten a real haircut. Just haven't had the money . . ." Not to look like a loser, he quickly adds, "Not to mention the, uh, time."

"Oh really." She laughs. "Tell you what. You said you wanted it short, right? Wasn't *manageable* the word you used?"

"Yeah," Gary embarrassingly admits. On the walk over he had concocted a little speech in his head and repeated it many times. *A little long on the top and short on the sides, shaved in back. A little long on the top and . . .* But when he sat in the chair and faced this attractive girl looking back at him, smacking a piece of orange bubble gum and waving a pair of scissors like a pistol, he froze. "Uuuhhhhh" had been his response at the time.

"Well, you said you wanted it short, like a buzz, so this is the thing I use." She holds up the shaver and turns it on for a second, the low-end hum starting then stopping. "I need to know what number, so I'll know how short to go."

"Oh," Gary says, as if he knows what in the hell she's talking about. "Um, actually, I'm really not sure."

The girl fondles the back of Gary's large head, running her fingers in his bushy hair.

"I guess a number three will do the trick." She turns him in the chair, getting a look at him in the mirror from all sides. "Well, we'll *start* with a number three, and if nothing else, we'll just take off a little more if you want it shorter, okay?"

Before cutting his hair the girl runs her hands over his head again, trying to feel the thickness in different areas, scoping out beforehand any patches that might pop up later like a crop of weeds. Gary revels in the attention, wondering if he should ask her to do the same with his chest hair when she's through up there, but then he opens his eyes, sees the other customers sitting in the barber chairs next to him, as well as those sitting in the lobby reading magazines. He frowns, the reality setting in.

"Real haircut?" she says after the first couple of passes with the whirring shears.

"Hmm?" Gary asks, trying to read the backward headline in an issue of *People* magazine an older woman is reading in the seat next to him.

"A second ago, you said 'real' haircut." He notices her voice is lower than most girls' he knows. When she laughed at a coworker's joke a few minutes earlier, it reminded him of Kathleen Turner, breathy, husky, deep. And sexy. "What do you mean?"

A picture flashes through Gary's mind: four months ago back in Kitty, sitting on a milk crate in the kitchen of his apartment with an issue and a half of a newspaper spread out underneath him as his roommate James circled around him brandishing a pair of ordinary paper scissors, continually asking, "Well, does it *feel* straight?"

"Oh, nothing." He waves his hand under the blue plastic cape thrown over him, making it look like something had suddenly burst up from his chest.

She's a tall girl, perhaps five eight, and a good match for Gary's own gangly frame. She's wearing black clunky shoes with a big silver buckle over the front, little wisps of his dark hair clinging to the rubbery soles. Her jeans are tight and fairly new, which Gary scoffs at, and her shirt actually looks brand new.

*Could have got something like that at the thrift store,* he thinks, reaching under his bib to tap his wallet, fastened to a belt loop with a chain, thinking back to all of the dollars he's saved over the years on secondhand clothes.

"Straight or tapered in the back?" she asks, switching the electric shears for a large razor as seen in the opening scenes of Kubrick's *Full Metal Jacket.*

"Straight, please," his voice cracks.

As Whitney (he spotted her California cosmetic license in the corner, her address covered in Wite-Out) runs the buzzing mechanism across the bottom of his hairline, he can't help but inch up slowly in the chair, wanting her to run the razor down both sides of his neck, down to the beginning of his shoulders, getting rid of the small tufts of hair that had sprouted since his last proper haircut. With each swipe of the machine he thinks she's going to do it. He can just imagine the clean feeling of the razor clearing out the path and then sitting back and enjoying the light fall breeze as it splays across his fresh, white skin. But each time he thinks she's going to do it, she doesn't. It reminds him of a heavy make-out session. Every time a girl makes a pass over the front of his jeans, he's chanting in his head, *Zipper, zipper, zipper.*

"Want me to clean up the neck?" Whitney finally asks.

Gary nods his head up and down. The razor feels just as good as he imagined it would. And as Whitney's bending over to get that just-right angle, Gary wonders if she is thinking about the haircut at all. He notices that the customers to the left and right of him have all disappeared, paid their money, and been replaced by new ones. And, is he crazy, or was she especially leaning into him as she snipped his bangs once and then, perhaps just for her own pleasure, leaned in and snipped them again? What's making her take so long unless she's, somehow, enjoying it?

*Nah,* thinks Gary in his head, shooing away the thought that she's attracted to him, even though he's attracted to her. *That's crazy. She does this all day. It's her job, getting this close to guys, making them sweat so they'll buy the high-priced gels. Besides, what would she want with a scrawny guy like me? No, no chance in hell.*

Instantly his spirit's wings melt in the glaring sun of self-doubt and he kicks himself as his soul sinks back into the maze. *This is going to end up just like the other night.* He crosses his arms underneath his apron, only no one can tell. *I'm getting all worked up over this girl, and I don't even know her.*

Trying to get his mind off his already aborted romance with Whitney, he thinks of a new song he'd started writing earlier in the week. He mumbles the words slightly off-key even though he's never too on key to begin with.

"What?" Whitney asks.

"Nothing, I was just humming a new song I'm working on."

"Oh, really?" She swings him in the chair to the left and finds his proxy eyes in the mirror instead of looking straight at him. "You write music?"

"Well, songs, I guess. You see, I'm in this band and we're from back East." Gary would kick himself if his feet already weren't stuck to the stirruplike pedestals of the chair. Like she couldn't already tell he wasn't from around here? "Anyway, I've been working on a new song, so I was, uh, just sort of humming . . . so, when you, er, asked . . ."

"So, *you're* the singer?" Whitney asks, trying to imagine Gary's thin voice amplified, shouting over guitars and drums.

"Nah, I just play bass. Mark, he's our guitar player and singer. I'd just give him the words and he would sing it."

"Uh, yeah," Whitney says, as if no longer interested. She unbuttons the collar of his cape, shaking it out and sending a rain of hair to the floor.

"Well, anyway"—Gary gets up awkwardly, his neck already feeling itchy—"I guess, uh, I mean, how much do I owe you?"

Gary fumbles as he slips a few bills from his wallet.

"No." Whitney stops him, placing a soft pair of hands on his shaking ones. "You pay the cashier."

"Oh," Gary squeaks, turning and walking away. Whitney follows him halfway, stopping to call for her next customer, who she then ushers to her chair. She smiles at the man graying at the temples as he starts in on his haircutting request.

"Just a trim, little girl . . ."

Gary kicks at the ground as the cashier rings up the total on a pocket calculator and not a big register.

"That'll be thirty dollars."

"Hmmm?" Gary says, not hearing the total. He's trying to catch another glance at Whitney from the corner of his eye, but she's too far down the corridorlike room. He can hear her husky laugh and he feels sad that she didn't laugh that way for him.

"I *said*," the cashier repeats, somewhat impatiently, "that will be thirty dollars."

"Oh."

*Thirty dollars, for a fucking buzz?* He scrambles for his wallet. *What kind of city is this?*

Sandwiched between coupons for Stefano's Pizza back in Kitty, a business card for Robert Hernandez, *The Amp Man,* and a condom, are a $20 bill, a five, and two ones.


"What are you doing?"

Mark asks this as he sits on the bed, *Details* magazine dropping to his chest for a second, affording him a view of Corinne through the bathroom door as she stands before the mirror, applying Clinique lipstick.

"I'm putting on some makeup," she answers in a funny voice, her lips stretched out flat and not puckered, the way Mark thought girls did it. "What's it look like?"

"Yeah, I *know* what you're doing," he says, exasperated, the caffeine from earlier flowing through his veins, speeding up his heart rate, making the corners of his eyes twitch and setting his nerves, again, on edge. "But what I want to know is, *why?*"

"Why what?"

Corinne examines her painted mouth in her reflection. She turns her head to one side, then the other, getting a view from all angles.

"Why are you putting on makeup when we're not going anywhere?" Mark rearranges the large pillow behind his head, giving his upper body more support so he doesn't have to crane his neck while he rereads the think piece on Drew Barrymore that he scanned earlier in the day. "I mean, we just got *back* from going out, and you know we're not going out again. So why, I'd like to know, are you getting all spruced up?"

"It's just a little lipstick, honey." She tosses the light pink pencil into the basket of cosmetics that sits above the toilet and then switches off the light with an acrobatic sweep of her right foot. "It makes me *feel* better."

Mark groans, turns over in bed, and throws the magazine to the floor, where it lands on a pile of other magazines Corinne likes to keep by her bedside, calling the stack her night reading. The pyramid of pulp is capped off with the freshly discarded *Details*, merging into *Mademoiselle, Sassy*, then a layer of *Entertainment Weekly, Cosmopolitan, Bikini*, ending with a hearty foundation of *Vogue, Paper, Buzz, Interview*, and a special double back-to-school issue of *Rolling Stone*.

"*Time* magazine?" Mark says, surprised, as he spots the bold logo from underneath the corner of the trendy font-splattered *Raygun*. "How did *that* get in there?"

"You say something?" Corinne asks as she slides into bed.

"Yeah, I said you should have run that shade by me"—he slides over, nuzzling up to her—"since it's all going to end up on my face anyway."

Corinne nibbles on Mark's ear, then withdraws to see she has indeed left a temporary madder rose scar on his earlobe.

"Nice." He takes the soft flesh between his thumb and forefinger and transfers the greasy lipstick from his ear to his hands. "Great."

As they begin to shuffle under the covers, Mark's eyes catch a glimpse of Corinne's underwear, a brief vision of satiny sheen, before her body disappears completely beneath the bedspread.

"What in the hell are those?" Mark points with his hand, in which is a lit cigarette with a caboose of ash about an inch long, precariously dangling above the fresh sheets.

"You mean *these,*" she says coquettishly, folding back the covers and waving her hand over her boxerish drawers. "These are my brand new pajamas. You like?"

Mark sort of grunts, unable to take his eyes off her embroidered top, only buttoned once in the center and, like a tent flap, exposing a triangle of flesh just above the belly button.

"I like, I like."

"Thanks, they're from Victoria's Secret."

"Geez, and I used to think that the secret was that nobody ever looked as good as those models in this stuff, but you've proved that wrong."

"Stop," she says, even though she wants him to continue.

Mark reaches out a hand but stops an inch short of the bottoms, afraid to touch them the way you'd like to run your finger over the ripples and grooves of the long-dried oil of a van Gogh in a museum but can't. He hesitates for another second before running his hand, from the top of her elastic waist down, over the material. He feels the underside with his callused fingertips, her hipbone sticking out, which gives way to a sloping, crescent-shaped curve leading to the beginning of her pubic hair, which feels like crushed grass underneath a picnic blanket.

"Smooth," he finally announces.

"Thanks," she says proudly, as if she produced the garment herself instead of just ordering it over the phone on a lunch hour last week when she spotted the catalog sitting on Quincy's desk. "It's made out of Jacquard silk moile, and both pieces are finished with French seams."

"Really," he asks, not raising his eyes, his fingers still making circles in the soft fabric, "what are French seams?"

"I don't know, actually." Corinne laughs. "But that's what the catalog said."

"Oh, and I like the belt," he says sarcastically, fingering one of the soft and frilly tassels looped around her waist.

"You mean you don't like it? I thought it was cool." She moves back a bit and angles down her head so her chin is buried in her chest, examining the satin cord laced through the skinny hoops.

"Are you kidding? You look like a Turkish pillow. And a *double* knot? Is this some sort of a chastity belt?"

"No." She blushes again, but for a different reason. "It's just I . . . you know, usually wear heels or mules, so when I wear sneakers to jog, I guess I always double-tie . . ."

"Don't worry about it. I think it's cute." He takes a long drag and then taps the cigarette against an ashtray. "Come here."

Mark turns back to Corinne and takes her in his arms. He runs his hands up and down the back of the pajama tops, which are just as soft as the bottoms. He pauses for a second to pull the hair from her face, pinning a tuft behind her left ear.

"Ooh, yuck." Tasting his tar-flavored saliva, she pulls away. "Cigarette breath."

"Hey, you smoke too," he defends.

"Yeah, but only when you do. You're a bad influence."

Mark turns and stubs out the nearly spent cigarette in his hand, gets out of bed, and goes into the bathroom. He takes the green toothbrush he'd bought from the Thrifty's on La Brea and covers the head with sparkly toothpaste. He can't believe he's doing this again. He was beginning to feel pussy whipped. There was no end to what a man would do for a woman, and he figured the brushing of his teeth twice a day was just the beginning.

Corinne looks to where Mark is standing over the sink, vigorously scrubbing his teeth made yellow from years of cigarettes and coffee. His hand jerks back and forth quickly, as if he were giving his mouth a shoeshine. She realizes this is the same view he had minutes before. She concedes that she must have looked ridiculous putting on makeup, just to go to bed. This makes her think of Brandi and Quincy, how she never thought she was as shallow or boring as her friends, but maybe she was. Mark pauses for a second to spit pink into the sink even though the toothpaste is baby blue.

It stings when he brushes his teeth, his gums cut by the hard bristles, and this annoys him. He preferred to be unhealthy on the inside, where he could hide his afflictions. Instead, he is bleeding on Corinne's bath mat the way he bled from shaving earlier in the week. He wondered if he'd ever run out of enough blood to ruin a woman's things.

"You didn't have a very good time tonight, did you?"

"Honest?" He spits again into the sink, blood and mucus stringy like cheese on a pizza. "No, I didn't."

"If it's any consolation, I didn't have a very good time, either."

Mark places the toothbrush back into the plastic holder and then rinses off his hands. He rejoins Corinne in bed and she startles at his cold touch.

"But what did Brandi mean, at first, when she said you hadn't been out of the apartment in months?"

"Weeks, for chrissakes, *weeks.*"

"Whatever."

Corinne pauses before answering. She had been bored enough lately to make Mark her boyfriend, but still, how much should she divulge? Facts were definitely facts; she was once with Tim, but now she was not. She was willing to let Mark know about her past, and had already mentioned Tim in passing. But the real answer was what the breakup had done to her, how it had nearly completely devastated her. And how could she explain to Mark that just talking to him on the sidewalk that day, walking half a block and then agreeing to go out with him, was such a victory after the days she had spent crying and the vows she had made to never touch another man again? And how would Mark, especially, understand this, since it seemed he left his girlfriend back home and was suffering no pangs of regret or remorse, while Corinne was only beginning to make scant progress in getting her life back on track? And Brandi was right, it *had* been months.

"Well, it's like this . . . ," Corinne uneasily begins. "Brandi and I dated the same guy. Sort of."

"That Tom guy?" Mark says, trying not to feel jealous, even though it's rising already.

"*Tim,*" Corinne corrects, unsure whether to think it's sweet that Mark even remembered or if the only the reason he did is because Tim had crowded in on his territory. Corinne often thought that men had the memory capacity for the stupidest things, lists of baseball statistics, song lyrics to the *Alice* theme, the name of every piece of junk in their car, and the names of their girlfriends' former lovers, which they considered yard-sticks to their own manhood. "Only *I* really dated him while *she* just fucked him."

Mark makes a hissing noise.

"Sorry, sorry. I guess I'm still catty about it, but I mean, I really loved the guy. It's over now, don't worry. He ended up being a jerk, but she was just using him."

"Using him for what?"

"To get back at me, to get in good with his friends, to prove something to herself, Quincy, *every*body."

Corinne turns to Mark, who's trying to look concerned, only it's not working very well. She can see in his eyes, almost as if they were a movie screen on which his thoughts were projected, herself having sex with another man. It doesn't matter that they have only known each other a short time, or that he hasn't even begun to really care for her. The image remains, and Mark tries to smile, to caress her hair, say how, "Yes, yes, I under*stand,*" only the thoughts continue and his blank drive-in eyes prove it: *You were once fucked by somebody other than me.*

Corinne reaches up and turns out the light.

"What do you say we go to sleep?"

"Sure." Mark scoots back underneath the covers. "Sure."

He kisses her cheek, then her mouth, moving to her neck. The toothpaste has helped but he still smells like smoke.

**Corinne reaches across her cluttered desk, grabbing at** the square clock-radio that sits under her brass lamp with the stained shade and only one working lightbulb. She takes the cube-shaped electronic device, the top of which is a speaker, shooting out the music coming from the radio straight into the air like a megawatt searchlight used for movie premieres, and tilts it, resting the side with the green LED display on the edge of her boomerang-shaped split computer keyboard.

"What are you listening to?" Quincy calls out from the next cubicle, noticing the slight rise in decibels.

"KCRW," Corinne yells back, distracted, missing a line of one of her favorite songs, which is being performed live in the station's studio, which is just a few miles away on the campus of Santa Monica College. She loses the beat for a second, her foot, tapping underneath her glass desk, lost for a moment and forced to stop, raised in the air like a drawbridge. "The *Morning Becomes Eclectic* show."

"Oh!" Quincy replies, as if surprised, even though it's what Corinne listens to every morning.

"Me? I'm listening to Howard Stern," she continues, even though Corinne didn't ask.

"Yeah," Corinne replies quickly. Anything to get Quincy off her back. "Great," she mumbles, fumbling with the cord antenna that's looped around the on-and-off switch of the lamp. The signal keeps coming in and out, fading and then reappearing, only to fade out again a second later. Victoria Williams's voice keeps advancing and then retreating, the lyrics to "Summer of Drugs" hanging in the air for a second, then dropping out just as quickly.

"Guess what?"

Corinne tosses the black cord to the desk and, looking up, sees Quincy, her blond hair pulled back into a ponytail, poking her face over the side of their tomato-red wall/space divider.

On the radio Corinne can hear that the song's ended and Victoria's now chatting with the host in an annoying whine, warbling on about meeting Lou Reed, Evan Dando, and how she doesn't have any medical insurance. Bored, Corinne picks up the clock and slides it to its usual position, skirting the base of the lamp, scooting it between a black plastic computer disc holder and a Rolodex.

"What?" Corinne says, looking past Quincy to the round clock on the wall. Ten-forty-five.

*Fuck, another six hours to go. Why do Mondays always seem to drag? I think that clock is slow.*

"Well . . . ," Quincy begins, stopping for a second to stick a clear green lollipop into her mouth, swirling it around and bulging out her cheeks before yanking it out by the white cardboard stem, "I heard that the boss is calling an employee meeting for around three and we're all going to have to stay late."

"Tonight?" Corinne wearily replies, glancing again at the clock. Ten-forty-six.

"Yeah, tonight." Her coworker stops for a second, sucks on the candy, pulls it out with a *smack,* and then reconsiders. "Or maybe it was tomorrow."

Corinne sighs and turns back to her desk. Sandwiched between her Syquest hard drive and Performa color monitor is a stack of faxes waiting to be answered, including a few that were addressed to her boss that Corinne intercepted earlier in the morning. She shrugs her shoulders, thinking of all the work that has to be done.

The DJ's now plugging a pledge drive set for that weekend,

going into the usual begging-for-money spiel. Corinne always means to send in $20, $30, $50, whatever, but somehow never gets around to it. Like that old commercial for the Control Data Institute used to go, "I can always start my training tomorrow," and then the sorry-looking guy's voice echoes into the eternity of never-was: *Tomorrow, tomorrow, tomorrow . . .*

"And it sucks, too," Quincy continues, "because what is she going to tell us in person that she can't spell out in a memo? You know what I mean?"

She flashes her green lizard tongue before dropping behind the divider to avoid her own work for the day.

Corinne continues to position the antenna, for some reason unable to get a clear signal. She gets up and pokes her head over her cubicle wall and sees Elliott leaning against it, propped up on one foot, aimlessly reading *Wired* magazine, his lips moving along as his finger glides over the text as if it were braille. Elliott shifts a little to the left for a moment to scratch his back, and for a second the signal on the radio comes in clearly, but it fades out just as Victoria clutches her acoustic guitar, launching into a new song.

"Oh, forget it." She whips the cord across her desk. She glares at the clock. Ten-fifty-one.

"Hey, Quincy, I just can't work under these conditions. You want to head downstairs and get a snack?"

"What? Oh, sure. Just let me get my purse."

Corinne reaches toward her foot to get her own purse, a jet black leather satchel with a brass buckle and gold chain-link strap. It's a little too dramatic for the simple suit she's wearing, but she was tired this morning and didn't feel like rummaging through the closet to find something more apt. She also didn't want to wake up Mark, who liked to sleep in.

As they leave their respective cubicles Corinne notices that Elliott's now gone and that her radio reception is coming in crystal clear.

"Ready?" Quincy asks, her high forehead wrinkled.

Corinne glances at her cluttered desk, then to Quincy. Now

Corinne would rather catch the last couple of songs of the radio show, holding out until lunch to make a break, and then maybe not come back at all, but she figures since going downstairs was her idea, she'd better just stick with it.

"Sure."

They walk through the reception area across the dark gray marble floor, passing an area of construction to the left, where more offices are being added next to the break room, and enter an empty elevator.

"Why can't *Die Hard* or something like that ever happen in *our* building?" Quincy whines as she pushes the blue button marked *L*. "It's just so *boring* around here. Nothing exciting ever happens."

"Uh, geez, Quincy, I don't know," Corinne says as she tries to avoid her reflection in the brass elevator doors. Her eyes are sagging, her brown hair limp and up in a bun to hide its loss of life, a textbook bad-hair day. Her bones feel weary and her suit, which really needs pressing, seems to be hanging at odd angles all over her body. As she tucks a strand of hair back into the pile on the back of her head, her sight shaves the face of her watch. Ten-fifty-seven.

*Only ten-fifty-seven.*

It's been a rough month. The faxes keep rolling in, wanting to know what happened to the unanswered faxes of the week before, the ones Corinne had been hoping to get to that day. Her boss, an illiterate twig who speaks French because she lived for years in Paris and speaks Spanish because she's lived with servants, swarms around the office like a queen bee checking on her workers, yet rarely presses Corinne about her work flow. She is completely clueless as to the secret drawer full of near emergencies that Corinne keeps, all printed on cheap thermal fax paper that curls up into inscrutable scrolls when the roll is nearly spent. Every day Corinne just smiles, puts in her nine hours (sometimes ten and twelve), and keeps filling the drawer, making a mental promise to get to the drawer some other day, perhaps tomorrow.

Corinne's enthusiasm began its downward spiral not long after Tim's father's golf partner had got her the job. At first she was eager to make a good impression so favorable reviews would be telegraphed to Tim, his father, and the golf partner. But after a few months of answering meaningless faxes, picking up the phone, making countless copies, and getting caught in the cross fire of office politics, Corinne became bored. After she lost Tim, she kept the job. She and his father were still on good terms. Every once in a while she found him on the other end of the phone she hated to pick up or else would find a card from him in her mailbox; he insisted she keep the job. She was not happy, yet knew that she would probably not be happy anywhere else. Because she was unsure of what she wanted to do for the rest of her life—devote herself to that "career" her girlfriends talked so much about—Corinne never really held a job; she just holds each one at bay.

"I talked to Ron who works up in accounting on forty-five, and *he* said he was trapped in one of the elevators here and it *wasn't* so glamorous." Corinne stops for a second to nibble on her thumbnail, spitting out flakes of red nail polish. "Maintenance finally rescued him, not some swarthy, unshaven renegade from the bomb squad who's a rebel and plays by his own rules. It was some middle-aged janitor with a Mexican accent who got pissed off when Ron called him Jesus. *Hey-Seuss*, the guy said."

"All I'm trying to say"—the elevator coasts to a stop, the doors sliding open to reveal a bustling lobby—"is that we could use a little excitement around here."

"Well, with *that*"—Corinne follows Quincy into a small gift shop and looks over a cart filled with fat-free muffins—"I agree."

Quincy returns from the back of the store with a bottle of Snapple mango-flavored iced tea.

"You know who is in the back, trying to decide on a Häagen-Dazs ice cream bar?"

"Who?"

"Elliott. What should I do?"

Corinne looks to the back of the store where Elliott, a maga-zine rolled up underneath one arm, is putting the three choices in his hand back into the freezer. When he turns to walk away he notices his tie is caught in the freezer door.

"Simple, Quincy, just say 'Hi' or 'How are you?' You know, something easy. Small talk."

"Small talk, okay. Okay."

Quincy steps into the aisle, which Elliott's going to pass through in a second. She's surrounded on one side by various mugs with slogans like OVER THE HILL and ALLERGIC TO MONDAYS, on the other with cheap pens, desk sets, and fake trophies with placards that read BOSS OF THE YEAR. Quincy's trying to pick a certain topic of small talk with which to confront Elliott but is unable to decide between the weather or an assess-ment of his weekend. Elliott retreats from the freezer, stumbles into a large yellow tank filled with helium, and then into Quincy.

"Hey."

"Hey."

In the ensuing silence, as Quincy watches Elliott fold into the crowd of the lobby, Corinne says out loud the words appearing in her head.

"Was it Eliot's toilet I saw?"

"What?"

"Oh, nothing," Corinne says quickly, mentally chastising her-self for letting loose a literary reference in the presence of Quincy, who, Corinne correctly guesses, is disappointed she's missing the Stuttering John segment that's flickering out of her radio sixteen flights above.

"No, really, what did you say? Something about Elliott? Is it gossip?"

"No, no." Corinne files into the line, turning her head to talk to her friend, who's positioned behind her. "It's not *our* Elliott, it's *T. S.* Eliot. The poet."

"Never heard of him."

"You know, 'We are the hollow men, the stuffed men'? Or

how about 'The Wasteland'? Anyway, Eliot was married to some publishing magnate's daughter." She fingers her chin, trying to recollect the facts. "Maybe it was one of the Simon & Schuster girls."

"Carly Simon?" Quincy springs to life, a recognizable face on her cultural horizon.

"No, you dummy, this was in the twenties or thirties. Maybe it wasn't even Simon & Schuster. Anyway, that's not important. The thing is, some guy was being shown around the offices where Eliot used to work, and he spotted this bathroom in the corner and said, 'Was it Eliot's toilet I saw?'"

A man at the head of line pays for his coffee and doughnut and exits the store with inexact change. Corinne and Quincy advance a few steps in silence.

"Uh, I don't get it."

Corinne sighs, wondering why she's even pushed it this far.

"It's a palindrome."

"A palin-whatsa?"

"Palin*drome*. It's any word or sentence that means the same thing spelled forwards and backwards."

"You mean like *god* and *dog*?" Quincy stops for a second, spooked at the ramifications of her example.

"No, no." Corinne rubs her stinging eyes. "Those words have different meanings when you reverse them. A palindrome means the *same* thing. Like, Napoleon once supposedly said, 'Able was I ere I saw Elba.' You see how that works? How *able* at the beginning is *Elba* at the end? The same with *was* and *saw*, and the *R* in the middle of *ere* is sort of like the pivot point of the whole thing. You see?"

"Uh, yeah," Quincy says, not really seeing.

*Not even with glasses,* Corinne thinks, reaching into her purse for a couple of dollar bills to pay for her muffin.

"So how did you know about all that?" Quincy races to catch up to Corinne as her coworker weaves in and out of the bustling lobby traffic. "You know, all that pallinwhatever stuff."

"Tim," Corinne says, not even conscious of the name. The

information had been with her for so long that the point of origin had been lost, and now that it had been suddenly found, it struck her with an alarming acuity and also a searing pain.

"Tim?" Quincy asks, unwrapping a Tootsie Roll lollipop and sticking it into her mouth. The candy was something she ate during the day because she could not smoke, and she told herself the only reason she needed cigarettes was to keep her hands off the sweets at night. To her, it made perfect sense.

"You know, Tim," Corinne says sarcastically.

"Oh, you mean Brandi's old boyfriend."

MADAM I'M ADAM.

These three words are laid out on the silver metal rim of Corinne's bathroom mirror in rainbow-colored plastic letters, each one with a little brown magnet on its belly, causing it to stick to the silvery surface. She picked up the cache of letters at a flea market in the Valley as part of a Fisher-Price desk set that came with a small blackboard, a yellow spongy eraser, and a handful of nubs of varied colors of chalk. She paid the $1.50 for the set, ditching everything but the letters in a trash can just outside the gate that read *Keep Encino Beautiful*.

"Madam, I'm Adam," Mark keeps whispering to himself as he shaves. "What in the fuck does that mean?"

He shakes out the disposable razor underneath the steaming water flowing from the tap. The mixture of shaving cream and sheared whiskers garnishing the sink looks like cookies-and-cream ice cream, black flecks suspended in the gooey white.

"Maybe Adam's an old boyfriend." He makes another pass with the razor, up his jawline, trimming the bottom of one of his sideburns. "Maybe he's that guy in the photo in the living room. The one she's posing with, looking almost *too* happy. Or is that Tim? Jesus, how many have there been?"

In midspeech, one of his cheeks, bulging and not laid out smooth the way it should be, causes the thin metal blade of the razor to cleanly slice into it, as if his flesh were an apple being pared.

"Adam, Adam . . . Adam," he's mumbling as the flowing blood mixes into the white lotion, turning both a bright pink. "Adam, this is all *your* fault."

Reaching out for some toilet paper, he spots a small container of floss, and the object stops his actions as if it were a rattlesnake appearing out of nowhere on a hiking path, poised to strike. For a minute he just stares at it, his body frozen, blood still flowing, now off his chin and onto the white bath mat he's standing on. The hot water coming out of the tap hisses and the steam continues to rise, fogs up the mirror, the plastic letters stuck to the quartz surface seemingly hovering in clouds.

It's just an ordinary dispenser of floss, waxed, mint flavored, plastic white container with red lettering and a wisp of the string peeking out over the shiny metal cutter at one corner. Run-of-the-mill floss.

He picks it up from the Formica top of the toilet as if it were a million-year-old dinosaur bone or some artifact equally old and steeped with mythological lore. He turns it over a couple of times, then brings it close to his nostrils for a smell. Its sterile odor, sort of twiny and plantlike at the same time, brings him back to another era. Laura used to use this stuff.

Remembering the mail he picked up the day before, he tosses the plastic *T* into the sink and runs into the living room and grabs a letter from his blue duffel bag. The beige envelope reads, *Mark Pellion, c/o The Mondrian Hotel, 8440 West Sunset Boulevard, Hollywood, California.*

Mark had recognized the plain, printed writing the second Hanes handed it to him the day before, along with a letter from his parents and some forwarded bills from home.

Now, alone in Corinne's apartment, he tears open Laura's letter.

*Mark,*

*Where does one begin after such a long silence? It seems to me that it's been over a month since we last spoke—that morning when I dropped you off at the airport. I won't ask if all is well. Steve calls Jim and Jim has been filling me in on most of the details. I hope the recording is going smoothly and, may I say I'm proud of you?*

Laura's scribbling is small almost to the point of illegibility and Mark wishes he had brought a letter or two from home to compare it to.

*Perhaps the strain of depression?* he wonders, trying to find a cause for the compacted letters and minuscule sentences running like dashes and dots along the off-white page. *Or maybe she's writing this using some guy's ass as a desk.*

Mark's biting his lip when the phone next to the couch he's sitting on rings.

"Uh, hello?" he tentatively says. He still feels weird about answering her phone.

"Hey, it's me. What's up?"

"Oh, Corinne, um . . ." He glances down to the card and then nervously runs his hands across his frosted cheeks, the lotion now congealed. "Shaving, yeah. I was, uh, shaving."

"Shaving?" She laughs. "You mean you just woke up?"

Mark looks across the room to a clock with a round face housed in a silver square. Eleven-thirteen.

"Well, not exactly. I watered the plants like you said and did the dishes so I, uh, was just getting ready to take a shower. How's *your* day going?"

"Boring as hell. I'm sitting here choking on a stale muffin I bought while Quincy and I were—hey, that reminds me. Quincy told me that there might be some sort of a staff meeting tonight . . . so I may be a little late."

"Oh, that's . . . too bad. But I'm in the studio today, so don't worry about it."

"Don't sound so crushed. Anyway, I thought I'd let you know so you wouldn't worry. And maybe when I come home we'll order in some food?"

"Yeah, sure, Corinne. Actually, I'd better go . . . I'm . . . I'm getting shaving cream all over the phone."

"Oh, okay. Well then, I'll see you whenever I get home."

"Sure, sure. I, uh . . ." The impulse to say *I love you* comes more out of habit than a great outpouring of emotion. *I love you*. I was such a typical send-off when he was dating Laura, but saying it to Corinne now seems unimaginable to him. And little does he know that fifteen miles across town she is crossing her fingers, praying he doesn't say it, because, regardless of her own feelings, she knows she would be obliged to say it back. "I, um, will see you then . . . then, okay?"

"Okay. Bye."

Mark slams down the phone without wiping off the mustache of lather that's now attached to the receiver, and as it slides back in its cradle a few whips of the lotion spray onto the floor.

He reads the card again in his hands.

*My life has taken quite a turn since you left. I got a new job with the college radio station as an advisor, this time a paying position! No more interning. I know it's nothing compared with what you've got in store for you out there, but then again, we all can't be rock stars living life in the fast lane. Back here in Kitty, if you'll remember, even the Interstate 95 only has two lanes, and both of them are slow. Ha, ha.*

"My life has taken quite a turn since you left"? *What in the hell does* that *mean? Is she living with some guy? Is she a lesbian now?* Mark paces through the apartment. *What?*

He sits back down on the couch and finishes the rest of the note.

*There's not much else going on now. I hope your muse stays with you. If you get the urge, drop me a note.*

A large dollop of shaving cream drops like a tear from his face to the card in his hand. Quickly wiping away the creamy substance, he sees that the soaked print underneath is smeared and illegible. Not much of the letter is lost, in fact, not a single sentence, just the sign-off. But now Mark can't tell if she jotted down a plain *Sincerely* or a suggestively reunional *With Love*. Only the phantom curve of her signature, an errant *r* and *a*, remain at the bottom of the card, the rest of her farewell lost.

On the way back into the bathroom Mark sees a picture standing on a built-in bookcase he's never noticed before. It's of

Corinne and some guy. They have their arms around each other and are smiling. Corinne's hair is shorter and her smile is not like any he's ever seen.

*I guess we all have our sordid pasts.* He fingers the photo in its expensive hand-painted, oval-shaped frame and leaves a trail of soap scum around the beveled rim. *I guess we're all haunted by the certain faces*—he rubs a hand over the documented fragment of two lives merging for a brief period of time—*people we can't forget.*

Mark goes back into the bathroom, quickly finishes shaving, and turning to leave, catches sight once again of the floss. He picks it up quickly and tosses it into the makeshift brown-paper-bag trash can, its rim folded over to give it some shape.

From a drawer opposite the sink he takes out a couple of the plastic magnetic letters and, turning back to the medicine chest, adds a few and takes away others.

"There," he says, marching out of the bathroom, "two birds with one stone."

The mirror catches the reflection of him stomping into the other room, the rainbow letters like a tattoo on his tense back.

MADAM I'M MARK.


Steve picks up his snare drum and brings it close to his face. He breathes on the shiny, silver band of metal and scrubs off the fog created by his warm breath with the bright green sleeve of his T-shirt, examining the whiskers on his chin and upper lip. He laments that the hair feels only a step or two away from the peach fuzz he encountered his freshman year in high school. His burgeoning goatee, which is really just strands of sandy brown hair here and there, looks more like the beginning symptoms in a werewolf transformation, the pointy ears and fangs to follow.

"Mark here yet?"

Steve quickly replaces the snare drum on its tripitched stand and looks up. He sees Gary entering the studio; behind him Kenneth and Paul are having coffee, discussing the day's schedule.

"Uh, no, not yet. I mean . . . I haven't seen him."

"Damn." Gary slams down his bass and goes to run his hands through his hair. He's alarmed to find he has none. Well, *almost* none.

At another sound at the door, Gary turns, figuring it's Kenneth, there to bitch them out because Mark hasn't arrived, or Paul, here to deliver the news that Kenneth is just too pissed off even to tell them that work for the day was canceled.

"Hello boys," Mark says, jovial. His band mates glare back at him, still pissed off that they've been working so hard while he's been lounging around. In the harsh stares that follow, he notices their changed appearances. "Well, well, well . . . Daddy's away for a few days and the kids go crazy."

"What are you talking about?" Gary says, but then turns away, as if to hide.

"You know what I mean." Mark reaches out and pinches Gary's chest through his royal blue T-shirt, which reads BODY BY NAUTILUS, BRAIN BY MATTEL. "Now wait, don't tell me, don't tell me." He points first to Steve—*"On the Road"*—and then to Gary—"and *Revenge of the Nerds*. Am I right?"

"You guys want to come in here for a second?" Kenneth's voice booms through the studio monitors.

"M-m-moonraker," Steve mumbles into Mark's ear as they enter the booth, and Gary, just behind him, shakes his head and says under his breath, "I'm a geek, *not* a nerd."

Kenneth stands in the center of the room looking over a schedule in his notebook while Paul rips inch-long strips of white masking tape from a roll and attaches them to the studio's long, button-riddled console.

"Now, today we're going to start getting the guitar down because I figure that's as good as the drums and bass are going to sound. At least, that's as good as you guys can *play*. There's a few fuckups, but I'd rather get those later as quick overdubs right before we mix because you guys are already losing the momentum of this project. Come to think of it, so am I. Mark, it's your turn."

Steve and Gary take a step back and eye Mark with a look that silently says, *Busted.*

Mark shrugs his shoulders and heads into the studio, where his gear is set up in the room between the drum studio and the vocal chamber. A Crate amp faces the wall, his Fender Jaguar sits on a guitar stand, and between the two is a large baffle, a carpet thrown over the amp to ensure no other sounds leak into the microphone, which is aimed, slightly off center, at the speaker's cone.

"Let's try and get the rhythm guitar down on 'Parisian Broke,' clear out the work tracks from preproduction, and then we'll maybe try and nail the solo before we call it a day, okay?"

Mark puts on the headphones and twirls his arms around like windmill blades, trying to loosen some of the tight muscles in his neck and shoulders. He picks up his guitar, heavy in his hands, which have not held it for days, and loops the leather strap over his head, where it falls diagonally across his back.

"Okay, Mark." Kenneth's voice appears in his headphones. "The first pass is going to be for me just so I can get up a good headphone balance, so bear with me if things sound a little wacky."

Clicking appears as suddenly as Kenneth's voice disappears. Steve knocks together his drumsticks, counting off the intro to the song (a stray sound Kenneth assured them would be removed during the mixdown, even though the boys sort of like having it there), and then the beat starts, followed closely by Gary's bass, which overpowers the drums until Paul adjusts the fader, lowering the signal in the mix. Behind all of this is the temporary guitar track Mark recorded during preproduction. He catches up with the song halfway through and plays the shuffling chord progression, dreading the complicated solo that will follow later in the day.

"Okay, Mark. Let's try a couple."

The first two tries Mark fucks up, but on the third Kenneth stops him, saying there's a problem inside the booth that has nothing to do with the way he's playing. On the fourth take Mark feels he nailed the part. Kenneth's voice in his headphones afterwards confirms what he suspected.

"That was pretty good, Mark. Why don't you come in here and we'll have a listen."

Mark scampers back inside the booth, where Steve and Gary sit on the couch and Paul is rewinding the tape. The song plays back, Mark's newly recorded guitar a little higher in the mix than everything else, just so they can examine it.

"What do you think of the sound?" Kenneth asks. "Does it sound like you?"

"I don't know." Mark looks confused. "I guess so. I mean, I think I hear myself differently."

Kenneth, already exhausted, turns to Steve and Gary.

"Does it sound like him?"

The bass player and drummer quickly nod their heads in the affirmative even though they, too, can't be sure. They've never heard themselves sound so clean. For the past couple of years they had played either in shitty bars or their practice space, recording a few times in a friend's garage, and there they sounded the worst ever.

"Well, I'm happy with it," Kenneth finally announces, since no else seems to want to speak. "The sound, anyway. You were stuttering a little on the opening, and the chorus wasn't as in the pocket as I'd like it. We'll keep this track just in case, but I'd like to try it again."

Mark walks back into the studio and puts on his headphones. Returning to the small space from the air-conditioned control room, he finds the room warm and slightly damp, the smell of his shaving cream hanging in the air. He places a hand to his face and it feels scraped and still sort of sore. He remembers seeing those white spots under his chin when he got out of the shower, streaks of soap he hadn't managed to rinse off, and his skin was dry, so he applied more shaving lotion to his already perfumed face. Now the scent is beginning to choke him.

Halfway through the fifth take, the music is abruptly cut.

"What's the problem?" Mark asks.

"I'm getting a hum on the guitar."

"Well, it sounds perfect in here," Mark protests.

"I don't give a shit what it sounds like in *there,* Pellion," Kenneth's voice booms in Mark's headphones; "in here I'm getting a hum, and in *here* is where it counts."

Mark just nods okay through the glass. Kenneth has his left hand to his face, a black felt pen in his hand, two fingers in his mouth. He looks as if he's eaten something sour.

By the time Mark had heard "Parisian Broke" forty times over the span of seven hours, he was sorry to have ever written it.

Gary and Steve had been sent out to have a late lunch, while Kenneth and Paul stayed behind with Mark to try and get his guitar solo down on tape, but even after a leisurely meal at Carney's and some quick window shopping at a tattoo parlor (the old theory was correct; Gary was finding it habit forming), they returned to find Mark still in the studio, still trying to get down his part.

"One more time," his voice came through the control booth. "I'm sorry."

Kenneth held his head in his hands.

*"He's* sorry?"

No one noticed when Gary quietly picked up the phone and made a call. He would have preferred to have called from home, but the conversation had been on his mind all morning, and as Mark blurted over the studio's monitors, "Sorry, sorry, my fault," yet again, Gary didn't know if he'd ever make it back home.

Five minutes later he slams down the phone and turns to Steve, who has been staring intently at Mark, who he sees is beginning to sweat.

"I got a date," Gary says over and over again. "I got a date."

"You got a what?"

Gary twists and turns on the couch as Kenneth tells Mark to try the solo yet again.

"I said, I got a date."

"That part I heard, but with who?"

"Whitney, that girl from the other day."

"The barber?"

Kenneth turns around and angrily shooshes them. Steve and Gary recoil slightly from the reprimand, remain silent for a second, but then turn back to each other, this time whispering.

"She's not a barber, you moron, she's a stylist."

"And she's going out with you?"

"Yeah, well, she had to get her money back somehow."

"Huh?" Steve asks. "I didn't catch that last part. She needs to get her *what* back?"

"Her money, okay?" Gary says quickly. "I didn't have enough money, so she lent me some. No big deal."

"So this isn't a date as much as it is a payoff." Steve begins giggling.

"I could have wrote her a check, but *she* suggested dinner."

"Yeah, right." Steve chuckles. "She just wanted cold hard cash. She probably thought a check would bounce."

Mark's guitar solo echoes throughout the room until it stutters slightly, stumbles, and then disappears altogether.

Before asking what went wrong, Kenneth sighs heavily, wringing out his rectangular head with his hands.

"Uh, Mark? Why'd you stop?"

"The . . . tone." Mark's disembodied voice floats through the booth. Gary sits up to see his friend, catching only a glimpse of Mark's back and his hair, which sticks up under the confines of the headphones.

"What's wrong with the tone?"

"It doesn't sound bright enough."

"Bright enough?"

"Yeah."

"Well, give us a second, we'll see what we can do from in here."

As Paul starts to fiddle with the controls, taking the low end out of the equalizer, Kenneth turns to Steve and Gary.

"Mark's been playing in bars too long. The noise has finally started to get to him and he just doesn't hear the upper register as well as he used to. So when he says it doesn't sound bright enough, he's right. It doesn't sound bright enough to *him*. But in here, it's fine." Kenneth turns back to the console. "Okay, Mark. We've made a few adjustments. Let's try it again."

As Mark waits, yet again, for his cue, he tries to figure out why the ability to perform his guitar part is eluding him, especially since it has never seemed to elude him before. They practiced the song at least five times a week, and sometimes he stumbled while he played it or transposed a note or two, but nothing as bad as he was doing today. On their recent tour (except for that lengthy hiatus in Kentucky, when they were stranded for three weeks and did not play a show at all), night after night he played the solo, and it always sounded fine. In fact, drunk in a club, he found it easier to play. He could immediately sense the impact the frenzied notes had on the people in the crowd. Or maybe that was just his imagination. It wasn't the liquor that liberated his fingers and made them scale the guitar's neck with rubbery ease; maybe it was all those drinks before the show that didn't make him notice all the fuckups during the show. Often after a gig he would stumble down off the platform and find Gary and Steve at the bar after their gear had been torn down (ever since that first show Mark had tried, usually successfully, to weasel out of setting up or tearing down the stage), and he would proclaim the previous performance to be one of Bottlecap's best . . . ever. Steve and Gary always seemed to think it was one of the worst. As Mark passed out in the back of the club, some poor girl trapped underneath him, he could never figure out how this could be true. *But that solo,* his last thought would be, thankful to be forced into sleep just as the room was beginning to spin, *what about the solo?*

Back inside the booth, Kenneth is worrying.

"If we don't get this down on tape soon," he leans over and whispers to Paul, even though both Gary and Steve can hear, "we're going to have to start again fresh in the morning, and by that time Mark will be totally burnt out on it."

"One more time," Mark begs. "I can get it. I swear."

"Okay," Kenneth says into the talk-back mike. Paul punches in a few numbers on the tape remote. Mark tosses his head back and forth, like a boxer about to enter the ring, trying to corral his concentration. The music starts again in his headphones, the way he's heard it, it seems, a thousand times already today. The way he knows he's going to hear it in his head tonight and the next day for months, or at least until the next troublesome solo that will take him just as long to record.

He readies his fingers on the fret board, his palms getting sweaty, and he's afraid he's going to drop the pick the way he did when he was first learning to play the instrument five years ago. When he starts in on the solo this time, though, he seems to be playing it perfectly. His hands slide up and down the neck, his eyes closed, his raw fingers find their marks expertly, achieving perfect clearance and allowing each note to sing fully before being replaced with the next (even if it still doesn't sound bright enough). He's almost done when, in order to get into his performance, he starts moving his shoulders and swaying backward and forward and accidentally steps on the guitar cord, which pulls the heavy body toward the floor and out of his grasp. Two notes away from the end and he blew it.

"Fuck!" Mark screams.

Steve and Gary rise off the couch just in time to see Mark take the guitar off his back and, swinging it by the neck, smash it against the first of the sliding glass doors. The guitar recoils upon impact, causing the glass to crack but not shatter completely.

"What are you doing?" Kenneth yells.

Mark bursts out of the studio and begins pacing around the control room.

"We could have just edited that last bit out and punched in the ending." Kenneth continues to shout. "We're not working with your little friend's four-track here. When in the hell are you going to stop being such a moron and realize that you're wasting other people's time? I don't give a rat's ass for you *or* this shitty solo, but I've got a job to do and I'll be damned if I let some little nobody from nowhere ruin my . . ." His words trail off as he marches out of the studio, followed first by Paul, then Gary, then Steve.

# 11

***Corinne stares into the heavy cast-iron skillet, not*** believing how hot it is for October. Sure, this is southern California and it's not as if she expected snow to be on the ground (a winter spent in Manhattan four years ago convinced her that anyone who put up with the constant barrage of extreme weather year round was crazy, and deserved all the crime and traffic they got), but still, here it is nearly November and the morning is warm enough that she's making a big breakfast for a picnic on the roof.

She turns the scrambled eggs over and over again in the hot pan, not wanting them to burn, surprised at how adroit she is with her left hand though she's actually right-handed. Before her eyes the eggs (the only thing she can cook for breakfast, or so she says) turn from a gooey yellow-and-whitish substance into a lumpy but palatable solid. Mixed in are slivers of cheddar and bits of American cheese, her trademark secret passed on by an old cleaning lady who lived with Corinne and her parents until she left the cat and dog on their own for a weekend and was fired. In a pan diagonally across from the eggs on the stove top are a dozen pieces of Polish sausage, cut from two long links and frying up in a thin layer of oil, and the juice from two lemons. With her right big toe Corinne turns on the toaster, which sits beneath the microwave on a rickety black cart that was intended to hold a TV and VCR that she bought from IKEA. Mark, whose sole job was to pour the orange juice, is sitting on the couch in the other room, staring out the window.

"Honey? I'm getting close," Corinne calls out, as if it were a sexual climax around the corner and not breakfast. "Could you give me a hand?"

Mark just sits there, comatose. He keeps thinking of his failure at the recording studio, how he'd been so swept up in Los Angeles and his new life with Corinne that the guitar in his hands felt alien, except for when he brandished it like an axe and cost the band $850 damage to Starmaker Studios. The next couple of days hadn't been much better. No matter how hard Mark tried to concentrate, he kept fucking up on the most elementary of chord changes, on even the one-note solos that the guys used to laugh at him for including in their songs; he was forgetting tunes that he himself wrote, and he figured that if he couldn't remember them, who could?

Kenneth shot dirty looks through the studio's glass doors (now decorated with an X in heavy gray duct tape since they couldn't waste the day it would take to repair), and Gary and Steve glared and gave him the silent treatment. That is, when they weren't impressing upon him how important this all was, how they weren't looking forward to going back to Kitty a failure, and that if Mark couldn't do the job, maybe they would try to find someone who could. Forget that Mark wrote these songs, cajoled Gary and Steve into playing them in front of people in the first place, not to mention dragging them three thousand miles to record them. A week of Mark making mistakes and they were whispering about replacing him, but how could they do that? It would be like firing your mom when you're still in the womb. Adding to the stress was the fact that on Monday they were going to start recording his final vocals. Henry kept warning that if they didn't turn in the record by the deadline, they'd be taken off the release schedule, postponed indefinitely.

"Mark?" Corinne calls out again, the eggs turning hard and crumbly in the pan. A few of the sausages are more black than a deep red, a crusty charcoal soot covering both the meat and the bottom of the pan. The toaster oven is also smoking, the bread barely cooked but the coating of apple turnover filling from

Mark's late-morning snack a week ago going up in hazy smoke. "Could you, uh, help me?"

"I don't even *want* orange juice," he calls back, torn out of his apocalyptic thoughts.

*My life is going down the tubes and she's talking foodstuffs?*

"Well, could you, you know?" Her voice is erratic, bouncing off the walls as she twirls around, switching pans from lit burners to cold ones, trying to get everything under control before the smoke alarm goes off. She doesn't know that Mark took out the nine-volt battery two weeks ago and put it to a better use powering his Boss Super Overdrive pedal. "I could use a . . . hand."

Mark thinks about clapping but gets up instead, thinking Corinne wouldn't appreciate the joke. He yawns as he enters the other room, sad to see it is already Sunday, that in twenty-four hours he will back at Starmaker Studios with headphones on and Kenneth behind the broken glass, glaring at him along with his two once-best friends, who were on the road to becoming what they were before they were his best friends: strangers.

In the kitchen, Corinne still can't believe how hot it is. Her face in various sizzling pans and toes pulling down the glass door of the toaster oven, where a glowing red grill lies behind it, makes her sweat. Her hair is pulled back and she can feel beads of saltwater breaking out on her upper lip and forehead the same way she saw on the sausages when she began frying them twenty minutes ago.

"Juice, right?" Marks says as he enters the room, which even in his self-absorbed state he notices is at least ten degrees hotter than the rest of the house, already warmer than usual.

"And plates, please." She motions toward the cabinet above the counter strewn with food, half an onion, the remaining bits of a diced bell pepper, and a Pyrex bowl containing half an inch of the runny egg concoction.

Mark complies, fetching two plates and placing them onto separate teakwood trays on the table, each with its own napkin, set of silverware, and half-an-orange decoration, the center cut into sharp angles and crevices by a device Corinne ordered from an infomercial late one night. As soon as the plates are down she scoops some of the scrambled eggs onto each one, following up with pieces of sausage. She cuts the long slices of sourdough bread in half, places two on Mark's plate, then two on her own.

"Ready?" She picks up her tray, hoping Mark will follow without being told.

"What? Oh, sure." He clumsily grabs at his tray, tipping over the little pair of salt and pepper shakers that Corinne stole from a hotel last summer.

Corinne leads the way out the front door, which is propped open with a copy of Harold Brodkey's *The Runaway Soul*, a book that Tim had left behind. Her door was propped open constantly in the summer months in order to air out the cavernous apartment, which seemed to keep pockets of warm air trapped in the corners of rooms unless she flushed them out by opening the windows in the living room and keeping the front door open, achieving the mythical cross ventilation. It felt strange to employ the tactic this far into autumn, not to mention that it took her twenty minutes to find the Brodkey book, a novel too long for her to ever consider reading.

At the end of the hallway, past a row of metallic mailboxes, a staircase leads to the roof. Mark follows as Corinne takes each step slowly, not wanting to overturn her breakfast. Slightly off center, skirting the southwestern corner of the roof, where a two-foot ledge is the only protection from accidentally plunging to one's own death, sits a card table. The rubber-capped, outstretched tubes of thin, battleship gray painted metal that form the table's legs rest unevenly on the gravelly surface. Covering the table is a blue-and-white checkered tablecloth. In the center is an empty Diet Coke can stuffed with four yellow daisies and two makeshift name cards (converted cardboard inserts from a pack of five Maxwell cassettes she bought earlier in the week). One reads MARK, the other CORINNE. Metal folding chairs with couch cushions sit tucked into the table.

"Quite a spread," Mark says, just to be polite.

"Thanks." Corinne sets down her tray, nervous that she forgot something, nervous that the eggs have not been cooked enough, this fear quickly replaced by the anxiety that perhaps they have been cooked too much.

She pulls out her chair, which skids slightly and leaves a groove in the gravel. Mark follows, sitting down quickly and applying generous amounts of salt and pepper to his breakfast before taking a bite. This hurts Corinne's feelings; it's as if he's deemed the meal tasteless before giving it a taste.

*At least give it a chance*, she thinks, lightly applying some salt and pepper to her own eggs.

"Good," he says, pausing to stuff a wedge of sausage in his munching mouth, "real . . . good."

"Thanks," Corinne says, her own plate so far untouched. She has been planning the picnic for the last couple of days, the idea springing up when she was at lunch with Quincy and then later, at her desk, when the idea was something to occupy her time and stave off boredom until six o'clock mercifully arrived. When the weather held through to Saturday and was predicted to reach into late Sunday (not a cloud in the sky), Corinne snuck out of the house and went down to Farmer's Market to get fresh fruit, eggs, and juice. She snuck out not because Mark would have noticed—he was too wrapped up in his own problems— but because it added a bit of suspense and intrigue to her Saturday morning, when she usually only had a hangover.

"Nice day," he grumbles, the toast cracking his mouth. It is slightly stale and after being toasted is brittle. When he tries to butter it he puts his knife right through it, as if he were trying on a woefully small pair of pants made of paper towels.

"Yeah, it is. Even though it's still a little hazy."

The city is ensconced in thin clouds, but the light still glints off the sides of buildings and makes you squint. It's the kind of day where you don't think it will be too sunny so you don't wear a hat, only to look into the mirror the next morning and find your entire face sore and burned red. In the background, birds chirp and stereos and conversation are heard far away, and the omnipresent buzz of traffic, a low, soothing hum.

"Come here often?" Mark laughs at his own joke, as if the point of everything was to dig himself out of the mood he was in instead of trying not to drag Corinne down with him.

"Not really." Corinne looks around, examining the roof, looking beyond to the next couple of buildings. As far as the eye could see no one in Los Angeles was having breakfast on the roof. She was sure people in the city right now were fucking or fighting, making and losing money, murders happening and humans being tortured under the same sun they found themselves enjoying. But breakfast? It didn't look like it. "We used to have barbecues up here all the time, but the manager got real freaked out. He said he couldn't risk the chance of someone falling over the side. Like that's going to happen twice?"

Mark perks up then settles back down, the energy not in him to ask the question. As he digs back into the rapidly disappearing pile of eggs (which *had* been cooked too long) Corinne continues: "So after that I'd just come up here every once in a while to think or sort things out. You know? But it started to get cold, so I stopped."

"What made you think of coming up here today?"

"I got the idea when Quincy and I were having our lunch in the park on Friday. I had forgotten how nice it is to sit outdoors and enjoy a meal. In fact, a kid came up to us with a couple of water balloons in his hands. He was selling them for two bucks each. Can you believe it?" Corinne laughs at her story, the food she just swallowed making her mouth dry and throat scratchy. "I mean, what happened to a good old-fashioned lemonade stand? Hey, that reminds me . . . where's the orange juice?"

Mark stops in midchew, places his fork on his plate, and heads downstairs.

Sam has been painting all night and by the next morning his fingers, knuckles, and hands up to his wrists are covered in paint.

"Got to get some fucking turpentine," he mumbles as he

places a box of Frosted Flakes cereal upon the kitchen table, "and stop using those goddamn oils." He tosses a banana alongside the bowl, then heads to the fridge for the milk. "Water-based acrylic paints, now *that's* what I need." He grabs a spoon from the dish dryer sitting next to the paint-stained sink, streaked with various colors from the night before, when he tried to wash the paint off both his brushes and hands. "Water-based, not oils. Right now I look like some goddamn mechanic."

He sits down at the table and pours the cereal into the white bowl with a dark blue circle around the lip. He grabs the banana and makes a small incision with the tip of his knife horizontally across the skin, just below the neck. Pulling the tip of the stem, he drags it down like a zipper, peeling off the rubbery sheath.

"Goddamn bruises," he mumbles, noticing two or three black-and-brown mushy spots along the shaft of the banana. He slices off half-inch sections of the fruit and sighs as he sees each one is slightly streaked with a dark turquoise trail of paint, courtesy of the still-wet spot on his thumb. "Aw." He pours in the milk and then scoops up a spoonful. "Who cares?"

Across the courtyard a phone rings, its computerized, staccato *beep-beep-beep-beep-beep* a long way from the ancient ringing of old rotary phones with an actual bell inside.

"Hello?" Steve jumps at the black, polished receiver. "Hello?" he says eagerly to the dial tone. Two apartments away the phone is still ringing. "Damn." He slams down the hand piece.

Disappointed, he slumps into the large, soft couch.

"Sure, *they're* not even home to answer the phone and I'm just sitting here, bored, *waiting* for someone to call. How ironic is that?"

Steve sees a pair of Mark's shoes on the ground. "Hmph," he grunts, "Mark's out with his little Hollywood girlfriend." Steve turns his head, noticing the Frogger Atari cartridge Gary picked up earlier in the week. "Sure, and Gary's out shopping for something to wear on his date tonight with that haircutter-type person. Well, Joker . . ." Steve crosses his arms over his chest to keep himself warm as, two apartments away, the phone begins to ring again. "It looks like you're fresh out of friends."

Steve gets up and begins to head to the kitchen but stops for a moment, remembering there's nothing in the refrigerator. "I think it's Mark's turn to do the shopping," Steve says disdainfully as he pulls on his shoes, "but he has a date today. Or maybe it's Gary's turn." He laces them up, tying them in tight double knots. "Either way, they *both* have dates."

He grabs his keys off a small end table and heads out the door, crossing the courtyard sidewalk. Steve approaches Sam's apartment, stopping for a second to admire the mat outside the door, which says in white-on-black lettering in a cursive script, GO AWAY. Steve knocks three times.

"Come on in," Sam shouts, too lazy to get up and answer the door.

"Hey, Sam." Steve slowly opens and then closes the door behind him. "It's me, Steve."

"So I see." Sam concentrates more on his cereal, which is getting soggy, than on his visitor. He searches the bottom of the bowl for another slice of banana like a treasure hunter vacuuming the sea floor.

"Been doing some painting, huh?" Steve notices two thick squares of wood, both the same size, about three feet by four feet, covered with what looks like fresh paint.

"Good guess."

Steve pokes at one of the paintings with the toe of his black Vans sneakers, a gold, chipped letter *S* that's strung through the unraveling shoelace of his left foot flopping to one side.

"What's it called?"

"*Don't Look Back in Anger.* No, wait." He takes another bite and then sniffles. "It's called *You Can't Go Home Again.*"

"Well, whichever it is," Steve says more to himself than Sam, "it's original."

Steve scrutinizes the painting. Wild brush strokes cut deep into the layers of paint, where Sam must have led the thick brush (or maybe even his finger) all over the surface like the course of a racetrack. The subject of the picture seems to be half a face, mostly just the chin and nose, neck, and a shoulder. The head (outlined in dark blue, green, and aquamarine in the center) is turned, as if glancing back over the red, white, gray, and purple kaleidoscopic landscape.

Unable to think of anything else to say, Steve says, "Uh, nice."

The second painting is done in a more realistic style, but the eyes, nose, and mouth are still just lines, facial features reduced to slashes or curves. It's a full head with long, foppish black hair almost covering both eyes, right cheek incredibly round, left ear like a pear, and a dimpled chin below a slightly smirking dash of a mouth. The paint is still wet and the vibrant colors of dark blue, dark green, black, with streaks of red and white, make the oil look like glistening frosting, decorating the surface of a sheet cake.

"That one's called *Self Porthate Number Two*."

From what Steve has seen, Sam's limited *oeuvre* seems to consist mainly of abstract heads, barely drawn, all facial features washed out.

"Pure emphasis of form," Sam explained when Steve first asked him about it two weeks ago. Steve's explanation was different. He would bet that Sam just couldn't draw.

"Port*hate*?" Steve asks, confused.

"Yeah, like *portrait*, only *hate* instead of *trait*. Get it?" He takes another mouthful of cereal.

"Yeah, but the *trait* in *portrait's* more of a *trit*, not a hard *ate* sound."

Sam hunches his shoulders, exhausted.

"Will you just fucking sit down?"

Steve crosses the room and pulls out a chair, sitting down at the table. He notices little bits of paint smeared everywhere.

"Where did you get the wood? I like that."

"Garage next door. I noticed them sitting behind that gold-and-black hatchback, underneath a stack of old two-by-fours." Sam lifts the entire bowl to his mouth, a trail of milk running down his chin. "I pulled them out in the middle of the night when most of the lights in the unit were out, especially those back units, the two-storey ones that have windows facing the carport. So I grab these big ol' slabs of wood, right?" Sam starts to laugh, remembering his adventure from the night before. "And I'm being all sneakylike, walking quietly, wearing a black T-shirt and black jeans. I finally get them inside and turn on the lights, and I see that both of them are covered in old leaves, mold, and spiders. There was this humungous daddy longlegs just inches away from my fingers. Anyway, it took me just as long to clean them up as it did to paint them."

"Hmmm," Steve says, glancing around the messy room. "Think anyone will miss them?"

"I doubt it." Sam pours another bowlful of cereal. "Care for some?"

"Nah," Steve declines, noticing that Sam's hand has accidentally blotched out Tony the Tiger's face with a splotch of bluish paint. "But hey, I was wondering if . . . wait a second. What's that smell?"

"Oh." Sam nods toward the wooden blocks. "That's the paint. Gross, huh? I don't know why I bought oils, but I did. Yeah, they stink like nothing else and take three weeks to completely dry. I'm really nauseous this morning after inhaling that shit all last night." He glances down to the bowl. "Plus . . . I think this milk has gone bad."

"Like I was saying, Gary and Mark are doing other stuff today, and I was wondering if you wanted to do something."

"Do something?" Sam tries to decide. He looks around the cluttered room, the slightly rotten, sulfuric funk of oil still hanging in the air. He scratches his temple with his forefinger. "Uh, why not?" He moves his hand back down to the table to pick up the spoon and feels a wet spot on his forehead. He dabs at the area with the corner of a white napkin, returning with a thick, wet, mauve stain.

Sam owns an old Chevy hatchback, the kind that looks like an American version of a Japanese car, which always seemed strange to Steve since America invented the car in the first place; we were copying them copying us.

Sam's car was at one time bright red but had faded over the years to end up looking like a dull tomato. Steve figured the California sun was as powerful as he'd been led to believe; the car was just a couple of years old, and sitting in the sun had accelerated its aging at an exotic-disease pace. Or maybe Sam just didn't give a shit about the car, the way he didn't seem to give a shit about anything except sitting on his porch and getting stoned.

"So, you paint *and* act."

"Well, I'm sort of a jack-of-all-trades. That is, providing Jack did things half-assed. Seriously though, it's tough to get a part, so I get by however I can. The thing about being an actor is that it's all about waiting. You've got to have patience." Sam stops for a red light at Franklin. The light turns green and within seconds he's leaning on the horn for the driver in front of him to move. "Sorry. So, where was I? Oh yeah, *patience*."

"Patience, got it. So, where are we going?"

"Well, it's such a nice day." He leans his head out the window, which is rolled halfway down only because he can't roll it all the way up. In California, this was not such a problem. "I thought we'd go for a drive. Check out the view."

"The view," Steve says, wondering if he should have just stayed in the apartment alone and watched TV.

As they continue west on Sunset, Sam mumbling something about heading into the hills, Steve can see a fair amount of the city stretching out on the left.

The skyline of L.A., which was what the whole world saw in the opening credits of half the shows on TV and countless movies, was located downtown, a sector of the city that catered exclusively to daytime business. At night and on weekends the area was a ghost town, bereft of traffic on the sidewalks or streets. People like Corinne and Sam and Whitney, who had spent their entire lives in Los Angeles, never set foot downtown; there was no reason to. Sure, every once in a while a relative would drag them to see *Cats* or some other horribly large stage production at the cluster of theaters that skirted the outcropping of tall buildings aimed at the sky, or else they might go to a big party at one of the imitation New York lofts, which were found amid the sweatshops of the garment district, but other than that no one wanted to bother getting on the freeways. The meager Chinatown, the Museum of Contemporary Art, and the other, smaller museums with the more eclectic collections and the bars and cafes that indubitably followed were called downtown, even though they were nowhere near that village of skyscrapers everyone thought of as being the heart of L.A.

Los Angeles seemed to be laid out as if each of the city's sections had been a die rolled by the hand of God. It spread from the coast to deeply inland and was left to sprout up from the land wherever the die happened to tumble to a stop; it was a hell of a roll from heaven.

"So, tell me, kid. What's your family like?" Sam takes a right onto a winding road, the city, momentarily, disappearing. "You got any brothers or sisters?"

From the tone in his voice Steve figures that Sam is curious about a sister as a potential fuck and the brother as a potential roadblock to that fuck; unless Steve was wrong and it was vice versa.

"No sisters. One brother. Older."

"Is he cool?"

"Let's just say we get along about as good as the brothers in *Bright Lights, Big City.* If there were subways back in Kitty, we'd have chase scenes in them and he'd always leave me on the platform, sweaty, searching for a token. Left behind."

Sam grins, thinking of the movie and not the book, which is what most people do.

"My brother says he doesn't understand me, and I don't understand why he doesn't understand me. He thinks I'm just in this, the deal, the band, for the money, or the girls."

"Well, why *are* you into it?"

Steve had explained this to his brother on countless occasions, sometimes just to hear what he himself would say. Steve, not Phil, was often the one who needed convincing.

"Before Bottlecap I didn't really exist. I mean, I did, you know, but I didn't know who I was. Where I was going. I wasn't quite sure what the world was going to do with me . . ."

For years it seemed Steve could sit back and let life happen to him. Right after he graduated from high school, he got his own apartment and began taking classes at the local community college. His mother passed on the child support money that his father continued to send, even though Steve was over the legal age, and that would continue to flow as long as reports were sent back to the old man that the kid was in college. Never mind it was a junior college and that he scarcely attended classes and even when he did he was either hung over from the night before or, in fact, still drunk. He was young and on his own for the first time. His old friends from Kitty High, the ones who had yet to con their parents into subsidizing their freedom, used to hang around Steve's apartment as if it were the center of the world, headquarters for fun. He was constantly upsetting his neighbors, but their displeasure was more than outweighed by the great joy he felt inside. He was happy for the first time in his life, and it felt odd. It was like recognizing a face you've never seen before.

Not only were there guy friends who more than supplanted his fickle and tough-to-get-along-with older brother, but there were women as well. At one time he was having casual relationships with three different girls, which meant sex on almost any night of the week, no questions asked, no strings attached, delivered straight to his door. Squeals on wheels. It was like Domino's Pizza with a hard-on, and the best thing was, they called him. If Friday night rolled around and he didn't have any concrete plans, he was never worried because he knew the phone would ring at midnight or one or two or even three in the morning, and it would be a girl, maybe drunk, maybe not, asking if she could come over. He came to rely on the sexual spontaneity, which he knew was a bad thing to do, but he just couldn't help it, because it just kept happening!

Until it stopped happening. Whether his luck simply ran out or discovered it never should have visited him in the first place, it stopped altogether. He lay in bed at night, alone, sober, watching the minutes of the clock tick by, hoping for a call that never came.

He figured his friends had moved on, began getting their own apartments and the lives that inevitably followed; while the girls got real boyfriends, which was what they had wanted all along. None of them really liked calling that late. It was usually the alcohol that made them dial and drive, and then fear that stopped them from demanding some sort of commitment from Steve once they arrived. Miraculously, he never got the clue, and even more miraculously, none of them ever got in an accident on the way to his apartment.

After growing up with Phil and then those first few years after high school, which blew by in an inebriated blur, this period was the first time Steve found himself totally alone. It did not take long for Steve to deem himself one of the most boring people he'd ever met.

He began to talk to himself. Since no one else was around, two-way conversations used to sprout up at all times. If he was watching TV and something entered his mind, he'd say it, only to counter with a different view. Steve didn't go so far as to do separate voices, but he felt the need to fill the air of his apartment with something other than the noise of the television, stereo, and his own burps and farts. At one point he began to talk to himself so much he considered taking up writing, since he figured that's how most writers originated and formed the bulk of their ideas. "Chapter one," he found himself saying, walking around the apartment, repeating, "chapter one . . ." When it came time to follow these words with a story, characters, and dialog, he was stumped. That was why he did not take up writing.

Pathetically, he began to master recipes for one, developing an uncanny ability to chop just the right amount of lettuce for a salad, and reach into the large sacks of spaghetti he bought on sale every other week and grab just the right amount of the dry stick pasta for his dinner that evening. Steve wasted very little. He became a pro at cooking three tacos, or two eggs, or one hamburger. For dessert he even began baking mini chocolate cakes, using muffin tins, covering each with caps of frosting.

He ate most of his meals in front of the TV, but sometimes would sit at the table in the kitchen and read. Around the beginning of every month he'd spend a few nights reading the various music magazines he had subscriptions to or that he'd picked up at DISContent. Novels were slightly more difficult, especially if the print was small and the prose dense; and if the author was aiming for literary awards, this always entailed big words and long sentences, dancing around the point instead of just stabbing it. Big hardback books worked well because Steve could crack their spine and afterward they would lie flat on the table, pages spread as if arms open for a hug. Small paperback books kept wanting to clam up, and he often had to use a tub of butter to weigh the pages down. This was a hassle because if the butter was covering a passage he was trying to read, any narrative momentum was broken by the time he moved the tub, found where he was in the text, swallowed, and continued reading. Sometimes this method was so tedious that if he was reading a mystery he would forget, as he fumbled about with the container, who had been killed.

The perfect book during these awkward years was *Bonfire of the Vanities*. It met all of the requirements: it was big, relatively easy to read, broken up into conveniently sized chapters (each one almost perfect to ingest during the course of a meal), and was also buoyantly enjoyable. The book made him, for a brief spell, want to move to Manhattan, even though it should have had the opposite effect. Often he found himself laughing in his kitchen, the sound of his chuckling bouncing back at him. He loved the book so much he read it twice (something he'd never done before or since), and he even liked the much maligned film version, which he often rented and would watch while eating. He once tried to explain to Gary what a great book *Bonfire* was, explaining at first the volume's more apparent qualities: brilliant satire, large wit, invective prose, Wolfe's stellar observations. But when Steve tried to describe how the inanimate object had been the best dinner companion he'd ever had, Gary just laughed.

The few acquaintances to whom he confided how lonely he was all had the same suggestion: get a cat. Even though Steve truly loved cats (during his brother's many silent treatments growing up and their working mother's long hours, Frisky was sometimes the only friend he had), to get one now would have been too great an admission. Let him cook and eat and live alone, but there was no way he was going to get a cat. Steve wasn't exactly ready to throw in the towel. He decided to get a life instead. He borrowed his brother's drum set, started playing drums again, and joined Bottlecap.

"W-w-w-what was that?"

Somewhere, deep in the canyon, an animal has let loose a bloodcurdling cry. The hairs stand up on the back of Steve's neck, bristling in the warmish late afternoon air.

"Just a coyote."

"Like a . . . wolf?"

"Sort of." Sam spits on the ground.

The cry comes out again, echoing down the canyon.

"Uh, you come up here a lot?" Steve asks, overlooking the Valley from the promontory that Sam has chosen, somewhere along the curving stretch of Mulholland. He searches the brush for a pair of glowing eyes.

"Used to," he says, getting up from the weeds he's been squatting in. He swats at the dirt on his motorcycle boots and then looks out onto the blanket of white, gold, and red blinking lights in the land below. "It's not real safe anymore. Used to bring girls, you know, the hug-and-cuddle stuff. Now it's just me. When I want to be alone. Well, you know." He picks up a rock from the hill and hurls it toward the freeway even though it's a laughable stunt, the eight lanes of cement easily miles away. The stone glides for about twenty-five feet before falling out of the sky, silhouetted by the moon for half a second before plunging into the dry trees and jicama plants on the hill below, making a rustling that sounds like an approaching snake.

"So tell me," Sam begins, turning and facing Steve, "about the other guys in the band. That guy Mark, who's never around, and Gary. How'd you guys meet? You guys get along?"

Steve had been confronted by this question from Sam on numerous occasions concerning a variety of people; he always wanted to know how you met someone and if you actually liked them thereafter. This seemed to be his philosophy, that life was all about being able to stand the humans you happened to be trapped with. Steve figured Sam's life must be a continuous showing of *Lifeboat*.

"When I first met Gary, years ago, he was real nervous about everything. Out of sorts. Like, he was the type of person who took eight bites to eat a Reese's peanut butter cup. And a jerk, too. He once told me that handicapped people had it good because they could park wherever they wanted to. One time, I can't remember where we were, maybe on tour, but he pointed to some horrible pile of a woman who was being lowered to the sidewalk outside a restaurant on this forklift attached to the back of a shitty old van. Gary turned to me and said, 'Sweet.'"

"So what happened to him?"

"I guess he was like me, sort of drifting, before the group got together. He didn't quite know who he was." Steve concentrates on the horizon and not the words coming out of his mouth. He scrutinizes a large hotel, the word HYATT glowing red from the sign in the center at the top of the gray-and-silver mirrored building. "But after Bottlecap had been together for a year or so, really working hard and touring and playing show after show to audiences who cared less and less, he found out who he was. Or else what he wanted to be. We all did. I guess it was because of that thing, that saying, about looking into the abyss? Facing the abyss, you know? Nothing staring back at you but you?"

"*The Abyss*?" Sam says, once again referring to the movie, like a good Californian.

"No, no. Anyway, after all that work, we finally found our mettle. You know, that word that sounds like *metal* but it's spelled with a *T-L-E* instead? It was heavy, to know you've finally grown up, facing the world alone." Steve reconsiders. "But we *weren't* alone. We had each other. We were best friends back then, and that's what makes all this bullshit we're going through now so hard to take."

Sam gets up at an approaching pair of headlights but the car passes by, heading down the hill.

"Heavy mettle?" he says.

Steve shrugs his shoulders in disgust but completes his thought anyway, more for himself than for Sam. Steve feels like he's back in his apartment, years ago, before Bottlecap, eating a frozen dinner alone and talking to himself with his mouth full.

"Having the guys really helped back then. No matter how cold or poor we got on the road, we were still this tight little unit, the group. Someone to talk to. It's like, I'd rather have a friend in prison than be alone in paradise."

"Paradise? You're *in* paradise, and you're not alone." Sam says this as if to imply, *What about me?* But it makes Steve think of Gary and Mark.

Steve has been left cold by his remembrance earlier in the day of his pathetic life led not long enough ago to be completely forgotten; he still looks like himself in those photos despite whatever had changed inside. Mediocrity might still know his face and come after him again. He had tried for years to forget about how ashamed of himself he once had been, but his grip was so like a child's he could not let go of things.

"But that was then." Sam picks up a rock and hurtles it out onto the road, where it skips about twenty feet over Mulholland, resting at the base of a street lamp. "This is now. Fuck all that negative bullshit. You're going places, right?"

Steve, feeling colder still, looks at his watch.

"Yeah, home. It's chilly."

"What? It's only five." Sam notices Steve's beginning to shiver. "Fucking winter. Daylight savings ruins everything. It always does."

The week before, at two in the morning, the guys were supposed to set their clocks back an hour, but forgot. They managed to coast through their Sunday without noticing that they
were an hour off from the rest of world; after years of living on
society's margins, an hour didn't seem like much. Since then the
days had become shorter and the nights longer and the lingering
stretches of darkness extinguished any notions the boys in Bottlecap had of California being a magical place.

Sam rises off the dirt ground, wipes his ass off with three or
four pats to the seat of his pants, and passes by Steve on the trail
back to the car. He says, "Goddamn day cut in half."

It seemed lately that all Mark, Steve, and Gary were given were
directions: do this, do that, go here, go there; follow these directions. A few months into their stay it was apparent that some
were better at following directions than others.

"Okay, you know where the Vista Theater is?"

Gary stared at the pink Post-it note he grabbed from the coffee table, nervously clutching a blue ballpoint pen. Whitney's
voice on the other end of the phone was shaky, as if she were
deciding in her head if the entire idea was a mistake.

"Not, uh, really."

"Well, you know where Silverlake is, in general, *don't* you?" A
few miles away she leaned back in an odd-sized rocking chair
her mother bought her when she was visiting from Arizona last
summer. "Okay, look. You know where Sunset is? You know,
Sunset *Boulevard*? They made a big movie and a musical about
it?"

"Yes, yes, I know about Sunset."

"Take Sunset, let me see, from where you're coming from,
take a right and head down Sunset. Just past, like, Vermont and
stuff, Sunset will veer off to the right."

Gary, suddenly coming alive, began scribbling.

"Okay, hang on," he said slowly, repeating the words he was
writing down. "Veer off to the . . . right."

"Good. Follow that to Lucile. You know, like Ball?

"Yeah, Ball. Which way do I turn?"

"No." Whitney sighed. "Lu*cile*. Jesus, take a right. Not at Jesus Street."

"Jesus Street," Gary said as a joke. "Got it."

Whitney also laughed, reassuring herself that the night might not yet turn out to be a disaster.

*Geez, a lot of liquor stores,* Gary notices as he drives down Sunset, cruising through the light at Ivar. He notices vendors, mostly Hispanics, standing on street corners peddling various kinds of merchandise, ranging from Power Ranger helium balloons to rugs, flags, and cheaply framed artwork. On the concrete islands between lanes the more standard fare of peanuts and oranges, housed in plastic and stacked in supermarket shopping carts, is being offered, most often by women, sometimes with one or two children in tow, playing on the metal grid below the basket of the cart.

After a few more blocks he's stopped at the light at Berendo Street. To the right is a massive compound, a building set back behind a large parking lot, colored in passive yellows and blues. A giant rectangular window opens into a lobby patrolled by weary volunteers trying to look busy. A huge sign atop the building reads CHURCH OF SCIENTOLOGY. On the street a large sign with an electronic face flashes a menu of messages meant to coerce the idle or curious passersby into the building for a free personality test or complimentary tract.

"Ooh," he coos under his breath, as if the telephone poles around him contained sensors that could read his mind, something he actually suspected, "religious cult. Spooky."

In the next block he spots a few thrift stores and makes a mental note to check them out sometime, gets honked at for drifting into the left-hand lane while going through Vermont (as he was trying to look in the window of the Children's Hospital Thrift Store), and then, ahead of him, he sees it, the Vista Theater. The neon-lit marquee stands at the edge of a confusing five-way intersection, streets sprouting from one another at odd angles while traffic signs are cluttered with bent arrows and diagrams of which direction it is legal to turn from in what lane.

"Let's see, Hollywood is this way, no, don't want that. Uh, Virgil." He clutches at his little Post-it note scribbled with the directions. "She didn't mention *that* one. Uh, veer to the right, no, wait, is this okay?"

Honking from behind makes Gary drop the directions and lose them momentarily on the floor.

"Move it, you fucking asshole!" a woman in a red Toyota screams as she pulls out from behind Gary and goes straight, down Sunset Drive.

"Oh, green light." Gary, still a little startled, leans lightly on the gas and crawls through the intersection. He jerks the car hard to the right, the tires screeching against the gray concrete patchy with clumps of lumpy blacktop.

As his eyes scan the street signs, looking for Lucile, his chest begins to tighten. His breath becomes short, exiting his body in short bursts like the exhaust from a car that needs a tune-up. His old first-date anxiety is kicking in. It's been a long time since he's been on one of these. It had been years since he'd been in love, and he had only been in love once. Whenever he thought about that relationship, and how messily it ended, he remembered why it had been years since he'd been in love or on a date.

Her name was Sharon. He met her shortly after Bottlecap played their first show. In fact, it was the night of their fourth gig (and their first one played well) that he knew he was seriously falling for her.

He had invited her to come see his new band, proud of both his friends and their music, wanting to show them off as much as he wanted to show her off to his friends. Gary was almost as excited at the prospect of a life with her as he was at the prospect of a life in rock and roll. Thinking it would be quite amazing and maybe even a record if he could seal the two fates in one day, he later asked her if she would go steady with him. Never having been in a relationship before, he didn't know if that's what was done. She informed him, laughing sweetly, that that was not the way things were done, but she appreciated the sentiment.

One morning, when Sharon had to leave his bed early for class (she was studying education at the community college, wanted to be a teacher), he carved their initials in his wall, putting between the duo of letters a gigantic misshapen plus sign that looked more like a cross. The wall was forever scarred and powder and bits of plaster littered his floor, but he did not care. Who thinks about a security deposit when they're in love?

After he discovered that she slept with one of his friends while Bottlecap played their first out-of-town gig (Atlanta, a disaster, a baker's dozen in attendance at the beginning of the show, leaving just the baker by the end), he covered the engraving with one of Warhol's prints of row after row of the electric chair. Unfortunately, this did not solve anything. Even though Gary could not see it, he was still disturbed by the carving's presence; it hurt every time he passed by, which was several times a day. He began to avoid his room altogether since it also housed the bed where she fucked him, but so did the living room possess the couch and the bathroom the shower where they also had sex; to carry his pain to its conclusion he would have had to have moved out, something he would have done if he'd had the money to do so.

Every day the picture of death reminded him of his love. He felt he could see through the lithograph under dusty glass to the wall, as if he were Superman, where the two sets of initials sat encircled by a heart and an arrow that was not cut straight. It was no use covering something up when you knew what was underneath.

He hadn't thought about her for years, had forced himself not to (avoiding records they used to listen to, restaurants they'd eaten at, and even shared friends who formed bridges between them), and yet the struggle to forget seemed to often outweigh the little bit of effort it would have taken to just resolve the problem on the inside. He sometimes thought he spent too much time putting distance between himself and his failures, and other times felt he did not spend enough.

It bugged Gary how Mark was always whining about his various romantic obsessions, how much he missed Laura when they were on tour and how sick of her he got when they were home; it was as if no other member of Bottlecap could ever invite women into his heart, only to see them not arrive. But then again, Mark's problem was that he thought he was the only one who had problems.

After a few blocks he finds Lucile. The street slopes upward, the houses made of wood and not plaster like in his neighborhood. Almost all the buildings have bars on every window, doors covered by thick metal cages and not thin aluminum screens, protection against humans and not bugs. He quickly spots Whitney's address but ends up driving around for fifteen minutes trying to find a parking space. When Gary finally parks (heinously scraping the front of the car on the concrete of a driveway in the second part of a three-point turn), he's almost half an hour late.

"I was getting worried," Whitney says as she answers Gary's tepid rapping on her door. "I thought maybe you weren't coming."

"Traffic," he says, as if out of breath, but why would being stuck in traffic make him out of breath?

"Well, come on in."

As Gary enters, he turns and looks at her. She's wearing a pink angora sweater whose fuzziness makes the garment seem to glow, along with black pants that taper toward her feet, which are capped with black shoes fitted with heels that look like square pegs. The pants scratched against the back of his hand as she passed, and he wonders if this is a sign of quality or of junk; whether she owned silk or if he deserved silk even if she did. Polyester was fine for first dates.

"I said, could I get you something to drink?" Whitney says again, Gary lost in his thoughts the first time she asked.

"What?" he says, startled. "Yes, please. Whatever it is you're having."

Whitney steps into the kitchen directly behind the living room and Gary ventures further into the apartment. On the wall directly opposite the door is a futon folded up into the couch position. A quilt of varying colored hexagons is draped over the black futon cushion, which looks worn and is probably a throwback to Whitney's college days, going on almost ten years ago now. To the right of the couch is the doorway leading into the bedroom, where another futon lies stretched out as a bed, at the foot of which is a milk-crate nightstand crowned by a black Sony phone identical to one back in the rented house. To the left of the couch are stacked a number of books; on the wall next to this, two large speakers balance a piece of unfinished pine, which supports a CD player, receiver, tape deck, and a turntable (which duly impresses Gary). A stick of strawberry incense slowly burns on a drafting table in the corner, depositing its slate gray ash on a dark brown scoop of wood.

"It's sort of a homemade tea, with some cloves and licorice and other spices." Whitney hands Gary a pyramid-shaped mug with a rubber coating on the bottom. "Hope you like it."

He takes a sip, the sweet tea quickly calming him.

"Wow, this is good."

"Thanks."

Whitney's hair is down, where before it was up, and he can see she's wearing a touch of makeup, where the other day she was wearing none.

Looking at her, Gary is still a little amazed. She's darting around the apartment, pointing out things, complaining about the low counters and lack of hot water in the morning, showing off the paint job in the kitchen and the painting yet to be done on the trim of the window in the bedroom, but Gary just stares at her.

*She's making an effort.* He feels ticklish inside. Then he glances down at the Pac-Man watch that is beeping, a timed alarm set by the previous owner interrupting her explanation of a lightning-bolt crack in the living room wall. *I should have made an effort, too. But I've just got to be honest. No sense in acting like a knight in shining armor during courtship when that's not really what I am. Why disappoint her later?* He gulps, the tea caught in his throat for moment, spit back in his mouth. *So does that mean I'm disappointing her now?*

"Anyway, the landlord said he'll fix it, but I'll believe it when I see it, right?"

"Right."

Whitney excuses herself to the bathroom and Gary continues to look around the apartment, peeking into the corners, scanning every inch, trying to glean aspects of Whitney's personality from the items she has chosen for her decor. He spots a record sleeve peeking out from a stack of art books in the corner. He leans closer, examining the two-inch stretch of familiar-looking cardboard.

The background of the sleeve is dark but is not a painting. Blue, pink, and green circles peer out from the hazy purple backdrop. Barely detectable is a shock of black hair and maybe an elbow, the rest hidden by a book.

"Wait a second. Is that . . ." Gary has a hunch, but he doesn't want to be incorrect and look stupid. Not yet, at least. "Is that Kiss *Alive*?"

Whitney, who has just reentered the room, recoils, half amazed and half pitying, wondering how in the hell Gary could know any record sleeve so well as to identify it with so little a clue.

"Why . . . yes," she says slowly, still astounded. She crosses the room and eases into the rocking chair as Gary sits down on the beige carpeting, fingering the record.

The band, perfectly captured in their prime, is poised on the stage of the Michigan Palace in Detroit. Peter Criss is behind the drums, his feline-themed makeup crowned by sandy brown and silver hair, his arms up, drumsticks pointing like a lightning rod to the four capital letters spelling out, in bright lightbulbs, KISS. To Criss's left Paul Stanley is strutting behind his star-face design, sporting black feather boa sleeves and Gibson guitar. Lead guitarist Ace Frehely, with his spaceman costume and silver eyes, is clutching his custom Les Paul upside-down, only one of the three pickups wired, the other two just holes where the smoke bombs fit. On the opposite side of the stage is Gene Simmons, replete in gargoylesque face design, Spandex pants with cutaway holes rimmed in chrome studs, and his perennially and supposedly bovine-supplemented tongue hanging over lip and chin. Flanking the stage is a candelabra, and the air is filled with a hazy, ethereal fog. The hottest band in the land, indeed.

"Did you know this photo was taken, like, six hours before the concert even started?" Gary turns over the cover and sees the photo of a filled arena, two teenagers holding up a sheet painted with images of their rock 'n' roll heroes, one of their fists raised and clenched in a head-banger salute. "Yeah, they put on their makeup and just posed. Can you believe that? Here it is, one of the best live albums ever recorded, *ever*, and there's not even a real live photo on the cover. It's a shame."

"Uh, yeah, a shame."

"Do you know that if we went to my apartment back in Kitty this very second, I would have this record on the turntable? I swear." He looks up to her, wide eyed. "Isn't that crazy?"

"Er, crazy, uh-huh. Say, shouldn't we get going?"

Gary's not listening. Instead he's drumming on his thighs with his palms, mumbling under his breath the chorus to the first song on the record.

"*You know your man is working hard . . . he's worth a deuce.*" He finally looks up. "What? Oh, dinner. Sure."

"Nice car," she says as she slips inside the rented Plymouth, surprised to see Gary's holding open her door. "Yours?"

"Sort of," he replies, his statement not sounding like the truth even though it is.

As he pulls away from the curb the car embarrassingly jerks out of the tight parking space. His old car in Virginia used to fight him; to steer felt like rowing. After a month and a half he still isn't used to the power brakes. As he turns the corner he says, "You look beautiful."

He hated to say it because it sounded so clichéd, but it was true; at least, it was how he felt. But when Whitney is silent, nervously staring at the road and not her date, Gary thinks back to what he has said. He slaps himself mentally when the three words float into his mind. *Shit. I'm a stupid idiot. Stupid. Stu-*

*pid. Stupid.* He had skipped a step. He had meant to say, "You look nice," saving *beautiful* for later, anytime they weren't driving, for a moment when it might get him someplace. Three lousy words and he had managed to fuck them up. It was no wonder he hadn't had a long-term girlfriend since Sharon.

"How was work this week?" he asks, his tone trying to sound casual, yet interested.

"Okay, I guess. But the chemicals I work with are starting to get to my hands." Now she turns back to the interior, scanning her companion in the dark. His black polo shirt is small on him and tight. As they pass under streetlights she can see bulges of flesh at his waist, and his chest sticks out in lumps where his shoulders meet the trunk of his body. She grins, glad to see Gary is at least brave enough not to cover up. She then considers that maybe he's just not smart enough to wear a jacket. Now there are two people in the car wondering if Gary is stupid.

He feels her sideways glances like a warm X ray. He knows she's checking him out and he wishes he could squirm out of the path of her laser-beam eyes, but he can't because he's driving and strapped into his chair.

As her gaze takes note of the clothes he's wearing he becomes hyperaware of their presence on him; every stitch turns coarse and itchy, fomenting a revolution of dissatisfaction in the choice he had made earlier in the evening. Again Gary thinks he should have tried harder, but then thinks, as a guy on a casual first date, how hard could he have tried? When he was young he had come to the conclusion that men simply did not have enough tools to work with.

One night, years ago, he ran into an old girlfriend at a club where one of his favorite bands was playing. He spotted her seconds after entering, the ink on the back of his hand still wet, and he was glad it was there because he needed a drink. His heart started to beat fast but his breath almost stopped altogether while his confidence flat-lined. Their relationship had ended badly, as most of them seemed to end, so many of them that Gary was beginning to think that maybe the problem lay with him and not the various females he had dated. Maybe. This one was standing against the wall of the entrance to the floor of the club, sipping on a drink, bopping her head to the tune being belted out by the opening band, a band that Gary had dragged her to see at the Scene almost a year before, and now here she was, rocking out to the music as if she were their number one fan. It just wasn't fair.

She was wearing a short black dress that left plenty of room above the knee, gray tights, black shoes. Her hair was longer than when he saw her last (it would have had to have been; she never liked getting it cut unless something traumatic in her life warranted the change, but breaking up with Gary did not), and it looked healthy, full, lush, gorgeous. The hair made her gorgeous. No, Gary kicked himself, that was ridiculous. The hair only helped, added, assisted in her overall appearance. The other men in the club would have agreed; all of them were checking her out, undressing her with their eyes while he had once undressed her with his hands. Maybe he was not alone in this fact. Maybe someone else in the room had fucked her; maybe it was the guy next to her, who was also sipping a drink, also bopping his head. It killed Gary to consider this.

Despite the smoke atmosphere in the club (Gary contributing with his own cigarette lit with shaky hands to calm his nerves, but it was not working), he could tell she smelled nice. A smell he could still remember even though he tried so hard last year to wash it off, figuratively and literally.

Looking down he saw himself in everything used: old Levi's, tattered canvas shoes, and a white T-shirt upon which someone had scrawled CUB IS GODDESS even though he did not know why. His hair sat in clumps all over his head—he had not worked that day and so had not bothered to shower. Besides, it was a concert, his favorite band; he was heading straight for the stage, he was looking forward to the sweat. No one dressed up just to stand in the pit all night.

His ex-girlfriend, on the other hand, looked so attractive and presentable she could have been out celebrating an anniversary, and maybe she was. Gary got drunk fast and never did find out who she came or left with. She was wearing makeup, leaving bright red lipstick on her glass, her eyes lined in black, subtle amounts of color on her cheeks creating highlights even in the dim club. Gary cursed the meager weapons men had been given to fight the battle of the sexes. It just wasn't fair. Gary sometimes thought that if he could line up all the things that weren't fair, end to end, he'd be able to walk clear to the moon on the backs of his troubles.

Thinking back to Sharon earlier in the night, and then to the ex-girlfriend at the concert (he didn't even like to say her name), he was glad to see he had been so profoundly affected and disturbed by a number of women in his life. It put him, he figured, within the ranks of great men because great men always seemed to be a little fucked up.

"Take a left here," Whitney says.

His mind still elsewhere, Gary takes a few seconds to react. Three blocks later his hands crank the wheel and he asks, "Here?"

"No, back there. At Hillhurst." She surveys the residential street, which steeply slants upward, loud music pouring out of the open windows of unseen houses, lost in the early darkness. Underneath the pulsating music, heavy with bass and the occasional shouted curse and racial epithet, lay the quiet hum of menace. "I don't know where we are now."

"Should I turn around?"

"Um, yeah. Maybe. Or this might dump into Griffith Park or something. But I'm not sure. Is that a dead end?"

As Gary's hands tightly clutch the wheel he remembers the plot of a book that Steve told him about years ago: a man and woman take one wrong turn, end up in a bad neighborhood, and from that small mistake their entire lives are ruined.

"Guh-ree," Whitney says his name strangely as he again scrapes the front of the car as he turns around, heading back down the hill, the great mistakes of the evening and his life hopefully not already made. Save some for later.

•    •    •

Halfway through the meal Whitney was still waiting to be annoyed by Gary. So far, it hadn't happened. Whenever she was on a first date, there came a point (sometimes sooner, sometimes later) when she became bored by the man sitting across from her. Whether it was because of looks or the conversation that flowed through the first date's mouth, which she doubted she'd be kissing later, Whitney not only could not manage to foresee any type of relationship with the person, but she usually didn't even order dessert. But with Gary the minutes kept ticking by and she found herself interested in what he had to say, laughing at his jokes, and intrigued that he was from Virginia, sent to California by a record label she'd never heard of, recording a major-label debut with his band. Not that he was by any means the man of her dreams, the dashing gentleman little girls dream of and are supposed to wait for, but Gary was nice and cute in an age where nice and cute were about as close as a girl could get to dashing.

Because the dinner and the conversation are going well, she feels stupid because the day before the phone rang but hung up after one time. She had hoped it was Gary, canceling the date, erasing the worry and stress from her life, which, she felt, she did not need. Life was hectic enough. Her friends at the salon all encouraged her to go out on the date, and even though all of them were present at their initial meeting, none could remember exactly what Gary looked like. It was true that eyewitnesses were often very unreliable. They kept offering slogans such as "Give the guy a chance" and "See what happens." Her coworkers felt stupid for giving such vapid advice, and it only reinforced Whitney's suspicions that no one in the world knew what in the hell was going on when it came to love.

"More wine?" Gary asks.

"Sure, why not?"

Gary waves down their waiter and asks for two more glasses of Chablis. He feels self-conscious for a second, wondering if, since they were having Chinese food, he should have suggested sake at the beginning of the meal. At the time he had been nervous and still a little bit shaken from their wrong turn, his chest hot in the short-sleeve shirt even though it was cool out. He did not want to make yet another wrong turn. After introducing himself, the waiter ran down the specials for the evening, one of which sounded delicious to Gary, but he feared ordering that as well because he wasn't sure how much it cost. Gary thought that was the way they got you: entice you with a mouthwatering description but conveniently leave out the price. It could have cost thirty bucks for all he knew, and if so, then there wouldn't have been enough left over for the check, and he and Whitney would have to make a run for the rental car. It was not the first date he was hoping for.

"How's your noodle thing?" Gary asks, trying to sound interested in her dish, something with noodles and vegetables; he didn't catch the name when she'd ordered it with a convincing accent half an hour ago. Afterward she had told him that she was a vegetarian and this at first worried him. He had met too many women who were utterly humorless about their vegetarianism, who blathered endlessly about tied-up baby cows and scolded others for not adhering to the same lifestyle. In California, Gary suspected, this kind of thinking must be in overdrive. Besides, girls who didn't eat meat sometimes didn't even smoke or drink, and Gary wondered what he could possibly have in common with a person like that.

"It's good. Really good. How's your sweet and sour chicken?"

Gary glances down at his plate filled with deep-fried nuggets swimming in sweet, gooey sauce. He had ordered it by number, and then asked for more sauce as if asking for another miniature pitcher full of syrup while eating pancakes. Is he really being tacky? Is she offended that he ordered something with meat in it? Is she really trying to ask, "How's your sweet and sour murder?" Whitney grins, twirling a brown noodle over and over the teeth of her fork as if it were a strand of hair around her finger. Gary thinks the evening is going nowhere when it's actually picking up speed.

"What? Oh, this . . . It's okay. Tastes like chicken. Ha ha. You know. Well, maybe you don't."

"It's okay, Gary." She puts down the spring roll she had grabbed for and instead touches his hand, the tips of her fingers wet with drops of oil. "Just because I choose not to eat meat doesn't mean you can't."

"Really?"

"Really."

"It's just, some vegans act like born-again Christians, always trying to get people to join the flock. They've always got some gruesome veal story or photos of a slaughterhouse. Disemboweled cows galore. You know, blood and guts everywhere?" Gary pauses for a second, realizing he has strayed far from his original point. He looks for the tracks that lead back into a pleasant conversation. "But, uh, I digress."

The waiter refills their glasses with wine that looks too yellow, and as Gary takes a sip, he's glad he skipped lunch that day. He begins to feel light-headed, gulps half the glass, wishes he had a cigarette even though he's not yet through with his meal. The restaurant, like most things so far this evening, impressed Gary. The large wooden door decorated with a brass lion's head with a hoop through the mouth for a doorknob and the fact that all of the waiters were Asian seemed authentic. Because of his lower-middle-class upbringing, the expensive entrees signaled quality. They were sitting in the corner, underneath high vaulted ceilings, bordered on one side with a large aquarium, inside of which were two brilliantly blue fish with long graceful fins. When Gary commented favorably on the place, extending the compliment to her neighborhood, Whitney stopped to laugh.

"No, this isn't technically Silverlake. Chi Dynasty is in Los Feliz."

"Los Feliz? Jesus, how many parts of this city are there?"

"Lots," she replied. "The trick is finding the one you like and staying there."

"Los Feliz." He stopped to glance at her, and then smiled. "I like."

Slightly drunk—and maybe he shouldn't have driven, but he did—they went back to her apartment. He tried to seem surprised when the offer to come in was extended, even though he would have been heartbroken if it hadn't arrived. After all, he'd spent so much money on dinner. He hated thinking this way because he knew it was the road that led to not taking no for an answer, and it sent a chill down his spine to identify, if only for a second, with the true assholes of the world.

"Should I make some coffee?" Whitney asks.

"None for me, thanks."

Gary declines because he's got a nice buzz going and he doesn't want anything to put it out, not yet at least. Whitney doesn't want coffee either. The only reason she offered was because it seemed like the mature thing to do.

"Shall I put on a record? And we'll just sit on the couch?"

"Yes, shall. I mean, please."

"No Kiss, though."

"No kissing?"

"Kiss." She laughs. "The band. Kissing, we'll see."

"We'll see kissing?"

"Maybe."

Whitney puts on a compact disc instead of a record because she has a good idea of where they'll be in twenty minutes and she doesn't want to have to get up to lift and flip and drop the needle again.

"Thanks for dinner. I had a good time."

"Me too."

Gary sits on the couch and Whitney joins him, sitting a few feet away.

"So, tell me more about the guys in the band."

"There's not much to tell. Mark's big and roofs houses. I mean, he plays guitar, Steve plays drums, and I play bass."

"And you're making a record, right?"

"Yes, and hopefully it's in something other than the hundred-yard failure."

They were having a normal conversation, and yet they

weren't. Each were running their hands through the other's hair. Whitney was astounded. Gary was just drunk. This really seems like a signal to her, that she's reached some sort of comfort level with this man, where she can relax and be herself, something that was like being shot out of a cannon; it sounded easy to do but was actually quite difficult. As he keeps talking about the record, how much of a recluse a guy named Steve was when they first met and how Mark had been emotionally downsized years ago, Whitney keeps running her hands through Gary's hair. She realizes it's the second time she's done so; the first time, the other hand held shears. She folds his tufts of black hair between her fingers, as if measuring her own work. He does look good, she concedes, but that could be due to the combination of the wine and his charm at dinner and nothing to do with her haircut. She always wondered what kind of effect, if any, her talent had on the men who sat in her chair.

"So I guess it's all really their fault," Gary says, releasing a handful of Whitney's hair so he can pull her closer.

"What?" She's more drunk than she realizes. She notices that Gary has pulled her alongside him and been kissing her ear while relating stories of his band.

"I said, it's all their fault. Everything. Steve and Mark's. Hands down."

"Yes." She smiles, grabbing his wrists, which are caressing her shoulders. "Hands down."

He relents while she playfully reduces his arms to the sides of his own body. He wiggles his hips and scoots under her, feeling the fuzziness of her sweater against his chin. All through the meal she kept rolling little clumps of pink fluff off her forearms and pinning them on Gary's black shirt. Now, because he is so close to her, the little wisps of fabric begin to get caught in his nose, making it hard to breathe. Making him want to sneeze.

"So," Gary wheezes, "do you like me?"

"Maybe."

"Maybe yes? Or maybe no?"

She turns to him and smiles, offering her two lips.

"Let's just say you're worth a deuce."

As they lie back on her sofa, Gary has a thought. Isn't there a country called Angora? A place, Africa, Latin America maybe, where horrible things happen to the horribly poor, much-trodden-upon citizenry? Someplace with a despot in charge, a ruthless dictator, a fascist junta (a word he'd always loved, pronounced *hoon-tah*) who lives in a palace while the populace live in shacks? A small stamp of land you see on the news every once in a while, or in a Pulitzer Prize–winning photo; a dead child, armies of flies buzzing over the still-warm corpse, and the photographer, as he clicks the shutter, asking himself, *Why?* Filled to the brim with refugees who cross the border of neighboring countries and then back again, like live tennis balls except people care about the outcome of tennis games but no one cares about them. But as Gary buries his head in the face of Whitney's fuzzy sweater with her warm and solid chest behind it, he forgets about every other place on earth except for the island that he and she have created of the couch in her apartment in Silverlake, which he didn't think was heaven but he may have been wrong. He'd have to look at the directions.

**Hanes is wondering. He is in the mail room on the third** floor of the Pacific Media Arts office on Sunset Boulevard, sitting around with the other two company runners, Ray and John. Ray is feeding letter after letter into the large Pitney Bowes mail machine, which is applying metered postage with a rhythmic *chugga-chugga*, sucking letters on one side and spitting out stamped envelopes on the other. John is sitting at the lone desk in the room, filling out an international Federal Express airbill, glancing at the commercial invoices laid in front of him for the address. Above the postage machine thin horizontal slots have been added to a regular bookcase, and below each slot is an employee's name. Inside each slot are a few assorted bits of mail; a canary yellow memo sent out by Henry James earlier that month announcing the signing of the label's latest band, Bottlecap, still sits in every one. It's almost ten, but still no one's arrived for their mail. Hanes thinks to himself, *That's the ticket.*

He imagines himself at home in his apartment just off Wilshire Boulevard, an Art Deco building built in the twenties with a neighborhood to match: immigrant families crowded on front porches below lines of drying laundry as if they were all Irish and this were the Lower East Side of Manhattan, the smell of Ellis Island still on everyone's skin. The kids, always with the kids, and where did they come from? The running and the screaming and the piñatas, almost every day, knocking candy to the ground and yelling, even though there couldn't be that many birthdays in the world; the cars on cinder blocks, exoskeletons of vehicles littering lawns; landlords constantly coming around trying to collect the rent, met by pregnant women with baleful eyes who speak no English but still somehow promise the rent next month, always next month; and every evening, just past seven, the converted ice cream truck arrives with the novelty horn that blurts out "La Cucaracha" and sells produce and Mexican bread from the large window cut into its side. Hanes suspects it's selling something more, something illegal, because who would buy lettuce from the back of a fucking truck? Despite all of this he'd rather be home than here, the sleepy office building not yet come alive, the stale scent of the antiseptics left over from the cleaning crew who invaded under cover of night. He often wondered what they did when no one else was around. Did they have sex on John's desk? Jack off into Ray's postage meter? Discover the stash of *Hustler* magazines behind the Saran-wrapped rolls of thermal fax paper? If they did all these things, would he really care? Hanes shrugs, figures no, and wishes he could be just like Henry James, at home, still sleeping.

Hanes always thought the great thing about brains was that once everyone was convinced you had them, they were rarely needed. James was a perfect example. Having worked his way up from the mail room (which was one of the reasons he liked Hanes; in him he saw himself), Henry had been present at most of Pacific Media's larger accomplishments, although as a passenger, not the engineer. He always managed to be in the background of anything successful. If there was a photo filled with the top brass engaged in fervent congratulatory handshakes, Henry would be found at the corner edges, head and shoulders peeking into the action. After a while people got so used to seeing Henry James around that they made him an executive; in fact, many couldn't believe he already wasn't one. Since then he's guided a few mildly successful artists through the system, distanced himself from the flops, and managed to stay in the good graces of whichever executives were in power that week. From this Hanes figured out that it's not that the triumphs had to be large as much as that the disasters had to be small. Like the impending disaster that was beginning to form around Bottlecap. Henry had already started to distance himself within the company, saying it was a previous A&R man who had scouted them, that if anything went wrong, it would be that other guy's fault, not his.

In the middle of all of this, Hanes is wondering.

*How far could I get on thirty thousand dollars?*

He looks over the three checks, each made out for $10,000, to Steve Haverkamp, Gary Reiger, and Mark Pellion, that arrived that morning from the New York accounting office in the daily Federal Express package. When he first spotted the checks he thought about accidentally losing them, at least for a couple of days. The power of being able to put someone's dreams on hold was such a rush to him, made him feel like God, whereas he usually felt like nothing, which made him act, in turn, a little like the devil.

But Hanes knew better. He knew that someone in New York would call Henry James later in the day to make sure the checks had arrived safely, and if Henry hadn't seen the checks, the first place he'd look would be the mail room. The New York office was always doing that, checking on things, not trusting, following up and generally making Hanes's life and job harder. Not that anyone trusted the mail room in the first place. He, Ray, and John were always being blamed, the higher-ups using them as scapegoats for everything from lost mail to beginning rumors to the decline of the price of Kobiyashi stock. Half the building was basically against them. You couldn't trust anyone above the fifth floor; Hanes had learned that much already.

After deciding not to lose the checks he considers an even brasher plan: cashing them.

All the girls in the Bank of America across the street knew who he was from his constant visits, various errands, making withdrawals and deposits on Pacific Arts' merchant account as well as doing a little of his own banking, and he was sure he could get away with some scheme like, "Look, Mr. James needs this cash for a party tonight, so if you'll just be a dove and give it to me in *small* bills, there might be something in it for you . . ." He looks up at Ray, who's been feeding mail into the machine for the past forty-five minutes without taking his eyes off the steady stream of white envelopes, making sure two don't get sucked in at once, just like Laverne or Shirley on the bottling line. Hanes glances over at the seated John, who's trying to figure out how much he should claim for customs for a few promo CDs. Hanes wonders again, *How far could I get on thirty grand?* He fingers the checks for another few minutes before coming to the conclusion, *Not far enough.*

"Hey, Hanes," John calls out, waving a black pen at him, "you'd better hurry up and deliver those checks, *pronto,* or else the boys on the sixth floor are going throw a hissy fit."

"Yeah, yeah." Hanes hops off the counter and fishes out his Thomas Bros. guide from one of the filing-cabinet drawers. "I'm going."

"And don't forget to fill out your mileage sheet today. We need to get them in the New York pouch this afternoon," warns Ray, who's barely audible above the racket of the mail machine. "And no more fudging. I know it's not thirty miles to the goddamn Valley, I don't care how lost you get."

Hanes has been at Pacific Arts for over two years now. Ray and John had been there when he started, and, Hanes sometimes thought, they would be there when Hanes's children were old enough to buy Pacific's records on whatever technological format would be popular at the time. To Ray and John, Pacific Arts was not only their job, but their life. Their identity. To Hanes it was just another in a long line of hack jobs he used to pay his ever-rising rent and the sundry costs of living that sprang up at the beginning of every month.

His job before Pacific was as a projectionist at the New Beverly Cinema, where he worked for three years from the age of eighteen, his first real job. He was fired by the owner, who possessed an eery resemblance to the late Abbie Hoffman, for showing foreign pornographic movie trailers after hours. At the time Hanes barely cared. After years of carrying around the heavy blue plastic cases that the film prints were shipped in, he found himself a twenty-one-year-old who already had a bad back and groaned like his father when he bent over. A friend who had vacated the runner position at Pacific for a better job within the company had suggested Hanes, and after lying profusely on his résumé, he was hired. He hadn't minded the job much until a few months ago, until the delivery of checks, guest passes, and new lives impressed him enough that he decided that he wanted to be on the other end. Hanes was sick and tired of taking lunch orders and wanted to start giving them.

"And on the way back stop off at Jack in the Box. Get me an Ultimate Cheeseburger, those Seasoned Curly Fries, and a chocolate shake." John looks up at Ray, who somehow heard the conversation even though he's got his head in the postage machine, trying to dislodge a bit of sticky tape from the large spool it's attached to in the ass of the machine. He nods once. "And get Ray that Jumbo Jack Combo, *with* cheese."

Hanes slinks down to the parking garage, trudging down the dirty gray cement steps, rounding each corner slowly, as if there is a firing squad waiting for him at the bottom.

"At least I've got a plan," he whispers to himself as he thinks of Ray and John upstairs in the mail room, giving each other high fives for sticking it to Hanes yet again, "which is more than those sorry assholes have got."

A few months ago when Henry James was looking for someone to help him in A&R, it was Hanes that he came to, not Ray or John. Not that Ray or John noticed. They were happy where they were, and always would be.

Gary sits on the couch, staring at the back of Kenneth's head. Kenneth sits at the mixing board with Paul, who tweaks the knobs as Mark stands behind a microphone in the vocal chamber, waiting for Kenneth's verdict on his latest vocal take. Mark waits uneasily, wishing he had taken Kenneth's offer to sit on a bar stool instead of standing in front of the mike. Kenneth tried to gently persuade him, knowing from experience that singers loved to get close to the mike, and that sitting down helped keep them from creeping up on it, but Mark refused. This is the third day of recording vocals, and only one song is in the can. Mark is feeling nervous, restless, but also a little happy knowing that vocals are the only thing left, save for a couple days of overdubs and a mixdown. They were almost done.

"That felt really good in here. What'd you think?" Kenneth says into the talk-back mike, his head like a shoe box waggling back and forth.

"It was okay . . ."

"But?"

"But . . . play the second chorus again, I think I fucked it up."

Kenneth nods to Paul, who glances down at the piece of paper where the entire contents of the song are itemized, punches the numbers into the remote, and waits as the twenty-four-track machine whirs into place behind them.

Gary munches on a box of pretzels Paul had bought during a break earlier in the day, running to a nearby liquor store to stock up on beer and snacks. Gary thinks that Kenneth's head is more square than round, and he's wondering how it got that way. Could it be Kenneth was actually born with a square head, or did years of sleeping with an odd-shaped pillow or no pillow at all slowly shift the separate pieces of bone in his skull to their present position, the way the earth's continents shifted a million years ago and continue to shift today?

"Actually, punch me in at 'using a saucer as an ashtray.'"

Kenneth looks over the flashing digital numbers before him.

"The *first* 'using a saucer as an ashtray' or the second?"

"The second," Mark says hesitantly, his voice scratchy over the monitors hanging above the mixing console. The music to "I Like This Frown" starts up again, guitars high in the mix and drums and bass, as usual, low. Mark is seen through the patched-up glass biting his lip, waiting for his vocal cue. Gary munches on another pretzel as Mark starts singing, and he's on his way back to examining Kenneth's head (now it looks more like one of those Easter Island statues) when something suddenly strikes him.

"Wait a second," Gary says, springing off the couch, "what did he say?"

Kenneth just waves him off, his cinder block head shaking, annoyed.

Mark chokes up on a line and stops singing, making a cutting motion across his throat, signaling to Paul to stop the tape even though he's already stopped it.

"Yeah, *I'd* like to cut his throat," Kenneth whispers, motioning to Paul to rewind the tape and cue it up for yet another take.

"Can I hear that back?" Mark asks, leaning away from the microphone covered in an inch and a half of ash gray foam padding. "I just want to make sure I'm on key."

"On key," Kenneth says snippily. "Yeah, right."

Gary wonders if, as he continues to attack Mark, Kenneth has forgotten he's there; maybe they think he accompanied Steve to the bathroom ten minutes ago and still hasn't returned.

"Tell me." Kenneth turns and finds Gary's eyes in the half dark of the room. "Does he *ever* sing on key?"

Before Gary can answer, Kenneth turns back to the board, and music floods the studio. Paul punches up the vocals, his hands racing across the console as he adjusts a rough mix.

"*Heaps of dead Ataris gathering dust, I read that book by Marina Rust, I just want to have sex with that girl Brett from* The Sun Also Rises . . ."

Gary drops the bags of pretzels to the ground.

"*I got nothing to do all day, I got a job but it don't pay, I hate the Clash so fucking much . . .*"

Gary runs into the studio, where Mark, satisfied, is putting his headphones back on.

"What in the hell are you saying?"

"Huh?" he asks, confused. "What do you mean?"

"This song!" Gary points back toward Kenneth and Paul, but not to Mark, who wrote it. "Those goddamn lyrics."

"What, you mean this part?" Mark closes his eyes and begins

to sing. *"I don't run and I don't jog, my least favorite Woody Allen movie is* Shadows and Fog." His eyes reopen, as if he'd been deep in character. "You mean *that* line?"

Gary finds it hard not to scream. "That line's even worse!"

A sound is heard at the back of studio. Someone's just entered, and both Mark and Gary turn, hoping it's Kenneth to mediate the argument. Instead, it's Steve.

"Hey, I had to take a leak. What'd I miss?"

Gary approaches Steve. "Have you ever listened to the lyrics of this song?"

"What, you mean, *'She thinks she knows the cause, reading books by Octavio Paz, but I don't think that she knows shit'*? You mean *those* lyrics?"

Kenneth turns to Paul in the other room and says, "Jesus, can't anyone in this band sing?"

"No, no, no," Mark says, "that's 'Trojend.' A *completely* different song."

Gary's hands clamp down over his head, trying to squeeze out the migraine headache now firmly lodged there.

Early in Bottlecap's existence each of them had a notebook, an ordinary three-ring binder filled with college-ruled white sheets of paper divided into three categories: Finished Songs, Unfinished Songs, and Song Ideas. Behind each yellow card-stock separation lay song lyrics, each printed out on Mark's cheap Stylewriter from his ancient Mac Plus at home. At the back of the notebook was a supply of blank paper to jot down ideas whenever they happened to arise in a jam session. The covers were individually designed by Mark with a felt-pen outline of a bottle cap and the words USS GARY and STEVE floating against a background of musical symbols the names of which he did not, at the time, know. Each band member had his own notebook and used it to take notes for the current song they were working on. Mostly, it was just so no one would lose his place.

"Right *here*." Mark would point at a group of four lines with an outstretched index finger, the tip mashed in from pressing against the guitar strings all day and the pick stuck between his front teeth. "*That's* the chorus. That's where I hit the distortion and we go into the change I just showed you."

Steve and Gary would sort of nod and mark any sort of symbols that would help them remember their respective musical accompaniments. For Gary this usually meant the numbers of a fret and string, a long series of double digits that ran down the page like DNA code. For Steve the device was usually more mnemonic; a phrase like "From Grindcore to Madchester" would help him remember to go from the dirgy heavy metal drone into the faster shuffle beat that Mark had requested.

Gary even found an old music stand in the Love Is Christ thrift store, and he would place his notebook on it, flipping from song to song as Mark called them out. Steve balanced his on the tip of his bass drum, leaning it back on the metal tree that supported his two tom-toms. Mark placed his notebook above his amp until an especially long practice session nearly melted the vinyl cover, and after that he just put it on the floor, bragging how good his eyes were, able to pick out the lyrics from six feet away.

The notebooks were so important during those early practices that Mark was often chastised for wanting to introduce a new song without the requisite three copies of the words for everyone's notebooks, and when Gary left his at a girlfriend's house one afternoon, Mark responded with, "A lot of good it does there."

As Bottlecap became more musically proficient, the notebooks were rarely needed. Each band member eerily began to feel the changes in the music seconds before they occurred. With just a look Mark could signal to Gary that a guitar solo was forthcoming and that he should keep the rhythm until Mark twitched his face, which would lead them back into a reprise of the first verse. Even Steve, who looked squarely into Gary and Mark's backs, could sense when the song was about to take a turn; he kept his eyes on Mark's foot as it was about to descend on a pedal, or Gary's shoulders, the way they would rock up and down whenever a slower part was coming from around the bend. Ever since the notebooks hadn't been needed, Steve and Gary never received printouts of Mark's lyrics. Since then neither of them was really sure what it was exactly that he was saying.

"Jesus, Gary," Steve asks, "what's your problem?"

"My problem," he says, wearily, as if it should be apparent to everyone, as if the entire world should be on his side but never is, "is that those are the stupidest fucking lyrics I've ever heard."

"Gee, Gary, thanks." Mark's shoulders droop a couple of inches.

"No, I'm sorry . . . it's just . . . I never thought I'd be in a band that would have lines in a song like *'Rabbit Run and Rabbit Redux, I feel like Rabbit with my new hairdo.'* Besides, *hairdo* doesn't even *rhyme* with *redux*. I think it's pronounced *re-ducks*."

Inside the booth Paul turns on the microphone the three of them are arguing around and records their fight onto one of the open tracks, figuring he'll bury it in the mix later for a laugh.

"I really don't see what you're getting so worked up about." Mark tries to reason with Gary. "We've been playing these songs in our set for a while now. It's not like I've been hiding anything from you."

"Yeah, but . . . when we're onstage there's so much fucking noise from the drums and your Twin Reverb that I guess I never really knew *what* you were saying. Like, I had my little cues on when to go into the chorus and whatever but I just never imagined that . . ."

"What's the big deal?" Steve says. "Mark's not a great poet, so what? So we don't print a lyric sheet. Let's just get on with it."

"I agree with Steve." Mark moves to put back on his head-phones.

"But what are we," Gary continues, "the guys from *Ishtar*?"

Mark rests the headphones around his neck, the cool padded leatherette cups rubbing against his cheeks like a thick scarf.

"What are you saying, Gary?"

"I'm saying that I literally despise this song."

"Literally?" Mark chuckles.

"Yes, literally, and what's so fucking funny?"

"You can't literally 'despise' something, you moron."

"Why not?"

"Because, to despise something is just to not like it, it doesn't have another meaning. Like, if I said that Whitney crushed you, literally, I would mean that she actually, physically, crumpled up your body, not that she stopped dating you. That's what *literally* means." Mark turns to Steve. "And he thinks *I'm* the one misusing words?"

"But still, I mean . . . it's just . . ." Gary's mouth opens to form a rebuttal, but nothing comes out. He shrugs his shoulders, walks out of the room, followed by Steve.

"Okay, Mark, that last take was good," Kenneth says into the talk-back mike, "so let's move on to the second verse, although I may want to try that first verse again later. It felt like you were too behind, because last time you were right on top of it."

Mark steadies the headphones on his head and signals Paul with a thumbs-up from the studio. Paul cues up the tape and again the song fills the booth. Steve taps out the song's drum parts on the dusty arm of the brown couch and Kenneth is glad to see that at least one member of Bottlecap isn't disgusted with its music. Inside the vocal chamber Mark bobs his head to the tune, leaning into the microphone.

*"I call her Vene, she thinks it stands for Venus but it really stands for venal, she says she wants to stage a bacchanal but she's really just banal . . ."*

Gary twitches on the couch as if he's been electrocuted.

"But those words *don't* rhyme!"

"Sssh." Kenneth turns around and scolds.

Gary just leans back on the couch, trying to bury his head under the cushions. The sound still seeps through, but the words are muffled, the way they'd been for the past twelve months, the way they were when Mark first played them the song in the rehearsal space, and Gary liked the tune so much he jumped right up and figured out a bass line with Steve following closely on the drums. They played it seven times that day, then played it the next week during their gig at the Scene. Since then they've probably played it fifty or sixty times, but he'd never really been able to hear the lyrics.

"Wait a second." Gary sits forward quickly on the couch. "What did he just say?"

Steve, sitting next to him, is finishing off the pretzels, holding the bag to his lips and channeling the last couple of broken stems and sea of salt flakes into his mouth.

"I think it was something," Steve says between bites, "about the moon landing."

Next to the couch the door opens and Hanes enters, a couple of small envelopes under his arm clothed in a plaid shirt. When Mark sees him through the glass of the recording studio, half his own image staring back at him, he loses his place in the song, the words get stuck in his throat, and he fucks up the take.

"Sorry, Kenneth," he says, stepping away from the microphone, "sorry Paul."

The music halts, suspended in midair, then rewinds sounding like a chipmunk singing backward. Hanes saunters to the middle of the room and flaps the envelopes back and forth in his hand.

"Hope I'm not . . . interrupting anything."

"What is it now, Hanes?" Kenneth says, annoyed.

Mark sees Hanes holding court in the middle of the control booth, so he takes off the headphones, places them on the microphone stand, and exits the vocal chamber.

"Just a little something for the three of *you*," Hanes addresses the members of Bottlecap, who surround him in a semicircle. He hands each of them his check.

The guys quickly tear into the envelopes, shoving their fingers under the gummed flap or splitting the papery seams with a fingernail. The plastic rectangle on the front of each envelope crackles as they mangle the thin parcels, struggling to get at their contents.

"What is it?" Steve asks, even though he's staring right at the check. It took Hanes half the day to deliver them, despite the fact that the Pacific Arts building is less than ten minutes away.

"It's a check." Gary slaps the back of Steve's head with his discarded envelope, now just trash, the real treasure in his hands.

"I *know* it's a check. But what for?"

"It's probably for signing, or like a bonus." Mark looks over the check quickly. "Or a signing bonus. Yeah, that's it."

While Hanes strikes up a conversation with Kenneth, and Paul heads outside for a smoke, the guys examine their checks. The paper is divided into two: the actual check and a sort of receipt with columns for gross amounts and federal and state withholding taxes. Under the heading of PAYEE, computerized type reads *Mark Pellion/Bottlecap* and next to this *Advance on signing*, above which is typed DISTRIBUTION OF NET AMOUNT. Next to each amount written in a line of boxes are two sets of initials in a different-colored ink, a quartet of letters that Mark cannot translate into either a face or name.

On the bottom half nothing has been written by hand. Their names, the date, and amount are printed in slanted, computerized script. Even the signature is by proxy; instead of a John Hancock there is IBM, a tricolored computer-generated stamp of a Japanese name, which starts in blue, dissolves into white, and then bleeds into red. At the top of the check is the Kobiyashi Entertainment Group logo, a globe separated into grids with a number of them filled in to form a *K*; underneath this is the address of a New York bank.

"Wow." Steve gasps, practically drooling. It's more money than he's ever seen in his entire life, even if he is staring at a check and not the actual sum. He can barely handle the concept of what is in his hand. This little slip could be a new car, a trip to Europe, his rent for a year. It makes his knees buckle just to consider the possibilities. He is by no means alone in this fact. Gary and Mark are also in their own private freak-outs.

The money, a long time in arriving, it seemed (they'd been in California nearly two months now), could not have come at a better time. The boys had all but totally spent the small private reserves they had arrived with. Steve blew half of the two hundred he brought from Kitty the night they went to the Roxbury. Gary was looking forward to courting Whitney and did not want to have to constantly add up the price of meals in his head for fear the totals would be larger than the amount he held in his thin wallet. Later in the day Gary will try to Xerox his check in order to cherish it forever, only to find the photocopy riddled with the word VOID.

Mark, whose mother slipped him five $100 bills in a greeting card that she found under the heading of *Best Wishes* at the Hallmark Hut in Moore's Mall, thus making him the richest member of Bottlecap, was rapidly running out of cash because he was spending it on Corinne. Ever since their first date, when she used her credit card to pay for the hotel room, it seemed that she automatically expected the dinner and movies and drinks that their dates usually consisted of; and his dwindling ability to provide for her only accentuated the chasm that he suspected existed between them. When they lay in bed and she told him about her childhood (trips to Hawaii, several servants, a family apartment in New York, and a summer spent traveling throughout Europe before she was even of an age to enjoy it), it tasted to Mark like sin. Even though his own family was rich by small-town Virginian standards, Mark had always known that his parents were not truly wealthy. They had planned well for their later years, which, it seemed, had started to arrive (wrinkles appearing on his father's face, where before Mark had noticed only confidence and a smooth, tanned exterior; and his mother's hair showing ivory white roots, her usual diligence in smothering them with dye fading slowly, exposing an unwillingness to care for her body that had never existed), but they would never live in the luxury that Corinne's parents perfunctorily surrounded themselves in. The irony was not lost on him that Corinne, if he had met her on one of his summer vacations while growing up, would have been one of those girls who made him uncomfortable. Nervous. Now he was dating her. It felt like both a coup and a sham.

"Hanes, I'm confused."

Hanes, annoyed to have been interrupted, turns from Kenneth and focuses on Mark, who is still intently staring at his check.

"If we haven't signed the contracts yet, what is Pacific doing giving us thirty thousand dollars?" Mark asks this even though he'd yet to question the house, car, or hours of studio time he and the boys were devouring like Pez. "I'm just saying, what happens if we don't sign the final contract?"

"Oh, you will." Hanes laughs. "Trust me. You will."

**"Hey, hey."** **Steve accosts Gary while he's still in the** shower.

"Jesus, Steve." Gary leans out, covered in suds, his eyes mere slits in a lathered-up face. "Use the toilet downstairs. For chrissakes."

"No, no," Steve says, turning away from the vinyl shower curtain only sparsely covered with fluorescent, floating fish. "I wanted to know what you're doing tonight."

Gary accidentally drops the bar of soap to his feet, squints to find it, then kicks at it with his left toe, sending it careening the length of the tub, hugging the curved corner like a bobsled, and back along the other side into his right hand.

"I'm going over to Whitney's. She's making dinner. Some sort of lentil crap. I told you."

"No, you didn't." Steve tries to sound dejected. "It's just, it's Saturday night, and yesterday you said . . ."

"Yesterday I said I was busy." Gary pokes his head out again, this time rinsed off, what's left of his dark hair slicked back as if he's just come up from a dive.

"Oh, well," Steve says, exiting the bathroom. "I guess I remembered it wrong."

Gary climbs out of the shower, applies some Speed Stick to each underarm, but not too much. A dab of cologne behind each ear, a dollop of gel in the hair, and Gary goes into his room, where he's got two shirts to choose from, a 1950s brown polyester button-down that itches against his skin but makes him look like a private investigator on his day off, or else a knitted pullover that's a little more mod, bean green, but may be too warm for staying indoors all night.

"It's just, Mark's over at Corinne's"—Steve, sitting on the edge of Gary's bed, has been waiting for him—"and it *is* Saturday night."

"No shit." Gary sighs, moving past Steve and to his closet. "That's why *I* have a date. Don't blame me that *you* don't."

As he turns to look in the mirror, placing each shirt over his bare chest and imagining what it would look like (he doesn't want to actually put either of them on because all that pulling on and off would just muss up his hair and make it puffy), he sees the hurt look on Steve's face.

"Look, man, I'm sorry. I know it's tough. Mark's all tense about the record and is hanging out with Corinne, and now *I've* got Whitney and . . . I mean, we're all still buds and all, it's just . . . some of us have more time than others."

"Just because I don't have a girlfriend doesn't mean I'm a complete fuckup. I don't even *want* one. And who says I couldn't get one if I did?"

As Steve stomps out of the room, Gary pulls the green shirt over his head, calling out, "Yeah, right!"

Gary continues laughing as he heads downstairs. He sits on the couch, careful not to flatten the back of his hair, which is still wet. He looks at his Pac-Man watch, then the clock on the wall. As he waits for Whitney to pick him up, he places a hand over his grumbling stomach. He knew that Whitney was going to cook for him, but also that she was going to cook something exotic, something Gary had never even heard of, and, he was betting, something he wouldn't like. Over the phone Whitney had mentioned things like curry, sautéed vegetables, humus, all of which was alien to him. He kept thinking of his favorite foods: pizza, spaghetti, or, at his most daring, an item from one of those Americanized Chinese food places, sweet and sour chicken or noodles, which reminded him of eating Top Ramen in his highly budgeted days back in Kitty. Whitney had laughed at Gary's story of being sent to the store for some spinach and returning with romaine lettuce because the sign in the Food King misled him and he truly had no idea what spinach looked like when it wasn't in a Birdseye box, frozen into a swampy square. She had twirled the phone cord around her finger and called him "adorable," and Gary was afraid she meant in the quaint, cutesy sense (which she did) and not in the virile, sexy way (which she did not). He tried to laugh off his culinary ignorance, blaming his Virginian meat-and-potatoes upbringing, stressing the good ol' way of eating down South, even though this too was false. His mom, a single mother, was often working late and didn't have the time for the traditional biscuit-and-fried-chicken meals Gary told Whitney he had been raised on. More often than not his diet growing up consisted of fast food, McDonald's, Burger King, or bologna sandwiches with Fritos or Ruffles on the side. Processed meat and potato chips would have been more like it.

"You're precious," she had cooed into the phone.

"Precious as in, 'I'd better hang on to you'?"

"Uh, no."

So Gary couldn't decide whether to starve himself all day or have one of those mythical four-course breakfasts he'd been telling Whitney were a staple of his upbringing. If he went to her house hungry, he figured he'd have to eat anything she shoved in front of him simply because his body would be weak and begging for food. But then again, if he had a big breakfast and then the dinner didn't appeal to him at all, at least he would have had one good meal that day and he wouldn't spend the remainder of the night (which he was hoping would overrun into Sunday) covering up the not so precious or adorable sounds of his gurgling intestines, wondering where the dinner was that Gary refused to ingest.

Figuring he'd better just go hungry, he had starved himself most of the day. As Whitney now checks her hair in a compact on the sidewalk before ringing the doorbell, Gary has his hand on his rustling stomach, amazed at the churning and bubbling of his empty insides.

"Who is it?" Gary lamely calls out even though it's exactly seven o'clock.

"Me," she says, embarrassed. "Whitney."

Over the past couple of weeks she had grown to find Gary's clumsy behavior charming. Although she was drawn in from the beginning, she never thought she would feel much for this funny-looking guy who was a few years younger than her and thought he was right about everything when he was, in fact, mostly wrong.

Her last boyfriend had been an intelligent and brooding sculptor who worked in sheet metal and was as unforgiving as he was talented; nights out with him seemed more like tests than dates. Gary seemed like a logical antidote.

She didn't think about him much, but when she did, she did a lot. During the day, when she was cutting other men's hair, she found herself still feeling what was left of Gary's hair in her skilled hands. In the past a lot of her boyfriends had been jealous when it came to her job; they didn't like the way she leaned into the customers or the way men leered at her in the mirror. She was being asked out all the time, but Gary trusted her. He knew there was nothing he could do about the thoughts of other men, so he instead concentrated on making Whitney happy so she would continue to turn down their offers. Even though it had only been a few weeks, it felt to both of them like months. But in a good way. There were times when it was nice that time stood still.

Scrambling to his feet, he catches sight of himself in a full-length mirror in the hall. He wishes he'd worn the other shirt but decides it's too late and answers the door.

"Hi."

A kiss on the cheek.

"Hi."

She moves past him and into the apartment.

"Wow, nice place."

Gary follows a step behind Whitney as she pokes her head in and out of the kitchen and living room, and peers up the stair-case.

"I love the furniture"—she runs her hand over a credenza of unfinished pine, atop of which sits a terra-cotta vase painted in a colorful Southwestern design—"and all of the little touches."

"Yeah, well." He rubs his fingernails against his shirt.

"The space is so . . . ergonomical. It really"—she searches for the words—"it really . . . *breathes*. You know?"

"Oh, I know," Gary says, caught off guard. For potential con-versation he'd prepped himself on topics such as the weather, local sports teams, and the fact that crimes were on the uprise, but not anything intelligent. "Very, er, archi . . . *textural*. So, uh, shall we go?"

"Oh, sure."

Gary leads the way out, locking the door behind him even though Steve's upstairs, sulking, creeping to the bedroom win-dow overlooking the walkway, trying to check out Gary's date as they leave.

"Is this one yours?" Gary gravitates toward a black, late-model BMW parked at the curb.

"Uh, no," Whitney says, crossing the street and heading toward an off-white Dodge van.

"*This* is yours?"

Whitney unlocks the door, climbing inside, while Gary just stands in the middle of the street, too shocked to move. For some reason he never envisioned himself dating an older woman who cuts hair for a living and drives a van that had been on earth longer than he has.

"You got a problem with my car?"

"Uh, no problem. No problem at all," Gary says as he finally enters the vehicle.

"Oh, watch out," Whitney warns as he climbs up and into his seat, "I have a couple of tubes of gel on the . . ."

Gary plops into the black vinyl chair, feeling a hard, lumpy pressure under his ass. He sits up quickly to find one of the tubes has leaked a gelatinous stream of the thick, gooey substance.

"My brand new chinos." He wipes his hand over his backside and discovers a wet, quarter-sized mark on his rear.

"Those aren't new; you bought them the other day when we were at the Salvation Army."

Gary scrapes away the goop from his pants, tosses the tubes to the back of the van, and sits in the seat, grabbing for a seat belt that does not exist.

"Yeah, well, they're new to me."

Whitney starts up the van, heading north and then east, toward her apartment.

"Thanks for taking me to that thrift store the other day." She tries to make the light at La Brea but doesn't, and as she leans on the brakes all the debris from the back of the van slides toward the front, an empty can of mousse beaning Gary in the ankle. "I hadn't been there before. I had a good time."

"Me too!" Gary has to speak up to be heard over the loud rattling of the ancient engine that sits between them.

"Although I still can't believe you fought with me over that Luke Skywalker baby T."

Gary says plainly, "Why can't you believe that?"

"Because, it was for a small child, therefore it'd be sort of snug on me and look cool. But you . . . *you* would have ripped it at the seams."

Gary beams, thinking he's the Incredible Hulk, muscles bursting from his chiseled torso even though the shirt would have cut off the circulation of an underdeveloped sixth-grade boy.

"You're just lucky it was from *Return of the Jedi* and not *The Empire Strikes Back*, otherwise I never would have given it up. Goddamn fucking Ewoks."

"Yeah, thanks, lucky me."

Gary reaches into his pocket for his cigarettes, pulls one out, and sticks a bent Marlboro between his lips. His lights it, cupping the flame with his hand against the wind flowing in from the open window. Searching for an ashtray, he grabs at a slat of wood connected to the dashboard in front of him with hinges you'd see on a pair of shutters, only to find a gaping hole leading down to the rushing street.

Whitney points to an old ashtray set in front of her, one of those with the golden tinfoil top and the tartan fabric underneath, filled with sand and easy to balance anywhere, a beanbag for those who wish to die young.

"So, how's the studio been the last couple of days?"

"The studio?" Gary tries to get comfortable, to lean on the door, only there's no armrest on his right so he crouches over to his left, hunched over, shifting half his weight to the engine housed in a large black metal box that rises from the floorboard. It reminds him of the little bump on an otherwise sleek submarine. "Jesus, don't ask about the studio."

"Why not?" Stopped at another light, Whitney turns to look at him, the van slowly making its way through crosstown traffic. "Things not going as planned?"

"Not unless we planned this to be a total disaster. Oh, I guess it's not as bad as all that. It's just . . ."

"Just what?"

Whitney wrestles for a second with the gearshift, which is attached to the steering column and not the floor. Three on the tree.

"Well, Mark's totally fucking up, and Steve and I are starting to get on each other's nerves. I don't know what in the hell this producer's doing with our sound, or what in the fuck the label's going to do with us once the record's done." He takes a drag off the cigarette, inhaling the smoke deep into his lungs. Since his stomach is empty, he gets a quick buzz off the tobacco and it makes him feel like he's back in junior high school, to be catching anything but a cough off a regular cigarette. "I guess I should be grateful I'm even out here, right?" He feels light headed, his face flushed. "To be making a record and to have some money in my savings account for the first time in . . . ever. But still, I feel like Han Solo when they jumped into that trash compactor in *Star Wars*."

They stop for a light at Normandie. Off to the right, a group of about six or seven rough-looking kids mill around outside a run-down liquor store. Another kid approaches them and is met with shoves and jeers, pushed around from one to the other like a metal ball against the bumpers of a pinball game.

"Why?" Whitney asks, her eyes on the oil temperature gauge and not the scene on the sidewalk. "What did Han Solo say?"

As the van lurches through the intersection, asthmatically picking up speed, Gary sees the kid thrown to the sidewalk, where he finds a beer bottle in the gutter and smashes it against the curb, holding it by the stem with the rest jagged, turning quickly toward the others.

"He said," Gary begins, the scene on the sidewalk drifting out of view, "'I've got a bad feeling about this.'"

Corinne looks up from the work she had to bring home as Mark barges into her bedroom, his electric guitar in one hand, nothing in the other.

"I can't find a heavy pick."

"What?"

"I brought home the Jaguar from the studio to practice some overdubs for next week and I *need* my pick."

"Well, I saw a bunch of them on the dining room table," Corinne says, remembering the half dozen or so little pointy triangles of plastic splayed on top of an antique jewelry box her grandmother bequeathed to her from the deathbed.

"Those are all *thin*," Mark says angrily, as if that fact would be readily apparent. "I need *heavy*. If they're thin they just fold against the strings and it's like playing with a pat of butter and I can't . . . I just can't practice with those. How many fucking times do I have to tell you? Heavy, electric. Thin, acoustic. Jesus Christ!" He drops the guitar to the ground and it falls with a clatter, the strings painfully humming for seconds afterward.

"Yeah, I bet Laura knew all about your goddamn strings."

Turning to leave, Mark halts in his tracks.

"What?"

From underneath a stack of papers, Corinne pulls out a Pacific Bell telephone bill, page seven, long distance.

"Not real cool, Mark, calling her from my house." She throws the piece of paper his way and it lands on top of his guitar, muffling his still-vibrating high E string. "It's bad enough you're not over her and I have to put up with these childish antics, but I've got to literally pay for it, too?"

Mark, dazed, reaches for the bill. Instantly he recognizes the four or five numbers with the same 804 area code, Laura's smack dab in the middle. He had made these calls about three weeks ago while Corinne had been working late in the office and he had had another bad day in the studio.

"But who says I—"

"Don't even try to deny it, Mark." Corinne doesn't even look up, even though she's lost the concentration on the work in front of her. "I called them all, three guys, one girl; the others were a record store and a radio station."

"But . . . look." He points to the bill. "I never said anything." Under the MINUTES column all of the Kitty numbers read one, except for the call to WKIT, which read two because he had for some reason called to request a song from three thousand miles away. "All I did was hang up. See?"

Corinne snatches the bill from Mark's hand, glances at it, and tosses it aside.

"Same difference," is all she says, turning back to her paperwork.

"What?"

"Whether you said anything or not is beyond the point. The fact is that you called. Or, no, that's not even a big deal. If you had wanted to call and say hi, I could have lived with that." She finally looks at him. "The fact is . . . you lied."

"How did I lie?"

She laughs, then mumbles under her breath, "Men."

"Huh? Don't just sit there, tell me!"

"You think just because you didn't tell me, you didn't lie? That it was just yours and the telephone man's secret? You lied by omission, Mark. Just because you didn't create some fanciful story to cover your tracks, look . . . you still lied."

"I didn't say anything! I just wanted to hear her voice and—"

"Fine, you rationalize it any way you want to. You say anything to make yourself sleep better tonight, but I know that what you did was wrong. Not the act in and of itself, but the childish way you didn't mention it. What, were you just hoping I'd write out a check and not even mention it?"

Yes, that's exactly what he'd hoped. He'd been meaning to intercept the bill when it came, and had been expecting it for some time now. Of course it came on one of the days she got off early and he was stuck in the studio getting down a solo. Goddamn Kenneth. Goddamn phone company.

"And it's not just *this*." She waves her arm toward the bill. "It's a whole bunch of things that's been happening lately."

"Like what?"

"Like . . ." Suddenly Corinne draws a blank. Where was the list she'd drawn up with Quincy just days before as they lunched at the Chinese restaurant down the block from their office? Quincy nearly dropped her fried shrimp into her kung pao chicken at hearing a few of Corinne's horror stories with Mark. Corinne, surprising herself, was able to laugh, as if it were someone else's life she was dissecting and not her own, her growing disappointment just a line on a graph heading south fast with nothing real behind it. "Well, for one thing, the dishes."

"The dishes?" Mark walks in little circles, anything to work out the anger growing in him. "What about the goddamn dishes?"

"Well, the few times I've asked you to do them, since you *are* practically living here now, well, they're never done right."

"Done right? What in the fuck's that supposed to mean?"

"You know . . . cleaned properly. Like one time I was going to make coffee and there was still a little bit of the grounds in the bottom of the pot."

Mark shakes for a moment before answering, as if he's a pistol that was loaded and had to go off.

"Well Jesus Christ! Heaven *fucking* forbid that the coffee tastes a little like, the horror, *coffee.*"

Corinne pulls back, Mark's breath like a wind trying to catch a sail.

"Now, that's not it, Mark. It's the point. If you'll stop shouting for a second and just listen . . ."

As Corinne begins recounting how his stress from the recording is beginning to affect her, Mark tunes her out. Her lips are moving but his ears are just taking in *blah-blah-blah.* He wonders if he was wrong about Corinne; maybe she wasn't as laid-back and cool as he had previously hoped, suspected, and then prematurely confirmed.

"Are you even listening to me?"

He just stands there.

"Hello? Mark?"

"Look, don't treat me like my goddamn mother. I don't need your fucking bullshit right now. Quit being such a bitch!"

The volume of Mark's voice rises higher than she's ever heard. She jerks back, alarmed, her hands thrown in front of her face out of instinct.

"I'm going out," Mark says, his voice calmer now but still slightly crazed, harried, as if even he didn't know what he was going to do next.

Corinne follows the sound of his footsteps down the hall, through the living room, and finally out the door and down the front steps. She counts a minute or two go by in her head, using the old *one-Mississippi-two-Mississippi* method she learned when she was a child, until she's sure he's gone.

Outside, Mark works out his aggressions on the pavement. His angry feet push against the ground.

He can't believe any of this is happening: the recording going down the drain, his friends unraveling into not being his friends, the trouble with Corinne. Each problem seemed to feed on the other until he found himself at odds with everyone; he couldn't discern between Corinne's tired eyes, trying to get some work done, or the deep, black sockets in Kenneth's ill-shaped head as he yelled at him to do it again, reminding him that the deadline was approaching.

Trudging over someone's lawn, he remembers something about answered prayers, something about how they were worse than the wishes that didn't come true. The phrase is fuzzy, and he keeps mixing it up with that Rolling Stones song about not getting what you want but getting what you need. This leads into humming the chorus to "Sympathy for the Devil," and he finds himself singing, "Ooh, ooh . . . ooh, ooh," into the black night, puffs of cloud appearing before his mouth as he does so. Crossing the street, drawn in by the tractor beam of a liquor store's neon sign, he starts whistling the opening bars to "Tumbling Dice." He smiles. It was only rock and roll, but he liked it.

After trying for another hour to add up columns, Corinne keeps arriving at a different answer every time. She heard Mark come back almost twenty minutes ago and has been waiting for him to apologize. Figuring it's not going to happen, she gives up on the work she'd brought home and goes into the living room.

The hall is dark and there's only a lamp in the corner of the living room turned on. This is doused with one of Mark's T-shirts, only a muted half-light permeating the room.

"Out of candles, wanted it dark," she hears his voice say as she crosses the room.

In the background, music is playing, *Exile on Main Street*, an old record he'd brought over a couple of weeks ago. She hated it when he did that. As if she had no taste of her own. As if she hadn't existed for twenty-four years before he'd come along and put her under his musical tutelage. Sometimes she really feels he thinks she's seriously stupid.

"Went out, bought some beer," he calls out again just as she's entering the kitchen. She looks back to him, his body sunk down deep into the armchair, his feet raised up on the ottoman and a drink in his hand, just like that guy with the butler in those Maxwell audiotape ads.

"Me . . . drink one . . . tasty beer," she says, mimicking his pained, clipped sentences.

"Yeah, real funny." His face, in shadows, is illuminated for a half second as he takes a drag from a cigarette that is almost burnt out to the butt. Has he been crying? *I just want to see his face.*

Corinne moves to the couch, grabs one of the cigarettes, and lights it. She takes three sips of the Corona and smokes half the cigarette before saying anything.

"You okay?"

She finishes half the beer and starts on another cigarette before he answers.

"I don't know."

"What's wrong?"

"It's this record. The deal. Everything seems to be turning around on us."

"Well, if it doesn't work out, I'm sure Bottlecap will stay together. Maybe you could go back to your old record company."

Mark's head jerks so fast toward Corinne that he almost cramps his neck.

"I mean, you've just got to trust your instincts."

Corinne takes another sip of the sudsy beer, the carbonation floating into her nose.

"Yeah, but it's my instincts that got me *here*. And now it's getting all fucked up."

"Well, there's nothing you can do about it tonight. So why don't you try and relax?" She leans forward and places her hand on his arm, but he flinches when she does so.

"You know what I heard?"

"What?" Mark says, dully.

"I heard on NPR today that a comet was going to enter the earth's atmosphere tonight, and that it was so big it might even be visible to the human eye."

"I read about that, too, and the *Times* said it'd have to be a couple of miles wide to be really visible, not to mention dangerous. And anyway, those things are mostly just ice, and they dissolve the second they hit the atmosphere. We'd never see anything."

"Well, it might be fun trying." She places her hand on his arm again and this time he doesn't remove it. "You know, get a bottle of wine, maybe some cheese and crackers? It could be like a picnic."

"A picnic . . . ," he slowly says, "with a comet?"

She just grins, her own smile sort of a comet, the straight-line white of her teeth a color streak against the darkness of the living room.

Gary was right. Steve did want a girl. He wanted to do the things that Mark and Gary were doing with their girlfriends, the same things he'd done with his in the past, things that went beyond sex, like shopping together, holding hands during a movie, cooking together, a soft perfumed female holding out a wooden spoon with a puddle of sauce in it and a hand below to catch the drippings, as she smiled and poured it into his mouth, warning, "Be careful, it's hot."

But in the meantime, he'd settle for getting laid. Having the guys out of the house gave him plenty of time to jack off; not like when they were on tour, and half the time they thought he was holed up in gas station bathrooms with another bout of diarrhea, he was actually in there masturbating, working off the tension caused by both the road and celibacy. It had been a while since he'd had in his arms a real-life girl. Too long, he figured.

"Gary," Steve says snidely, reaching for the television remote control. "He thinks he's so funny."

He watches about ten minutes of a made-for-TV movie (he's not even sure what it's about, only that it stars one of the Golden Girls) before scampering across the room to the kitchen table, where he fetches the *L.A. Weekly*.

Steve slowly examines the back of the paper, which he's only glanced at in the presence of Gary and Mark, never wanting to seem too interested. Now his eyes scan the various personal ads, massage-parlor, escort-service, phone-sex listings.

"*Bored housewives. Wet horny babes in heat. Shaved, tat-tooed pussy.* So many, uh, options."

WHY HAVE SEX ALONE? LIVE B&D! *I'm gonna love you with my lips.* "HARDCORE" LIVE 1-ON-1 GIRLS. THE HOTTEST, HORNIEST, BADDEST, GAYEST BOYS AROUND. *Please don't tell my mother what I'm doing . . .*

"What's a pre-op TS? And what does this one mean, 'Greek freak'? Hundred-dollar in call. Hmmm."

Steve looks closely at the closely cropped photo of a woman's chest, a, full bust pressed together in a lacy bra, above one breast the words NO TIP and above the other, ACTUAL PHOTO. He runs a hand over the front of his shorts, his penis actually small and tucked into his boxers, the idea of shelling out five $20 bills for a quick, anonymous fuck leaving him cold.

He throws the large paper to the ground, an insert on Los Angeles's top fifty restaurants falling out of the center. "I haven't paid for sex before, and I'm not going to start paying for it now."

As he settles back into the couch and a new TV movie (an inspirational tale based on a true story starring a woman who used to be on *Dallas*), Steve thinks back to a girl he dated years ago named Kiva.

Kiva was an out-of-work artist. Actually, she was an out-of-work waitress who sometimes filled large canvases with paint, sometimes not even covering them, just applying deep gashes of color here and there but always leaving room for a scrawled sig-nature in the corner. She would wander around Kitty in paint-splattered overalls with gobs of cerulean blue and permanent green light on her fingernails as if polish, mumbling under her breath, which was scrubbed with a vegan diet, words like *chiaroscuro* and *fauvism*. Once, for two days, all she would talk about was the Viennese painter Egon Schiele. Egon Schiele this. Egon Schiele that. How tragic his life had been, how great his art still was. It was a hell of a way to spend a weekend, but Steve fell for her immediately.

Gary and Mark were always giving Steve a hard time about the fact that he was such a sucker for those dark, moody, artistic types. Steve never fought back because it was true. There was just something about a girl with a studio apartment stuffed with Dalí and Picasso books, volumes of Rimbaud or Sexton or Plath, black sheets on a futon mattress laid simply on the floor with experimental music playing in the background that just knocked Steve off his feet.

One night, Steve conned his boss into letting him leave the office job he held a little earlier than usual. He swung by Kiva's apartment to pick her up. They were headed for a six o'clock reading over at the Novel Idea Cafe, where a mutual friend of theirs, Darren, was going to read from a novel in progress.

Once at the reading, they sat at the bar. Darren was set up in the corner near the double-door entrance, sitting on a stool behind a podium equipped with a Radio Shack microphone and about twelve pages of his handwritten text. Throughout the reading Steve couldn't decide what to be more upset about: the fact that Kiva had ordered two slices of cheesecake (for herself), an iced mocha, a caffé latte, and finally a gelato, or that Darren had a bullet of white spittle on his bottom lip, which sometimes attached itself to the top lip as well, where it would waggle back and forth like a string of mozzarella cheese before returning as a glob just above his chin.

"You mentioned dinner?" Kiva said before the perfunctory clapping that Darren did not deserve died down.

"I don't know"—Steve glanced at his watch, looking for an excuse—"it's almost eight already, and my friend's band goes on at the Scene at nine. Maybe we'd better just stop by my place for something microwaved."

"Oh, nonsense"—she hopped off the bar stool and headed for the door—"we've got *plenty* of time."

As Steve followed her to the door, where Darren was surrounded by a semicircle of attractive women with, Steve figured, bad eyesight, he looked to see if Kiva had even bothered to bring her purse. She hadn't.

At dinner she ordered an entree, appetizers, and drinks, having to take most of it home. At the club she was on her third mixed drink of the evening ("None of that well stuff. *Tanqueray* and tonic," she had berated the bartender over the din of the Deer Park's debut show) before Steve shoved the last remaining $20 bill to his front pocket, claiming he was out of money.

That night, as Kiva asked him in and as he was pissed off but followed anyway, Steve couldn't help but look back on the evening as an investment whose future he was about to collect. Kiva leaned back on her pitch black comforter, pushing a paperback copy of *Delta of Venus* out of the way, making room for Steve beside her among numerous journals and sketchbooks. As they fumbled through the motions of sex, Steve kept thinking that she was just doing it because she felt she owed it to him, not because she found him particularly attractive or even really liked him. Kiva just stared at the ceiling, her meter running, wondering if that new, expensive-looking Thai place had opened up yet in Moore's Mall, and if so, was Steve busy Saturday night?

Steve decides that yes, at one point, he had paid for sex. Then he thinks of all the money currently idling in his newly opened bank account, and of the automatic-teller-machine card sleeping in his thin wallet, a tattered accessory whose days of being thin, Steve hoped, were permanently over.

*It may not be the coolest thing in the world,* he figures, contemplating hiring a prostitute, *but I've got ten grand in the bank and this big, gorgeous house all to myself. I deserve it. No, I owe it to myself.*

The *L.A. Weekly* on the floor catches his eyes, and they are drawn to it in direct proportion to the gnawing feeling lurking in his jeans.

On the VCR clock he sees it's now past nine o'clock. He decides he'd better go out and get some cash since he doesn't have a credit card and he doubts a hooker will take one of his newly issued checks. He grabs his wallet and keys and heads out the door.

Hanging a right onto Sunset Boulevard, he notices a license plate holder that reads at the top RESPECT AND PROTECT and underneath THE BLACK WOMAN. This is attached to a white

Lexus, the model of which isn't even listed to the left side of the italicized *L* within a circle logo, the way it would be with a cheaper car.

He tries to get a look at the driver of the Lexus, to make sure it's at least a black woman, but the tinted windows prevent him from doing so. He thinks about the license plate holder, about how ironic it would be to buy one and slap it on his car back home, imagining the stares he would get when women of color would pull up alongside him and immediately put down the clenched fist they'd raised in solidarity before seeing the scrawny white kid at the wheel.

He wonders what Henry James would think if he returned the rental car with a RESPECT AND PROTECT THE BLACK WOMAN license plate holder surrounding the white-with-blue-lettering California plates.

Steve heads for the 7-Eleven on Vine with an automatic teller in the back so he can extract the needed cash and also so he can purchase some cigarettes to help him deal with the situation he's about to immerse himself in. He also decides to buy some liquor to make sure he won't try and weasel his way out.

As he pulls into the parking lot he notices a man curled up in a ball, directly in front of him, and for a moment he seems like a deer caught in the headlights and Steve can actually make out the grayish color of the man's steely eyes. Shutting off the head-lights quickly, he remembers to lock the doors, heading around the trunk to enter the store.

"Wash your windows for you, sir?" an elderly black man asks him as he clutches the door handle, a half-empty bottle of Windex in his hand and a jumble of crumpled-up newspapers in the other.

"Uh, no thanks."

"Then maybe some change on the way out?"

"Er, we'll see."

Steve goes right to the back of the convenience store and withdraws $300, just to be safe. He grabs a six-pack of beer and asks for a pack of Marlboro Lights, in a box.

"Eight thirty-five," the man at the counter says in a heavy Indian accent.

He pays for the items with one of the crisp $20 bills stuffed in his wallet, which has never held so much cash and won't for much longer.

He slides the $10 bill back into his wallet, pockets the cigarettes, and keeps the change in his hand, ready to hand it off.

"Here you go," he says as he gives the change to the man with the Windex bottle, the beer in his other hand.

"Thank you, sir," he says upon receiving it. Even in the darkness and the man's dirty face Steve can see egg yellow eyes light up. He opens Steve's door for him, bumping him slightly, taking the beer from his hands but only to place it on the backseat, out of Steve's way. Anything for Steve. "You have a good night, you hear? You wear that seat belt and make sure you be careful—"

The old man is continuing even as Steve gets in the car and starts up the engine, revving it to drown the man out. Pulling out, he's sure not to turn on his headlights until he's out of the spot, not wanting to torment the other homeless man, crouching in front of the car, though he momentarily feels bad for not giving him money, too.

Driving up Vine back to Sunset, Steve smiles, reflecting on his small humanitarian gesture. He thinks back to the way that his and the old man's eyes had locked for a second as the money was exchanged, and the way Steve realized that it could have been him on the other side, reaching for the handout, and not the other way around. The only thing saving that alternate reality from being so was the minuscule set of details of where he was born, who his parents were, and, to a degree (and this was continually argued everywhere), the color of his skin. He feels guilty for spending who knows how much on an anonymous fuck, but only for a second. Hanging a left onto Sunset he forgets about the homeless man. The image that seemed to rock his world only moments before now faded into his memory and is replaced with the image before him, the way you change a channel and there's no trace of where you had been before.

As he travels the short distance back to the apartment, something feels strange to him. He looks in the backseat and sees the beer in the brown paper bag, a rip already appearing toward the seam on the bottom. In his front left pocket he can feel the cigarettes jutting into his thigh, a tube of lip balm, and pack of gum in his right. But nothing else. He steadies the wheel with one hand while his other tentatively reaches behind and taps each of the back pockets of his jeans, only to find both hollow. Panicked, he tries again, this time with both hands (knees barely keeping the car in its own lane), only he again comes up empty. He turns onto Sierra Bonita and locks the brakes as he parks in front of the apartment complex.

Steve quickly gets out of the car and turns on the overhead light set into the felt-covered interior. He searches the gap between the seats, underneath the floor mats, the drink holder just below the radio, hoping that the wallet fell out as he was getting back into the car and not when he was at the . . .

"Seven-Eleven," he says ruefully.

He figures it came from behind, the moment most likely captured on a security videotape somewhere, him standing outside the garishly lit convenience store, and if it wasn't the greasy hand of the homeless man who relieved him of his night of debauchery, it was his own stupidity.

"And I even gave that fucking bum some money . . . I was being nice"—he slams a fist against the roof of the car—"and this is how I'm repaid? God*damn*."

Steve turns to the night sky, which has forsaken him.

"I want my whore!" he screams, beginning to cry. "Can't I ever just get fucked, the right way?"

He shrugs his shoulders and drops the pack of cigarettes into the gutter, where it lands in a trail of green antifreeze. He leaves the beer in the car, gaining his composure enough to drag himself up the steps to the rented apartment.

"Early night, huh?"

Steve turns to see Sam standing on his front step, the door

open and music pouring out from the inside. In the shadows of Sam's apartment Steve sees a silhouette he think he recognizes. The third person's identity is barely concealed by Sam's grin.

"What?"

"All dressed up?" Sam points to Steve's jeans and T-shirt with the butt of a lit joint. "Nowhere to go?"

Sam takes a long hit, and by the time he exhales, Steve is at his door, about to enter.

"Why let the night end here?" Sam pokes the amazingly long joint behind his left ear, where it stays without singing his sideburns. He pulls a handful of color out of his pockets.

"What have you got there?" Steve asks.

"Ba-ba-ba-looons," Sam sings it like the song of the same name. "On the house. For you and your buddies."

Steve takes his keys out of the door, considering for a second, but then shakes his head and steps inside.

"This is crazy, this is crazy, this is crazy."

Mark keeps repeating this as he tries to stay warm on Corinne's roof, wrapping up his chest in his crossed arms. "We're *never* going to see anything out here."

"It's just cloudy, that's all." Corinne's scanning the purple night sky, patchy with gauzelike clouds. "We *should* have driven out to the desert. It would be pitch black. Here in the city"—she waves her hand over the hundreds of thousands of lives lying stretched out in grids beneath them—"it doesn't even get dark anymore."

"No, Corinne, what we *should* have done was caught that revival of *Dr. Strangelove* at the Nuart. I read that it's even a new print."

"By the way, Mark, it's pronounced Nu-*art*. It's not supposed to rhyme with *Newark*."

"Well," he says, rubbing his hands together for warmth, "I didn't know. And why's it so cold out here? It's autumn and we're in California. A few weeks ago we were having breakfast up here, and now I'm freezing my ass off. I thought it *never* got cold out here. Isn't that why everyone moves here? Why, back in Virginia at this time of year, it's . . ."

Corinne's not listening to Mark, who's now doing a little dance, hopping around in circles, trying to get his blood circulating again and droning on about the weather.

"And even if it *wasn't* cloudy, Corinne, there's no way in hell that we'd be able to spot that comet with our own eyes. I read in the *Times* that even with the most rudimentary of telescopes it would be barely visible, so I don't see how—"

"Oh, Mark, will you just stop it for one second?" Corinne cuts him off, slapping at him as he glides by her in a low-temperature-induced jig. "Why don't you just use your imagination a little bit?"

He stops for a second to turn and look at her. Her pale cheeks are turned a ruddy red from the cold, a trail of glistening mucus beginning to seep out of her sniffling nose.

"Seriously, I just don't see how you can be so creative with your music and yet be so close-minded about this. It's like all you think about is—wait a second, did you just hear something?"

"Hear something like what?"

"Like a sort of . . . wait, there it is again!" She sprints across to the roof to the southwest corner, staring into the sky.

Mark looks at Corinne, then into the air, then back to Corinne, making the connection.

"Oh no." He laughs. "You don't think you actually *heard* that comet hitting the Hollywood hills, do you?"

"Well, it sounded just like—"

"Just like a comet hitting a planet? How would *you* know what that sounds like? Like, when's the last time you *ever* heard a comet hit a planet?"

"Jesus, you're such a fucking downer sometimes."

"Maybe, Corinne. But come on, you're being crazy."

She whips around quickly, tearing her eyes from the stars and locking them on Mark.

"Why do you keep *saying* that? 'This is crazy. *You're* crazy. Stop acting so *crazy.*' I mean, if you really think I'm truly insane, how come we're even dating?"

Mark slowly crosses the roof and takes Corinne in his arms, where, he's surprised to find, she's trembling even though she's wearing a long coat and scarf. He tightens his hold in a hopefully reassuring manner before beginning the process of digging himself out.

"I'm sorry, Corinne. You're right. I'm being a grouch about all this. It's just, I don't see how this whole comet thing has anything to do with us."

"God, you're so selfish!" She wrestles out of his grip and walks away. "You think *you're* the center of the universe? I swear to God, you probably sit around and think a meteor's going to hit *you*, as if *you're* so fucking special."

Mark's afraid to say he actually did have that nightmare when he was about ten, in 1980, when Skylab was falling out of space like a fly ball.

"How can you be so solipsistic?"

Mark fights the urge to reply, *Easy.* Instead he chases her across the roof, trying to take her back in his arms, only she refuses.

"Come on, Corinne. I'm sorry."

"Sorry? Sorry for what?"

"For, uh . . . whatever it is you're . . . mad about . . ."

"Yeah, *real* sincere, Mark."

"Okay, okay," he replies quickly, staring unbelieving at the breath appearing in front of his face in small gusts of white wind. "Maybe we *can* see the comet from out here. Happy?"

"That's not the point, Mark. This isn't about the goddamn comet. This isn't about not being able to see what we know's happening out there. This is about the fact that *I* wanted to at least *try*." Her voice becomes strained. *Don't cry,* she's telling herself. *Don't start . . .*

Mark looks into Corinne's eyes, which seem clouded up, fogged over, panicked.

*Oh great.* He sighs inside. *Now I suppose she's going to cry.*

"This is about something *I* wanted to do, Mark. And the fact is that you just didn't want to have any part of it. You've been pissed off since the second you got home. Then you yell at me because of your goddamn guitar picks, and then you act like I'm *dragging* you up here, as if spending a little time with me were torture or something." She stops for a second, listening to the air whistle through her head. "You know how that makes me feel?"

Instead of answering he just stares back.

"I guess not."

"Now wait a minute, Corinne. This has gotten totally out of hand. You have no idea what I'm going through, so I don't think you should—"

"So why don't you *share* it with me? Jesus, Mark, you walk around my apartment like you're some kind of victim. Can't you see that I'm here to help? That I *want* to help?" Her words trail off and she loses her thoughts.

"You think this is funny?" he asks as he notices Corinne holding back a laugh, she doesn't know why.

"No," she says ruefully, her voice now drained of any feeling. "This isn't funny at all."

"Look, Corinne, I just don't know what you want." Mark stalks the rough surface, kicking at a small bushel of fluffy pink insulation streaked with tar and peeking out from a flap of roofing. "I just don't know what you need."

"All I need is for you to be honest with me. To tell me how you're really feeling and to maybe try and guess how *I'm* feeling some of the time."

Mark turns back to the ledge, looking down to the bustling street rather than the sky, imagining that the cars rounding the block are instead planets in orbit around him.

His silence slaps Corinne in the face. She hunkers down in her jacket, wraps her body with her scarf as it if were Mark's sinewy arms, comforting her, telling her things he can't express in words even though he somehow manages to write all those songs and play that damn guitar; only his arms are huddled around his own midsection, each paw suspiciously kneading the flesh around his scapulas the way she wishes he would hold her.

As he finally, and then only lamely, because he feels he's expected to, takes her in his arms, Corinne still imagines she can hear something. Over the irregular beat of his heart that she wasn't quite sure existed, she hears a low roar, like the screaming of a jet engine, even though the sky is momentarily free of planes, and then an explosion.

*Maybe Mark's right,* she thinks as he tugs her closer to him. *Maybe I am crazy.*

Mark leans into a yawn and Corinne tilts her head to one side, looking out over the Hollywood sign and into the sky, each star like a tiny hole in a black cloth that's being held up to a light.

# 14

**MONTEIL PARIS.**

The bag says this over and over again. MONTEIL PARIS. It is written at straight angles, on its side, upside down, right side up. Above every set of words is a small gargoylelike figure, maybe a griffin, sporting a lion's tail and a set of feathery wings.

The bag feels like vinyl, its color a dark gray or dirt-clod brown. Mark can't really tell in the half-light of the overcast morning, the sun struggling with the clouds outside while shadows dominate Corinne's drafty apartment. A zipper divides the top of the rectangular bag, which is slightly larger than Mark's closed fist. He tugs on the beige zipper, and the flap opens like a closed mouth opens to speak, only instead of words pouring out little cosmetic items poke up their heads, silver, dusted with powder, smeared with the color of the lipstick next door.

"What's Monteil Paris?" Mark asks the empty room. "Is that a company or a place?"

He picks up the bag and sniffs it, catching a whiff of perfume, and he wonders if there's a small vial of cologne in the bag or if the scents of all the accessories conspired to make one rosy odor.

He pokes around the wide assortment of lipsticks, tubes of mascara, pencils with varying earth-tone tips, and compacts with dusty mirrors on one side and chalky pools of color at the other. He imagines the colors the way he's seen them on Corinne's face, a little beige under the eyes to mask the purple bands that stretch above her cheeks right about Wednesday, the weekend still two days away, or some color in the cheeks, powder on the forehead to take off the shine. He thinks of how Corinne looks with makeup and without, like two different people, and that it feels like cheating on one to fuck the other. Corinne with makeup has a depth that the Corinne without cannot touch; the eyes, when painted, seem deep, penetrating, and her eyebrows swoosh over her face. Without makeup her eyes sort of run into the rest of her face like an egg whose yolk has broken and skidded across the pan, her face flat and not a mass of hilly cheekbone dunes, and he can see that tiny river of a scar on her left cheek that is usually filled with a neutral-colored base.

"What's this?" Mark had asked a couple of nights ago as Corinne pulled out an instrument that looked like a scissors on one end, with hoops for a thumb and forefinger, while the opposite end looked like an inch-long nail clipper curved in a gentle arc.

"I use it to curl my eyelashes, silly," she said as she brought the thing to her face and like a helicopter pilot landing on shifting ground, carefully inserted her delicate dark brown lashes between the two pieces of chrome, then gently flexed the muscles in her hand, bringing the pieces of metal together with her hairs caught in the cross fire.

Mark saw Corinne's eyeball through the shiny bars of the contraption, the metal holding her eyelashes to be effective the way you keep pot smoke in your lungs as long as you can. "That looks like something out of *A Clockwork Orange.* Hang on a second, I'll get my Beethoven records." She just laughed, brought down the small machine, and then did the other eye.

He goes to the closet, swinging the door wide open. The first thing that catches his eyes is the small black jumper dress that Corinne was wearing the night before. Where eight hours ago it writhed and shimmied on her body, bent with her movements and shaped to her figure, the dress now hangs four feet off the ground, and clear plastic sticks through each hole where

Corinne's shoulders should go. Even in the half dark of the room Mark can make out the tag that would sit at the base of Corinne's neck: RAMPAGE. The word is in big black letters against a white background. Mark closes the closet, the image of the dress shifting slightly as the vacuum from the closing of the door kicks up air and shoots up the hem of the skirt, only there's no stretch of leg or thigh to catch a glimpse of, only more air.

He holds his face in his hands, the flesh seeming rubbery to his kneading touch. Over his feet he feels a current of cool air spiral around each toe, an undercurrent of icy wind flowing through the inch-and-a-half gap between the front door and floor.

"Have got to be cooler to her," Mark says to the empty room. "Have got to get this record bullshit off my mind."

The phone rings and Mark, without hesitation, reaches to answer it.

"Corinne?"

"No, you mamby-pamby asswipe, it's Gary!"

"Oh, uh, where are you?"

"Where am I? Where are you?"

Mark, still in a daze, looks at a clock in the hallway and discovers it's past ten. He remembers Corinne setting the dual alarm on her clock radio, seven-thirty for her and nine for him, and he remembered hers going off; he jarred awake for a moment as she, as if a figure in his dreams, crept quietly out of bed and into the shower. But nine o'clock must have come and gone without his notice, or did the damn thing actually go off and he just swatted at the off switch before any of his senses dragged him completely out of sleep? He cannot remember.

"Oh, shit, sorry," he mumbles into the receiver, feeling disoriented, irresponsible, out of place.

"Yeah, well, get your ass over here and all is unforgiven."

"What was that? *Un*forgiven?"

"Just get here." Gary hangs up the phone.

Mark gets into the shower, feeling like a zombie, like without the streaming hot water all over his body he'd never completely thaw. He leans up against the wall of the shower and points the nozzle directly at himself, sitting there with his eyes closed and thinking back to Saturday night, to when he glimpsed the inevitable unraveling of his relationship with Corinne back into two separate lives, the way he has always thought cynically would happen. The other night was the first night they'd slept together without having sex. They met in bed about an hour apart, him staying up to watch MTV, waiting for her to fall asleep so he wouldn't have to say anything after she broke free from his grip on the roof and ran back down the stairs. Whether he knew it or not she was still awake when he finally came to bed, but he hadn't noticed that, either.

"Don't want to fuck this up," he says, receiving a mouthful of water as he does so. "We've got Thanksgiving at her parents' house in just a few days . . . got to make a good impression . . . got to . . ."

It's not until the hot water runs out and he's standing under a cold stream, trying to get the soap out of his eyes, that he reluctantly gets out of the shower, puts on some clothes, and heads to the studio.

"You know, Gary," Mark says when he sees his bass player sitting in the swivel chair behind the large mixing console, Kenneth in the corner talking to Henry James, "you're going to have to be a bit quicker with those Swoosie Kurtz wake-up calls. You almost let me go till eleven."

"I would have let you go, *period,* except that Henry's here to talk about—"

"Hey, what's that on your chin?"

Gary places his hands self-consciously over the Band-Aids applied just below his bottom lip.

"It's nothing . . . So, like I was saying, Henry's got this idea for the—"

"It is not nothing, because you keep hiding it. What is it, like a shaving thing?"

"Yeah, shaving." Gary drops his hands, the mystery solved.

As he listens to Gary drone on about Henry James's visit, how Steve is beginning to get spooked, the feeling that Henry's not one of them beginning to crystallize, Mark focuses on the two-and-a-half inch cut on Gary's chin, the bulk of which is covered with a regular sized Band-Aid, with two smaller ones on each end. Mark decides that Gary is lying, that no one could cut himself that badly while shaving.

"So, Steve says that Hanes said to call Henry James, and I said go ahead because we're meeting with him right after Thanksgiving anyway, right? So then I—"

"Cut the shit, Gary. What's up with the lip?"

Gary is silent for a second, considering telling Mark the fictionalized story that had already worked on Steve. He decides on the truth.

"I got it at Whitney's." His eyes find the floor, whole head dropped. "Saturday night."

"That new girl you're dating?" Mark barely holds in a growing laugh. "She punched you?"

"No, no. *I* did it, to myself. In her . . . bathroom."

"Wait a second." Mark reconsiders. "So you actually *were* shaving."

"Not exactly."

Gary pauses before continuing. He looks around the room, makes sure Kenneth and Henry are still deep in conversation, Paul is in the kitchen down the hall, and Steve is in the studio, fiddling on the bass, working on his stupid song.

"I was doing a push-up and, well, the bathroom's like this triangle, stuck in a corner, so I was all cramped and I slipped and cut my—"

"Wait, what? A push-up?"

"Yeah, you know." Gary brings his hands to his chest and juts them out and then back, an example. "A push-up."

"But why?"

"Well, we'd just had sex, and I could tell we were going into heavy cuddle mode, even though I was, as usual, tired and just wanted to go to sleep. I was taking a piss and I thought I'd do a couple of push-ups to, you know, beef up the old biceps, pump up a tad so I would actually have some arms to hold her in."

"And instead you bled on her sheets?"

"No, no, I wadded up a mess of toilet paper and did that direct-pressure thing to stop the bleeding. But I was in there for about twenty minutes. She kept hearing the water run and me take toilet paper from the roll. She probably thought I had the shits or something."

Mark chuckles, imagining the sight of Gary straining to perform a push-up in his date's cramped bathroom.

"Why are you exerting so much effort?"

"You don't understand," Gary says dreamily, as if no one else in the history of mankind had ever been in love. Gary was not delusional enough to think he loved Whitney, but there was still a warm feeling in his chest whose origins could be traced directly back to her and the way she touched him. "You don't understand what kind of a night it was. We were up till six in the morning . . . just talking."

Mark stands there, unimpressed.

"So?"

"So? So when's the last time *you* stayed up till dawn talking with a girl?"

"What did you talk about?"

"Everything. Our pasts, old-girlfriend/boyfriend type stuff."

"Gary . . . you should be able to have a good time without knowing anything about the other person." Mark places his hands on Gary's shoulders and tries to shake some sense into him. Hanes enters the room, handing Henry James an envelope, a devilish grin aimed at Mark. "*That's* the real test."

"Oh really?"

"Yeah. You need to start at the top and work your way down. You need to dress nice, laugh at whatever the other person says, and be totally agreeable. Like, what'd she wear on your first date?"

"Pants."

"Pants? Oh, man, what's next? Jeans? A pair of shorts? Sweatpants?" Mark chuckles while Gary scratches at his injury, quickly tiring of the conversation. "And you don't talk about your sexual pasts and old boyfriends and stuff. That's all for later, once you're really sure they like you. On a first date you need to act as if you were just hatched *that* morning, wearing nice clothes and with absolutely *no* past at all."

Gary stares at Mark, not wanting to believe the words his friend is saying. He and Whitney had just entered that sexual common ground trod upon by countless others in the world's existence, and even millions right now, right here in this city (at this very second even), were laying their bare feet into the balmy soil. But the odd thing about sex is that it makes one wonderfully egotistical, as if he or she alone (and their partner) had discovered a door to a brilliant and exciting world, blithely failing to notice that the lock has been busted thousands of times before, and maybe even a dozen or more by the foot of your own lover. Not only did he feel that Whitney was different, but after the weekend, he felt that he was different, too.

Kenneth motions for Mark to join him and Henry James. Hanes is loitering off to the side, trying to act as if he's not eavesdropping. Mark drifts over, but not before he grins at Gary and undoes an imaginary zipper running down the length of his body, as if he were a body snatcher crawling out of a pod.

"Well, well, look who graciously decided to pay us a visit. *Mr.* Pellion."

"Well, I figured it was the least I could do, Kenneth."

"I'm glad you're here, Mark. I've got some ideas I wanted to show you and the band." Henry sounds like what passes in his universe as excited. He motions with the package Hanes has just handed him, sitting down at the mixing board and opening the manila envelope. He takes out a large, heavy sheet of paper, which is backed by a slate of dark brown cardboard.

"I just got this from the graphic design department. Mind you, it's just a low-res output from the Syquest disc, so it's not as sharp as it will be, but you get the idea."

Mark, unhappy to be brought back to the reality of the car

crash happening all around him (he'd rather make fun of Gary some more, to hear about *his* problems), walks over to Henry. The remaining two thirds of Bottlecap crowd around.

"What is it?" asks Steve.

"It's the artwork," Henry says, pride in his voice, as if he were showing off his small child who was walking and talking, both ahead of schedule.

"F-f-for the record?" Mark stutters. "Because I'm still working on that . . . remember?"

"Of *course* I remember," Henry answers, referring to a discussion they had the other day when James had woken Mark out of a deep sleep even though the A&R man warned him he'd call first thing in the morning. Mark thought Henry meant around eleven, and when the phone rang loudly at a quarter to ten (James in the office early rather than late for a change), Bottlecap's lead singer was sure the call was some sort of emergency, news that someone close had died.

"We had our monthly production meeting yesterday," Henry James had begun as soon as Mark was conscious enough to embark upon the conversation, "where we introduce our new records to the rest of the staff. I played them a little bit of the upcoming Bottlecap record. And everybody loved it. Just *loved* it."

"But the record's not even ready yet. What did you play them?"

"Oh, just a few snippets. Don't worry, I told them you were still mixing and had a few overdubs to finish, but I couldn't wait. They all knew it was just a rough mix . . . but you're missing the point."

"The point?" Mark turned in bed, staring at the swirling pattern of the plaster ceiling. He tried to imagine the meeting Henry was describing, the boardroom in which it took place, which he figured was large, white, and sterile. He tried to picture men in suits sitting around a long rectangular table at the end of which stood Henry and a stereo, the A&R man popping Bottlecap into the cassette deck. Mark tried to see in his mind's eye the grimace on the faces of the men in their forties, fifties, one even in his sixties, as the noise from the speakers, which they wished would just go away, assaulted them.

"The point I'm trying to make is that they loved it. And the boys in graphic design are frothing at the mouth to get started on the cover. But then I remembered you mentioning that you'd like to take a crack at coming up with some ideas for the sleeve."

"Uh, huh, yeah."

"And, well, have you?"

Mark turned over in bed and tried to kick the door shut because he could hear one of the guys taking a piss down the hall; the sound of urine splattering against the still water bounced off the hardwood floors and reverberated through the house.

"Yeah, yeah, Henry. I'm getting to it."

"Getting to it? Getting to it when, exactly?"

"Soon, soon."

"Listen, Mark. I don't believe in pushing artists, but we're going to be running into deadlines soon. Deadlines which, if ignored, will affect the release date of your record. Is that what you want?"

Mark was still too sleepy to become angry at the fact that he was being talked to like a child.

"No, Henry, I'm sorry. I'll get right on it."

He could now hear one of the guys burp, fart, and then something solid fall into the toilet bowl, followed by a contented groan and the gargling noise of water and waste being flushed out to sea.

Steve now tries to shove Gary out of the way in order to get a clearer view of the proof sheet sitting on the mixing console. "If it's not for the new record, what is it for?"

"This is for . . . the single." Henry tries to put some *ta-da* in his voice, but no one notices.

"Hey, Mark," Gary says, "what'd you finally choose as the single?"

"We haven't decided yet," Henry says quickly.

Steve fingers the heavy paper, where the front and back of the single's design are laid out, each square skirted with black cropping marks, a color bar in the lower right corner next to some note scrawled by the designer in precise, comic-book-style handwriting, the kind you see on blueprints.

"Hey, this doesn't look like five inches to me," Steve says, stretching his thumb and forefinger to the opposite points. "It looks bigger than a CD."

"It's seven inches," Henry says.

"Vinyl?" Kenneth says, speaking for the first time in ten minutes. "Pacific hasn't pressed vinyl for years. Why start again now?"

"It's to establish the band's street credibility, Ken. We'll do a platform release, servicing college radio first, sending out copies to all the little fanzines, and getting the records in all the mom-and-pop stores. That'll get a buzz going. Hell, to make it look really legitimate, we won't even be using WEA, our normal distributor. We're going with the Alternative Distribution Alliance, to further distance ourselves from Pacific."

Gary looks over the front of the design, a sepia-tinged black-and-white stock shot from the nineteen fifties of a packaging plant, square-jawed men with crew cuts overseeing a parade of bottles as they jangle through a curvy assembly line. The word BOTTLECAP is printed, off center and crooked, at the top, in standard type, the print scratchy, almost blurred. Near the bottom, in the same type, only smaller, it reads, *If there was a song title, it would go here.*

"Why's the lettering so fucked up?" Gary asks, running a finger over the shiny proof.

"Yeah, I thought those design guys of yours were so good," Steve says.

"They are," Henry says blandly. "It's *supposed* to look that way. Remember, we're going after a young demographic. We've done studies on this type of thing. We wanted this to look as punk as possible."

Steve says, "But we're not punk. I mean, we sound like—"

"That's not what I meant," Henry interrupts.

"What he means," Mark interjects, "is that he's got a team of graphic designers working round the clock with hundreds of thousands of dollars' worth of equipment, trying to make it look like it's two guys with an X-Acto knife in their kitchen. All to fool the kids, right, Henry?"

The A&R man looks over the half dozen people in the room, all waiting to hear his answer.

"Well, of *course*. You think we want the kids of America to know that Pacific Media also puts out polka records, or that the Kobiyashi Group has a large interest in at least four military research firms down in Long Beach? We need this whole operation to look as, uh, Seattle . . . as possible. Because if the kids knew that a major record label was behind all of this"—he waves his hand over the mixing board as if above the entire project— "they wouldn't touch it with a ten-foot pole bought at a thrift store. No offense. In fact, you'll notice that Pacific's name is nowhere near any of this artwork, or any of the ads we're going to place in every little magazine from coast to coast. Hell, we do such a good job covering our corporate tracks that most of the editors only charge us half price because they think we're an indie."

Mark looks over the proposed artwork, scanning the backside, which is another Eisenhower-era photo, this time of three kids between the ages of ten and thirteen, passed out drunk on an Art Deco–ish street in Chicago, a dozen bottles strewn around the trio's inebriated feet. He finds only a smallish logo of a crudely drawn square package wrapped in string, underneath the word SUBTERFUGE, along with the Sunset Boulevard address, but no mention of Pacific Media Arts International, or the name stamped on the large checks they received a few weeks before, the Kobiyashi Entertainment Group.

"I don't know about any of this," he slowly says, his stomach beginning to turn over violently.

"Look, Mark. We need this. *You* need this. We plan on making a lot of money off Bottlecap, and this is the way we need to start. After we build a little bit of a groundswell in the minor leagues, we'll bump you up to the majors. With that kind of leverage under your belts, it'll be easier to go after a wider commercial audience. After all, alternative is the format du jour these days, right? The bottom line is, a major-label release that bypasses college radio and goes straight to commercial alternative has no track record, no momentum to get it into heavier rotation."

"Heavy . . . rotation?" Mark mutters, his stomach now in heavy rotation.

# Verse

# 15

**Breaking the blue-and-silver paper seal between the** neck and cap, Mark unscrews the top of the vodka bottle with one hand while the other tucks a tail of his green-on-red plaid flannel shirt deep into his patterned boxers.

"So, where are we going again?"

"The Valley," Corinne says, rushing around the room trying to find a pair of earrings her mother gave her for her birthday last year. Corinne hates the earrings, small disks of gold inlaid with oval opals, but her mom has a pair just like them, so Corinne's trying to be nice. *Protocol,* she reminds herself.

"The Valley?" Mark cackles, sitting on the arm of her cobalt blue chair and taking a swig from the vodka. "The valley of what? Of the dolls? The mutants?"

"Strip malls, is more like it. Are you ready to go?"

He stiffens up, turning quickly to look at a mirror, and pleased with what he sees, turns back. "Why, don't I look ready?"

"Well, you *look.* Let's just leave it at that." Corinne disappears into the living room, still in search of the earrings.

As Mark hears her going through various drawers of the other room he turns again to the mirror, examining his faded blue jeans and tucked-in flannel shirt. *Tucked in* had been his major concession a half hour before, the battle that Mark had lost and Corinne had won even though he was sensing that she wanted more, maybe even a tie.

"So, when's the last time you saw them?"

"Who?" Corinne asks, reentering the room, putting on the found earrings.

"Who do you think? Your parents."

"Oh, *them.*" She shrugs as she struggles with the clasp on the left earring. "I guess I saw them a couple of months ago."

"Wow."

"What?"

"Well, it's just funny that it's been so long since you've seen them, and they live less than an hour away."

"I'm busy a lot, what with my job and all." Corinne flips her shoulder-length brown hair, continuing to search for an explanation. "Besides . . . none of us really likes each other."

Mark laughs, hiding the bottle of alcohol between his legs.

"Look, Mark, I'll warn you right now that we're not the happiest family on earth. I don't think we're the first and we're definitely not the last. They're good people, it's just . . . we don't get along."

"Why not?" Mark asks just as an excuse to take another swig of the vodka. Corinne catches a glance of him taking a drag off the smallish $18 bottle of Absolut she picked up at Greenblats on her way home from the office a few days before but never got around to opening. She fears her father will smell alcohol on her new boyfriend's breath. Corinne's chest heaves because it won't be the first time it's happened.

"My parents are very . . . overprotective."

"About what? You?"

"No"—Corinne sighs, wrapping a gold Chanel chain-link belt around her waist—"home security. Of *course* about me. My mother's never satisfied, and my father, well, he's never interested."

"Hmmm." Mark sighs, sliding into the couch with the vodka bottle, splashing a portion to the back of his throat and gargling before swallowing. Hearing Corinne talk about her parents' various faults, and struck by the similarities of her situation to his own—only child and so forth—he prepares a list of his own parents' deficiencies: they're boring, close-minded, self-involved, and petty, but Mark still misses them. After all, it is Thanksgiving. Mark thinks of his parents, probably sitting down to eat at the country club, or else Father carving the turkey amongst a few friends in their spacious house. Lost in thought, Mark brushes his thumb against a wet spot on his chest and finally notices a thin trail of vodka running over his shirt, beading at first, then racing toward his cardboard belt, but soaking in at his slightly bulging gut, looking as if an ulcer was seeping right through his skin.

"You know what?" Mark calls out to Corinne, who's standing in front of the full-length mirror set into the closet door. "I'm going to put on a better shirt."

Corinne loops the belt yet again around the waistband of her black cashmere skirt, trying to get just the right amount of slack so the intertwining double-*C* logo dangles at the base of her stomach and not between her legs.

"Perfect," she mumbles, spotting Mark in the background, buttoning a starched white dress shirt. She marches into the bedroom as Mark fumbles with the stiff neck of the garment.

"Now don't be afraid, Mark, but those little *white* things all over the front of that are buttons. Repeat after me, *buttons.*" She laughs, poking her head into the closet, trying to find her black Manolo Blahnik flats.

"Hey, what's that for?"

"Oh please," Corinne says, her voice muffled as she leans into her business suits, reaching for some rectangular boxes in the corner, "half the time I come home you're wearing a T-shirt, and if you *happen* to be wearing something with long sleeves, like that flannel shirt you were just wearing, you *still* don't button it, because you just pull it on and off over your head all the time." She emerges from the closet with a shoe dangling from the crooked index finger of each hand. "Those flannel shirts might as well be a damn parka."

"Well, I'm sorry," Mark says before he hiccups.

The smell of alcohol wafts across the room to where

Corinne's sitting on her hope chest, slipping into her shoes.

"Did you open the vodka I bought?"

"Why, were you saving it?"

"Well, no, not for Thanksgiving, but maybe for the weekend."

Mark struggles yet again with the top button of the shirt, folds of his already turkey-necking throat getting caught between the plastic and the slit it's supposed to fit into.

"I'm sorry, I'll replace it."

"No, Mark, that's not even the point." Rather than get up off the chest and find her purse with the strap to match her belt, like she had planned to a minute ago, in an effort to arrive at her parents' on time for a change, Corinne just sits there. "It's just . . . you know, maybe I don't want my new boyfriend drunk when he meets my parents for the first time."

"Who's . . . " Mark says but hiccups again before adding, "drunk?"

The heels of her shoes clack against the hardwood floors as she goes into the bathroom and slams the door behind her. She looks into the mirror to check her makeup. Corinne lets the crookedness of the mascara encircling her eyes and the disparity of the amounts of base on each cheek go unrepaired, matching the gaps and droughts in her own life.

"Honey?" she hears Mark call out from the bedroom. The word, a pleasant little nickname that he's grown comfortable enough to call her after their two months of dating, is a tag that made her feel special up until a week ago, when he tried to schmooze with the attractive Israeli maître d' at the Formosa Cafe by calling her "honey" as well. This time it is punctuated by that *glug-glug* sound made when impatient liquid cannot leave the bottle fast enough. "You okay in there?"

*Two months,* Corinne thinks as she leans into the mirror, noticing that bags are still visible under her eyes despite the amount of makeup she used trying to cover them up. *Two months.* The relationship flashes before her eyes the way it's always been said your life does in moments of impending death: bumping into Mark on Melrose in front of Bleecker Bob's, him looking cute and dazed; how she was attracted to his boyish good looks and her interest was piqued by the fact that he was from back East, Virginia, a state she'd never given much thought to before and never visited; how the fact that he was a musician cutting his first record with the backing of a major record label impressed her, since the limit of the ambition of most of her friends was to try and make it out to Century City or the Beverly Center on the weekend to *buy* a record, let alone record one. Besides, Mark neatly filled the gap left when Tim suddenly decamped at the beginning of the summer. Corinne sighs and again thinks, *Two months*, knowing that her parents are going to completely hate him. At least their dislike of him would leave them little time for picking on her.

Now nearly suffocating due to the amount of Escape she applied behind her ears ten minutes before, she finally opens the bathroom door. Standing in the middle of the bedroom, like a small child with a grocery list pinned to his sleeve, is Mark. The white shirt is finally buttoned, painfully, all the way up, and a blue tie with red-and-yellow flowers looks like it's cutting off the circulation to Mark's face, which is reddening like a beet.

"Hey, how long do I cook this thing for?" Gary asks, staring into the oven, where the large turkey has been cooking for almost three hours already.

"I don't know," Steve calls back from the table in the dining room, where he's breaking white bread into squares for a stuffing recipe Gary's mother gave him over the phone the week before. "Why don't you try reading the directions?"

"Don't be a smart-ass," Gary calls back as he begins to root around in the garbage for the small white paper packed in a plastic bag that was stuck inside the bird's chest like a pacemaker. "It says to bake it at three hundred and twenty-five degrees for four hours if it's an eight-pound turkey."

A second passes before Steve answers.

"Uh, yeah, so?"

"Well, the thing's *ten* pounds."

Steve still doesn't understand the problem.

"And?"

"Well, fuck, man, don't make me spell it out for you!" Gary marches into the room, the tattered KITTY CAVALIERS T-shirt he's wearing as an apron already smeared with stains, and it's barely noon. "Don't you remember that I'm the guy who always asks Mark what time it is back home, and he says just to add three hours and I *still* can't figure it out!"

"Okay, okay." Steve shuts his eyes and does the elementary-school-level math in his head. "Cook the thing for six hours."

"Thanks!" Gary shouts back. "Now was that so hard?"

"Yes, it was," Steve mumbles as he hears someone approaching on the sidewalk.

"Knock knock," he hears a semifamiliar voice say, the sound of boots scraping against the doormat.

"Come in," Steve shouts, thinking, *Sam?*

"Hey, you crazy kids, Happy Thanksgiving."

Gary comes out of the kitchen to ask Steve what he should do with the heart and dildoesque gizzard, but turns when he sees Sam standing in the living room, in a loose-fitting brown leather jacket over a worn black T-shirt, a set of raccoon eyes and pasty pallor. Gary heads back into the kitchen, tossing the mounds of turkey parts into the garbage.

"What's up?" Steve asks.

Sam crosses the room and sits down at the table. He reaches over and picks up a can of cranberry sauce and rolls it around the table, his eyes not on Steve's face but the corrugated tin can filled with jellied fruit as it rolls between his thin hands.

"Nothing." He sighs before continuing. "What are you guys up to?"

"Oh . . . we're just getting ready for dinner. You know, turkey, stuffing . . . all that crap."

"Turkey?" Sam's eyes light up for the first time since entering. "I haven't had turkey in a long time. No, me, I was just going to get a pizza." He stands to leave, fishing around in his pockets for a second. "Do you know if Rafallo's is delivering today?"

Steve rises from the table, dropping the hard disk of bread in his hand.

"Hang on, let me go check."

Steve heads into the kitchen, where Gary, even though he's delicately sliding the turkey back into the oven, is shaking his head back and forth.

"Oh, come on!" Steve says loudly, with as much force as he can put into a whisper.

"No, Steve. No. No."

"But why not? We've got more than enough food. And Whitney's going to be *your* guest. Why can't I have one?"

"Because *I* bought all this crap. *I'm* the one who's been stressing out all morning hoping this shit's going to turn out. I'm not saying he can't stay here and have dinner. That's fine. But you can join him for a slice of pizza. I'll just make this whole meal to go and eat it at Whitney's."

Steve steps back and leans against the counter, which is riddled with cooking utensils, spices, and even a brand new turkey baster, which Gary had bought at the store the day before.

"Look," Gary says softly, "I know he's your friend and all, but . . . I don't like him."

"Why not? It's not like you've ever really spent any time with him. Come on . . . so it won't be the day you planned . . . so what?"

Steve knows he's hurting Gary's feelings, that this day is something Gary has been looking forward to for a long time. Recipes had been clipped, food bought days ago, and it was bad enough that Mark dropped out at the last second to spend the day with Corinne's parents. He wasn't even Sam's biggest fan, but Steve didn't want to be alone while Gary had Whitney.

"He's not going to ruin it, is he?" Gary asks warily. "Because I really want to impress Whitney, and I'm not going to go to all the trouble just for him to—"

"No, no," Steve cuts him off, trying to reassure, "I guarantee . . . we'll still have a nice meal. There will just be one more . . . that's all. Okay?"

Gary weighs the decision in his head and, going against his better judgment, acknowledges with a slight shake of his head: Yes.

"Thanks, Gary," Steve says, a smile on his face.

As Steve and Gary enter the living room to give Sam the verdict, they catch him going through a small box of curios collected by the house's owner, Gary spotting a suspicious bulge in Sam's leather coat pocket that wasn't there before.

"Good news, Sam," Steve says, taking a step back and elbowing Gary in the side.

"Oh, yeah," Gary says, pissed off that Steve's making him do the asking. "Since you're not doing anything today, and in the Thanksgiving spirit and all, we wondered if you wouldn't mind joining us for dinner."

Sam takes a small Lalique crystal sculpture of an elephant from the wooden box and begins tossing it from hand to hand.

"Well, that all depends," he says slowly. "What're you having?"

"It's Thanksgiving," Gary angrily responds. "What do you *think* we're having?"

In his mind's eye Gary spots himself rushing for Sam, knocking him down with one swift punch, and then stuffing his prostrate body into the garbage behind the spider-infested laundry room.

"Yeah, sure, I mean, I *guess* I can stay," Sam finally says, as if mulling over all of the day's invitations in his head, ruefully concluding that in life there are just so many social engagements and so little time. "But I don't want to be a freeloader or anything. Why don't you let me run out and get something for the meal. We need anything else?"

Gary's both touched and surprised by Sam's offer.

"Actually," Steve says, "wasn't Mark going to get us something for dessert before he bailed?"

"Speaking of, where is the Stravinsky of Stratocasters?"

Gary crosses the room to where Sam has just put his feet on top of a cookbook opened to the section headed FOWL, and grabs the tome from beneath his boots.

"He plays a Jaguar, and he's at his girlfriend's parents' house."

"He got a better offer," Steve says lightly, trying to defuse the look Gary's shooting across the room to their guest.

"A better offer?" Sam says sarcastically. "Geez, that's hard to believe."

There's silence for a second as Gary retreats into the kitchen to check on his meal. He emerges a minute later.

"Okay, a pie. Why don't you get us a pie? Apple." He shakes his head slowly as if he'd considered the matter a long time. "Yes, an apple pie."

"Sounds great." Sam claps his hands as he gets up. "I know a great little bakery that's not too far from here." He points his fist in the shape of a pistol at Steve. "Hey, kid, you want to ride shot-gun?"

Steve looks at Gary before answering.

"Yeah, go, it's cool. It'll give me a chance to finish everything. I'll see you guys in a little while."

Sam begins heading out the door, with Steve trailing along behind him.

"Be back soon!" Steve calls out.

"Yeah, yeah." Gary turns and heads back into the kitchen, where he thinks he smells something burning.

Outside, Sam has a sly look on his face as he slips into his Chevy. They get in, and without a word, Sam pulls away from the curb, heading down Sierra Bonita, then making a left at Fountain. It's not until ten minutes into the trip that either of them says anything.

"So, how's the record coming?"

"It's not. Well, it is, sort of."

"Trouble"—Sam reaches an arm out the window and waves it in the warm air—"in paradise?"

"You could say that."

"Tell Sammy everything." He takes a right at Vermont.

"It's just, I'm beginning to think this whole thing was a mis-take. I have no idea what's happened to Mark. He can't cut it in the studio, and he'd rather hang out with his new girlfriend than with us. It's like, you start a band with your best friends, only to slowly start to hate them."

Sam pulls his car in front of the Skandinavia Bakery, which has a wedding cake in the window along with a tray filled with cookies, croissants, and loaves of fisherman bread.

"I think you deserve a break today."

"A break?" Steve asks. "Today?"

Sam just grins and opens his wallet wide, exposing two twenties, a five, and a ten. He reaches in and hands Steve the ten-dollar bill.

"This'll cover the pie. The rest is for heroin. Don't forget, apple."

Steve gets out of the car but, standing on the curb, pokes his head through the window.

"Apple . . . heroin?"

Sam begins laughing.

"Yeah, apple-heroin pie." He takes the last cigarette out of a pack, lights it, and throws the empty container into the street. "You're funny, kid."


Traveling over the hill on Cahuenga Boulevard, Corinne calls out names of towns as they pass through each set of city limits, though nothing really changes.

"Okay," she says as they cruise through the light at Bareham, "Burbank." A minute and a half later she announces, "Toluca Lake."

"Nice, I guess."

"Don't get used to it, it ain't going to last, *oops,* you see? Now we're in North Hollywood. See Hanna-Barbera? See Jerry's Deli?"

Mark sort of hums, glancing out the window at the packed restaurants, the strip malls overflowing despite the holiday. Even the outskirts of a twenty-three-theater multiplex, perched atop the same hill that boasts Universal Studios, an amphitheater, and state-of-the-art video, record, and souvenir stores, is clogged with traffic, too many cars and not enough space.

"Sherman Oaks," Corinne says as a hot dog stand Mark recognizes from a Tom Petty video comes into view, followed on the opposite side of the street by an old movie theater turned into a Gap clothing store. "Woodland Hills. Ah, now it's probably safe to hop on the freeway."

"Wow," Mark finally says, amazed. "In Virginia there's a town, then some fields, grass, trees, maybe a cow or two, and then another town. They're all at least ten minutes apart. Like, if you miss the turnoff after Mechanicsville for Kitty, you have to go clear to Ellerson before you can turn around and head back. If people are afraid to merge on the highways in Virginia, it's because they don't know how. There's maybe a dozen off ramps in the whole state. But here . . ." He glances up at a green sign with reflective letters as Corinne hops onto the freeway for the remaining miles. "De Soto, Winetka, Topanga, there's not a minute that goes by without some jerk with a *Welcome to California Now Go Home* bumper sticker dumped in front of you with his blinker on, wanting in." He leans back into the deep, contoured seat and closes his eyes, the alcohol putting him close to sleep. The various brake lights flashing on and off all around him and the headlights of the oncoming traffic, barely peeking over the formidable center divider, seep through even his closed eyelids and appear as floating pinpoints of light in his dark world.

"God," Corinne exclaims, just to make sure Mark's still awake, "the sun's setting at *four* in the afternoon now. Can you believe it?"

She downshifts prematurely as she cruises down the off ramp at Woodman. Mark jolts forward, caught by his seat belt, which locks the second he's sent careening to the dashboard.

"Well, we're here." She pulls up to a large two-storey house with French shutters set on a quiet side street, two lefts and a right from the hustle and bustle of Ventura Boulevard. "A half an hour and five zip codes later."

They both get out of the car and meet at the grille of her radiator, where her VW hood ornament would be if it hadn't been stolen a week ago.

"You sure you're ready for this?" Corinne asks, moving in to straighten Mark's tie, only it's pushed up so tight there's not any slack and it won't budge.

"Sure." Mark gasps for a breath. "Why do you ask?"

Corinne just grins and takes his hand, leading him down a winding inlaid stone path skirted on both sides by white flood-lights housed in black plastic cones.

"Nice place," Mark says, looking around at the well-manicured lawn, a rose garden peeking out behind a stiff-as-a-crew-cut hedge, "nice, nice place."

Corinne shrugs and rings the doorbell, which chimes a semi-familiar tune.

"Yeah, I guess," she says, checking her hair in the beveled glass set into the oak door, "but it's not like *I* grew up here. They only moved here two summers ago."

Footsteps are heard from the inside, a set of high heels clattering on the dark parquet floor, and the song from the doorbell only now stops chiming.

"Jesus, what *was* that?" Mark asks.

"'Theme from *Love Story*,'" Corinne says as she sees a small shimmering figure wearing an apron through the frosted cut glass, "my mom's favorite song."

Before Mark can reply that his mother also had a favorite song, but you didn't see her programming her goddamn door to spew it throughout the whole house every time the paper boy needed another two dollars, the door swings open and an older, smaller version of Corinne stands wringing her not-too-wrinkled hands on the edge of a red-and-white checkered apron that reads WORLD'S GREATEST DAD.

"Merry Thanksgiving!" the woman says, beaming, craning her neck for a kiss on the cheek.

"Hi, Mom." Corinne gives her a perfunctory peck, and then says, "And it's 'Merry Christmas,' Mom, *not* 'Merry Thanksgiving.'"

Mark sort of nods, unsure if he should offer his hand or not. Instead he wipes his feet on the doormat and enters, Corinne's mother closing the door behind him. She turns to Mark, acknowledging his presence even though he hasn't been formally introduced, and says, "Well, why *can't* it be 'Merry Thanksgiving'? After all, we've got so much to be *merry* about. Right?"

Mark laughs at the bounding spirit of Corinne's mother, the way it seems he's already been accepted and hasn't even said a word.

*Geez, she's really nice,* Mark thinks as he smiles, nodding along with Corinne's mother, who's still laughing and still wiping her hands. *She's not at all like Corinne described her. She doesn't seem so bad.*

"Hey, what's all the noise in here?" A voice booms from another room. "I can barely hear the ball game."

"Oh, Martin, our guests have arrived." Corinne's mother finally leaves her apron alone, joining her husband by his side.

"You must be Mark," Corinne's father heartily says, switching a rocks glass from his right hand to his left in order to greet Mark. Mark shakes Martin's hand and is relieved to discover he's not one of those men's men who feels that a simple handshake is a wrestling match with fewer rules and tries to crush every bone in your wrist to claim victory. Martin's grasp is warm, if not slightly wet, snug enough to register confidence.

"Yes sir, that's me." Mark laughs as Corinne stands awkwardly by.

As they all stand there in the foyer, Mark compares Corinne to her mother. He can spot where a few of Corinne's traits have been derived from her father, her eyes, mostly, along with the square shape of her shoulders, but her nose, mouth, and jawline look exactly like her mother's. Even their hair, a deep brown with natural blond streaks, is nearly identical, and if Corinne had gone with her first instinct of wearing it up instead of pulling out her tortoiseshell hair clip only minutes before they left, mother and daughter would have been able to pass as sisters.

"Forget the *Mr.* bologna, Mark. You can call me Marty. And this is just Pat," he says, putting his arm around his wife. They make a good couple, all smiles and clean, healthy complexions.

Mark wonders how much of the picture is accurate. "You know, we've heard a lot about you."

Mark sort of laughs, thinking, *Why does everyone say that in every situation? And why am I always left to say, "Well, I hope it's been good"?* He sighs and plays along with the script that was written too long ago to be argued with.

"Well," he ventures, "I hope it's *all* been good."

The three of them laugh on cue and finally it's Corinne's silence that signals the rest of them to restrain themselves.

"Corinne, why don't you show him around," her mother says, returning her hands to the wringing of her apron, "and then come on in the kitchen and give me a hand while the boys get to know each other a little better?"

"Okay, *Pat,*" Corinne snidely says, turning and grabbing Mark by the starched sleeve.

As they begin up the stairs her father heads back into the den, where the game is waiting for him, and her mother calls out to Corinne's retreating figure, "Oh, *you.*"

"Boy, Corinne, I don't see what you're always complaining about," Mark tries to whisper, unsure of the acoustics of the house. "But your mom seems cool to me."

"Sheesh," Corinne says in a huff as she leads Mark up the stairs. "Did you see the way she kept clutching at that damn apron? Like it was a security blanket or something?" Corinne absentmindedly swings her Chanel belt buckle in a small orbit around her belly button. "Man, I tell you, one of these days that old facial tic's going to come back and then she'll be sorry . . ."

As Corinne continues with her matricidal monolog, Mark marvels at the artwork hanging on the walls.

*They have so many paintings that they hang them in the god-damn stairwell?*

He comes to a large Impressionist oil painting of a woman holding a small child, and he swears he's seen it before on a postcard in a museum gift shop back in Virginia. He leans in close and runs his fingers over the canvas, poking at the deep grooves of paint with his fingers, thinking, *Is this for real?*

Corinne stops suddenly on the top step and turns to Mark, who's picking at the *C* in *Cassatt* with his thumbnail.

"Besides, she's just pissed off I didn't buy *her* an apron. I think she wears it just to spite me."

"Take it easy, Corinne." He places his hand in the small of her back and rubs it in circles, trying to calm her down. "I think you're just being touchy."

"Touchy, my ass. Oh, there's a guest bedroom, a bathroom, a linen closet, I guess. No big deal."

Mark breaks away and heads down the hall, heading for a set of double doors.

"What's in here?"

"That's *their* bedroom."

Corinne glides in front of him and opens the doors, which lead into a room larger than the entire floor plan of Mark's rented house back in Virginia.

"Wow," he gasps, pouring into the room like escaping steam, clinging to the walls, searching out every corner. "These windows are cool"—he points to a large pane of glass that looks out over a well-tended backyard with a gazebo but, he's surprised, no pool—"but can you open them?"

"No," Corinne says, bored, "the whole house is climate controlled. It drives me up the fucking wall every time I come here. You can't get any *real* air. It's disgusting."

"Yeah," Mark mumbles, examining the point where the window meets the frame, sealed with a thick line of black rubber.

He walks around the bed and through the mazelike bathroom, where two sinks are set into a large countertop, which looks like real marble.

"Is this a bidet?" he screams to the other room, where Corinne is sitting Indian-legged on the Persian rug. "I've never seen one of those before. Can I try it?"

"Real funny, Mark. Come out of there."

"Aw, you're no fun." He emerges a few seconds later, wiping an imaginary stream of water out of the seat of his pants. "Hey, what are these?"

Corinne turns and sees he's discovered the fireplace, which is aligned with the large bed. Atop the mantel are the usual embarrassing childhood photos: Corinne in AYSO soccer, all freckles and braces; her junior high school years painfully documented in various pictures of geeky poses. On the end is the largest photo of the bunch.

Her hair is strawberry blond and her skin almost pink, delicate; like Bible paper, it might rip if you tugged on it too hard. Her smile is huge, as if propped open with a roof beam, her eyes just a squint because she's clamping them so hard, her cheeks fleshy blushing hemispheres with each dimple a small cave. On top of her head is a paper crown, the fake gold glinting off the blue satin strips of ribbon that intertwine with the lacy white cotton of the dress. She's probably about five in the photo, taken, Mark hopes, on an Easter or a relative's birthday (or was she dressed up like this *every* weekend?), and the photo has aged and yellowed in the ensuing two decades. The glass is dull and the gilded frame needs Brasso in the ornate corners. Fresh fingerprints on an expanse of shiny metal shows where the item is picked up regularly.

"I'm his little princess," Corinne coos as she puts the frame aside and moves on to another, a family portrait during her high school years, her brown hair dyed orangish blond and her long bangs parted in the middle and feathered back like two wings, covering each ear.

At the end of the photo-covered mantel Corinne sees an oval wooden box painted a deep hunter green, the lid of which is decorated with a trim of white lace around the edge and a decoupage of cutouts from a Rembrandt postcard on top. She opens the container, finding inside, along with an extra set of house keys, a broken watchband, and a few batteries of various voltages, a small packet of photos stuffed inside a Thrifty's envelope. Corinne remembers sending it to her mother a week before she met Mark. It contains every photo of Tim and Tim and her together, save for the one in the living room of her apartment. She spots the note she'd scrawled on the back in all capital letters with a pen so black and deep it looks like a brand on the white-gummed flap of the envelope:

*MOM, DON'T THROW THESE PHOTOS AWAY BUT DON'T LOOK AT THEM EITHER. JUST HANG ON TO THEM FOR ME. I CAN'T HAVE THEM IN THE HOUSE RIGHT NOW. THANKS.*

"Something wrong?" Mark asks, grabbing her from behind, his arms around her waist and his head on her shoulder.

"No." She fumbles with the photos, stuffing them back in, then the lid of the box, whose size seems at odds with the base and doesn't want to fit. "No," she repeats, finally squeezing the thin wood of the box to match the shape of the top, "not at all."

Mark nestles his nose between her earlobe and neck, nibbling at the soft skin, making wet trails with his tongue, and then lightly biting with his two front teeth. Corinne smiles. It *does* feel good, but she's sad at the thought of her former life stuffed into the box on the mantel like something being buried alive.

"Well," she says, "better head downstairs."

She leads Mark out of the room and down to the first floor, uncomfortably holding his hand the entire way.

"See you in a little bit?" he says in a light tone.

"Hopefully," she answers back.

Corinne watches as Mark walks down a hallway, still visibly affected by the alcohol, following the white noise of a crowd cheering before he disappears through the doorway that leads into the den. She swallows hard and heads in the opposite direction, finding her mother in the kitchen, placing a green, white-cottage-cheese-specked Jell-O casserole into the refrigerator to cool.

"So," her mother says tentatively, avoiding Mark, the obvious topic of discussion, "how's . . . work?"

"Work's . . . good." Silence. "Oh, Quincy finally got the courage to ask out that guy Elliott." Corinne hops onto a stool at the square island that contains the stove in the middle of the large room. "I told you about all that, remember?"

"Oh, yes," her mother replies, crumbling sausage over a pile of dried and cubed white bread. "I think I remember you saying something about that."

Corinne catches sight of the kitchen sink, which is immaculate even though her mother's been cooking all morning. The KitchenAid mixer she used for the pumpkin pie this morning is already scrubbed clean and sitting in its place on the shelf behind the wood-and-glass cabinet doors, along with the double boiler she used for the homemade cranberry sauce (chilling in the fridge since eight) and the sparkling Cuisinart that aided in slicing and dicing all of the vegetables for the dressing.

*Everything in its place* — Corinne sighs — *as always.*

"So, uh, how have things been around here?" Corinne asks as she pulls down the oven door and bastes the turkey, emptying the contents of the large plastic eyedropper over the cheese-cloth-covered bird.

"Oh, fine, fine," Pat says as she takes a frying pan from the stove top and pours the sizzling sautéed celery and onions over the bread and sausage. She sprinkles salt, pepper, and poultry seasoning over the big bowl before mixing it up with her hands, smarting at the still-warm touch of the butter on her fingers. "I've been thinking of taking some classes, so . . ."

Silence fills the room until a buzzer goes off and Corinne rushes for the oven, pulling out a pumpkin pie from the wire rack beneath the turkey.

"Ah ah ah," her mother says as if the word were skidding. She slaps away her daughter's hand, leaving a grease mark on Corinne's wrist, and sticks a butter knife into the top of the pie. Pat retracts the knife a second later, some of the pie's terra-cotta filling clinging to the silvery surface. Corinne's mother frowns and turns back to the stuffing without a word while Corinne slides the pie back into the oven.

Five more minutes pass before a word is said, and then it is only an innocuous subject changer, anything to throw the light off them, and it is Corinne: "So, I wonder what the boys are up to . . ."

•   •   •

Mark stands poised in the antechamber to the den, a small vestibule decorated on either side with dark green-and-red prints of fox hunts and mallards, the plaid brown-and-blue wallpaper matching the flannel shirt he almost wore. He can see Martin's hand poking out from the side of a wing chair, fingers gripping the padded arm as he cheers on the advancing team.

"Is this still the Detroit game?" Mark asks, holding back a burp.

"Huh?" Corinne's father sticks his head out from the highback chair and sees his guest, not recognizing him at first. "Oh, no. Now we've moved on to the Cowboys. Come on in here and sit down."

Mark scoots in between Martin's long legs, resting on an ottoman, and the television, and plops down on a deep brown leather couch.

"You *like* football?" the man asks.

"Oh, sure." Mark, trying to get comfortable, leans into the soft couch, which squeaks with every centimeter he moves. "My dad used to drive me out to RFK for Redskin games on my birthdays when I was a kid, but I don't get a chance to follow it as much now as I used to."

"That's a shame, Mark. A shame." Martin says it as if Mark had admitted that he couldn't read. "I *used* to play, you know. For the Bruins."

"Really?" Mark says politely, crossing his legs. As Corinne's father drones on about his glory days—wishbone offense, team spirit, and Hail Mary passes at both wide receivers and coeds—Mark slowly tunes out the man's voice, his own thoughts racing in his head. He stares into Corinne's father's eyes, which are darting around the room, on Mark one second, on his old high school track-and-field trophies the next.

*The things I've done to your daughter,* Mark thinks. *The things other men have done. And will do.*

Martin gets up and moves to the bar, which is festooned with photos, these even older than the ones upstairs, predating Corinne's arrival. The liquor in Mark's empty stomach that

Corinne had warned about earlier is taking over. When Mark moves to uncross his legs he slides halfway down the leather couch, the long hair on the back of his head sticking on the upholstery as his body cruises for the floor. Quickly he scoots up, his hands squeaking against the oily grain as he hoists himself back into position. Martin turns to see what all the noise is but only finds Mark, his legs still crossed, a strained smile on his face and a few strands of hair on the back of his head frizzed out wildly.

"As I was saying . . ."

Mark hasn't been listening, so when Corinne's father puts down the photo of himself and his wife standing on the banks of the Seine, fading blue ink in the corner reading *Honeymoon '64,* and approaches him, bending at the waist and leaning into his ear to speak, Mark nearly jumps to the bearskin rug sprawled out on the floor.

"One word," Corinne's father says.

"Huh?" Mark stumbles, trying to catch up. "Excuse me?"

"One word," the older man repeats, desperately trying not to lap himself in the joke and crack up before delivering the punch line, like he usually does.

"What?" Mark says again. He feels at once drowsy and light-headed. The few inhibitions he has are beginning to peel away, held up only by the last restraints of his dwindling sobriety. "Your daughter is hot . . . ," Mark has to stop himself from saying. "Great in the hay, great . . . in . . . the . . . hay."

"One word," Martin says again, beginning to prematurely articulate, the guffaw already on his lips. "One word: plastics."

Mark sits there, silent, hands on his knees. Corinne's father marches around the room, laughing uproariously. Noticing that Mark is not joining him, he stops and turns to his young guest.

"Don't you get it?"

"Get what?"

"What I said? It's that line from *The Graduate.* You know, out by the pool, the friend of the father's? Sure, I know I'm *the* father and not the *friend* of a father, and you're not graduating

and are even a little older than Benjamin was"—he's going in
mental circles, trying to explain the connections—"but still, I
thought it apropos."

"Oh, *The Graduate*. Nope, I never saw that. I'm not that into
*older* movies."

Martin looks wounded, as if stabbed with the arrow of Mark's
youth.

"Well, geez, kid, I'm not talking about the silent version of
*Napoleon*. This was the sixties, for chrissakes."

"But, uh . . . ," Mark begins, unsure if he should volunteer the
date of his birth. "I wasn't even *alive* in the sixties." He watches
as Corinne's father licks his wounds in the corner of the room,
examining a photo of himself in his UCLA football uniform,
fake-throwing a pass for the camera, and it must be going on
thirty years ago now. Mark licks his lips, and the acidy alcohol
still lingering from before stings a cold sore on the upper part of
his mouth. For no reason he goes in for the kill.

"Sir, what does *apropos* mean?"

In the kitchen Corinne's mother folds her apron neatly into
eighths and says, "I like him."

"Let's not start, Mom," Corinne says, as if exhausted. "We've
been down this road before and it just dead-ends, remember?"

"Who's going down a road?" her mother innocently asks. She
takes a sponge from the sink and wipes down the countertops
even though they're still clean from when she scrubbed them
ten minutes ago. "I was just saying that I like him."

"Well, you don't *need* to like him."

"Really?" her mother says slyly, her patience paying off. "Why
not?"

"Because he's not staying around."

"Not this one, either, huh?" Corinne's mother says slowly.

"He's a musician. He's only in town to make a record. Then
he's, uh, leaving. I guess."

Corinne moves to leave herself, but the stiff arm of her
mother stops her.

"Tell me, how do you find them?"

"Find *who*?" Corinne asks, biting her lip.

"These men of yours." Her mother jerks her head in the direction of the other room, where Mark's loud laugh can be heard along with her father's. "The ones that are always, you know, 'Sorry, love, can't stay. Shipping out in the morning.' The last one ran off to Arizona to make some movie, and now this one's just passing through town *and* your life. My heavens, I'm waiting for you to meet a man in the French Foreign Legion."

"Mom, don't."

"All I want to know"—her voice is steady and calm—"is why you lead your love life like any young man walking down the street has the right to kiss you and move in for a couple of weeks."

"Mom, that's not what's—"

"Happening? Let me tell you what's happening, *Corinne,* because you've kept me on the outside for so long that I've got a hell of a view from where I am."

"You know, Mom, there's still really a lot to do." Corinne quickly turns to the counter. "You haven't even *started* the potatoes, and Daddy must be dying for the relish tray about now."

Pat crosses the kitchen and gets close to her daughter at the counter, grabbing a still-dirt-encrusted brown potato, off-white twinelike strands growing out from a few eyes, and tosses it into the sink along with a pile of carrot peels.

"Listen to me, Corinne, you're twenty-four now and I think it's about time this *Love for Sale* attitude of yours came to an end. You hear me?"

"Love for sale? Jesus Christ, what in the fuck are you talking about?"

Her mother's eyes fly open and bleed red.

"Don't you talk that way in my house!" Pat nearly screams, as if Corinne's saying the word *fuck* were as big a crime as wasting her life, which, to her mother, it is.

Steve's hands are trembling as he sets the pie down on the floorboard of the Chevy and Sam speeds away from the curb, bald tires squealing and failing, at first, to connect with the pavement.

"So, wh-wh-where are we going?"

"To score." Sam takes a drag on his cigarette, which is two puffs away from being just a filter.

"And, uh, what is it we're scoring again . . ."—Steve shifts uneasily in his seat—"exactly?"

Sam makes a left-hand turn but leans his face in the opposite direction, toward Steve.

"You heard me."

"But . . . I don't know if I should . . ."

"Look, kid, you turned me down the other night. I won't take no for an answer. You hear me?"

Steve watches as the neighborhood segues into sleazy, run-down tenements and risk-your-life liquor stores. Sam hops on the 101 Freeway, getting off at Alvarado Street, hanging a left. He gets caught behind a bus momentarily stopped to unload and load holiday travelers, and Sam, already edgy, leans his head outside the window and yells, "Goddamn it, you assholes, get out of the fucking road!"

A minute later Steve asks, "So, where do you get the stuff?"

"Bonnie Brae," Sam says plainly.

"Oh, is that like a, uh, store?"

Sam laughs, "Geez, kid, you really do crack me up." He turns to face him for a second. "No, it's not a store, it's a street. Bonnie Brae, a few blocks south of Beverly. *That's* where we're headed. In fact . . ." He grabs the wheel with his right hand and sends his left digging into his back pockets for his wallet. He hands it to Steve.

"Let's get three balloons. That way I can have two, but you'll just need one."

"Yeah, uh, okay, three." Steve stares at the gaping wallet. "So how much would that be, like, all together?"

"Fifteen per." Sam sighs, disappointed by Steve's inexperience. "Forty-five. Okay, here we are."

On the far corner is a liquor store, the front of which is home to a phone booth without a receiver or directory and a few kids wearing gang attire and sitting astride low-rider bicycles.

"Now, the first block is crack. The second block is smack. You got that?"

"Why are you telling me this?"

Sam grins, turning right onto Bonnie Brae, heading past the cocaine dealers.

"Just in case you want to come here yourself someday."

"Don't count on it," Steve says slowly, trying to sink down into his seat. "This is going to be a one-time thing, I hope. Just for the hell of it and nothing else."

"Okay, now we're getting into H territory." The car comes to the top of a gently sloping hill and coasts down the next block. "Okay, where's my guy? Where's my guy?"

Sam's bloodshot eyes scan the sidewalks, which, to Steve's amazement, are also filled with families casually strolling, some even with baby carriages in tow, weaving in and out of the youths peddling drugs from their ten-speeds.

"Aha." Sam pulls his car over to the side of the road. "Bingo."

Sam's dirty car is not stopped for more than a second before a Latino youth rushes to the window.

"Three," Sam says plainly, as if to a maître d' at a restaurant.

The kid outside the window takes the $45 and then leans in and spits into Sam's palm. The youth disappears back into the shadows of the sidewalk and Sam pulls off, hanging a right at the bottom of the hill.

"That's it?" Steve asks, somewhat amazed.

"That's it. Here, you hang on to these."

Sam dumps the contents of his hand into Steve's lap. Steve picks up the tiny balloons one by one. Each is slightly wet, barely a quarter of an inch in diameter, the drug obviously scrunched at the bottom of the rubbery receptacle, tied off at the end. One is blue, another red, the last an off-white.

*Fifteen bucks apiece?* Steve thinks. *For this?*

"How come he had these in his mouth?" Steve asks as he wipes off each balloon, storing them in his shirt pocket.

"That way, if the cops come by he can just swallow them. And retrieve them at a later date, if you know what I mean." The Chevy stops at a bustling intersection with a McDonald's on one corner, while families cluster at an overcrowded bus stop. "I heard you can even score at this intersection."

"Here?" Steve asks as they pull away, turning around to see a young black girl in a pretty yellow dress be dragged by her mom into the RTD bus that has heaved to a stop at the red-striped curb.

"Yeah." Sam sighs. "But I prefer good ol' Bonnie Brae. That is, when my dealer doesn't return my fucking pages, like today. Oh, wait"—he guides the car into the parking lot of a 7-Eleven—"one more stop."

Sam quickly hops out of the car, leaving the engine running and Steve feeling paranoid with the drugs lying against his chest. A minute later Sam hops back into the car and tosses a blue-and-pink rectangular box of aluminum foil onto Steve's lap.

"What's this for?"

"You'll see." Sam backs out of the spot with a devilish grin on his face.

Back at the house Sam and Steve run into Gary and Whitney just as they're heading out the door, about to get into the purple rental car.

"Where are you two headed?" Steve asks, holding the pie in his hands.

"I forgot to get stuff for gravy. I thought I could just make it from the drippings and some flour, but I put the turkey a little too close to the heating coils, and, like, there *are* no drippings. Whitney says there's a Mayfair market around the corner that's open."

"It's expensive," Whitney says, trying to make a joke and seem easygoing around Steve, whom she's never really talked to, and Sam, a total stranger, "but it *is* open."

"I'm just going to get some gravy in a jar, and a can of Easy-Off oven cleaner." He spots the foil held between Sam's arm and body. "What's that for?"

"Leftovers." Sam grins, leading the way into the house.

"Yeah," Steve says awkwardly, "see you in a, uh, bit."

Once inside, Sam rushes for the couch, breaking the seal on the foil, little pellets of dried glue underneath the flap above the metal serrated cutter.

"Why don't you undo the balloons while I get the pipes ready?"

Steve sits down opposite him as Sam tears off four squares of foil and spreads them on a coffee table in the middle of the living room. He then gets up and marches around the apartment for a second, looking for something.

"What do you need?"

"A pen, like a regular ballpoint pen."

"There, on the table."

"Huh?" Sam twists and, scanning the room, finds it. He sits back down on the couch and pulls two of the four squares toward him. He places the pen at the lip of the curling foil, places his fingers against the edge of both the aluminum and the pen, and rolls the metallic material toward Steve, using the pen as a spine. Then he slides out the pen and hands the delicate layered cylinder to Steve. "There's your pipe."

"Look, Sam, I don't know if I should."

"Why shouldn't you, kid? Gary's got his girlfriend. All *you've* got is *me*. So let's have some fun. How's your little task coming?"

"Huh?"

Sam points to Steve's hands, where he's just been holding the three balloons for the last five minutes.

"It's hard to smoke the shit when it's still in the fucking balloons."

"Oh, yeah," Steve apologizes. "Sorry."

Steve fiddles with the knot on the neck of the first balloon. After a few seconds he gets a good grip and untangles the rubbery pretzel. He then holds the open balloon over the table, trying to shake its contents out.

"It's easier if you just turn it inside out, or else cut the fucking thing open, but the way you're doing it," Sam says, his voice containing an edge not present before, "you're never going to get it."

"Heh, heh," Steve sort of mumbles and then takes Sam's advice and turns the balloon inside out, finding inside a smallish clump of something wrapped inside a blue square of cellophane. He discards the sky blue sheath and finds a gooey mash of black licorice.

"Now, let's see if they dicked us over." Sam leans over and inspects the portion. "No, it doesn't look too bad. Let's just hope it's at least seventy percent pure or else we'll be puking our guts out."

"Puking?" Steve asks.

"Yeah, or rather, *you'll* be puking. I'm pretty used to bad shit, and the worse thing that will happen for me is that I just won't get stoned, which, actually, now that I think about it, *would* be a tragedy. Now, we need either a CD case or, what works really well is, like, a video card."

"Oh wait, I've got one of those." Steve perks up, finally being able to be a help. He draws from his wallet his mother's membership card from the Video Express, back in Kitty.

"Perfect," Sam says. "Now, why don't you fetch me a little knife from the kitchen, and a lighter for yourself?"

Steve jumps up and grabs a smallish utility knife from the cutting board, where it sits alongside a squash that's only half julienned, and a violet disposable lighter from a drawer beside the stove.

"Now, what you do is . . ." Sam takes the semihard pellet of heroin and smears it onto the smooth, laminated surface of the card. He then takes the knife and, as if cutting himself a slice of brie to slather upon a Ritz cracker, cuts a small portion of the substance from the larger whole and then wipes it on the foil square placed in front of Steve. He then repeats the process, cutting himself a bigger portion.

"Okay, now . . . get your pipe and lighter. You've got enough there for a few hits, but don't blow your wad all at once. Hold the pipe between your lips because you're going to need both hands."

Steve takes the metallic straw in his mouth, careful not to squash the opening.

"Hold the foil just below the end of your pipe, with the opening just over the hit. Put some flame underneath, and when you see it smoking, inhale."

"Sure," Steve says, nervous. "Simple."

He steadies his pipe over the black wisp of heroin wiped onto the foil, then puts the lighter beneath the hit and lights it. The drug sizzles quickly, like a pat of butter tossed into a hot pan, smoking and shriveling up. He reacts a second too late, most of the smoke rising to the ceiling, leaving Steve to grasp at the tail with his pipe pointed upward like FDR in those photos with his cigarette clenched between dying teeth, aimed toward the heavens.

"Good start, kid, but you've got to be quicker. Light and inhale at the *same* time, otherwise you'll miss it. Watch."

Sam takes the pipe in his lips, lifts up the foil, and flicks the dial on his own lighter. The drug crackles and shrinks like it did for Steve, only Sam takes in every shred of toxic air, his pipe twirling around in a Hooverish motion.

"You see?"

Sam dishes out another hit for both of them. Steve readies his lighter and pipe and tries to concentrate. This time, just as Sam had said, he combines both actions that he had kept separate before, inhaling the second his thumb grinds the flint wheel of the cheap lighter, sending the flame grating against the foil, on the other side of which lies a small dollop of heroin. He gets a pretty good hit, his mouth filling quickly with the drug, where it stays for a half a second before he swallows it into his lungs.

The taste is at first totally disgusting, then hearty, like ashes from a fire, then curiously citrusy, fruity almost.

"Is this like a pot thing?" Steve asks in a croak, trying to not let out air as he speaks. "Where I hold it in as long as I can?"

"Of course, dumb shit."

Sam takes a long hit and, while the smoke is still in his lungs, cuts off a slice of the drug and streaks the blade of the utility knife against his swatch of foil just a half an inch away from his last hit. He holds the square taut and brings the lighter to the underside, taking a gigantic hit.

Steve exhales and marvels at the unpleasant aftertaste.

"Jesus, man, this shit *coats*."

"What do you mean?" Sam's already readying two more hits for himself and another for Steve, the contents of the first balloon almost already gone.

"It's like, it tastes really gross at first, like industrial, but then it softens and tastes really organic. Sort of chocolately, almost. Or like teriyaki."

Sam takes another hit and considers.

"I never really thought of it like that, but now that you say so, sure, I can kind of taste that." He smacks at his gums. "Anyway, open another balloon."

Steve takes another hit, sort of getting used to it, and reaches for the knife, this time just cutting off the top of the balloon and easily getting to the insides. He takes the contents and smears it onto the back of the rental card, in fact, just across his mother's name and address. He gets wistful for a second, seeing the contraband slicked across both his mom's name and signature.

*What would she say if she could see me now?* Steve wonders. *What would she think?*

They sit in silence as Sam dishes out a few more hits for himself and another one or two for Steve, which he politely obliges, one time burning his hand because the lighter is too close to the edge of the foil where he's holding it, and another time sucking at the dry air above a hit of the smack that was already exhausted.

"No, no," Sam says, "if it doesn't smoke, it's done. Cut yourself a new piece and move on. The portions I'm giving you are good for only one or two hits each. Quit milking it."

Ten minutes later there's a just a speck of the third balloon attached to the video rental card. Steve's square of aluminum foil is filled with about a dozen burned-out little circles of expired heroin, while Sam's, who moved on to his second piece after five minutes, is littered with charred streaks, perhaps twenty of them. Sam, content, leans back into the sofa while Steve gets up and puts the foil in the kitchen, taking the tubes and card and knife and stashing it all in a drawer off the dining room.

Outside the door there's a rumbling, and then Gary appears with a bag of groceries, Whitney trailing behind, a smile still on her face, as if she's been wearing one her whole life. Gary enters the room, eyeing both Steve and Sam suspiciously.

"What's that smell?" Gary asks, his nose sniffing wildly and his olfactory senses picking up a scent above all of those emanating from the kitchen.

"Just the turkey, man," Sam says, his eyes just a slit, his body sinking into the warmth, his mood twisting like a leaf in slow motion, this way, then that.

"The turkey?"

Gary tosses the key ring onto the dining room table and then unloads the sack of groceries onto a counter in the kitchen. He sniffs again, but this time all his nose picks up is the stale, charcoalish smell of the burned bird.

"Uh, Gary honey, I think they're right," Whitney says, lifting her chin in the air and sniffling at the smoky air.

Gary reaches into the brown paper sack and grabs for the jar of Heinz Country Style Gravy before disappearing into the kitchen.

Whitney, left behind, tries to make conversation.

"So, what did you guys do while we were gone?"


Throughout the dinner Mark could not concentrate on the small talk that Corinne and her mother and father were engaging in, guilelessly leaving Mark out of the details, which involved friends of theirs whom he could not possibly know and which they did not explain. Instead he thought of the photo he had seen upstairs, the photo of Corinne as a small child.

"I can't believe he told that damn junior high story *again*," Corinne says gruffly as she pulls out of the driveway.

Mark just stares at Corinne's parents, standing on the lawn

waving good-bye, both with a drink in their hand, as the preprogrammed sprinklers go on, and they have to rush inside the house, their calves drizzled with wet spots. He thinks of Laura, his last girlfriend, as a child.

In the photo he had seen, Laura's hair was practically glowing bright yellow ("From playing in the sun," she had said when she discovered him looking at it one afternoon at her grandparents' house), parted in the middle and sternly pulled back, bobbing pigtails barely visible. Her smile, like Corinne's, was also fierce, as if recrimination lay ahead for the girls who did not put one hundred percent effort into their grins, and the front row of her teeth, jutting out slightly due to a mild overbite, bit lightly into her incredibly pink, fleshy lips, a tooth missing a space away from her two chalklike front teeth.

Then there was Tricia, an old girlfriend from high school. She was the one he lost his virginity with, and for a while he thought he might spend the rest of his life with her. Then he saw her as a child; the photo was of Tricia, about five years old, standing with a shirt but no pants on in a pile of mud outside a double-wide mobile home somewhere in a Virginia forest. Her cheeks were soiled with mud, her look almost frightened, her hair frizzed. The surroundings looked like a junkyard, skeletons of cars and an old washer and dryer in the upper corner, behind where the entire house could be hitched up to a truck and just hauled away. "Camping?" Mark asked hopefully when he saw it. "No," Tricia replied, deadpan. He broke up soon after because he knew he'd always be ashamed, that with every look at her then, or in twenty years, all he would see in her face was the ghost of that scrubby kid, a rube who could never amount to anything more.

"And damn my mom, cornering me in the kitchen like that." Corinne slaps it into fourth gear heading down the quiet street, the trees on either side of the road high and intertwined, blocking out the moon and stars. "Like *she* should talk."

Corinne glances at him queerly as she hangs a left, heading down a side street, on her way to the freeway.

"What's with you? You seem deep in thought. Or rather, deep in something."

Mark takes a second to react. The street signs keep passing, Cahuenga, Vineland, Tujunga, but the landmarks remain the same, McDonald's, Target, Blockbuster Video, the Gap. On the corner of Ventura and Selma a youngish bum, male, white, with a sign that reads WHY LIE? NEED A BEER, stumbles into the path of traffic, and the cars speed up, barely swerving to avoid him. Mark thinks, *Hell of a way to spend Thanksgiving,* referring to himself and not the man in the street.

"I'm not thinking of anything, I guess," he lies. "I'm just . . ." He curls up in the seat, trying to get comfortable. He shuts his eyes and blocks out the scrolling picture in front of him. The cars around him whisk by, the sound of traffic slow and constant, like breaking surf. "It must be the combination of the drinks and that drug in the turkey. I'm just sleepy, that's all."

Corinne looks over at him at a stoplight. He looks cute, curled up in a little ball, not much different than he must have as a small child, in bed with Charlie Brown sheets, waiting for his mother to come tuck him in.

"Is it my parents?" she asks. "Did you really hate them or something?"

"No, no, it's not that. I was just thinking . . . of you, in that photo. The little princess." He laughs ruefully. "And the way your father kept calling you *pumpkin* all during dinner. Pass me the potatoes, *pumpkin.* More turkey, *pumpkin*? How about some more pumpkin pie, *pumpkin*?"

"Oh?" Corinne asks, deeply interested. "And what did you figure out from all that?"

Mark puts his feet on the dash, much to her dismay.

"That you're, you know, Daddy's little girl."

Corinne absorbs this for a second before adding, "I *am* Daddy's little girl. So?"

Mark brings his feet back to the gray floor mat stitched with an embroidered black *VW* in the far left corner. He hooks a finger in the collar of his shirt, pulling it down about an inch to reveal three scratches that have left his skin red and raised in burning, bumpy trails.

"Does Daddy's little girl do things like this?"

"Well," she grins, clamping onto Mark's knee instead of the stick shift, "not that Daddy knows."

"But still." Mark chuckles again. "That photo."

"Oh that," Corinne says in a funny tone. "Well, I wouldn't give *that* too much thought. After all"—she removes her hand and turns the wheel, switching on the radio with the other— "that was with my *old* nose."

Sitting in his infant buzz, everything in the room annoyingly clear and his thinking almost maddeningly lucid, Steve thinks that the most exciting part of the evening so far has been when he said yes to Sam's offer to do the heroin. The decision made his heart run faster than the inhaled, black tarry drug.

"It's your first time. Don't sweat it, man," Sam had said when he breezed by Steve in the kitchen as they both got out of their seats to dish out potatoes au gratin that Gary deemed too hot to bring to the table. "It'll kick in. Just give it time."

Now Steve's sitting at the dinner table, wolfing down the meal, which is actually pretty good, while Sam just picks at his and Gary, a little pissed off at Sam's lack of hunger and fretting over Whitney's impression of everything, runs back and forth to the kitchen every couple of minutes, trying to make everything perfect.

Steve feels dulled, sure, but that could have come from Gary's lecture on the difference between stuffing cooked inside the bird and stuffing cooked outside the bird. Steve feels high but not stoned.

"I need a drink," he says, rising from the table, wanting a further drug boost out of the eery gravity of the smack. He goes to the kitchen and gets a bottle of Sutter Home white zinfandel. He's always liked this brand but Corinne had made fun of it when she was over a week and a half ago.

"Sure, it doesn't cost much," she said as she examined the label, turning up her nose, "but you get what you pay for."

Steve fumbles with the foil cap, looking for a corkscrew and a knife to break the seal. He opens a few drawers before coming upon the aluminum-foil pipes, hit-streaked squares, the utility knife with still a few smudges of heroin on the blade.

"What are you looking for?" Gary calls out, about to rise from his seat.

"Nothing," Steve shouts back, quickly closing the drawer and running back into the pantry, where he finds the corkscrew lying amidst the spices and a bag of flour.

"Anybody else want some?" he asks when he reenters the dining room, setting down his glass and the bottle right beside it.

"No, thanks," Sam croaks.

"Yeah, none for me, either."

"I'll take a glass," Whitney says, the first time she's spoken in over ten minutes. Half the time there was no one to speak to: Gary was in the oven checking on the green bean casserole (which, an hour into the meal, was still cooking), and Steve and Sam were wedged in their respective drug-filled hazes.

Steve stumbles over to the side of the table, where Gary has positioned Whitney's chair within inches of his, as if tacitly claiming ownership and signaling that she is off-limits to anyone but himself. Whitney politely raises her glass and Steve begins pouring, only his aim is off and a peach-colored line of cool liquid spills out of the glass and onto the table and then Whitney's crushed-velvet sleeve.

"Oh, sorry," Steve says plainly, moving to his own side of the table and filling his wineglass to the brim. Whitney makes an apology, even though she was not to blame, and excuses herself from the table.

Gary assesses the situation, trying to figure out why Steve's acting so strangely and why Sam's reaction to everything is just a wry laugh.

Steve gulps at the wine, pausing only to scoop out portions of the food laid all around the table. He's almost finished with the bottle of wine and his third helping when it first happens. His stomach sort of gurgles. He passes off the sensation to his quick ingestion of the meal, figuring he is experiencing gas bubbles and nothing more. After all, Gary had confused the recipes for ambrosia and succotash and ended up adding whipped cream to the lima beans while folding corn into the grapes and coconut slivers. But then, a few minutes later, it happens again, the pit of his chest violently shifting. He looks around the room and sees Sam in his own little world, sitting silent, while Gary recounts his favorite Thanksgiving memory and Whitney tries hard to seem interested. It happens again, and then a fourth time.

"Be right back," he tries to say in a normal voice, excusing himself and heading for the restroom.

He puts a hand on his gurgling stomach, feeling the movement inside the way he imagines a pregnant woman feels her progeny kick and turn. He kneels in front of the toilet in anticipation, but the moment passes. He stays a few extra seconds to make sure, then gets up, splashes some cold water on his face. While he's examining his dilated pupils in the mirror the symptoms hit him again. His stomach overturns, a gyroscope in the center of his body gone haywire, and this time it's no false alarm.

The wine shoots out of his mouth, leaving his palate soaked in a warm sheath that smells not of grapes but of peaches and apricots. Thinking of the orangish tint of the wine in the bottle and not the blood red it looks now, all mixed with the acids of his stomach and his partially broken-down Thanksgiving dinner, he wonders, *How in the hell do they make white zinfandel, anyway?*

For a few minutes he throws up the wine, followed by varying-sized chunks of Gary's meticulously planned dinner.

Floating like an iceberg on the toilet's shimmering red surface is an almost untouched chunk of stuffing, a large nugget he must have swallowed without chewing that managed to make it back up in one piece and that didn't, to as much surprise as he can muster, choke him.

"You feeling okay, Steve?" Whitney asks when he reenters the room, a large water spot still visible on her dress.

"Yeah, why?"

Gary looks over his roommate, noticing Steve's pasty white face, some dried spittle clinging to the left side of his cracked, chapped mouth.

"You look . . . out of sorts."

"I'm okay," Steve lies.

Sam continues to stare into his plate of uneaten food, the fingertips of one hand each capped with a black olive.

In the next half hour Steve leaves the table four times, three to really puke and another just to roll around on the bathroom floor.

"That's a lot of pisses," Sam says, pushing around an untouched piece of turkey on his plate.

"Well, he *did* drink almost that whole bottle of wine pretty fast."

"Yeah, sure."

Gary begins clearing the dishes when Steve returns from yet another restroom excursion.

"Hey, what are you doing?" Steve asks.

"What the fuck's it look like?" Gary angrily grabs at the large tray holding the turkey, deposits it on a table in the kitchen, and marches back into the dining room, collecting glasses. "Dinner's over."

"But I haven't finished with my ambrositash, or succotasia . . ."

"Ha ha," Gary sarcastically says as he grabs Steve's plate, heads into the kitchen, and tosses it into the trash. Whitney stays in her chair, nervously picking at a jellied fillet of cranberry sauce.

"What did you do that for?"

"Do you really think I don't know what's going on?"

Steve's eyebrows shoot up.

"You honestly think I'm that fucking stupid?"

"No, wait, Gary, let me explain . . ."

"No, Steve, just shut the fuck up for a second. I don't really care that you and that dumb shit got stoned, but why did you have to do it when Whitney was going to be here? Huh? Answer me!"

Whitney pops her head into the kitchen, the palm of her left hand placed horizontally over the fingertips of her right hand.

"Time out, you two. Uh, Gary, I'm going to go. Thanks for dinner."

"No, Whitney. Stay, please?"

"No, really, I'd better be going. That other guy is lying face-down on the couch, and since you two are in here shouting at each other, I'd better just . . ."

"No, please, Whitney." Gary's voice softens, almost cracking. "Stay?" Out of the corner of his eyes he catches Steve clutching his stomach, spit bubbles coming out of his mouth. Gary begins shouting again. "Stay just so you can hear Steve's apology!"

Steve turns to Whitney and tries to speak, but the only thing that comes out is a thin trail of blood red mucus that drips down his chin, clings briefly to his shirt, and falls, finally, onto the floor.

Whitney averts her face and exits the kitchen, the sound of her heels clacking on the hardwood floor of the living room, the sound getting smaller as she heads for the front door.

"Are you happy now? Are you *completely* happy? Making me look like a total asshole in front of my girlfriend?"

The clacking sound stops for a second, then increases in volume and pace.

"Girlfriend?" Whitney says, her head suddenly appearing behind the door.

Gary says shyly, "I didn't want to assume, but . . ."

"That's cute. Call me?"

"You bet."

Once Gary is sure Whitney is finally gone, he leans in close to Steve and whispers, "Since when did you start choosing that asshole over me?"

"But I *didn't* choose him over you."

Steve's defense emanates from the base of his sick chest, and he's hoping the words won't be a trip wire for another violent turn of his already exhausted stomach.

"I don't see you puking up *his* apple pie, or, I forgot, you were too busy throwing up to *have* any dessert."

"Guys, I think I'll leave," Sam says from the other room, picking up his box of foil on his way out the door.

"Gary, I'm sorry."

"No, Steve, fuck you. Wow, what a really great Thanksgiving. Thanks a lot."

Gary turns and stomps out of the kitchen. Steve tries to follow but catches his foot on the legs of the butcher-block table, and the force of his movement sends both him and the table to the ground. He feels the black carcass of the turkey bounce off the small of his back and then skid across the tiled floor. He throws up again, jerking his head forward so as not to bury his face in the warm liquid and choke, a typical drummer's death.

He looks up to see where Gary's gone, and in front of the turkey body lies the wishbone, a three-inch horseshoe with an epiglottis on top, the magical symbol of wish-giving power.

*Did I throw up that? How could it have gone down, much less back up?*

He reaches for the wishbone in front him and closes his eyes, composing his wish.

*Please, Gary, don't be mad at me. Gary* will *not be mad at me. Gary . . . mad . . . no . . .*

He grabs at the greasy wishbone but it is too slippery in his twitching hands, covered with his own vomit, and will not break.


"They hated me, I know it."

Mark exits the bathroom, wiping at the deposits of chalky toothpaste collected at the edge of each side of his mouth. He smacks his gums and grabs for a black tube of Chap Stick sitting on Corinne's dresser.

"No, they didn't hate you." Corinne tries to reassure, even though their meeting couldn't be called a complete success.

"Okay, maybe they didn't *hate* me." He kicks off the thick gray socks that had made his feet sweat all day, crammed in the loafers he only wore to make a good impression. He's sad now to see it didn't work. "But I doubt they liked me much, either."

"Oh, who can tell?" She tries to be vague, hoping he won't

press the issue and ask for details. "Anyway, they're crazy, I told you that. Who cares what they think?"

Mark sits at the edge of the bed, scratching at his stomach, digging his left hand underneath the elastic waistband of his boxers for a better grip.

"I care."

Her eyes dart to the living room, where the photo of her and Tim sits on top of the VCR.

"Mark, have you decided on whether or not you're staying in Los Angeles?"

"I don't know. I mean, things aren't going very smoothly, so—" She cuts him off.

"I'm not talking about the record. I'm talking about *us*. I'd like to think of myself as more than just a groupie, but maybe you don't."

He reaches out for her, pulling her into his body. "You're not a groupie. Groupies only last for a couple nights. We've been together almost a month now, right?"

"Real funny." *A month? Try two.* "But seriously, what's going to happen to us?"

"*Us* isn't going to worry about it so much. *We* are going to enjoy the time we have together."

"No, Mark. No." She gets out of bed, shrouding herself in a light blue robe that she grabs off of the doorknob. "I'm not going to be your toy for a couple of months while you play the brooding artist. Muse is one thing, but mattress, no."

Mark gets out of bed and tries to comfort her, pull her back toward him, but she resists.

"Come on, Corinne, you're being dramatic."

"I am not being dramatic." She slaps his hand away. "Why is it when some woman finally stands up for herself she's accused of being *dramatic* or something?"

Mark sinks back into the bed, amazed by the vitriol she's showing him. After eight weeks of exploration in bed, he finally knows her body, her curves, and how to make her come, but the contour of her mind and personality is not so easily seen or learned. He watches now as she stomps about the room, swatting herself in the shoulder, mumbling something under her breath.

"I just don't like the feeling that, any day now, you're going to be leaving. Back to Virginia, back to your old life." She pauses for a second at her dresser, looking over a jumble of items, checkbook, the tube of Chap Stick, her birth control pills, searching out the debris for a pack of cigarettes. "Even back to that old girlfriend Laura."

"Don't be ridiculous, *Corinne*." He says her name as if to reinstate his preference. "I'm not going back to my old life, *or* my old girlfriend. That's all over with, trust me. You know how much I like California, how much I'm thinking of staying."

"I sure hope it's the *climate* that's the deciding factor." She stops suddenly and looks him hard in the eyes, her voice drenched with irony. "You *do* know about the steep property taxes in this state, don't you? I'd hate for you to make any *rash* decisions."

"Oh, stop that." He grabs the edge of her robe as she paces around the floor, but she yanks it free, continuing to circle around the room. "I want to stay here because of you and nothing else. Although that place, what's it called? In-and-Out Burger, that's it, is *awfully* good."

She stops for a second and grins even though she doesn't want to. Mark takes advantage of her stalled position and manages to grasp the hem of her robe.

"Come here." He drags her onto the bed even though she's still resisting him. She falls stiffly, giggling but not wanting to show it.

As Corinne lands on the bed the robe flies open, showing her calf, ample thigh, and the beginning of her chestnut pubic hair. She playfully pushes Mark away as he starts from the very bottom, nibbling on her toes, which tickles her, chasing away most of her anger. He runs his tongue up the arch of her foot, and her pleasure is mixed with curiosity for why anyone would want to lick her *there.* Mark repositions himself, one knee painfully on the hardwood floor and another shoving onto a small plateau on the corner of the wooden box spring beneath the mattress. He leads with his hands as reconnaissance, the tips of his fingers clearing away the path for his mouth and tongue, now swishing back and forth like a windshield wiper, leaving a slick, sinewy trail.

He finds the skin beneath the topsoil of curlicuing hair and follows it down, separating the two sides of flesh, a small bud at the top announcing the beginning emergence of her clitoris. Mark pauses for a second, running a tongue around it, teasing it, nibbling on it, coaxing it to stiffen and grow, the way his thumbs are doing to her nipples just a foot and a half above.

At first he swears he can smell peach between her legs, and wonders if it's not from some female deodorant she'd sprayed on earlier, the types of products he always sees advertised on television but, for obvious reasons, has only half noticed. Then, as he probes deeper with each pass, using his whole mouth now, her musky scent begins to envelop him.

"Mmmm," Mark says, moving his whole head while his tongue sticks out, his mouth already tired, "you even *taste* like a pumpkin."

"Stop it," Corinne says, burying her head in the pillows and pushing back farther into the bed, allowing Mark more leverage, to go deeper, "that's not . . . oooh, there, there . . . funny."

Mark, now quiet, buries his head between her legs and in the process of bringing her to the edge of an orgasm, slurps once or twice. Rather than be disgusted by the sound, Corinne is turned on, as if their act had entered yet another dimension, their sex having not only a motion and a scent but also a *sound*. She leans back even farther and ignores the fact that her head is bumping into the wall slightly each time he thrusts forward, her legs now draped over his shoulders. Her juices, which run down his chin, mix horribly with the minty taste in his mouth from the toothpaste just minutes ago, almost as bad as orange juice, but not quite.

"Daddy's little"—Mark mumbles, his mouth full—"girl."

Even though he's been silent for well over a minute and is

making figure eights with his tongue between her legs, Corinne hears Mark's words in her head and no matter how much she tries to force it out of her mind, the connection has been made: sex = Daddy.

"Aw." Corinne closes her legs with a scissor motion, at first pinning Mark, then forcing him out. "You ruined it."

"I . . . I . . ." He's pushed to the edge of the bed by her kicking feet. "I didn't mean to."

"Well, you did."

Mark dabs at the wet ring around his mouth and wipes it onto the sheets. He turns and looks back at Corinne, who's already covered herself with the tails of the robe and pulled up the covers to her midsection. She misses the humming sensation that had been growing at the top of her inner thigh.

"I didn't know you didn't grow up in that house." Mark turns to Corinne, who's sitting up in bed, gnawing on a few strings from the belt of her robe, pouting. "You know, that's something we have in common. My parents suddenly upgraded after I left the nest, too. They moved into a swanky new place across town, and every time I go there now I feel like a . . . like a . . ."

"Visitor?"

"Exactly." Mark slaps his thigh. "Like today, when you rang the doorbell. It's like, that's what *I* always do, and my mother's always telling me, 'This is your house too, hon,' but it just doesn't *feel* like it, you know?"

Corinne drops the moist fabric from her mouth and places a hand around Mark's bare waist.

"I know."

"And just being in your den with your dad, surrounded by all those photos and track trophies." Mark looks through the window on the other side of the room and over the city, still not asleep even though it's late. He thinks of his parents back in Virginia, how his dad sounded upset when he spoke to him earlier in the day, the San Francisco game blaring in the background. "I can't tell you how much he reminded me of my own father."

Corinne stays silent even though the conversational ball is in her court. She runs a hand up Mark's back, an act that usually sends him shuddering with chills, but in this moment of reflection he's still, eyes trained on a pane of glass that, due to the lights on in the room, doesn't even allow him to look out, and only stares back.

*Two months,* she thinks again. *Two months and this is the most he's ever opened up to me. I don't know whether to be pissed off it's taken this long, or grateful that he finally has.*

"Sometimes I just think they're both such fucking phonies." He adds quickly, "My parents, I mean. Not yours."

"No, no, feel free to include mine, too. They *are* phonies. They think just because they've got that nice house and some rich friends, they've finally *made it.* In fact, you didn't see the silver Mercedes because it was in the garage—excuse me, *double* garage—but the license plate reads M-A-D-E-I-T-T. Pretty annoying, huh?"

Mark just laughs and tries to get comfortable. He props a pillow against the wall and offers his arm to Corinne, who accepts it and lies alongside him, curling her face into his chest.

For the first time all day she feels relaxed. She stretches her legs, tenses the tight muscles in her back, and then releases, her shoulder blades now easily gliding apart. Not out of instinct, because she wouldn't do this if placed beside a stranger, but because she wants to, she reaches another arm under Mark's back, clutching him in a snug ring.

"See? Isn't this great? You see how alike we are?" He reciprocates by pulling her into him tightly. "What we need to do is forget about all that other bullshit—"

"It's not bullshit, Mark."

"I know, I know, bad choice of words. All that other *stuff* that we can't possibly solve tonight, and we need to concentrate on all the things we *do* have in common. All the things we probably never realized before. We need to focus on just being there for each other, I mean, yeah, don't you think?"

He shrugs his shoulders, trying to prod out of her an affirmation of what he's saying.

"Yeah?" He asks again, now twitching his whole left side. "Yeah?"

Corinne pushes Mark away.

"Yeah, whatever."

# 16

### *"I'm adamant about the mixes."*

Before Henry James and Mark on the shiny circular glass table are two Caesar salads and a cassette. Henry leans over to nibble at his lunch, taking into his mouth large chunks of romaine lettuce that leave whiskers of pasty brown dressing on his cheeks. Mark is too upset to eat.

The cassette sitting before them is the first rough mix of the album that Kenneth, Paul, and Henry assembled over the long Thanksgiving weekend and had Hanes, who seemed only too happy to oblige, deliver to Mark the day before. Mark and the guys sat around most of Monday listening to the tape, alternately wanting to throw up and smash the thing against the wall. Gary and Steve kept glancing at Mark, deciding it had been all *his* fault.

"Where's my bass?" Gary kept asking as he sat on the couch with his head in his hands.

"And where's my drums?" Steve asked, sitting next to Gary, nervously stroking his goatee, which was finally coming in.

"Fucking digital," Gary exclaimed, throwing up his arms before stomping out of the room.

"Digital," Steve added, with equal if not greater disdain.

Their songs had, it seemed, been washed out, or rather, *smoothed* out. All of the sonic ragged edges that they used to exploit live and in their rehearsal shed back in Virginia were removed from the recorded music they were hearing coming out of the stereo's speakers. Where the songs before had bite, they now seemed toothless. Where before they grabbed you out of your chair and smacked you in the face, they now lamely tried to shake your hand, politely introducing themselves. Bottlecap's sound had been made palatable, mass-marketable, watered down.

"The kids," Henry James assures him, "are going to *love* it."

"I don't care about the goddamn kids, Henry. It barely sounds like us."

"It doesn't sound like what you *used* to sound like. But this is what you sound like now." Henry takes another bite of his salad and motions to the waiter to bring another San Pelligrino. A busboy in a stiffly starched white jacket approaches them, unscrews the imported water, pours some into Henry's glass, and leaves just as quickly.

"Tribeca?" Mark had gulped upon hearing the name of the restaurant the day before. Hanes shrugged before repeating the name, having to spell it, and then jotting down directions. "You know, over the hill." Mark stood awkwardly in the doorway of the rented house that was beginning to crowd in around him and said, "Over *what* hill?"

"*The* hill. The *Hollywood* hills. You know, big mountain range? The one that separates us from them?" Hanes stepped back and pointed north. "Like, the Valley?"

Following the directions earlier in the day, he haphazardly took the curves of Laurel Canyon, the rental car swinging wide on sharp turns, either edging into the oncoming traffic or riding onto the dirt shoulder, kicking up clouds of dust. He stepped on the gas in order to make the light at Mulholland, and this seemed to signal the turning point in his journey. Instead of continuing up the winding road, the rest of the trip was down-hill. He took his foot off the brake, ignoring the WATCH YOUR SPEED road signs, trying to make up for lost time. Why was he always late these days? Whether it was going to an appointment or simply noticing one of Corinne's hurt feelings, his reaction time had slowed to a snail's pace.

When Mark had finally found the restaurant, another ten minutes down Ventura Boulevard, he valet-parked at some gym and sprinted half a block, only to find the restaurant's address was smack dab in a strip mall. Tribeca was on the second floor, the way a shoddy car insurance salesman's office would have been back home, tucked into the corner because of lagging business. Mark wandered in, was sneered at by the maître d', who couldn't believe the party he was there to meet actually had a reservation. "Wait at the bar," he was commanded upon being informed that Henry had called from his car phone and was running a little late.

Mark slunk off to the bar, lit a cigarette, and ordered an Absolut on the rocks, surprised to see some of southern California finally rubbing off on him. "No more Rolling Rock for me," he said as he took a deep drag on the cigarette, downed half the expensive and lethal drink, spotting Henry James in the mirror above the bar as he was deposited at the top of the stairs and gripped the handrail, entering the restaurant from the escalator outside. As they were being shown to their table the maître d' chastised Mark for trying to enter the main dining room with a lit cigarette. Hadn't he heard? Over the past few years almost all of southern California had been declared smoke-free. Restaurants didn't present the option of smoking sections. Employees had to huddle outside their offices in all kinds of weather for a quick smoke, and you couldn't even smoke inside cafes, where cigarettes once completed the traditional triumvirate of nicotine, caffeine, and philosophizing. In Los Angeles, a city long known for its health-conscious stance, smoking was beginning to be seen as a moral fault. It was preferable to stink of garlic than to smell of smoke, as if it were okay to have bad hygiene but not bad habits. Mark mumbled an apology and dropped the cigarette on the whitewashed hardwood floor inlaid with a ribbon of dark cedar around the edges, grinding his heel into the still-smoking butt. Sometimes he missed the East Coast, where people may not give a damn about their health but at least give a damn about having fun.

Mark now sticks his stainless steel fork through the sea green lettuce leaves the way he'd like to poke Henry James, over and over again.

"But Henry, *we* don't like the way it sounds."

The A&R man takes the powder blue linen napkin from his lap and delicately wipes the corners of his mouth before speaking.

"Mark, let me tell you something. What *you* guys think really doesn't matter."

Mark tries to get the waiter's attention, to order a glass of wine, no, a bottle, but the waiter, smart enough to know who's in charge, doesn't bother to notice him.

"Di-di-did you get the proposed artwork I sent back with Hanes yesterday? For the cover?"

"Yes, yes, I did." Henry swabs at a small dish of olive oil with the crust of a roll, popping it into his mouth. "And I'm afraid we just can't do it."

"Which? The cover or the name?"

Henry reaches down to his briefcase and pulls out a manila folder.

"Both."

On the glass table he sets the idea that Mark had spent all last weekend working on at the Kinko's on Sunset Boulevard, returning back to Corinne's for turkey sandwiches and reheatings of her mother's stuffing, which actually seemed to get better and better upon each resuscitation. He had sent the cover ideas back with Hanes for Henry to see yesterday morning, hearing Hanes cackle from just down the pathway a few seconds after he'd slammed the door.

"We just can't do it," Henry says grimly, as if he'd gone to bat for both Mark and the idea, when in reality he hadn't so much as lifted a finger for either. He hadn't bothered showing it to anyone. He'd had the art department working on ideas since Bottlecap stepped off the plane almost three months ago now, and his acquiescence to Mark a fortnight ago when Mark wanted to come up with a few suggestions for the cover was just a way to keep the singer feeling involved while strings were being expertly pulled all around him.

"Henry, I *want* the record to be titled *Into the Garbage Chute, Flyboy.*"

"Look, Mark"—Henry swats away a waiter trying to get at his nearly empty plate—"even if Lucas didn't try and sue over the title, I'm sure he would never approve *this.*"

Marks picks up the sample artwork he had created using the color copier, transparent overlays, and pictures culled from a coffee table book entitled *Great Science Fiction Films of the '70s.* The photo was a shot from inside the *Millennium Falcon,* Han Solo behind the controls, trustful Chewie by his side, with Obi-Wan Kenobi and Luke Skywalker looking on (C-3PO and R2D2 recharging their batteries in the back, Mark guessed), only Harrison Ford, Mark Hamill, and Alec Guinness's faces had been covered up with snapshots of Gary, Mark, and Steve, taken from one of those booths where you put in a few bucks and get three color photos from a chute on the side. Chewbacca, however, was still Chewbacca.

"It's like an homage."

"No, no, Mark, it's like a *copyright infringement,*" Henry says in a mock French accent. "And there's no way in hell I'm going to tangle with Lucas after what he did to Luther Campbell. The only thing worse you could have done would be to make fun of Disney."

Feeling like he's choking, Mark reaches for his glass of water, gulps it down.

"Look, let's not make this a totally negative meeting, Mark. There's a lot of things I *like* about the record."

"Like?"

"Well, I particularly liked that song 'Parisian Broke,' where you talk about how in the twenties all those expatriates claimed they had no money but still wore suits and top hats. I thought your rhyming of *Nastasse* with *Montparnasse* was, er, particularly inspired, even though I'm not sure where *he* fits in and that the other word is pronounced that way."

"You take liberties." Mark taps out a song against the salt-shaker, avoiding Henry's eyes. "You know, switch things around."

Henry wipes his mouth with the cloth napkin, sets it back in his lap, and picks up the cassette sitting on the table. He looks over the tracks and then shakes his head, as if something he's looking for is not there but should be.

"What? What is it?"

"Well, it seems to me you're missing *one* song."

Mark snatches the clear plastic case out of Henry's hand and quickly looks it over.

"But all the songs are there. At least, all the songs *we* decided to put on the record."

Henry slowly takes another bite of his salad, meticulously chewing as if he were chewing the words he was about to say.

"No, Mark, the single."

"Single? But there's plenty of songs on there that could—"

"No, no, no. It's not here, Mark. I've listened and . . . I just don't *hear* a single."

"Look, Henry, I thought we decided—"

"What *I* decided was that Bottlecap needed a potential radio song. I didn't hear it a few months ago and I don't hear it now. Mark, listen to me." Henry tries to smile, even though his patience is wearing thin. *Memo to my secretary: I just don't understand the kids today.* "All I'm trying to do is help your band achieve the widest possible audience and—"

"Henry, no, please."

"—and unless I get that radio-friendly catchy song, I'm afraid this project will have to be pushed back. Indefinitely. Anyway"—Henry glances at his silver Tag Heuer watch—"it's getting late, and if there's one thing I can't stand, it's being late for appointments."

"Oh really?" Mark pushes away his plate for good. "Where do you have to be?"

"Not me, *you*."

"What?"

"Didn't Hanes tell you about the time change?"

Mark remembers the photo shoot at a studio in Highland Park, three cities away. He was meeting Gary and Steve there, but he could have sworn it wasn't until later in the afternoon.

"Looks like you'd"—Henry sinisterly chuckles—"better get a move on."

Mark stands up quickly, ready to say something rude, only to find he's tucked the hem of the tablecloth deep in his jeans, thinking it was a napkin, and as he rises he jerks half the contents of the table to the hardwood floor of the restaurant.

By the time Mark makes it out to Highland Park and to the loft of the photographer, the shoot is already well under way.

"What took you so long?" Gary rushes out of the frame just as the flashbulb pops and a shadowy figure behind a tripod shrugs thick shoulders and sighs.

"Don't start with me, Gary." Mark rushes headlong into the cavernous room. For a second it's as if he's wandered into a movie theater, the bright yellow light of midday reduced to the murkily lit studio, only a patch in the corner lit up from hanging spotlights and others on tripods. Steve is still standing in place.

The rest of the room is a normal apartment, lime green couch lining the far wall, coffee table, set of weights, mountain bikes attached to the walls and sticking straight out. In the corner of a small kitchen a green wooden bookshelf holds spices and canned foods on the first couple of tiers, CDs on the next. Mark notices Hanes reclining on the couch in the darkness, invisible save for a scant shadow cast from the lit end of a brown, skinny cigarette. He appears to be grinning. Next to the couch is a stereo, blasting some sort of strange, electronic music.

"What in the fuck *is* that?" Mark says, taking off his jacket and setting it on one end of a weighted-down bar suspended on a metal T stand. He notices on the other end of the bar a number of jackets with price tags attached.

"It's the soundtrack to *Close Encounters of the Third Kind*," a voice says from behind him.

Mark turns and sees a stocky man, with a nearly shaved head, wearing a white T-shirt and baggy blue jeans, a light meter hanging from a black cord around his neck.

"Oh, yeah, sorry." Mark, feeling self-conscious, pats down his pockets and feels for his sunglasses. Relaxing a bit, he settles into the role. "I was, you know, coming from the other side of the hill. Tri*beca*."

The photographer nods sagely, as if he and Mark had just completed some sort of secret handshake.

"Oh, okay then."

The photographer steps back into the shadows, behind the camera, and then barks out an order to Steve, who can barely hear him over the alien-welcome-call tune blaring out of the speakers.

"Huh?" Steve calls out, bewildered.

"I said, move your head, left. Left!"

Steve tosses his head in both directions, a confused look on his face.

"My left . . . or your left?"

The photographer stomps away into the kitchen and an assistant pours him a glass of Thai iced tea. He angrily stirs the settling cream on top into the deep brown tea on the bottom while the assistant kneads his thick neck. The assistant has a wiry body, straggly hair, and a face that looks like it derives pleasure from pleasing others.

Mark tries to shake off both the nerve-racking meeting across town with Henry James and also the maniacal driving it took to traverse half a dozen towns in order to make it to the photo shoot while it was still daylight. He rolls down his sleeves, which lie in moist rings around his elbows. The last freeway he'd been on, the 110, was more like a roller coaster than a stretch of road. The curves came out of nowhere, every corner blind. An entire lot of abandoned signs to the right of the road (creepy, spider-infested Arby's and Burger Kings) loomed above the blacktop, which rose and then sank like sand dunes. On ramps were like starting blocks in a track meet, stop signs that emptied immediately into a lane of traffic, and the off ramps were clipped painfully short, so much so that Mark nearly sent the Plymouth into a brake-locked skid when he finally reached Avenue 60, a white sign reading EXIT 5 MPH while the road whipped around in a crescent shape in the space of perhaps fifty feet.

"'Scuse me, my name's Vedra."

Mark turns and sees an attractive woman wearing a tight, white, ribbed sweater tucked into black pants, a pen behind her left ear pinning back a sheath of curly brown hair.

"Oh, hello." Mark is still a bit shaken, slow to respond.

"Didn't Bryant tell you?"

"No. Wait, who's Bryant?"

"Why"—the woman laughs—"the photographer."

Mark looks across the room to where Bryant is peering through the lens, barking orders, focusing on Steve, who's desperately trying to find a set of friendly eyes in the dark.

"You mean the short fat guy? Well, we haven't been formally introduced. Why, do you work for him?"

"Sometimes. Actually, I'm the art director for 2 Hot magazine. I'm overseeing the shoot for today."

*Overseeing,* Mark thinks in his head. *Great, just what I need, another fucking opinion on my band.*

"I thought the three of you could wear these jackets." Vedra stands back and casts her hand over the multicolored garments Mark had noticed before.

"Why don't all three of us wear the *same* jackets, like collarless numbers?" Mark says sarcastically. He snaps his fingers before continuing. "No, wait! Why don't we all sit backward in director's chairs while we're getting our hair cut? Of course, that will be difficult, since Gary really doesn't *have* any hair, but your readers will get the idea."

Gary looks up from the kitchen counter, which is filled with roast beef and turkey sandwiches served on little croissants.

"You guys talking about me?"

Vedra smiles politely before walking away.

"Oh, *Bry*ant," she says in a singsongy voice, "I think we've got *prob*lems."

Mark rubs his hands over his face, beginning to cool down slightly, before walking into the shoot and joining Steve.

"Ah-ah-ah," yells Bryant's assistant, pointing at Mark's feet as he approaches. "Please remove your shoes."

Mark slides off his sneakers, stepping onto the gray, seamless backdrop, a huge sheet of heavy construction paper unspooled from a large roll hung from the ceiling with cords of rope and attached to eye screws twisted into crumbling plaster.

"Hey, Steve, how's it going?"

"Horrible," he nervously replies. Under the harsh lights his goatee looks wildly overgrown, stray hairs looping down over his lips and into his mouth, or else the opposite way, splayed against his cheek like some sort of shrapnel, and Mark wonders how Steve can stand it. "Until you got here he was just taking these portraits of us, saying he was going to put them together later. By the way, what's a triptych?"

"I don't know, why?"

"Because he kept saying it, over and over." Steve lowers his voice. "I think it's some sort of code they've got, telling them not even to use real film on me because I'm just the drummer. You know? Like, who ever cares about the drummer?"

Gary walks up to the perimeter of the backdrop, still munching on a sandwich, a bit of the golden brown crust flaking onto the long-sleeve Izod shirt he's wearing. He slips off a pair of Keds before stepping onto the backdrop.

"How'd the meeting go?"

"Yeah, how'd the meeting go?"

Bryant steps around a ladder and into the foreground, interrupting Mark as he's about to answer, "Not so good."

"Okay, here's the shot." Bryant clasps his hands together like a shot marker on a movie set, a loud noise to call the cast and crew to action. "Vedra wants you all lined up, but just sort of staggered, like we'll have the tallest in back, you know, in descending order, facing forward and, oh well, you'll see."

Vedra appears from the shadows with three different coats on silver crazy-straw hangers, the steel neck twisted in superfluous loops and twists on its way to the simple triangular design.

"Now, if you'll each grab a jacket."

"But why?" Gary protests, not wanting to cover up the prize shirt he found the week before at the Children's Hospital thrift store on the East Side for two dollars.

"Because," Vedra duly explains, not used to having to do so, "this is for our 'What's Hot' summer issue. And you guys may be hot, but so are these jackets."

Steve steps forward and fingers the coats, one in a thick blue corduroy with brown wooden buttons up the front, the next in a bright silvery fabric that doesn't give way when you touch it, and the last a knockoff of an old stock-car-racing jacket, a simple cotton design with two pockets near the waist, red and blue stripes running the length of the left side. Embroidered over the breast and sleeves of the jackets are the names of manufacturers that have yet to make their way to their Virginia hometown: Stoopid, Drawl, Yaga.

"These"—Steve turns to his band mates—"are hot?"

Bryant's assistant turns as he steadies a four-by-ten-foot sheet of foam-core hanging from the ceiling, pushing up the sleeves of the jacket he's wearing, which is very similar to those in Vedra's hands.

"Look," Vedra says, her voice growing impatient, "I told Henry that we are a snowboarding, hip-hop magazine with a slight emphasis on freestyle skating and surfing, with a dab of cyberculture thrown in and he assured me—"

Mark cuts her off with a laugh. "Wait a second. Hip-hop?"

Gary follows close behind with a remark of his own, punctuated by laughter. "Cyber . . . culture?"

Vedra stomps off into the shadows, returning a second later empty-handed.

"I'll make someone else wear the jackets. Happy? Now let's get this under way, the clock is ticking."

There's silence in the room and Mark thinks he can actually

*hear* the clock ticking, but it's just the incessant *click-click* of the record on the turntable, the needle stuck in the run-off groove. Bryant snaps his finger and his assistant runs over to the stereo, puts on another record, then runs back to Bryant's side.

"Okay, good," the photographer says as he prowls around Mark, Steve, and Gary, trying to figure out how to light the shot Vedra has concocted. "Farsheed, get me an orange gel for the spotlights. And tone down the soft box a touch."

The assistant runs to a corner of the loft and returns with a square foot of orange plastic, which he tapes over a spotlight hoisted onto a tripod. He positions this behind Bottlecap, an orange light cast on the gray backdrop. Then he pushes in the soft box, a flashbulb housed in a nylon sheath, white in the center and rimmed with black on the outside covering. He turns a dial on a power box that reminds Gary of his preamp, cords running in and out, dials and switches littering the steel top. The light dims slightly. Bryant takes the light meter hanging from around his neck (reminding Steve of the stopwatch his gym teacher used to carry like a necklace but never seemed to use) and holds it close to Mark's chin. Bryant signals to Farsheed, who hits a lit-up button on the box, triggering the flash, which bursts like an explosion of lightning, with an audible *pop* like those clunky cameras do in old movies. The photographer checks the LCD display, then moves behind the camera, adjusting the shutter speed accordingly.

"Okay." Vedra slips off a pair of clunky-looking clogs, losing about three inches of height in the process. "You in the back"— she tugs at Steve, placing him behind Mark—"you in the middle, and *you*"—she grabs Gary by the arm and shoves him in the front—"stand here." She stands back to survey the trio, sees a discrepancy, and picks up an eight-pound weight sitting on the ground. She shoves it with her foot onto the backdrop (Farsheed cringing as she does so, the weight cracking on one side and horribly dusty), motioning for Steve to stand on it. "Better."

Vedra positions them just a few inches apart, like the steps of a staircase, then clamps a hand on Steve's back and Gary's chest and pushes them together.

"Sorry, but we need you together . . . tight," she adds, "for the shot."

Mark feels Steve's chest and even the nib of his pelvis squashed into his back, and he tries to retreat into the small of Gary's back, only he stinks a bit, so Mark recoils slightly, arching his shoulders, sucking in his gut, trying to hold his breath. Bryant examines the shot, calls out to Vedra, who takes a look behind the lens.

"Well," she says, sort of shrugging, "let's shoot a Polaroid and just see what it looks like."

Bryant grips the Asahi Pentax camera by the wooden grip handle, tilts it slightly, focuses, and then presses the button, triggering the flash and opening the exposure. He then rips out a postcard-sized bit of film from an attachment stuck onto the back of the camera. "Just give us a minute while this develops, okay, boys?"

"But hold your positions," Vedra calls out as she and Bryant saunter to the kitchen counter to trade photography world gossip while waiting for the instant photo to develop.

As they stand sandwiched together, Steve about to lose his balance from leaning forward so much and Gary trying to keep steady at the waist with the pressure building at his shoulders, Mark looks squarely into the back of Gary's head. He notices at least half a dozen worm-sized scars on the back of his head and top of his neck. Each one is just a little squiggle, a zigzag of tissue, landmarks of forgotten pain. The thin slivers of black hair try to grow around the keloids but have to find alternate routes, redirecting themselves in crazy patterns that make the back of his head look like a tangled freeway. Underneath his ears sprout a few spots of bright pink bubble-gum acne, and a final scar, the longest one and almost half an inch wide, diving from the base of his neck and disappearing underneath the collar of his recycled shirt. Mark had no idea Gary's skin had led such an interesting life.

"Okay, let's try a couple." Bryant assumes his position behind the camera. He barks out a few orders to Farsheed before hesitantly snapping a few pictures. Vedra whispers something in his ear. Bryant nods, doesn't change anything, and takes more shots. After a few minutes he begins taking pictures more rapidly, the inside of the studio lit up every few seconds like a battlefield with the flamelike outburst of the flash. Bryant, beginning to sweat and out of breath, changes film constantly. To the left of Bryant's foot Mark sees cylindrical cases of Fujichrome 100 film canisters littering the floor like spent shotgun shells.

"Perfect!" Bryant shouts out, the flashbulb popping, the winding sound of the advancing film barely heard over the tinkling piano music in the background. "One more, perfect!"

Steve tries not to laugh, but he can't believe that photographers actually do say those things, egging on their models as if they were lovers in bed: *Fabulous, more, more, yes, that's it, that's it! Don't stop!*

Every time a picture is taken, Mark can swear he blinks. He tries to anticipate this, tries to keep his eyes pried open for as long as possible, denying Bryant the satisfaction later of running his grease pen through yet another shot on the proof sheets, blaming his neophyte model. Mark tries to sneak in blinking, snapping down his heavy lids like a nightshade, snapping them up in a flash, just to see the real flash against the nighttime backdrop of his eyes explode into a dawn of a *Damn*, and dilated pupils.

Bryant conferences with Vedra for a second, and then she approaches Bottlecap, positioning them side by side, Steve now in the center, still standing on the weight, with Gary and Mark flanking on either side. Mark looks above Bryant's head and spots a hole in the ceiling, flaking particle board, a black female blowup sex doll half set in the gap between the ceiling and the crisscrossed wooden slats forming the underside of the roof, a faded green name tag reading HELLO MY NAME IS scrawled on in black ink, *Randy*.

"Perfect, hold it, hold it. Purr . . . fect!"

At the rear of the room Mark spots an exposed heating system set into a ledge above the bedroom, billowing silver ducts with vents on their ends twisting like an octopus's tentacles over the makeshift living room. The warm air circulates the foul odor of his band mates, only accentuating Mark's desire to be someplace else.

"Let me get a couple of close ones." Bryant picks up the tripod and moves it toward his subjects. He fishes out a lens from a gray canvas bag of equipment and slides it on the nose of his camera. As he readies the shot Mark can see his own reflection staring back at him, convex, slightly circular, as if looking into a carnival mirror. He can't be sure whether it's just the unfamiliar surroundings or the generally fucked-up day so far, but he doesn't recognize himself and even has trouble placing the two faces next to him. The photographer whispers something to his assistant, who twiddles one of the dials on the power box, and the large light looming down on him fades, like his future, into blackness.

"And then she kissed me."

Gary lies on the couch, outstretched over three cushions, while Steve sits on the ground and Mark is slumped in the chair next to the television set, which is on with the sound turned down.

Gary has been taking advantage of the band's truce in order to relate yet another of his stories that involved Whitney. Steve couldn't stand these because he didn't have a girlfriend and thus had no stories of his own, and Mark was annoyed because he did have a girlfriend, but you didn't hear him boring people every other second with his own romantic adventures. Besides, his adventures lately with Corinne hadn't been romantic at all.

"This was on that Tuesday, after our first date. Remember the date?" Gary prods Steve in the shoulder with his foot and prods Mark by nodding his own head over and over, as if saying, "Get it?"

"Yeah, yeah, the date. We remember. You guys had a good time."

"Soul mates, big deal. Keep going."

"Well, that's the night I came home and found the note she had left on our doorstep."

The letter came two days after the phone conversation to which the letter referred. What she had said in both was that she enjoyed Gary's company, that she felt, even though she had known him only a short time, that he was special. To Gary, both communications seemed like veiled excuses for expressing something else. What that something else might be she did not yet have the courage to convey, and he became more and more anxious every day to see it arrive, whatever it would be.

Gary read the note three or four times, as he did with most correspondence. He read his own mail almost as carefully as he'd read somebody else's. The tone was the same as their recent phone conversations: a touch of vulnerability, a hint of longing, general interest around the edges but built on a sturdy foundation of independence. Gloria Gaynor could be heard in the background.

But as he reread the letter in search for emotional clues (the hand-drawn heart as a sign-off was food enough to feed him for a week), he noticed something odd. There seemed to be a peculiar amount of space between some words, with queer gaps between the end of one sentence and the beginning of another, which led him straight to the door of suspicion. As he examined the format of the note he could see that the paragraphs had been force-justified by her computer, a command that tightly evened out both margins of the text. This must have been chosen by her after composition, as she scrutinized her words in a way he thought only he was neurotic enough to do. Realizing the amount of attention she had expended, he grinned. It was small, but meant a lot. Nobody said victories had to be large.

"Do you want to hear again, about the kiss?"

Gary, hating to waste a good idea, manufactured a reply the next night, fashioning a card much like the one he left for the smoking girl, which had been returned with a fist in it by her steaming boyfriend. This time he used a Manet landscape, olive-colored card stock, and sandstone stationery. On the way to where he had to park the rental car earlier in the day, he broke off two roses that were growing from a neighbor's bush and slipped their stems into the white ribbon he'd looped around the card. He cut himself on a thorn and, sucking the blood, found it tasted sweet and not salty.

As Gary drove across town he slid through traffic quickly, without having to curse or being cursed at, and even found a parking space outside her apartment. His ease in reaching her seemed a good omen, convincing him that despite the emotional obstacles their own insecurities erected, there really was not much standing between them. An entire world existed for Gary, if he were only confident enough to grab it.

He crept up the stairs to her building quietly, but not so quietly that someone across the street would call the cops, thinking he was a burglar. At the foot of Whitney's door he planted the roses fastened to the card, and then turned to escape, only to find Whitney staring at him with tears in her eyes. Both were silent for a few seconds, wanting to cherish the moment. And then she kissed him.

"And then she kissed me."

The kitchen door across the room catches Mark's eye. He wonders if there's alcohol inside and, if so, how long would it take for him to get drunk, to drown out his chattering roommate, and forget his worries, forget about the mounting pressures, their debut record that was so completely fucked. *How long would it take,* he asks himself hypothetically, *to fly back home, right now?* He rolls his shoulders and then swivels his head in an attempt to crack the tense bones in his back.

While Gary tells his story, his eyes glazed over as if he'd been injected with one of Sam's drugs, Steve flips through a catalog of men's clothes that had been delivered to the house, the computerized name above the address reading OCCUPANT. The descriptions for the assorted pleated corduroy pants and linen-banded collar shirts were written in an irreverently hardboiled style, as if Hemingway had stopped living the Eddie Bauer lifestyle and gone to work for them. Paragraphs of anecdotes in purple prose lay beside the merchandise like fat thought balloons, trying to obfuscate the fact that they were selling you just pants and shirts. But what Steve found the most disturbing was that none of the garments were worn by models, but instead were held in place with steel rods or some other sort of armature. Yet the clothes did not hang lifeless. Invisible men seemed to be inside. Forearms and chests bulged with bumps of flesh, but at the necks and ends of sleeves there was only space, sweaters hollowed out as if they were Halloween pumpkins. It was creepy and reminded him of *Escape from Witch Mountain.*

"Did I mention that *that's* when she kissed me?"

"Yes, Jesus, she kissed you. Blah-blah-blah. You know, Corinne's kissed me, too."

"Well then, Mark, why don't you write something like that for a single?" Steve says, trying to stop a fight before one begins. It was only last week that he and Gary had made up over the Thanksgiving debacle; Steve did not want to see Mark and Gary more at odds with each other than they already were. "Something sappy, romantic. Henry James would love that."

"Something romantic?" He stares at the ground. "That's a feeling I've not felt since . . ." His voice goes raspy until it disintegrates into just breath.

Mark thinks of the most romantic thing he has ever done, depressed at both the memory and the realization that it's not very romantic at all. He and Laura were sitting in her Galaxy 500 in front of her apartment, kissing, clinging to each other, not wanting to say good-bye. Mark opened his eyes for a second and noticed the inside of the car windows had fogged. He took his right arm from Laura's side and, double-timing with his left, alternately making circles on her back and massaging her neck so she wouldn't notice the other arm gone, he scratched out three words on the inside of the windshield with the tip of his index finger in the fog: I LOVE YOU. Just as he was rounding the curve of the U, a rubbing sound of dry skin against glass gave him away and Laura looked up and noticed the words. It was the first declaration of his affection, and even though Mark didn't exactly pronounce the words, Laura still considered them said. She pulled away a few inches and Mark at first was scared, wondering if he had done the right thing and cursing himself for so blindly following his emotions and not stopping to think about what he was doing. *Damn, damn, damn,* he kept repeating to himself, fearing recrimination. Laura drew back even farther, then lifted a hand, Mark feared for a slap, but instead placed both arms around him and lunged forward, leading with her lips, pushing him down flat on the bucket seats.

The next morning, when Laura picked up Mark to go to breakfast at the Waffle House near the freeway, she pointed to the windshield with a grin and Mark noticed that you could still, if you concentrated, make out the three words scrawled the night before by Mark's trembling finger. It remained there for over six months until Laura took it to a car wash while visiting some friends in Arlington and an eager young employee, new on the job and hoping for an extra-big tip, washed both the inside and outside of the windows. Laura was furious, yelled, screamed, cried all the way home, and did not tip at all.

"Hey, Pellion . . . You okay?"

"Yeah, Mark, you alright?"

Steve turns to Gary and says, "I think we lost him."

Mark licks his lips quickly, then sits up straight in his chair.

"Guys?"

"Yeah?"

"What is it?"

"I've got an idea."

Steve climbs off of the floor and sits beside Gary, who has unwillingly relinquished some space on the couch.

"What?"

"If they want a single, why don't we give them a single?"

"Well, sure," Steve says hesitantly, as if the proposition were too good to be true. He remembered something about there being no such thing as a free lunch. It reminds him that he's hungry right now. "But I thought you had picked all of the songs for the record and they said no."

Mark's now grinning, a twinkle in his eyes present where it had been missing for quite a while. "No, I was thinking of an older song. One of our oldest. You know"—his faces breaks into a smile—"that *really* catchy one. The one that's so . . . romantic . . ."

Sitting behind his drum set in the recording studio, Steve wipes a few crusts of sleep from the corner of his eyes and then glances to the large clock in the corner. He can't believe that Mark dragged them here at one o'clock in the morning.

"Uh, 'I Want to Fuck You'?" he asks.

"Yes," Mark replies, sitting on the edge of the amp.

"Are you sure?" Gary asks. He scratches at his left breast being rubbed raw from the black polyester shirt he picked up the day before from a thrift store on Melrose. He bought it because Whitney had told him he looked like Douglas Fairbanks in it, but, she added sadly later, not out of it. "That's supposed to be your big concession? 'I Want to Fuck You'?"

"Yeah." Mark plugs one end of a cord into his guitar and the other into his tuner. "So?"

Steve and Gary slowly turn to each other.

"Uh, Henry James's not going to like that." Steve steps out from behind his drum set.

"Why not?" Mark innocently says. "It's got a funky beat, and you can dance to it. It's a good little song."

"Yeah, sure, Mark, you know that Steve and I both like this song . . . but you know Henry's just going to shit if we deliver this as the single he's practically staking our entire future on."

"I Want to Fuck You" was one of the first songs that Mark ever introduced into the Bottlecap repertoire, and consequently it was one of the early songs that Steve and Gary knew the words to. Mark had forgotten about the song a long time ago when, after their first East Coast tour, he had played the song dozens of times and finally got sick of it and was excited about the newer, more complex material he and the band were working on.

At first the guys were too shy to play the song live. During practice, it was called on by any of them to revive a lagging session because it was fast, loud, short, and almost never failed to put a smile on all three of their faces. Mark convinced them to play the song in front of crowds (demurring only one night at the request of his two band mates when they played a twilight semiacoustic show at the Novel Idea Cafe and there were children scurrying about), and it always proved to be one of their most popular numbers.

Mark had composed "I Want to Fuck You" the night after he had written *I Love You* on the inside of Laura's windshield. Yet another milestone of that fateful weekend was that Mark had talked dirty to Laura for the first time. He eased into the situation the same way he had eased himself into her body for the first time four months before, carefully and in measured strokes.

"You'll never know how much I like to fuck you . . . ," he began cautiously, ready to stay quiet for the remainder of the lovemaking session if Laura did not reply in similar.

"I . . . ," she began as cautiously as Mark had, I . . . love it . . . when you . . . fuck me . . . too."

Mark smiled as best he could with his head butting into a large pillow, his teeth brushed with a dirty cotton pillowcase smelling of sweat and hair gel.

"I want to fuck you . . . all night . . . fuck . . . you . . . hard," Mark continued, fanning the incubatory flame that was growing in her, while simultaneously hoping that the condom would not break and that dirty words placed in a salacious order would be the only thing growing in her tonight.

"Yes . . . please . . . fuck me . . . fuck me with your hard, hot . . . cock . . ."

Mark again smiled, thinking it was funny that, at the moment, his cock may have been warm, but was not so hard at all.

Afterward, Laura made a confession.

"That was like a dream come true."

"Why?" Mark asked even though he had the answer half figured out in his head. But, as during sex ten minutes before, he wanted to *hear* it.

"I've always wanted someone to talk dirty to me."

Mark grinned and drew Laura close, glad she could still be a virgin to him in some ways.

The next night, after he had finally relented and abandoned the cocoon of her cozy car imprinted with his newly declared emotion, he sat down with his acoustic guitar and wrote a semi-serious pop song about wanting to make love to Laura. Christening their new era of aural sex, he called the song "I Want to Fuck You." He practiced the song three times a day for a week and a half until he could both play it and sing it at the same time (back then either act alone was still a considerable struggle). Finally he decided he was ready to serenade Laura.

Her apartment was a queer trilevel dwelling that wasn't a traditional three-storey house, but rather ate into the hill at the back of the property, positioned into the earth like a staircase. She lived on the second level, while her roommate lived in the spacious atticlike quarters on the third; kitchen, dining room, and entrance were on the first. Mark knew she would be home on that Thursday night, calling ahead to make sure she answered the phone, which she did, at which time he promptly hung up on her. He then jumped into his brown Tercel and raced across town, cutting the engine when he was half a block away and gliding to within twenty feet of her house, silently, like a ninja. He quickly and quietly retrieved his guitar from where it was lying on the backseat (he didn't bring the case; he thought Laura might hear the snapping of the brass latches through her window, which he knew would be open, since it was summer). He crept around the back of the house, positioned himself on a small mound of wet dirt, softened by a recent thunderstorm, and called out to his beloved.

"Yeah, what is it?" Laura responded, sounding angry at first, thinking it might be Jim, an old boyfriend of hers who, it seemed, did not want to take no for an answer. When Laura saw it was instead Mark with his guitar, her face glowed and she rested hands against cheeks and elbows against windowsill, expectantly waiting for what she knew was going to follow.

Mark found it hard to swallow before beginning the song he had practiced so diligently to master. His mouth was dry and his heart was beating so furiously that he feared she would see the guitar, strapped across his fibrillating chest, rise and fall, rise and fall with every hammering pulse. It only then occurred to him that this would be the first time he had ever played guitar or sang in front of a human being. (The genesis of Bottlecap was still three months away. He, too, could still be a virgin.) Finally he mustered enough spit in his mouth to grease his teeth and unclench them from his gums so he could sing. He strummed the guitar strings once, then twice, and then began his song. Five minutes after playing "I Want to Fuck You" for Laura, he went upstairs and did.

From across the room Mark spots Kenneth enter the booth and talk to Paul in an agitated manner, to which Paul replies by plainly pointing toward Bottlecap.

"What in the hell do you think you're doing, getting me out of bed and in the studio at this hour?" Kenneth asks, sauntering up to where Mark is standing behind a microphone with his guitar strapped on.

"It's just, I had an idea, that's all."

"And it couldn't have waited until morning?"

"Look at it this way," Mark says dumbly, lowering his head and bobbing it around like a doll's, "the studio rates will be much cheaper."

"Yeah, well, who cares? You're paying either way." Kenneth crosses his arms, looks back to make sure Paul heard his witty comment, then turns back to Mark. "Okay, what's this great idea?"

"A single. We finally found our single."

Kenneth's face instantly softens.

"Well, now. I'm glad that you're finally seeing things *our* way."

This sentence strikes Mark like a slap. *Our way.* He feels like an idiot for not realizing that Kenneth has been on Pacific's side since the beginning.

"Okay." The producer motions to Gary. "Why don't you hop in the booth? Steve, we'll start with the basic drum tracks, then we'll get Gary back in here, and finally Mark with a—"

"No," Mark interrupts. "We're going to do this live. All of us at once. *Now.*"

Kenneth shifts his weight and bites his lower lip before answering.

"Okay, Pellion. After all, you're the boss, right?"

"I am now."

Kenneth walks back to the booth, mumbling something under his breath. Once inside he grumbles, "Goddamn prima donna," to Paul before ordering him to start the tape rolling.

A grinning Mark turns to his band mates. "Let's rehearse this once or twice so Kenneth can get some levels, and then we'll put down a take."

Steve crosses himself with the plastic tip of his Pearl ROCK STAR drumsticks before beating them together in the center and counting off.

*"Late at night I'm thinking about . . . all the things I'm gonna do . . . all the things that I want to do . . . I want to fuck you . . . fuck you hard . . ."*

Mark screams out the lyrics, only half in tune. Hard to sing with a smile on his face.

# 17

**Mark can't sleep. His head is fully awake, tingling with** too many ideas to herd into obedience and let the weariness in his body take over and permit him even an hour or two of slumber. He rolls over once, then again, switching sides every few minutes, even trying his stomach, then back, staring at the ceiling, finding odd swirling patterns in the plaster above. The clock by his bed reads two-forty-eight. Grumbling, he gets up.

*It's the record,* he thinks as he stumbles out into the hall to the bathroom, taking a piss. *I just can't stop thinking about our fucking record.*

He yawns, figures he'd better not flush the toilet for fear he might wake up Gary and Steve (themselves treading the thin ice of sleep after many hours under the same weight of concern as Mark), and he heads downstairs.

Rather than try to find something decent on TV at this hour (too late for the late movies and not early enough for news or morning chat shows—almost every channel is clogged with infomercials), Mark rummages through the sideboard next to the stereo and comes up with the object he hoped the house would have, though he'd never actually looked for them: headphones.

He slips the good old-fashioned quarter-inch plug into its receptacle, relieved not to find the skinny eighth-inch kind popularized by Walkman years ago. Those were usually attached to skinny plastic disks covered in cheap fuzz with a thin band of metal looped over the head like a pair of novelty bunny ears. Mark prefers the older style of headphones, the kind that resembled heavy-duty earmuffs, completely covering each ear and weighing down the head by a couple of pounds. The kind that might end the life of a small boy with a brittle neck. The kind that really felt like something against your head, forming a tight seal between its rubbery cups and the area around your ear, leaving you alone with your music and completely shutting out the world, which seemed the point of headphones anyway.

With the pair now firmly attached to his head, his hair sticking out wildly from the leatherette band connecting the seashell speakers, Mark looks for something to listen to.

*Something soft, obviously. Something soothing.* The headphone's cord is shiny, jet black, and curled like an old telephone cord, and Mark likes this, too. It reminds him of Pete Townsend's guitar cord, of the Who guitarist standing on a Vox amp and assaulting his Les Paul with a final windmill strum just before he smashes all of his rig into a million pieces.

His fingers trail over the collection of CDs he had brought from Kitty, a few dozen records stuffed hastily stuffed into an old blue duffel bag. *Maybe something sort of acoustic?* He puts a CD into the player and lies down on the couch, operating the machine from across the room with the remote control. Halfway through the first song, and just as Mark is getting comfortable, his body soaking into the receptive cushions and his mind drinking up the comforting song, he startles, momentarily paranoid. This always happened when he wore headphones, even when he lived alone and would listen to records at three or four o'clock in the morning—he was always sure someone would call or pound on the door or even break in and rob him blind as his feet tap-tapped away.

"Huh?" He pulls away the headphones from his ears and places the CD on pause. "What?" But the only sound in the room is a buzz coming from underneath the refrigerator.

He places the headphones back over his ears but midway into

the third song he gets that paranoid feeling, the audio equivalent of being watched but not able to see the eyes upon you. He grabs the phone, feeling for a vibration, but, of course, there's nothing.

*Who would call this late at night?* He places the phone back on the table next to the couch. *Man, I have got to relax.* Three songs later he can swear he hears something ringing above the music. Mark sees the clock in the hallway, its golden hands in an L position. *Three o'clock in the morning,* he reassures himself, settling back into the music. *There's no way in hell anyone would be calling me now.*

Mark's feet start twitching to the tune, trying to forget about that incessant ringing in the background that he knows isn't really there. That's one of the nice things about being paranoid; several times a day you get to roll your shoulders and sigh, relieved to find your apartment hasn't been robbed, that you had not been followed home, or that you've woken up once again and not died in your sleep, the way you're sure you would.

Unable to stand it, Mark throws off the headphones and is startled to find the phone actually ringing.

"Hello?" He lunges for the receiver, knocking the base off the table and sending it hurtling toward the floor.

"Pellion?" A voice says, long distance, a scratchy connection. "What in the hell took you so long? It's been ringing for five minutes!"

"Henry?"

"Yes, it's Henry, what took so long?" Behind the static in the background there's the sounds of a crowd, clomping of feet, and too many languages to count.

"Where are you?"

"I'm at the Tokyo International Airport. I'm on my way back to the States. I'm just getting out of the annual stockholders' meeting here, but Hanes was kind enough to FedEx me your new little demo tape."

It was late at night (or early in the morning, however you chose to look at it), but Mark knew that James was referring to the rough-mix cassette of "I Want to Fuck You" that Mark had sent over to Pacific Media on Monday.

"Yeah, and?"

"It's not going to work, Pellion." There's a scratchiness on the phone, Henry's voice drowned out by the airport's PA system making onboard announcements in half a dozen tongues.

"What was that last part?" Mark gulps.

"I said," Henry says slowly, to be understood more clearly, only now his voice is coming through perfectly and each word tattoos failure onto Mark's soul, *"It's . . . not . . . going . . . to . . . work."*

Mark's eyes clamp shut at the same moment his mouth becomes bone dry.

"Pellion, you still there? Anyway, I've got to go, my plane's leaving. I just called to say"—there's a pause, Mark hearing shuffling in the background, a businessman taking the phone out of the cradle next to Henry's and beginning to dial—"nice try."

Mark drives, with Steve and Gary, for some reason, in the backseat. He feels like a chauffeur, sitting in the front seat, watching them out of the corner of the rearview mirror while they badger back and forth and complain to him about each other. He half expects them to break out into the license plate game as he heads down Vine, making a left onto Melrose.

The day after the late-night phone call Mark got hold of someone who knew where Henry James was. The receptionist at Pacific Media said he was still in Japan; while his assistant said he was back in America, only he would be stuck at the airport until well past six; while someone in promotion that Mark had been accidentally connected to swore she saw him in the delicatessen across the street at ten, ordering his usual plain bagel, toasted, no butter, just cream cheese. Finally, they connected him to Hanes.

"Well, if it isn't the next big thing," Hanes said, the sound of him biting into an apple audible above general office noise. "I mean that literally."

Mark had to wait for Hanes's laughing to die down before he could continue.

"Listen, where's Henry?"

"Why don't you ask Sylvia?"

"I *tried* Sylvia and she gave me some bullshit about him still being out of the country, but I spoke to him last night and he was at the airport, heading back."

"Did he mention my FedEx?" Another bite.

"Yeah, thanks a lot, Hanes. You're a true friend." In the background Mark could hear the whir of half a dozen copiers. He figured that Hanes was pissed that Mark had at least a shot at fulfilling his dreams, while five years from now Hanes would still be stuck in the mail room, his feet on the desk, eating yet another apple, trying to hold up a phone conversation while the whir of the newer, faster copiers drowned him out. What Mark didn't know was that Hanes had a plan, one he concocted the day he met Mark, and that it was going perfectly. "Why don't you tell me where Henry is? You see, that way we can have a nice, embarrassing shouting match that *you* could tell the whole office about. You'd like that, wouldn't you?"

Hanes's eyes opened wider than they did when a new batch of Victoria's Secret catalogs passed through the mail room.

"He's down at Electro Vox studios. On Melrose"—he could barely say the words fast enough—"studio C."

Now Gary shouts from the backseat, "Quit kicking me."

"You're kicking *me*," Steve responds.

"Will the two of you shut the fuck up?" Mark screams as he nearly rams into a red Mazda as the far right-hand lane of the two-lane road dead-ends into a number of parked cars. He swerves quickly to the left, honked at by a bus, and holds on to the wheel with one hand, sweating, squinting, trying to read the addresses. Trying to find the studio. "Will you guys help, for God's sake?"

"Okay, uh, what's the address?"

"Fifty fifty-four Melrose."

Gary pipes up, "I think Melrose is another block south."

Steve slaps him on his crew-cut head. "We're *on* Melrose, you idiot. We're just looking for the number."

"Let's see . . . Larchmont. What was the address of the gas station back there? Shit, there it is."

Mark passes the studio, set into a small block flanked on one side by Al's Liquors and the other by Lucy's El Adobe, a Mexican restaurant. He turns right, parks on the street, and walks hurriedly toward the studio, followed by Steve and Gary.

Mark enters the building quickly, the mini blinds hanging from the back of the door clanging loudly as he slams it shut. There's no one at the reception desk, so he wanders down the hall, gray-colored carpeting inlaid with ribbons of red and pink. Around a corner and past a unisex bathroom he sees a placard on the wall, STUDIO C. He opens the door quickly as the tenants inside all swing their heads and look toward the intruder who has invaded their sanctuary. Henry James does *not* look happy.

In the booth are Henry, a couple of guys in suits hanging out in director's chairs toward the back wall, a woman with a clipboard sitting at the mixing console, who Mark guesses is an engineer. Through the glass he sees into the studio, where a string quartet made up of three men and one woman sit before music stands, their instruments in a state of at ease. They must be on a break. Also sitting at the mixing console, his large head in his hands, is Kenneth.

"Jesus, Kenneth, what have these vultures got you moonlighting on?" Mark good-naturedly asks.

Steve and Gary enter the room a second later. Kenneth is silent, just stares at the immense board in front of him.

"Kenneth's not moonlighting, Mark," Henry says as a way of greeting. After all, why waste time? "He's working on *your* record."

"What?" Mark says, shocked.

Steve and Gary just look at each other, not sure what to think. "*Why?*"

"Well, when Hanes sent me over the rough mix of the new song, it gave me a chance to reevaluate the whole record. And, well"—he takes a deep breath—"I just didn't think it sounded as good as it could have. So, I . . ." Henry sounds somewhat embarrassed, but not of the act, only that he's been caught.

"So you *what?*" Mark approaches him, still not sure exactly what's going on.

"So I booked some extra studio time to record some string sections that are going to go great on a few of your songs."

"No they're not!" Mark shouts.

"I hate to tell you this"—Henry's embarrassment suddenly shifts from himself to feeling embarrassed for Mark—"but yes, they are."

From inside the studio the string quartet watch the scene through the window into the booth like a silent movie. They watch as Mark approaches Henry yet again, who casually sits down in a chair and crosses his legs. Mark's arms are waving about, his mouth opening and closing though no sound can be heard on this side of the glass.

The heavyset cello player turns to one of the violinists and says, "This sure beats the Philharmonic, eh boys?"

"Look, Mark," Henry exasperatingly says, "all that's well and good, but in the end I don't give a rat's ass about what your songs sounded like when you wrote them. I mean, what in the hell does that mean? Pacific Records is in the business of making money, not your records the way you've always dreamed of them."

"But when you signed us"—Mark's voice is now shaking—"you said—"

"Yes," James cuts him off. "*Signed.* That's a good word, isn't it? Now let's use it in another context, like when you *sign* your contract, which states oh so very clearly that we own your name, we own your songs, that we own *you.*"

"He owns *us?*" Steve asks, turning to Gary.

"Well, not you two," Henry quickly says, "because you're just the drummer and bassist and never had any legal rights to the songs in the first place. But he"—Henry points to Mark with devilish glee—"is *all* ours."

On the other side of the glass the quartet, who put down their instruments five minutes ago, continue to watch the silent but animated debate. They watch as Henry James says something, drolly it seems, eyes only half open as he talks, as if he really couldn't be bothered with such plebeian tasks. Mark listens to what he's saying and suddenly his eyes widen, the muscles on the back of his neck tense, shoulders jump up. He makes for Henry but Gary and Steve hold him back. The four classically trained musicians watch as Henry and Kenneth laugh and Steve and Gary try to pin Mark down.

Mark wrestles his way free from his band mates and jumps on a couch, avoiding Kenneth, leaping onto Henry, the force of the blow knocking him and the chair over, sending them both to the ground.

"Hey," says the flutist to the other three, "good move."

**The date that Gary and Whitney began shortly after the** incident with Henry James on Friday was still going on well into Saturday, not that either of them minded.

Now, as they travel south on the Hollywood freeway, staying to the right in order to loop around a sinewy off ramp, transferring to the 110 heading toward Pasadena, Gary thinks back to the morning, how he spent another night with Whitney and how that unexpectedly turned into yet another day. It's funny, but after a lifetime of waking up and going to sleep, the pattern could still, sometimes, amaze. They woke first at nine. He turned and faced her clock, thinking it was still early, while she was alarmed they had slept so late.

"But it's Saturday," he groaned, trying to grab another handful of the covers, which she had to then pin down with all of her body.

"I *know* it's Saturday, and quit hogging the covers."

He drifted back into sleep, only to be jarred awake seconds later by a knocking motion upside his head as Whitney kept asking, "Is that what you are? A covers hog?"

Gary hesitantly separated his eyes, thinking another day had already passed.

"Wha?"

"I said, get up, it's getting late."

"No," he murmured, his voice an octave lower than usual and his throat covered in layers of gook, "that's not what you said. You called me a pig."

"A hog, but you're close." She tried a final time to dethrone him from the command he held over the bed, his legs open in a scissors position while his arms stretched out, as if he were making the shape of an angel in soft sand or snow. But Gary would not budge. Already he retreated into stentorian snoring, which had alarmed her the night before. She had wondered if he wasn't dying, a hair ball caught deep within his chest and the staccato noises sputtering out of his nose and half-open mouth the last gasps of an unrealized life passing away.

So they fell asleep again, and even though Whitney had initially protested the supplemental slumber, when they both simultaneously awoke an hour later she felt incredibly rested and had even dreamed (Gary spooning her, his furry calves warm against her now stubbly legs and his arms circling her waist, one above and, she did not know how he achieved this without waking her, one below).

"What's this place called again?" Gary asks as he fumbles with a book of matches, trying to light a cigarette dangling between his lips, which are rocking with the rest of his body as Whitney struggles to keep the lurching van above sixty miles per hour even though it doesn't seem to have been designed for such an event.

"Saint Vincent's!" Whitney shouts out, both hands on the wheel as she changes lanes, getting ready for the Figueroa off ramp, which lies on the left side of the road and not the right.

"What?" Gary shouts back, the match in his hand finally catching and flaming up, but he loses the sight of the tip of his cigarette as they enter a long, dark tunnel. He fumbles with the match until he feels the heat creep to the tips of his fingers, and tosses it out the window. Instead it flies into the backseat. Gary just shrugs, figuring the wind will blow it out before it lands on any of the inflammable hair-care products piled toward the side door.

"*Saint Vincent's!*" Whitney says again, distracted for a second, and she goes over one lane too far and is caught in the line of cars waiting to merge with Interstate 5. After she passes a large truck and switches back into the right lane, she turns and faces Gary, trusting one hand with the wheel, which feels like the reins of a horse not yet broken. "It's that thrift store I told you about the other day!"

Gary sees Whitney's lips move, but due to the rushing of the traffic around him and the rattling of so many loose parts of the van, he only makes out the words *thrift* and *store,* and that's all he needs to know. He smiles and nods, and Whitney smiles also before turning her attention back to the vibrating wheel.

They exit Figueroa, heading down a winding off ramp that dumps them into an unsavory-looking neighborhood. She takes a right, then another right, heading over a bridge, the road separated down the center by old and unused train tracks, and the van shifts from side to side, the too-skinny tires caught in the grooves. Whitney turns left into a large parking lot, across the street from which are a dozen or so homeless men, some sleeping in boxes or just on the curb, all of their possessions stuffed in ragged pockets or a shopping cart. Whitney parks in the corner of the lot, stealing the second-to-last space from a dark blue El Camino. She and Gary walk up a ramp and into the large building, which is bustling with activity. A Hispanic security guard checking customers' receipts as they leave checks out Whitney's ass as they pass, Gary catching this only because he glances back as the El Camino burns rubber, peeling out of the cramped lot.

They separate and Whitney heads instantly for the far corner of the room, where a long row of bookshelves is filled with both hardcover and paperback books. She examines every book, her head cocked to one side so she can scan each spine. Judging from the minimal amount of books in her apartment, Gary did not think she read so much, but a few days ago Whitney admitted that most of her books were in storage. She said that she was running out of space in such a small apartment, and Gary threw his hands up, saying he had the same problem.

He had felt like a fool when, the night before, they had begun talking about reading and writing and writers they liked. Gary, who had all his life immersed himself in music rather than literature, tried to conjure up the names of the books that he'd read in the past year, most of them recommended by friends or girls he was dating.

"Carver," he had offered. "I love Raymond Carver. Short stories. Great stuff. So *real*."

"Oh, yes." Whitney was so eager to respond that she nearly choked on the piece of food she was chewing on. "I *agree*. He's fantastic. Carver's adorable."

Pleased to see he had hit upon a mutually admired topic, Gary pushed it, dredging from the back reaches of his mind the books his girlfriend Sharon had turned him on to many years ago.

"What's that one book that's like a . . . collection? You know, of other stuff?"

Whitney swallowed and then wiped down the corners of her mouth with a heavy linen napkin, which did not seem to want to bend.

"Gary," she said slowly, "they're *all* collections."

"No, no, I know that, geez. *The New Yorker*, right? *Esquire?* Places like that. But this one was like a . . . a sampler of all his other books. Um, it's like a . . . reader . . . no, you know, an . . ." The word he was searching for was *omnibus*, the definition of which seemed to fit even though he always pronounced it as *on-the-bus*, losing the *m* somewhere along the way. But then again, all of Carver's books could be considered *on-the-buses*. He decided to drop the subject, bringing up instead Kurt Vonnegut, whom Whitney did not like. "Grumpy old man," she responded, and this provided a springboard to a different topic altogether: movies. Later, as he drifted to sleep by her side, the title of the Carver book floated to the surface of his brain like an Ivory soap bar in bath water. *Where I'm Calling From*.

Gary watches her drift into the crowd before hanging a right into a graveyard of recliners and used stereo accessories. After fingering a few eight-track players and even an old reel-to-reel that looks like something the Beatles might have used to record a demo, he looks across the cavernous hall to where Whitney has moved over only one bookshelf in nearly half an hour. He thinks how weird it is that this girl, blurry to him now, was unclothed and in his arms just a few hours ago. Even more strange is that a few weeks ago she was a complete stranger. It makes Gary look at the other men and women surrounding him and wonder what role in his life they could occupy, given a few months' time. He figures that along with the six-degrees separation there is also the two-ply tissue of what could have been, how a stranger glanced at on a street corner, the one you almost talked to but then demurred out of shyness, may have been the one who would have changed your life forever.

He looks over at Whitney and thinks how he walked around her apartment with no clothes on without thinking it was strange, and it might have slipped his observation completely if she hadn't greeted him upon his arrival from the kitchen, where he had been sent on a mission of water, "Why, Gary Reiger, I do believe you're naked." Gary just blushed and looked down, his slight paunch sticking out of his otherwise slim frame like half a basketball, his penis drooping below that and surrounded by a crown of pubic hair. He tried to cover himself with the glass, which, being see-through and filled with water, proved a bad idea. Instead of the glass shielding him, his embarrassed dick was visible through a carnival-like mirror, which made it appear skinny and slight, the way Gary always feared.

"It's funny," Whitney said as she opened her arms and her breasts drifted to opposite sides, "but I haven't spent this much time naked since my freshman year of college."

At about noon, boxers, panties, and a bra were put on, only to be pulled off by one o'clock. A little after three, Whitney lay on her stomach with Gary's legs over her back and tapped out ash into an ashtray advertising a Madrid casino and remarked upon the magical properties of waning daylight. Gary smiled before he could agree, feeling not only lucky to be in the arms of an attractive woman, but lucky he was with one who noticed such things. He watched as the curling lines of smoke from smoldering incense seemed to make mazes in the musty air, their own musky scents competing with the patchouli. Gary responded that the California sunshine had seemed different to him when sitting on the hardwood floors of the rented house, reading the paper on a bright Sunday morning with the shutters open; how the sun not only seemed to be in the room with him but surrounded him like amniotic fluid.

"Maybe the Beach Boys were really onto something," he said, simply because the words came into his head, but then felt stupid for not editing himself.

"You're right," Whitney was quick to respond, allaying Gary's fear that he had talked too dreamily, like an asshole. "I have a cousin from back East and I spent a summer there and it *did* feel different."

Gary smiled and filed the discussion away in the drawer of things they had in common, glad to see the bin was already full and that he'd soon be needing another.

"In fact, when I think of the future, I think of sunlight." Whitney rolled over as Gary raised his legs slightly, like a drawbridge, for her to do so.

"You mean, like Buck Rogers in a tanning booth?"

"No." Whitney giggled like a girl. "I mean, I close my eyes"—which she did—"and I think of a room. A strange room, but I don't know where it is. It could be in Paris, or Omaha, or maybe just down the block. But I never think of it at night, or in a rainstorm."

She paused for a second and Gary took the chance, while Whitney was lying on her back to examine the body he had only stolen glances at, or tried to make out the corners of in the dark or in clothes. He noticed she had a small pot belly, just a little pocket of flesh below her belly button, and he laughed because it matched the one that had grown on his own body recently, made fat by the doughnuts he ate while hanging around the recording studio and all of the pizzas ordered with twenties taken from the seemingly never-ending supply smiled up by automatic teller machines that seemed to be on every corner in Los Angeles.

"I think of this room." She shut her eyes even tighter and crinkled up her nose, cheeks turned into flesh pockets as if pinched by invisible hands. "I think of this strange room in the daylight. And *that's* where I'm going to be. That's my future. I don't know how or where, but there it is."

Gary loses his train of thought when he sees a number of old video game units sitting on a shelf above a pile of old popcorn makers and automatic can openers. He picks up an Intellivision video game unit, the two controllers set into the main console and facing each other, held down with masking tape, the golden disks still intact and wobbly to the touch. It looks okay when he examines it, but with electronic things all you need is a scraped microchip inside and no matter how bright and shiny the plastic is on the outside, the damn thing will never work. Gary had been burned before with an Astrocade system, and one time he even found the shell of a Vectrex, only to find the vector monitor had been completely ripped out and the unscrupulous proprietor of the flea market stall was charging ten bucks just for the black plastic casing and a joystick attached with a long red rubber band.

He turns over the Intellivision and spots a $10 price tag. He weighs the option in his head for a few seconds, but then places the system back on the shelf along with two others and an old Pong console with no controls.

*Last thing I need is an Intellivision right now. I can't believe I bought a 2600 from that kid at the garage sale the other day. I'd better just stick to trying to find some decent cartridges for that. The only thing the Intellivision was good for was sports games, and I'm not going to shell out fifty bucks for a bunch of cartridges just to have Steve and Mark constantly whip my ass in World Series Baseball. Besides, I'm Christmas shopping with Steve tomorrow. I should concentrate on gifts for other people. Like Whitney. What in the hell should I get for Whitney?*

An hour later Gary bumps into her in a white L-shaped room filled with toys that connects a section overflowing with drapes and tablecloths to one of the main hangarlike areas stacked with

TVs, desks, and what seems like a football field of washers and dryers. He loops his arms around her waist and scoops her up.

"Find anything?"

"Yeah," she says quickly, breaking out of his grasp to show-case the clothes draped over her left arm. "Check out this pair of corduroy bell-bottoms! They're a little tight in the hips, but I guess that's sort of the point, right? And here's this cool men's tuxedo jacket that I thought would look nice with this black mini I've got. And look at these shoes!"

Whitney shoves a pair of light-pumpkin- or dark-mustard-colored pumps in his face; Gary can't tell due to the too-bright lighting, and since she's madly waving the vinyl-covered slip-ons back and forth.

"Oh, uh, nice," he lies, thinking the shoes are godawful and praying she never wears them out in public when he's around. Hell, here he thought he might be falling in love and already he was acting like a jerk. "Um, what else?"

She shows him a pair of black-and-white striped leggings that remind her of that witch in *The Wizard of Oz,* the one that was flattened by the house, but she notices him looking wistfully off into the distance, one hand poking at a large bin raised off the ground, shoved full of assorted toys, while the other bangs repeatedly into his gut.

"I'm sorry, am I boring you or something?"

"No, I was just thinking."

"Of bad things?"

"No, good things."

Her faces cracks into a smile.

"Then why be sad?"

"Because it just makes me miss you, that's all. Like, you were wandering around getting your stuff"—he pulls his hand from jabbing at his love handles to motion toward her pile of stuff, returning it to his aching midsection only a second later—"and all I could think of was you walking around out there some-where, and how you still smelled like me."

She smiles and moves in closer.

"And it was like, you know how you go to a party with a boyfriend or girlfriend and you may be in the backyard standing over the keg shooting the shit with your buddies, but it's okay because you just know, you can just *feel* that the girl you, uh, *care for* is inside the house, and you've got this feeling that she's thinking of you, too?"

"I know what that's like." She places a few of the items on her arm onto a staggered white wooden rack holding assorted diplomas and picture frames, using the freed hand to rub the soft small of his back. It was funny, but even she had noticed him getting chubbier in the last couple of weeks, as the stress from the record deal became more apparent and he was honest about what he thought of her cooking; lately he suggested they just order a pizza. "And it's nice."

"I know . . . and I'm just going to miss you next week. At Christmas, with you going away to your sister's."

"I know, but it's just for a couple of days."

"And, you know, after."

She raises her head from where it had been staring intently at his chest, noticing how it was wavering back and forth and thinking that it was cute, hoping it was the sign of a heart but not a heart condition.

"After . . . what?"

"Well, you know what happened yesterday, right?"

"Yeah, sure. So?"

Gary waits as a family of Mexicans wades into the room, looks over the toys, and then scampers off as a group. Gary always feels bad to run into these sorts of families when he's scouring thrift stores or swap meets. He's only out for kitsch items, maybe a *Swat* lunch box or a set of *Mork and Mindy* sheets, while these poverty-stricken families treat the Salvation Army the way the rest of this city treats the Beverly Center. Gary often spied migrant workers, their faces hard and their skin tanned deep like leather, trying on Western-style button-up shirts in the aisles, and he was unable to tell which was the old shirt they had worn in and which was the old shirt they were trying on. Thrift stores are a joke to Gary and most of his generation, a place to find funky flannel shirts and knitted caps that read SIT ON IT, knowing such items will get a laugh when worn to a party or bar, while others shop at thrift stores because that is all they can afford.

"So that means that Bottlecap—I mean, Steve, Mark, and I— may have blown the whole deal. We may have to head back to Virginia."

She draws back, knocking a Speak-n-Spell onto the floor.

"When's this going to happen?"

Gary bends over to pick up the red plastic device, heavy in his hands, and he notices the yellow-and-white-membrane keyboard is in remarkably good shape. He wonders whether or not it still works.

"That's just it, Whitney. I don't know if I *want* it to happen. I mean, I like it here." He puts the toy back into the pile with the others, but tries to find a price tag before returning his eyes to Whitney's. "I like *you*."

"So you're going to . . . stay?" she asks, confused.

"That's just it. I don't even know how much of the decision is mine. Mark's talking about walking away from the whole deal, but I just don't think I can do that. I want to stay here. I mean, I don't want to seem presumptuous and say I'm staying for us . . ." His eyes dart bashfully to the ground.

Whitney raises up Gary's drooping chin with a crooked forefinger. "Do you think I let just any guy spend the night at my house and then take him all the way out here?"

Actually, Gary *had* been considering this, sitting up in her bed during one of the odd moments this morning when he was awake and it was she who was sleeping and snoring slightly (on her it was slightly cute).

"I don't know," he says dumbly, soliciting the response.

"No, I don't, goofball. You're special to me. I know it's been just a short while, but that doesn't mean I don't feel an awful lot for you."

Whitney looks in Gary's eyes and he looks back, but is then stunned by the moment and must look away. He hates feeling this mature, this much like an adult. He wants to think that his mother is outside, waiting for him, tapping her foot angrily because the dinner she has prepared for him is growing cold back at home, where he still lives. To avoid her eyes now boring a hole into his soul (what was it anyway with girls and eyes?), he engulfs her in a quick embrace.

"I just want to make sure it's not just me you're staying for," Whitney says, a tad heavy on the dramatics, as if a fake, movie-style rain were being brushed in her face. "I want it to be every-thing. The *right* reasons."

With his chin propped up on her shoulder he spots a tomato orange piece of plastic sitting atop the pyramid of junk toys.

"I mean, I want it be for me in some ways but, you know, not in *every* way."

The object is thin, with sharp right angles on one side and rounded curves on the other. As he narrows his vision he sees that is a video game cartridge, meant for the Atari Video Computer System. He holds Whitney tighter, but only so he can crane his neck out even farther, trying desperately to read the lettering on the face of the game.

"I can't remember when I've felt so much for someone after so little time, you know? Gary?"

Squinting, he makes out the words printed against a black-and-white checkerboard background. CHASE THE CHUCK-WAGON. Gary nearly jumps out of his skin. The game is considered the most hard to find in the large and completely out-of-print catalog produced for the VCS. It was given away for a brief time in the early eighties as a promotional item for Purina dog food, and now fetched a price of over $100 from collectors. Gary has never laid eyes upon the real thing, only heard whispers about it from geeks around the country he met who still actively collected Atari memorabilia. He saw it in a picture once, a sketchy Xerox a fan had mailed to one of the zines that devoted its contents to Atari, the photocopy grainy and mysterious, looking like the only blurry black-and-white photo the FBI has of a Middle Eastern terrorist.

"I just want to make sure we're right for each other." Whitney pulls back, only to find Gary gazing off into the distance. "Gary?"

In a rushed kiss he lurches forward, lodging one hand deep into her pants as cover while the other reaches out for his found treasure, a barely adhering price tag reading 99¢. "I am," he reassures her, trying to retrace the labyrinthine path of freeways that will lead him and his girlfriend home to his video game. "I *am*."

As he pulls Whitney even tighter he can feel the tip of one of her rings begin to dig into the bulging flesh of his waist. She pulls back, nervously laughing as she wipes the trail of blood from the jewelry. They kiss again and then she heads outside, to examine the As Is section, which lies in the parking lot next to the large building. After her decampment Gary feels his wound, looking at the bright red gash in his gut made from the gift he gave back to her just the other day.

She had left the ring, along with another and a barrette, at his house earlier in the week, after they had been to dinner at a Thai restaurant in Silverlake. She had planned to just drop him off, but took up his offer of coffee and came inside, even though both forgot about the coffee and headed straight into his room. Steve and even Mark were at home, each in their own rooms, the light on in Mark's, the sound of snoring coming from Steve's. While Gary and Whitney had sex, Gary wanted them to stay quiet so his roommates would not hear him, but also wanted to be loud so they would. The barrette was shaken loose while they were fucking, and this impressed them both, the noise emanating from Gary's room impressing Steve and Mark. The rings were removed only afterward, when Whitney decided she was too sleepy and her legs too wobbly for the drive home. She would stay the night.

Both were gold, one thin, the band plain while the top was knobby with serrations between each rising indentation. The other was more ornate. This one featured a large black globe surrounded by a dozen smaller black spheres, tentacles of gold sprouting up between each one. The height of the decoration nearly matched the circumference of the trim, squared band. Gary tried each on but found he could get neither past the first digit of any of his fingers, even his pinky. Whitney had truly small hands.

She placed the rings on the small table beside the bed, which was home to an alarm clock and lamp. Next to these Gary placed the barrette, which had come to lie in the middle of the floor. It was cheap, made of some spotted metal, a line of dried glue on top leading him to believe that at one point the thing had held on its surface an extra bit of something. In the morning, in a rush to make her first appointment of the day, she had left the pieces behind.

Before returning the objects, he deposited them in a burgundy velvet jewelry case, then wrapped the box, which was difficult since it was all fuzzy and not square. He thought she would get a kick out of opening the package as if something new were inside. This made sense to Gary, even though it had also made sense to Gary to spit on the bath mat.

Besides the two rings and the barrette she had left half a pack of cigarettes, which were housed in a gold-with-a-blue-cover box, which was square, the approximate size of a property deed in the board game Monopoly. DUNHILL, the container declared in block letters that were sandwiched between a crest flanked by lions above and the words *Superior Mild* in script below. She admitted that even though the cigarettes were expensive and looked pretentious, they were the only brand she could stand.

"Don't talk to me about Marlboros," she had said the night before, waving away his offer of a cigarette when she could, temporarily, not find her own. Her vehemence behind the comment made Gary believe that there was something other than the inefficiency of Marlboro Lights at stake. As she told him a story that culminated in the dramatic retelling of the worst day of her life, he tried to imagine what that secret might be. *Maybe an old boyfriend, that one that sounds like Picasso, maybe he burned her with the lit end of a Marlboro. Maybe a relative, that*

grandmother who lived out her years on that commune in
Sedona, maybe she died of lung cancer after smoking Marlboros
for years. Maybe her dad, who she's never really talked about
much, was one of those Marlboro men you see in magazines,
rugged good looks, and he mistreated Whitney's mother and her,
and she never forgave him.

Sitting down the next day with his coffee, which had turned
cold after sitting untouched in the large black bowl of the cup
for fifteen minutes, he grabbed for the box of blue cigarettes.
He took one out and tried to light it, noticing that he had to
actually suck in rather than just dangle the tip of the thing in and
out of the flame. The cigarette felt solid in his hand, heavy, as if
it were wound tighter than the Marlboros he had smoked while
growing up and that Whitney had chastised him for mentioning
the night before. He took a drag and found that in order to get
the smoke into his lungs he had to deeply inhale, but this made
sense. That which was more expensive was always more difficult
to take in.

Steve also had a girl forget jewelry in his apartment. For him,
it had been a pair of earrings. Faux pearl (he'd hoped, since in
the end he just threw them away) surrounded by shallow, chip-
ping disks of gold color but not, most likely, gold metal. Kiva,
the artist he sometimes dated, on and off like a light switch that
neither asked to be flicked, found them sitting on his mantel one
morning.

"Whose are these?"

Steve tried to be cool, but it came out like being an asshole.

"A friend's," he said plainly, as if Gary or Mark might have left
them and not some girl who'd removed them while they
screwed on the floor, the brass posts poking into the sides of her
neck. Sure, Mark did have pierced ears, but he'd certainly never
wear these.

"A friend," she replied. Kiva decided to drop the subject, for-
going the shouts and loudly vocalized proclamations of innocence she knew would follow. The argument was like a
Hollywood summer blockbuster that she felt no need to see

because she was sure how the entire thing would turn out anyway: after years of action films and fights with boyfriends, she figured out there was no point in attending either.

Kiva's hurt was tempered by the fact that her regulated reservoir of emotion for Steve was small. Since neither had yet to proclaim an amount of substantive emotion (you cannot name something which does not exist, unless one wishes to christen silence, which has already been named), she did not really care who he slept with. Their relationship, if an outsider could term it so, was casual, and if that casualness led to a casualty, she was damned if she was going to let it come by way of some eery canal of her own unprotected psyche, the last remnant of her girlish desire, which she had left unshielded from the barbaric, unfeeling nature of men. In fact, she was well aware that if she wore jewelry she might have been the one to leave something behind for another girl to find. Let Steve explain away one of her paintbrushes or that sketch of him in the nude, which she had done while drunk, on the back of a vinyl copy of the Beatles' "white" album in black charcoal, to one of the other women he had conned into letting him fuck. Let someone else possess the anger she tried to squelch after learning that Steve, the Steve she certainly did not own but leased from time to time, was having sex with another. That was when she learned the most important lesson of her life: the trick was not to care.

Mark had also been made curious by the pieces of themselves that women left lying around. Years ago Laura left at his house a thin silver bracelet and he wore it, for a month, as his own; and just a few weeks ago he had held Corinne's makeup bag as if it were Yorick's skull.

It seemed that the boys in Bottlecap could write an entire record around the emotions of watching for movement the possessions of women. Of the three, Mark, with his previous training, could write some especially strong material about these feelings. Feelings he'd already felt but just watched slink by, unexploited, afraid he'd be too touched by the magnification of the emotion once it'd been turned into song: words and melody and the force of his fingers against the strings; the force of the sound coming out of his amplifier, which would hit him like a slap, a realization. If he could write that song, it would mean that he could feel love. He was unsure of which to be more afraid of. Forget being a person; if Mark ever stopped being such a smart-ass, he might actually become an artist. Steve and Gary were just too lazy to try.

**Startled, Corinne looks up from the golden yellow**
polenta she's frying up with half an inch of olive oil in her
favorite saucepan, the one with the copper bottom.

"You did *what?*"

Mark nibbles on a corner of garlic bread, recounting Friday's
events.

"I choked him."

Corinne moves across the room and slaps Mark's hand away
from the bread the way his mother used to do years ago, so he
wouldn't spoil his appetite.

"You *choked* your A&R man?"

"Not a smart move?"

Corinne moves back to the stove, flips over the squares of
cornmeal and crushed garlic, browning them on both sides. She
then grabs an oven mitt in the shape of a fish, her hand sliding
into the mouth portion, and when she reaches for the oven's
handle, it looks like Jaws getting ready to take another bite out
of Quinn.

"It's not my own personal management style, but hey."

"And then, later that day, as if we hadn't had enough excitement, Hanes dropped by with a copy of the contract, hot off the
laser printer. Gary, Steve, and I sat down to read the fucking
thing, all forty-five pages of it, and you should see the shit
they've got in there. I bet they've got my firstborn and my—"

"So don't sign it." Corinne turns from the stove to Mark. "Rip
it up and move on."

"We can't do that. That deal memo I signed a few months ago was legally binding. We can either sign the contract or else try and fight it, but either way Subterfuge owns us."

"So you already signed a contract?"

"Sort of, only I didn't know it at the time. Steve told me yesterday that Hanes told him a few months ago that the letter of intent was legally binding. When I asked Steve how come he didn't tell me any of this until now, he sort of shrugged, told me he wished it wasn't true. But it was."

Mark sees red. His temples throb. Every muscle in his body seems to go loose, like a thousand old red rubber bands snapping all at once.

"Well, from what you've been telling me about this Henry guy lately, it doesn't seem like he's going to play any games with you. Especially with that contract he's got you guys tied into."

"Guys? Me! He's only got *me* tied into it. The others are just hired guns, practically. It's *my* songs they own, *my* name. Hell, Steve never even *liked* the name Bottlecap. Here I fought tooth and nail for this fucking moniker and now some stupid record company owns it. Owns my songs, too."

Mark turns to the place setting in front of him, lodging an elbow on either side of a large white dish with a caster in the center, holding his throbbing head in his hands.

"Oh, Jesus, I just *had* to have the quick money, didn't I?"

Corinne turns off the burners before reaching out and rubbing Mark's back with the oven mitt still on her hand.

"There, there."

He feels her presence, her hands now on the back of his neck, and for half a second it soothes him, until his troubles loom again on the horizon like a gargantuan hill, casting a shadow he fears he'll never be able to escape.

"Why don't you go put some music on while we eat?"

Mark grumbles and leaves the kitchen, returning a minute later after Corinne hears a half a dozen curses followed by clicks in the living room. Music fills the apartment as Mark slouches back into the room, sits down in a chair, and grabs for a different piece of garlic bread, gnawing at the edge like a squirrel bites at a chestnut.

"Who's this?" Corinne asks, pointing into the living room with a wooden spoon with a flat bottom, stained dark by the oil.

Out of habit Mark doesn't respond. Whenever Laura used to come over to his place and ask what music was playing as they cooked dinner or made love, he always hesitated to tell her either the band or the song's name. He would make her tapes for the drives she'd take out of state to visit old friends who had already married and moved away or whose jobs had relocated them to Atlanta or Charlotte, but he never made up a list of songs and bands the way he did with the friends he was trying to impress with live tracks or b-sides from the newest, coolest group. Mark never told Laura the names of the bands because he never wanted her to fuck some other guy while listening to music he had suggested.

"You don't know who this is?" Corinne says, nervously laughing when in actuality she's spooked at the way Mark's now zoned out.

"Huh?" He's shaken out of imagining Laura's phantom infidelities. Only they aren't phantom, and because he left her, they're not infidelities. He scans the room for his cigarettes, convinced he really needs one. "Oh, this is us. Well, sort of."

Corinne places a dish of marinara sauce on the table and puts her hand on Mark's shoulder.

"I thought I recognized that cute voice," she says playfully, even though she hadn't recognized the voice at all. Perhaps somewhere, Corinne laughs inside, there was a suit he fit, and that was the real reason they flew him out here. *I'm sleeping with Johnny Bravo.* It would have been a dream come true.

Halfway into their meal a bit of romaine lettuce falls out of her mouth as she gasps. She remembers something she wanted to ask Mark earlier in the day. He laughs as the green leafy vegetable falls onto the floor and she delicately picks it up and folds it into her napkin.

"What is it?"

"I talked to my parents . . . about Christmas."

Mark's stomach gets tight. He grabs another piece of bread just to have something to do, as an excuse.

"And, well, they invited you over. I mean *us*. I mean," she says, embarrassed, "of course I'll be there. But you can, too. If you want to."

"Wow." Mark pops a torn-off corner of the bread into his mouth. "I feel like this is a callback."

"I'm impressed with your handle of so-Cal lingo." She rides her foot up his thigh underneath the table. "Does this mean you'll go?"

"I don't know. After Thanksgiving the guys are sort of pissed at me, and things are tense enough as it is, so I sort of promised I'd spend the day with them."

"No, this isn't Christmas Day, just Christmas Eve. Trust me, you wouldn't want to be with my family on Christmas Day."

Corinne gets up and goes into the kitchen for the bowl of freshly grated parmesan cheese that she left in the refrigerator.

"Why not?" Mark calls out.

"Because that's when we visit relatives out in San Marino, and it's just really boring." She reenters the room, placing the bowl of cheese in the center of the table. "This would just be Christmas Eve dinner with me and the folks. I know things are shaky all around, even with us, but I need you there as a shield, okay? Please?"

"Sure," Mark says, even though he's not quite convinced. As Corinne scoops out another portion of polenta from the thick black serving plate, Mark thinks about the offer. Thanksgiving was all right, he guessed. He had been a little tense, felt out of his league, but in the end it gave him a perspective of Corinne that he never would have seen, even if he never left her side for the next five years. Seeing a girl around her parents just answered so many questions for him, made him see her in a different light. It was as if for the months he'd known her before, she was in black-and-white, but now she existed in color. Then he gets sad, figuring she'll never see him in his home environment, meet his parents, or liberate him from the grainy two-tone Chaplinesque image of him she had in her mind. Corinne is thinking the same thing. She feels as if he's now seen her naked but she's only seen him in boxer shorts and an undershirt.

"Wouldn't it be crazy if you just flew your parents here for the holidays?" Excited, she bites too hard on her fork, through the food and into the steel prongs feeling like a retainer between her rows of medically straightened teeth.

"Oh, no," Mark sort of cackles.

"Why not?"

"Who's got that kind of money?"

Corinne barely has time to swallow before answering, "You."

"Look"—he turns serious—"the money we got for our advance has got to last us a *long* time. I know that, and the guys know that. Especially now that things are getting hairy, and since most of theirs is already gone. This may be the last bit of money we get for a while."

"Yeah, I guess so. But don't you miss them?"

Mark just laughs.

"Jesus, Corinne, I've only been gone for three months. It's not like I haven't seen them in forever."

"But I thought right before you came here you were on tour, right?"

"Yeah." Another bite of garlic bread, mouth full. "So?"

"So, that means you haven't seen them for almost half a year."

Mark considers this as he chews.

"Yeah, well, I had dinner with them one night in between the tour and coming here, so"—he looks over the table still covered with food—"I've had my fill."

Corinne wipes down her plate with the polenta on the end of her fork, stabbing at its trails of grease.

"I guess . . . I just can't imagine being away from my family at Christmas, whether I like them or not. That's all."

Mark misreads her signs for the hundredth time and reaches out to her, rubbing her back consolingly, crumbs transferring from his fingertips to the back of her ribbed blouse.

"It's okay. You'll be with them soon."

She throws his arm off.

"No, it's not that. I wish I *weren't* with them half the time. Hell, I've met your little band mates"—she takes her own plate, nearly empty, and Mark's as well, even though there's a few bites left, and heads into the kitchen to drop them into the sink— "and I think I'd rather spend Christmas with *them.*"

She comes back into the room a second later, the clinking sound of dishes being dropped against her tiled counter reverberating in the room and competing with the sounds of Bottlecap still coming out of the stereo's speakers.

"Is that supposed to be a compliment?"

Taking away the serving plates, salad bowls, and the basket of bread, she says, "No."

From the kitchen she says, loud enough to be heard over the water running cold on her hand as she waits for it to get hot, "It's just that my family always plans out my Christmases, well, the entire holidays. Hell, my goddamn life if I'd let them. I'd just like to do my own thing for a change."

Mark just sits there playing with a crust from the bread plate Corinne left on the table.

"But do they ever *ask* me what I'd like to do for Christmas? No. It's always decided for me, as if I was still a child."

For the next ten minutes Corinne tells him about Christmas when her grandparents were still alive, how they'd drive up to Santa Barbara and she'd look forward to the presents she was going to receive on the way up, and admire them on the way back down, but how all that changed after their deaths, in the early eighties, and how her family became splintered and it was only a few aunts and uncles she saw on Christmas, while the rest had their own families. Mark looks around the room as she speaks, Corinne choking up, tears swelling in her eyes, but he can't tell because he's looking over her apartment, the one he's getting more used to day after day. How his things are cropping up on the tops of tables, on hangers in the closets. Half the toiletries on the bathroom sink are his, and his possessions lie almost everywhere and not just in the bottom drawer he was allotted just before Thanksgiving. It's funny, but it feels domestic. And what's even funnier is that it doesn't make him want to run.

For example, last Sunday as he lay in bed, Corinne was horrified to discover they were out of both coffee and cigarettes.

"What is it?" Mark shouted out as he rushed to her shocked side after she'd screamed out from the kitchen as if she'd discovered her parents mutilated on the dining room floor.

"We're . . . out . . . of . . ." Her words were swallowed up by a kind of horrified amazement, the tone implicit in her voice: *I know this sort of thing happens to others, but not to me . . .*

"Yeah, yeah?" Mark, surveying the situation, saw no bloody bodies, no unattached limbs.

"C-c-coffee," Corinne stuttered and then had to take a deep breath before continuing, as if being out of coffee on a Sunday morning was not bad enough, ". . . and . . . cigarettes."

"Yikes," Mark said, not very relieved. He had an encroaching hangover headache. The night had not been a good one sleepwise, and he had been looking forward to the prescription of the house's missing items all night long. He might have preferred murder.

"Look, don't panic," he said, taking charge. He ran to the bedroom and returned a second later, pulling on a pair of jeans, his shoes (no time for socks, dammit), and a royal blue T-shirt that read, in fading letters enclosed in a white box of peeling silk screen, MAX FACTOR *You're Beautiful.* "I'm going to go out and get some more, okay?"

Corinne was still sort of shaking.

"And I'll get some breakfast while I'm out." A slight smile began to appear on her stricken face. "Almond-filled croissants? Maybe a banana-nut muffin? Huh?"

She started to grin and Mark knew that, if he could just have some caffeine within the half hour, the worst would be behind him. Corinne walked him to the door and kissed him good-bye as if he were going on a dangerous expedition (the city on a Sunday morning was *still* dangerous). She noticed the large, thick-as-a-Norman-Mailer-novel Sunday edition of the *Los Angeles Times* on the doorstep but thought, *Without coffee, what's the point?*

Mark returned twenty-five minutes later with two bags, one filled with freshly baked goods and another with a pound of coffee beans, cigarettes stuck in his back pocket. As he entered he could hear the water in the sink flowing, Corinne washing up the dinner dishes from the night before as a way to occupy herself until she was able to satisfy her morning need for caffeine and nicotine. He could see her hands scrubbing the plates, hear the noise they made hitting the sink as she held them under the steaming water and the muffled sound emitted when she placed them on the wood holder to dry. He called out, "Honey, I'm home," not even as a joke, even though that's how she took it. She rushed into the living room, grabbing the bags out of his hands, more happy to see them than him, and as she scampered off to the kitchen, where the Braun coffeemaker already was filled with water and a waiting filter, he couldn't help feeling that, if they ever got married, this is how his life would be, over and over and over. And it wasn't that bad.

"Mark, I'm talking to you."

He looks up, distracted.

"What?"

She's wearing a pair of yellow Rubbermaid gloves now that she's washing the frying pans. They're supposed to make her look dumpy and housewifey, but instead she looks like Audrey Hepburn in *Breakfast at Tiffany's,* her hair pulled back and her slender hands in elegant gloves, on her way to someplace charming.

"You're still at least going to buy your parents presents, right?"

"What? Oh, yeah, sure. Sure."

"It's just that, after that talk of money, I wanted to make sure they were getting *some*thing."

Mark gets up, his back cracking as he does so. He kisses

Corinne on the cheek and fondles her left hand through the sweaty, humid plastic.

"Don't worry, the bags of coal will arrive right on schedule. I've checked with Parental Unit Express and they assured me that—"

"I mean, Christmas is just a little more than a week away and, well"—Corinne slaps him playfully on the arm, leaving a wet stain and suds on his shirt before heading back into the kitchen to finish up on the dishes—"I'd hate for you to forget anybody *special.*"

Mark just stares into the distance, barely feeling the sensation on his arm, and mumbles, "Oh, yeah."

He's too preoccupied to notice, but Corinne had been hinting about something for herself. She had bought a few presents for him and now wondered if she was foolish to expect anything in return. Of course, that's not why she purchased anything for him in the first place, hoping to get something back, but was she crazy to hope he had been sneaking glances at her dress size while she was in the shower or calling up Quincy and drilling her best friend for her favorite color or what kinds of shoes she was currently in the market for? Corinne had been in enough relationships to know that what she was hoping for, even expecting, was not only not outrageous but had better damned well happen, or else a head that kept saying, "Oh, yeah," over and over again, would roll.

She had for him two presents: the first was sort of a joke gift, a fake Hollywood Boulevard Walk of Fame star that she'd bought at a tourist trap gift store in the Farmer's Market, and it came with a sheet of letters with which to spell out a person's name, and she had written, of course, *Mark,* but had to sneak a look at his Virginia driver's license in his wallet to see exactly how many L's were in *Pellion.* The second gift was a Calvin Klein shirt because, judging from the flannel shirt with the bleach-spot holes he first wore on Thanksgiving, she guessed clothes were something he needed. And though the shirt cost $90 and the star only $5, it was the star that she was looking forward to giving him because it was the present she'd really put thought into. She figured any chimp with a credit card could wander into the Beverly Center and come away with something halfway decent (and after working at the Express over a holiday season three years ago for traveling money for her trip to Europe, she learned this was pretty much the case), but she'd spent time on the star. Corinne spent half an hour aligning his name, double-checking the spelling, contemplated adding his middle name (Lane), only the sheet of letters had only two *L*'s; besides, *Only your parents call you by your middle name,* she thought. *It sounds too much like he's being scolded.* She even spent an hour trying to draw an electric guitar and amplifier in the gold circle at the center of the star, and even if the amp looked more like a washing machine and the guitar had seven strings instead of six (she went crazy with the ruler), she still thought it was a good gift, and special because of the effort she'd put into it.

"Honey?"

Mark retreats back into the living room just as the last song on the rough-mix tape is ending. He's glad. He turns on "Brave New World" on KCRW, tries to relax, but can't help thinking again about the money.

*This money has got to last us a long time. I know that. The guys know it, too.*

Gary circles once. Then twice. Then, like a lady, for a third time.

"What in the fuck's your problem?" Steve calls out, fiddling with a new digital watch he bought, big, ugly looking, with so many features he'll never figure them all out. It was a present he bought for himself, a leftover reaction from the fallout of Gary's incredible thrift-store find of the Pac-Man watch, which he is currently wearing, and the infusion of all that cash from Pacific Media.

"Huh?" Gary answers, turning to where Steve is sitting on a bench, staring at an inch-thick book of instructions, the pages he's intently gazing at written in Swedish.

"Just go on in there," Steve replies, not even looking up. He flips through the book (the size of a small novel) trying to find English. He passes Italian, French, and Spanish before reaching thirty pages of bizarre symbols belonging to what language he's not sure.

"What makes you think there's anything stopping me from, uh, going in there?" Gary cocks his head in the direction of the store, a Victoria's Secret on the third level of the Westside Mall. In the window are large photo blowups mounted on cardboard of the same sort of pictures that are featured in the Victoria's Secret catalog. Whenever it landed on the bachelor doorsteps of either Gary or Steve back in Virginia, it would be pored over meticulously, the way a Joycean scholar performs an autopsy on *Finnegans Wake*. "It's just a store." Gary again tries to defend himself, even though he continues to hover a few feet away from the entrance that is bustling with traffic.

"Yeah, it's . . . just a store." Steve has to pause as small clumps of people pass between him and Gary. "A store . . . that you're afraid to go into."

"What makes you say that?"

"Because it's been ten minutes and you're mincing back and forth like a goddamned ten-year-old scared to raid his dad's *Playboy* collection. I mean, it's not like the place is a whorehouse or anything."

"Yeah, but," Gary whispers as he turns away from Steve and peers into the store for the ninth time in fifteen minutes. Inside he sees men and women, some couples, and even kids idly browsing through the aisles, examining the rows upon rows of satin, cotton, and silk bras and panties. The salespeople, all of whom are women (not to mention attractive women), cruise the floor looking for patrons to help, while a rosy potpourri scent lingers in the air and romantic classical music (tapes of which are sold at the front counter) massage your ears as you shop. Steve was, of course, right, but to Gary it *does* sort of feel like a whorehouse, and he still needs convincing that the women selling the lingerie are not also paid to model it for him and then fuck his brains out. "Goddamn all those James Bond movies," Gary chides himself under his breath. "And god*damn* that *St. Elmo's Fire.*"

"Bock-bock-bock." Steve begins making chicken noises, a tactic he learned from a kid he met in Mr. Fox's science class in the seventh grade. "Come on, chicken."

"Okay, okay," Gary says quickly, turning away from his friend for the last time. He shuts his eyes and forces his legs to move, crossing the threshold as if from being a boy into manhood. The second his wary feet cross into Victoria's Secret air space, a shrill alarm goes off.

"Excuse me, sir?" A woman runs to his side wearing a button that reads *Two for One Sale on Second Skin Satin.* "I'm not saying you stole anything, but perhaps you forgot about something in your pockets?"

Gary is mortified. His heart is beating so heavily he fears it might burst out of his chest like the creature from the first *Alien* movie and scamper across the floor and into a pile of stockings, which would get him into even more trouble.

"What? Er, no, I mean . . . I just got here . . ." He begins babbling. "Normally I wouldn't . . . been under stress . . ."

Standing alongside of them is a tourist with fat arms, laden down with many bags, who holds up a Garth Brooks CD with a white plastic square attached. The tourist (Gary can't even tell if it's a man or woman, only that it's wearing a Seattle Mariners sweatshirt) waves the CD in and out of the entrance to the store, where the sensor sets off the alarm once again.

"Sorry, sir." The employee releases hold of Gary's upper arm and shoves him into a section of multicolored Miracle Bras, released on his own recognizance even though she makes a mental note to keep an eye on him.

Gary wants to buy something for Whitney, something for Christmas, something sexy, but he's convinced that everyone in the store, customers included, thinks he's just a young dirty old man whose intent is to wrap the pink Emma bra around his dick and jack off into it while he watches underage girls play out in the street. He wants to buy something, but now that he's inside, he's not sure what.

"Got a girlfriend," he says to no one in particular. "Swear to God I do."

He walks through the store, trying to keep his head low enough to avoid eye contact with anyone else but high enough to be able to still take in the view of the merchandise. Along the walls are large pictures of gorgeous models showcasing the products hanging lifeless around him, and one or two of the images he remembers from back in Virginia or from a copy of the catalog lying in a gas station restroom in Kentucky while on tour, how he masturbated to the picture now looming in front of him, and the memory kicks his penis into a mild erection. He quickly shoves his hands in his pockets and puffs them out like a blowfish, trying to hide the bulge in his pants, an old trick he hasn't used since junior high school.

Around a corner he sees a rack of silk nightgowns in dark, dramatic colors: burgundy, black, jade. He swallows hard. Next to this he sees a line of panties hung on hangers and he has to laugh; in his closet not even the pants are on hangers. Deeper into the shop he sees a line of bras laid out, with the smallest sizes toward the front. Gary kicks himself for not peeking at Whitney's bra size earlier in the week. Instead he makes a cupping gesture with his hands, drawing the attention of several passersby as well as a small girl whom Gary is sure he has scarred for life.

Finally, overcome by embarrassment, he runs out of the store and is still breathing heavily, his chest heaving up and down, as he pays for a teal summer dress he finds on the sale rack at the Gap next door.

"Want to take a break?" Steve asks as he meets Gary back in the lanes of shoppers in between stores. Steve switches the heavy bags in his left hand to his right, the seventh time he's switched, the twinelike handle from a Banana Republic bag digging into the soft flesh of his palm.

"Good idea," answers Gary, whose feet are beginning to ache

in an ill-fitting but cool-looking pair of old sneakers he found last week at a garage sale outside an Art Deco–ish apartment building on Vermont. "Want to get something to eat? While you were in that electronics store I saw a couple of food places on the top floor."

"Sounds good," Steve answers, switching the bags yet again.

After two escalators and an elevator (glass, looking out onto the traffic of the mall, hundreds of people scurrying around with the same purpose, dwindling amounts of cash in their wallets and lists in their hands), they reach the food court in the top level of the mall.

"Look!" Steve shouts out, a small group of Japanese tourists looking his way.

"What?"

"They have Orange Julius out here!"

"Yeah." Gary's own eyes light up as he spots a franchise at the opposite side of the mall. "And there's one of those pretzel-and-cheese places!"

Steve looks at Gary, who stares back. They nod once to cement the tacit understanding that each is going in the other direction for food but will meet the other back where they are currently standing.

Five minutes later it is Steve who first arrives at the large group of tables and picks one near a ledge overlooking the five storeys of the mall, and Gary finds him sucking on a frosty drink while the blood flows back into his hands. Gary places his lunch of a large soft pretzel on a square of wax paper with a small paper cup filled with sharp cheddar cheese (with a Popsicle stick jabbed in the center and standing straight) on the table before sitting down, careful not to further aggravate the blisters forming at the back of his heel and on the hood of his little toe.

"Goddamn, this thing tastes good." Steve sucks relentlessly at his drink, the icy mixture of ice cream and citrus flavors reminding him of a melted-down 50/50 bar. "I almost got one of those Orange Julius wieners, you know." Steve rotates his finger over and over. He's referring to a row of glistening hot dogs rotating endlessly under glass, behind the counter. "Those ones that they serve on a sesame seed bun with slices of pickle, even though the sesame seed part doesn't sound all that appetizing and I don't even like pickles."

"So why did you want to get one?" Gary wipes on the surface of the pretzel small portions of the cheese, which is hard at first but softens as it comes in contact with the doughy heat of the food.

"I don't know. Memory, I guess."

"Memory?"

"Yeah. You see"—he pauses to suck another mouthful before continuing—"I used to always go to Orange Julius in this mall up in Charlottesville when my mom would visit our aunt, or I guess it was *her* sister and *my* aunt. Anyway, I always saw those hot dogs and they looked so good, at least they did then, but I could never get one because my mom said they were too expensive. She said all we could afford was the drink, and then she'd drill it into me on the way home that I was lucky just to have gotten that."

"Times were tough, huh?" Gary takes the first bite of his pretzel, engulfed by his own memories. He feels like he's twelve again, how when he didn't have the three quarters for the pretzel and cheese (or didn't want to waste it, saving the triumvirate of coins for video games instead), the cute blond who sometimes worked behind the counter would sell him just the cheese for a dime.

"Yeah, I guess. I mean, we never could have posed for Dorothea Lange or anything, but let's just say my house was cheap on the frills." He takes the second-to-last sip. "Not many extras."

"Atari but no Colecovision?" Gary puts down his pretzel long enough to point to his T-shirt, which reads FROSTBITE BAILEY'S ARCTIC ARCHITECT with the rainbow-colored Activision logo looming above.

"Yeah," Steve laughs, "and the twenty-six hundred only, not

fifty-two hundred. Hell, I never even got those little race car paddles."

"The ones you could turn all the way around, unlike the tennis ones that just went from side to side?"

"Exactly."

"Ooh," Gary exclaims as if he had been stuck with a rusty nail. He shudders in the thought, just the mere chance of a life not lived, as if witnessing a hideous car accident that could easily have seen himself fly through the windshield and not a stranger. *No Colecovision? That could have been me.*

Steve pauses from trying to suck the last little bit of frothy mixture through the straw and looks over the number of bags crowding around his feet. Inside the Banana Republic bag (along with the plastic casing from his new watch) was a pair of dark brown cotton pants and an Irish linen shirt that looked bronze, a little red, but seemed to glint gold when you rotated it underneath a light source. *The* L.A. Weekly *to get girls,* he scoffed as he modeled the new outfit for the three-way mirror that was ensconced between a bank of two dressing rooms on either side. *All I need to get a girl is some better clothes.* Steve had been feeling rather rickety in his Virginia thrift-store finds; those funny T-shirts that seemed such a laugh riot when he found them in a bin at the Love Is Christ thrift store back in Kitty seemed woefully insufficient for most tasks in the glittering and suntanned metropolis of Los Angeles. Hell, maybe he could sell all his old clothes to Gary. Next to the Banana Republic bag was a plain white box that housed a set of antique wineglasses, which his mother collected. And for his brother, whom he could never seem to satisfy and over whom he was once again befuddled as to a Christmas present, a phenomenon he had encountered ever since he began buying gifts at the age of six, when his father left and he began to receive an allowance, a $50 gift certificate for a music store that had a location in Kitty.

"And now that I've got a little bit of money in the bank, I just don't want to do anything to screw it up."

"You mean the record deal?"

Steve nods as he makes a slurping sound, the cup empty but him not wanting to give up.

"But that contract. Does this mean, then, that you're willing to do whatever it takes? Whatever they say?"

Before answering in the affirmative Steve caresses, as a man strokes his lover's thigh underneath a table, the sides of the bags, which house the best batch of Christmas gifts he's ever been able to afford. The other night was a lesson quickly learned—$300 disappearing in the blink of an eye. He knew then that he never wanted to be poor again.

Gary sits there, wiping more of the gooey cheese onto his snack, waiting for his friend's answer.

"Yes."

"Good. Me too."

# 20

**Mark pulls up to the circular driveway of the St. James**
Club and gets out of his car. An attendant runs out and trades
him his keys for a claim ticket and then rushes away in the rental
car. After almost four months of living in California, Mark is still
not used to valet parking. He feels he's just been very politely
robbed.

Mark runs his hands through his hair, straightening out the
clumps sticking straight up, and then places his palm in front of
his mouth and exhales, trying to gauge his breath. He only sniffs
at the rosy residue of Corinne's conditioner, still hanging on to
his hair after two days of having not been washed. He glides his
tongue over his teeth, trying to dislodge the caked bits of food
stuck between each one, a small Cheeto deposit in the crater of
one of his back molars and a mash of peanut butter still clinging,
like a dull stalactite, to the roof of his mouth. He'd forgotten to
brush his teeth today, too. He glances down at his pants, to
make sure he's wearing some, then his shirt, shoes, and socks.

He is meeting Henry James in the bar. Just through the
lobby, and to the left, the A&R man had told him. "And *don't* be
late," he had also warned. According to the clock in the dashboard of the rental car, which Mark imagined was now on its
way to a chop shop just south of San Diego, the thieves changing
all of his preset radio stations, he was right on time. He cuts
through the lobby, stands at the lip of the bar, and then enters.

Mark is in too much of a daze to notice the spectacular Art

Deco surroundings, the hotel a holdover from America's glorious past, a shrine to the artistic aesthetic of the early twentieth century and a place in which F. Scott Fitzgerald would have felt comfortable having a nervous breakdown, and probably did. Mark figures, now it's his turn.

Walking across the nearly empty room, just a few waiters and busboys getting ready for the Christmas Eve after-dinner rush that will invade in a few hours, Mark spots Henry James sitting at a round table sipping on a mineral water, his hair slicked back, wearing a white shirt, gray slacks, and a long, beautiful, black leather jacket. Pinned to his shirt is a cloisonné button Hanes had given him as a gag gift even though it had cost him $25 (*Expensive gag,* thought Hanes), which showed Santa Claus in a Mercedes 350SL, waving not presents but a bottle of Stolichnaya, two little black *X*'s for eyes.

"Wow, nice jacket." Mark sits down. "New?"

"*Brand* new," says Henry, stretching out his arms and admiring the coat.

"A Christmas present?"

"A present to myself." He grins, leaning over to add, "You don't *want* to know how much this sucker cost."

"Yeah," Mark says, already uneasy, "I bet."

"Here, listen to this." Henry throws a cassette tape onto the table as if a challenge.

Mark, wary, picks the cassette up and slips it into a Walkman Henry provides out of one of the pockets of his black leather jacket. Mark presses the play button. He recognizes the song. It's Bottlecap's new hit single. But then again, it's not. He pulls off the headphones and drops them to the table quickly, as if they were binoculars and through the fogged-up lenses he had just seen another man fucking his wife.

"We're not going to stand for this."

"I know." Henry chuckles, taking a sip of his mineral water. "You're going to lay down and play dead. *That's* what you're going to do."

"What are you talking about?"

"Let me show you something." Henry James reaches for a manila envelope sitting near his feet, and as he does so catches a glance at his new watch with the black leather band, bought to match his coat. He sees that it's getting late. He has three parties to go to tonight, the first in Beverly Hills, the second over the hill, and the third in the other direction, Palos Verdes, down the coast. Mark is just a dot of ink in his time, and as he rubs a hand over his cool, unbelievably soft leather collar, he really can't be bothered. "I take it you've spent some time *reading* this?"

"Oh, yeah, the contract." Mark stares at the envelope, which is now sitting on the tabletop along with Henry's drink and the discarded cassette player.

"Yes, good, I'm glad. Now, do you remember this?" Henry pulls out of another of the coat's pockets a legal-sized piece of paper, folded into fourths. Mark, as a distraction, wonders how many pockets the coat has. "This is the deal memo. Which *you* signed. Now, *this* little gem has no expiration date. If you don't sign this contract, Bottlecap *cannot* sign to another label or put out a record until Pacific says so."

"But you need us." Mark is desperate, trying to find his leverage in the situation. "If I don't sign . . . you've got nothing."

"Are you kidding?" Henry James laughs, dangling the deal memo back and forth. "We've got everything. We've got the masters. We've got the legal rights to the songs. The name. *Everything.* Didn't you hear this tape? He did that one vocal part and you can barely tell. He could do it again. He wants to. Hell, it was *his* idea."

"No." Mark's voice begins to shake. "We won't take this."

"We?" Henry takes a deep breath, vowing not to take another until he gets up from the table, an incentive to get this over with. "You think your little friends—what are their names, anyway? Oh well, it doesn't matter, but you think they're going to stand by and kiss a quarter of a million dollars away? I bet the Mondrian's the first hotel they've ever stayed at that didn't have the fucking coat hangers attached to the rod hanging in the closet. And if they *are* foolish enough to take your side and *not* play along, well then, we'll just hire a drummer and a bass player, too. And if that doesn't work out we'll just flush the whole project and write it off. Let the masters rot in a vault somewhere for all I care. I've got *other* bands to worry about. Bands who are *willing* to play by the rules and not fuck them."

Henry's watch begins to feel heavy on his hand. *Still have to change. Pick up Chris. Wash the BMW. Christ, will the car washes be open on Christmas Eve? They'd fucking better be. Fucking Mexicans.* His eyes focus on a busboy across the room, now sliding a push vacuum in lines across the brilliantly patterned carpet. *They'll do anything to make a buck.* "Look, here's the bottom line. You want to work with us, that's fine. But just remember"—he reaches out for the Walkman, takes out the tape, and gives it to Mark—"we're calling the shots. And you're doing things *our* way."

Mark stands up, the chair catching on the floor behind him. "Fuck you." Henry just shakes his head from side to side. "Mark, don't do this."

"Fuck . . . you . . ."

Now Henry gets up, still shaking his head.

"Okay, Mark, that's it. You're out."

Henry leaves the room humming "Jingle Bells" and wishing the busboys a *Feliz Navidad*, tipping them $20 of guilt.

Steve remembers an old photo taken on a Christmas morning, he's not sure how long ago, but he must have been between the ages of three and five, and his brother, who always seemed to be three years older, six or eight. Both of them are sitting in a cardboard box, the rim of which pinches Phil underneath the armpit while Steve can barely see over the sides. The box contained a large, amphibious, mustard-colored Tonka toy that their father had spent half the night customizing with various decals and pinstriping. On opening the gift the boys seemed more intrigued by the cavernous box and the seemingly limitless possibilities it afforded than the toy.

"Look, I'm stuck in a cave," Steve had shouted as he

crouched down, his hands grabbing at his Muppet-adorned socks.

"Shut up, dummy, this is a tank," Phil reprimanded, swatting his little brother on the head, "and I can't concentrate with all your yakking."

For the rest of Christmas Day Steve and Phil played in the box, sometimes one inside while the other dragged it over the avocado green shag carpeting, or else turning it upside down, changing it into a fort. The Tonka truck sat unused in the corner, already collecting dust, and their father stewed about how much time and money he'd spent on the gift, mumbling, "If all they wanted was a goddamn box, then I wouldn't have bothered with Toys 'R' Us, I would have went to the Dumpster behind the goddamn liquor store!" Their mother intervened, saying the point of Christmas was to make the boys happy, and as they cavorted with the box going on six hours, pausing only for quick bites of turkey and a mouthful of stuffing before returning to submarine adventures and war-torn danger, she could tell they were happy.

As Steve sits on the cool, hardwood floors of the record-company-rented apartment in Hollywood, the photo of his brother and him in the box is the only Christmas photo he can remember.

"Good wrap job, Steve," Gary says as he sits opposite Steve, busy cutting up a long strand of Scotch tape into inch-long strips and attaching them to the ledge of the coffee table.

"Huh?" Steve says, flipping over the large box and noticing a section in back where the paper ran out and is crumpled and serrated, not quite covering the package contents. "Damn."

The present is for Mark. Steve bought it a couple of days ago and smuggled it into the house, having to pass by Mark, who was, remarkably, at the house, and even more remarkably, watching CNN. Mark thought the large package that Steve was doing a bad job of hiding was another teddy bear, a treat for himself the way women splurge and buy themselves expensive lingerie. Mark didn't even suspect the object Steve was hiding was a present for him, didn't even think it was suspicious the way Gary and Steve were slyly trying to find out what records he might want or the amount of Polo left in the green bottle he'd owned ever since they first knew him. Never mind that it had been the week before Christmas and his roommates were trying to hide shopping bags from stores around town in the corners of hall closets or that he kept finding spools of ribbon and packages of bows when he searched for his lighter in the drawers of the living room credenza.

Steve cuts a long length of wrapping paper from a new roll (green-and-red speckles, clashing with the simple white snow scene with *Merry Christmas* in script lettering over and over that most of the package is already wrapped in) and slaps it onto the back of the gift, covering the bald spot.

"What did you buy him?" Gary asks.

"A CD holder," Steve replies as he grabs for a cardboard tag with Santa Claus wearing a sandwich board with the words TO and FROM and a space underneath each for a name. "You know, one of those plastic ones that holds, like, thirty or forty of them."

"Cool."

"Yeah, I thought it'd be nice since the CDs are everywhere and he's always bitching about how most of them are his, even though it's the truth."

Steve looks to the stereo, currently cranking out jazzy Christmas tunes thanks to the Peanuts Christmas record. The music is apropos because on the way home from shopping two days ago, Gary pulled into the parking lot of the Mayfair grocery store on the corner of La Brea and Fountain, a row of deep hunter green out front catching his eye. He picked up a Charlie Brown–sized Christmas tree, barely three feet tall, bare in some places, full in others, the inside needles brown and already falling off in clumps, but it possessed a certain charm. Gary also bought three strings of lights, two boxes of glass bulbs, and a package of gold tinsel. Racing back to the house, he was more excited about the tree than any of the gifts he'd just bought and even considered paying another $2 just to have the tree tied to the roof of the rental car with twine, the way his father did when he was a child, but in reality the thing was much too small to warrant such special handling and Gary was too embarrassed to ask.

When he finally set up the tree at home, Gary knew how Charlie Brown must have felt, except that Lucy, usually, didn't swear.

"Jesus fucking Christ," Steve said as Gary came bounding through the door with the oversized bushel of weeds attached to a twig, "it's a goddamn midget tree!"

As the two of them listened to Christmas carols, first *Wayne Newton's X-mas Jubilee* and then *A Holiday with Robert Goulet* (the Music Plus on Fairfax was having a sale), they both warmed up to and then began to love their little tree. It was the first one either of them had ever had outside of their parents' homes. Gary, living with James for two years, never bought one because James decried Christmas as overblown, commercial bullshit (but only because he was too poor to afford presents), while Steve, who lived alone, considered a Christmas tree in his apartment of one to be more lonely than festive.

"You're a good man, Gary Reiger," Steve said as his roommate impaled a homemade angel on the spiky promontory of the skinny tree.

"What did *you* get him?" Steve now asks.

"I bought him an automatic string winder."

"Cool," Steve nods, thinking his gift is better.

"Yeah, I thought he would like it," Gary says, thinking *his* gift is better.

In the silence after this exchange, each wonders what the other has bought for him. Gary had sort of arched an eyebrow when he saw Steve go into that vintage toy store, emerging with a larger-than-a-bread-box brown paper bag, and Steve had certainly noticed Gary creeping across the living room floor two nights ago with something obviously hidden under his newly acquired Members Only jacket.

Gary and Steve had both agreed to keep the gifts they exchanged slight, setting a ceiling of $30 as the most either could spend. Gary exceeded that with a set of wire brush drumsticks, and Steve was nowhere near the prescribed amount when he bought Gary a vintage steel *Stars Wars* lunch box from 1977, in perfect condition.

Each of them figured his gift was most likely stashed at the bottom of the other's closet, and both were right. Underneath a mound of dirty T-shirts (in Steve's case, mostly old jeans), the present for the other was neatly wrapped and awaiting Christmas morning, when they were going to sit in a circle as Gary made his soon-to-be-famous hot chocolate, play Christmas music, and open up the gifts for one another.

From time to time throughout the past week both Gary and Steve wondered what Mark had been up to pertaining to gifts for them. He was spending less and less time at the house lately, and in the past few days seemed to be in such a fog about the whole record company fiasco that even when he was around, it seemed as if he were someplace else. *But still,* they assured themselves as they got paper cuts on their thumbs from rough-hewn rolls of wrapping paper or poked themselves in the palm with unruly scissors, *Mark wouldn't forget to get us presents. Would he?*


Mark curses into the chilly night air as he parks the rental car half a block down from the apartment.

"Fucking parking spaces." He scans up and down the crowded street. Cars parked everywhere, even on lawns. "God-damn city."

He walks up the sidewalk toward the house, hearing numerous parties in the buildings around him. He can hear four different Christmas songs coming from four different directions at once, all of them underlined with the constant trafficlike white noise of flowing conversation, punctuated with laughs or gasps of gossipy surprise. He also notices smells drifting through the air, musty piecrusts and rich turkey scents, even a tad of cigar and cigarette smoke. And somewhere, just up the block, some poor person was burning their meal, a pan of twice-baked potatoes being cooked for the third time.

Mark drags his bones up the steps and heads toward the

apartment. He had even forgotten it was Christmas Eve. He remembers seeing the tree in the living room, even Corinne had one, and he knew he was due at her house later, something to do with going to her parents' house, something to do with dinner, he couldn't be too sure, because it was just blah-blah-blah whenever she spoke to him lately.

Mark can hear Steve and Gary from the porch. He can hear them laughing, Gary doing his Elvis-tinged rendition of "Silent Night," and Mark can see in his mind the vision of Gary with his curled upper lip, his chubby midsection gyrating as if suspending a hula hoop in orbit. Steve is in the background, laughing hysterically. Then there's the clinking of glasses as Steve pours each of them another juice glass full of eggnog spiked with brandy from the liquor store around the corner. About to enter the house, Mark feels like a highway patrolman who must inform the family inside that their parents have just been killed, died on Christmas Eve, but have a Happy Holiday despite it.

"Hey, look who it is!" Gary says as he turns around and sees Mark struggling to get his key out of the lock. He cuts short his bow, letting his Southern-drawled "Thank you very much" fade into the next Christmas song on the CD, and Steve forgets his joke about "Gary has left the building," both of them turning their attention to Mark.

"So, how'd it go?"

Mark crosses the room, sitting down on the couch. He notices a batch of the TO/FROM tags and thinks, *What in the hell are these for?*

"You remember Pearl Harbor?"

Steve looks at Gary, who looks back, and then looks at Mark.

"Yeah, I mean, I've *heard* about it."

"Well." Mark sighs. "It didn't go *that* good."

He tosses onto the coffee table, riddled with scraps of red and green satin ribbons, the cassette tape Henry James had given him an hour before.

"What's this?" Steve asks. Then his face goes white. "What is this, *another* mix?"

"No," Mark gently laughs. "It's our last chance."

Gary picks up the tape and pops it into the stereo, cutting off the last few bars of Robert Goulet singing "O Tannenbaum."

Bottlecap's "I Want to Fuck You" fills the air, and neither Steve nor Gary notices anything tremendously different in the way the song has been mixed.

"Sounds okay to me," Steve says, looking to Gary, who nods in approval.

"No, no, they like the song," Mark says, grinning. "Well, *most* of it."

Just as Gary's about to say, "What part of the song don't they like?" it hits him. He turns, horrified, to the stereo, where the chorus is just beginning to come barging out of the speakers.

*"I want to feel you . . . feel you hard."*

"What did that just say?" Steve asks.

"You heard it," Mark says calmly, no longer mad or even disappointed. He passed those emotions days ago. Now, as it is all coming down around him like a house collapsing, he's just numb. It is all he can do to keep his eyes open enough to watch.

"Shut up," Gary says quickly, "it's coming up again."

*"I want to feel you . . . feel you hard . . . feel you all night . . . all I want to do is feel you -ooh-ooh . . ."*

The voice, most of it, at least, was still Mark's, except that where he had recorded it as *fuck,* Kenneth had gone back in and spliced in the word *feel* in its place, Hanes doing the honors. Now it could be played on the radio.

Stunned, Gary looks at the plastic sleeve in his hand. Printed onto the J card in Helvetica script are the words ADVANCE PROMO CASSETTE NOT FOR SALE. Underneath this it reads BOTTLECAP and then, finally, bigger than anything else, I WANT TO FEEL YOU.

"But they can't . . ." Steve disbelievingly says.

Mark, the will to speak difficult, says, "They already have."

"'I Want to *Feel* You'? Who do they think they're kidding?"

"Us, Gary, they're kidding us. Or rather, they're *screw*ing us."

"So what do we do about it?"

"We fucking walk, that's what," Mark says, even though just thinking of the physical activity of walking tires him out. He likens a stroll to the restroom to running the Boston marathon in under three hours.

"You mean, rip up the contract?" Steve says tentatively. "Forget the deal?"

"Sure, we can rip up *our* copy of the contract." Mark waves his hand to where the Xeroxed document lies on the kitchen table. "But the problem is, they have copies of their own."

"So we're fucked?" Gary asks.

"No, *they're* fucked."

"How do you figure?"

"Let them have the goddamn album. Let them release it without us touring behind it, or making a video. In fact," he begins speaking loudly, gaining steam, "let them make Hanes and two other schmucks stars. See if we care!"

Gary and Steve both consider this. *Stars?* The word rings in their heads like the aftershock of a sonic boom.

"Uh, look, Mark, don't you think you're being a bit too hasty?"

"Yeah," Steve agrees. He walks over to the stereo and rewinds the tape, pressing play a few seconds later. "I don't think what they've done here is *too* bad. After all, a lot of bands have, like, the radio edit of certain songs, and then the album version."

Gary joins in.

"If we walk away now it'll screw us forever in this industry, and then what? Go back to Kitty, tell everyone how we grabbed for the brass ring, got it, but then *dropped* it? Hell, no." In the background, "I Want to Feel You" is playing, and Gary and Steve figure they can live with it. It doesn't seem like such a big concession, one measly song changed around a little. They figure that more people in this world make bigger concessions than this every day of their lives: trudging to an office job they hate to be lorded over by a boss they cannot stand; living with a spouse whom they no longer love; breathing the air of another day when they constantly want to die. Steve thinks, *If the worst thing that happens to me is some record company changes one word in a song I didn't even write, that's still a pretty good life.* It was a rationalization, sure, but it was also Christmas Eve. "Come on, guys, let's have some more eggnog. Everything's fine."

Mark gets up quietly and goes upstairs. After a few minutes he lumbers down the staircase enveloped in a number of black bags, his luggage draped over his arms, a blue duffel bag slung over his right shoulder. In the hallway he grabs for his acoustic guitar in its heavy black case.

"I've called for a cab. I'm leaving." He stops for a second before adding, "Moving out."

"Where are you going?"

"Corinne's. I'm going to live with her until I can get a job, or else move back to Virginia. I don't know. I'm just going to get away from you fucks."

Neither Steve and Gary can challenge him quick enough to suit them.

"What?"

"What?"

"You guys are just both fucking retards, and if you want to continue this band with some record-company asshole calling all the shots, then do it." He makes for the door. "But you can count me out."

Mark turns around slowly as he opens the door, his movements made difficult by the weight hanging from his chest. He sees his former roommates, band mates, best friends standing, stunned, in the living room of a rented apartment just off of Sunset Boulevard in Hollywood, California. He feels like asking them, like you do at a party when you're introduced to a stranger, with an extended hand, "And you are . . . ?"

The flapping of his bags knocks him repeatedly in the ass as he walks to the curb to wait for his cab.

"He'll be back." Steve turns to Gary. "Won't he?"

"Yeah, sure," Gary says, even though he's not sure.

Steve runs a hand nervously over his goatee, which was getting out of hand and longer on the left side than the right, a tuft of golden brown hair dropping off his chin sloppily like food scraps.

"I'm going to go see Sam real quick. Maybe he's got some sort of Christmas Eve special going. I think I need it."

Corinne is rushing around her apartment. She goes over the mental list in her head of everything she was supposed to do and bring.

On the way into the kitchen (yet again) to look for her diamond brooch, the Christmas tree catches her eye and it makes her stop in her place. She's had the tree for over a week now, so it's not as if she's not used to it yet. She'd buzzed by it over a dozen times since picking it up in the lot near the Hollywood Bowl from a stand that was supposedly run by Boy Scouts even though none seemed to be around and the proprietor was a suspicious-looking older woman.

But now, as she is passing by the tree, something seems different. Or rather Corinne, completely freaked out, figures that the problem is that something seems too familiar.

She's reminded of Christmas a year ago, when, at this same exact time, last December twenty-fourth, she ran around the house, double-checking on presents, the dish she was bringing (startled, she realizes it's candied yams, the same as last year). There was Christmas music playing in the background, a token tree in the corner with two strands of lights twinkling on and off, only last year it was Tim she was waiting for and not Mark. She's shaken so violently by the remembrance that she has to sit down, the crinoline sewn into her dress crinkling up and not giving way at first, until her hands sweep it aside and then move to her face, sweeping aside the tears that have begun to flow.

*Last year.* She whispers. *Last fucking year.*

She remembers how Tim had been a little late, which, even though Corinne had been ready, made them late to her parents' house. Her mother *tsk-tsked* disapprovingly, her suspicions con-

GENIUSES OF CRACK    [417]

firmed, as always, that her daughter was not a chip off the old block but instead a gash caused by an accident, while her father just blithely drank his scotch, already well on his way to becoming drunk. Corinne didn't want to start off Christmas Eve by being pissed off, but the later Tim was, the more angry she became.

"Sorry, hon, traffic." He tried to sweep her into his arms the second he entered.

"No shit, Tim, it's Christmas Eve." She pushed him aside, not willing to forgive and forget in a matter of seconds. "You thought perhaps the roads would be empty?"

Tim grinned, knowing he'd been caught, and said, "Corinne, let's not start this right now, okay?"

She growled while he disappeared into the kitchen. Corinne could hear the refrigerator door open and close as a decoy (*How stupid does he think I am?*) and then she heard the jingling of a bottle and the hollow gurgling sound from the alcohol inside.

Corinne just sat silent as Tim filled up a mug with two fingers of whiskey, as if Corinne thought he might be swigging on some sort of coffee that just happened to leave his breath smelling of gasoline. Why was it always a race between Tim and her dad to see who could get drunk the quickest? And why did either Tim or her father have to get drunk on Christmas Eve, anyway? She could never understand the way they both ended the evening singing carols off-key, as if "Jingle Bells" were the Notre Dame fight song or else "Walking in a Winter Wonderland" were "Over There" and they were a couple of grizzled doughboys. It was always up to Corinne and her mother to carry one of the men upstairs. Corinne took the other home, as if he were a life-sized present, even though spending Christmas morning holding her boyfriend's head as he continually threw up didn't seem like much of a gift to her.

Corinne sighs, still sitting in the chair, eyeing the tree. She wants to cut it in half and count the rings inside. Then she contemplates doing the same to herself, confirming that, yes, a year has gone by, that it was in fact 1993 and not 1992, and that it was going to be Mark walking through the door any minute from now and not Tim. She wants to count the rings inside of her because she feels a year has passed and she has not learned anything.

Corinne contemplates going to the kitchen and retrieving from the cabinet to the left of the sink the bottle of Wild Turkey (the same from last year, just another talisman in the apartment that haunts her), pouring a shot for herself, and downing it with a quick jerk of her arm. She wonders how her father would feel if he looked over and saw that his sweet little pumpkin of a daughter had joined the race. She wonders if Mark would carry her limp and inebriated body to the car, drive her home, and ease her rubbery limbs into a nightgown, tuck her in, and tilt her head to one side so she wouldn't choke during the night. She figures, with all of the problems of his own he's been wrapped up in lately, that he wouldn't. Mark would probably just get drunk, too, and sing the carols off-key with her father, and would even make her drive home, saying that even though they both were drunk, that she was still not as drunk as he was. As if no one in the world had ever loved, been hurt, or felt pain and happiness except for Mark Pellion.

*In fact*—Corinne glances at her watch—*he's already half an hour late.*

Just then she hears a rumbling outside her door, as if someone with cement boots were wiping off their feet on her doormat. It is Mark, struggling with the doorknob, the acoustic guitar case underneath his arm banging into the mailbox and all of the bags looped around his neck and slung over his shoulders shifting forward and knocking into the front of the door.

Corinne watches as Mark crawls through her doorway, deposits a number of shadowy objects just inside of her hall, and then meekly looks up, half smiling.

"Hey," he says by way of an explanation that he's late.

"Yeah," is all Corinne responds with, even though there are rivers of angry words swirling in her head. But then again, the feeling, same as last year's, courses through her body. *Don't start a fight. Not now. It's Christmas Eve.*

She can see, even in the darkness, that he is dressed even more poorly than he initially was on Thanksgiving, and she didn't think that was possible. He's wearing ripped jeans, a worn T-shirt, and a dark blue shirt over this. On his feet are a pair of old tennis shoes, gray socks with bits of skin visible through holes, and a cardboard belt, fraying at the buckle, toffee-colored flakes of paper shedding on her swept floor. Corinne figures Mark is underdressed to even get arrested.

"Geez, Mark, you didn't have to get all dolled up just for me," she says sarcastically, beginning to sniffle.

"What?" He's slow to catch the remark aimed at the clothes he's wearing but that seem to be wearing him instead. "Oh, yeah. Dinner with your parents, right? Oops."

Figuring he needs the new shirt, Corinne walks over to the tree, where the presents have been divided into two separate sections: one a modest pile of gifts for her mother and father and also the gifts for her relatives the next day; and there is a pile (if you could call it that, the two gifts, one of top of the other, forming an *X*) that consists of the presents for Mark. She picks up the boxes, each immaculately wrapped and topped with red ribbon, bows, and even small wreaths that she found at a store just off of Highland called Natural Things, Etc.

"These are for you." Even though she's more angry than sad, she begins to cry, the tears coming because she's sick and tired of being sick and tired.

"Corinne," he says slowly, taking the gifts as she hands them to him, "you shouldn't have."

*No shit,* she thinks.

Corinne looks over the bags he dropped just inside the door. Even though the apartment is dimly lit (she liked to sit on the couch and just watch the rainbow colors the flashing lights projected onto the walls, especially since in a week it all went back into the storage bin behind the building), she can tell that the bags are mostly canvas, black, with the exception of a blue duffel bag. None of them have a bow attached, or even a card.

"I wish I would have known that we were exchanging gifts . . . because I just didn't, I mean . . . well . . ."

"Jesus, Mark, why *wouldn't* you think we were exchanging gifts? I mean, most of the free world does."

Mark nervously kicks at a loose strand of silver tinsel on the floor.

"Yeah, I know, it's just, we never mentioned it, so . . ."

"So what? So you just couldn't put half an idea together and buy me a *little* something." She notices how the word *buy* sounds so harsh it's still hanging in the air while the others have already drifted away. "I mean, it's not about money. I don't care about being bought anything big, it's just, even a card. Something that shows you cared enough to think of me."

If Mark were invisible he would be knocking his hand repeatedly into the front of his face.

*I knew it, I knew it, I knew it,* he thinks. *I knew she'd expect some big present or something. All women are the same. Laura pulled the same thing on me last year. Wanting a gift. Sheesh.*

"Just forget it," Corinne says as she lets out a sigh. "Let's just go, we're late enough as it is."

Mark nods and then sets his presents down on the floor, figuring he'll open them in the morning, the first act of the new life he would be leading with Corinne by his side.

"Hey, I forgot to ask, my normally inquisitive persona totally eclipsed by *your* selfish behavior"—Corinne grabs her purse—"but what are all the bags for?"

"Oh," Mark says, as if he's been caught. "I moved out of the house. You know, the band house."

"*What?*"

"Yeah, I, uh, told Gary and Steve to go fuck themselves. The record company, too. I'm going to just let them do whatever they want. You know, to hell with them."

Corinne doesn't know how to react. She's putting the bits and pieces of fact together in her mind and trying to see where they lead. Moved out. The luggage. Him standing there with a puppy dog look on his face.

"You want to move in *here?*"

Mark just stands there. He had concocted a speech during

the cab ride in which he not only professed his love for Corinne but also laid down the life lesson learned from the Subterfuge debacle, but now he is nervous and feels the bits of ideas and words slipping away from him. He suddenly feels abandoned.

"Yeah, I mean, it's not like I don't spend a lot of time here anyway."

"That's not the point, Mark." She paces the room for a second before pulling up a chair and sitting down on it quickly. "It's just, I wish you would have asked first."

"I *am* asking." His voice squeaks. "I'm asking right now."

"Bullshit, Mark, you've already got all that crap sitting in my hallway."

"I'm sorry, Corinne, but the crumbling of my life hasn't been planned very well and I just wasn't given much advance warning. Of *course* I would have liked to consult you first, but this all came down today, just now. And also, I think that this will—"

She stops him.

"Why are you acting like this is a done deal?"

Mark motions with his head toward the luggage.

Corinne sits there for a few minutes, contemplating a decision. When it arrives, it feels heavy in her chest and her throat holds it down, her lips barely separating to speak it.

"No, Mark," she finally says. "No."

"B-b-but I just told the guys to go fuck themselves. In fact, I told Henry James the same thing. Hell, I even mouthed off to the cab driver." His eyes are open wide, scared. She has never seen them like this. "You don't know how many times I've used the word *fuck* in the last four hours. I don't have anywhere to go, Corinne."

"Yes, you do, Mark. Go back to the house. Even if you quit the band, Gary and Steve won't mind you staying there until the record company kicks them out, too. Then maybe you can all get an apartment."

Now Mark's tone turns from feel-sorry-for-me to furious.

"Sleep under the same roof with *those* back-stabbing assholes?" he screams. "Never!"

In the ensuing silence Corinne just watches the walls as the multicolored lights from the two strings wound around her modest tree blink on and off, on and off. She gets up and, with a hearty smile, orbits him twice, trying to get his attention.

"Mark?" Corinne tentatively speaks out.

He says nothing.

"Ma-ark?" Again her voice is good-natured, as if she were a ballet teacher to a young group of girls who were butchering *The Nutcracker Suite,* but what else could underdeveloped legs that didn't want to be there do?

"Huh," he sort of grumbles, more a shrug of the shoulders and a clearing of the throat than actual speech.

Corinne sits down next to where he has collapsed onto a chair. Exhausted, she wrings her hands on the fabric of her skirt the way her mother is always fiddling with her apron.

"I would give five dollars to see your tongue," she says slowly.

"What in the fuck's that supposed to mean?" he says, still not looking up.

Again she tries to laugh, inject some levity into her voice, but at this point it would take helium.

"It means, I don't know, that I want to see your mouth open. That I want you to talk to me."

He sticks out his tongue like a four-year-old.

"Great. Marvelous. Aces." Corinne gets up from the table and marches around the room, in time, as if to an imaginary waltz. Her nerves, so on edge for the past few weeks, are firing tonight as if cylinders in a motor climbing a steep hill.

"You know, Mark, I thought of something tonight I haven't thought of in a long time."

Seconds pass before he answers.

"Really?" He keeps his eyes averted. "What's that?"

Despite his indifference, Corinne continues, more for herself than for him.

"It's a line from this play, I'm not sure which. Tim just used to say it a lot, usually when he would get horrendously drunk after being on the wagon for a while, but the line is: 'When you start again you never know exactly how much you need.'"

Seconds. Almost a minute goes by.

"What's that supposed to mean?"

Corinne stops from her absurd pacing of the apartment, but even after she sits down she finds she cannot control her feet from following the same pattern over the rug beneath the kitchen table, as if she were running in place.

"It means that when you and I started dating a few months ago, well, I told you about Tim. How I hadn't seen anyone since we broke up. And how that was because I wasn't *looking* for anything. But you came along and things were feeling right where they hadn't been right in a long time . . . so I let myself go."

Mark can't believe the way she's dwelling on her own problems, on her own life. Couldn't she see the trouble he was in?

"But?"

"But . . . I think that I was wrong. That's when that quote hit me. You see, I started again. Or really, *we* started, in this relationship, and I tried to get too involved, to act as if things were hunky-dory when they were not. I tried to treat you"—her voice is now just a whisper—"the way I had treated Tim."

If there is something quieter than silence, imagine it here.

"Mark, I'm sorry, but you're *not* moving in with me." She pauses, almost adding, *At least, not right now you're not,* because it really isn't an absurd idea. She does care for him, and they get along well together, but at this second, under these circumstances, it just doesn't feel right.

"Well then." His voice is heavy. Is he crying? She can't tell. Too many shadows, just the dancing lights and decorations of angels in the room of two who aren't sure what they are. "What am I going to do?"

"I told you, just go back to the house and talk with Steve and Gary, I'm sure they'll—"

"I told you." He rises just as she's about to place her hand on his back. "I'm never going back to that fucking place again and I'm never going to talk to either of those jackoffs, ever!"

"Look, calm down." She twists around and reaches for the phone, trading the purse in her hand for the shiny black receiver sitting on the edge of the couch. "Let me call my parents and tell them we're going to be a little late."

"Fuck you, Corinne," Mark shouts, heading for the door. "And fuck your goddamn parents, too." He quickly grabs for a few pieces of his luggage, but as soon as he has one bag over his shoulder it drops to the ground when he bends over to retrieve another. After a few more tries he curses loudly and grabs just his acoustic guitar, heading out the door, down the sidewalk, away.

When Steve goes over to Sam's apartment not long after Mark's decampment, he thinks he has discovered a man being held hostage. Sam sits on an uncomfortable-looking square-back chair, each shoulder blade fitting snugly against the wood, while his feet are planted squarely on the ground about a foot apart and his arms are hugging the sides of his body, while each wrist sits like a satellite of obedience hovering around his hip. All of this is taking place in the middle of the room, Sam looking arbitrarily placed four feet in front of the TV, which blasts a sporting event into the air. It looks to Steve like Sam is tied up, even though he can't spot the thick blond lengths of rope or even the spaghetti straps of dark brown twine.

"Uh, Sam?"

"Oh, hey."

The head twists slightly, eyes begrudging a scared look of recognition. Steve half expects Sam to be missing most of his ear. In the background one of the teams scores, and the room is enveloped in the crowd's staticlike cheer.

"You okay?" Steve asks, forgetting for a second his own troubles, the ones he came to Sam's to escape.

"What, you mean this?" He gestures to the stiff chair and his unusual way of sitting in it. "I've been doing a bunch of painting and I sort of wrenched my back."

Steve pulls up a black wooden folding chair; one of the three slats forming the back is badly cracked and pokes through his shirt the moment he fully sits down.

"How does painting hurt your back?"

Sam leans a little to one side and nods his head twice in the direction of the kitchen. Steve looks over his shoulder and sees two large canvases on the black-and-white tiled floor, both halfway done and both more of Sam's abstract heads.

"Yeah, so?"

"So, I got these canvases but usually I just do small ones and put them down on the table and do them that way." Now he tosses his head in the opposite direction, toward the dining room. "But these were too big for that. I mean, they fit, sort of, but a corner would always be hanging off or the table would poke into the canvas and I kept knocking the little tubes of paint onto the floor." He stops, sighs. "It was a nightmare."

"Sounds like it."

"I had to do them on the ground, except the way I work is to crane over these things and paint with my face about six inches away from the canvas. The old story about the painter standing in front of his easel and checking out a picture with one eye closed and his arm outstretched and his thumb in the air, like he was hitchhiking, is bullshit. At least for me it is."

Steve's problems began to slowly rise to the surface: the deal, Mark, his own future. He suddenly remembers why he had come here, for drugs, something to slip him into a stupor and make him forget the world that seemed to have such a fun time slapping him around.

"I spent all night bending over these damn canvases like that, uh, like that . . . that half-blind cartoonist who hated women but loved dogs?"

"I don't know."

"Anyway, I get halfway through both of these paintings and by that time I was so tired I nearly passed out. I slept on the couch and when I woke up this morning I could barely move."

"Your back?"

"Yeah, my back." Sam twists his upper body slightly to illustrate his point, only it doesn't move. "And my neck. And my legs. *Every*thing hurts. So I was sitting here, just sort of trying to straighten myself out. It's funny, I finally got some of those water-based acrylic paints I had been bitching about, so there's no paint on my hands . . . but now I can't move." Sam stiffly holds up his hands, which are indeed free of the dark splotches of color Steve saw on him a few months ago, even though a silver chain-link bracelet dangling below his wrist is colored in a few places with whips of red paint.

"You know what the joke is? The paintings didn't even turn out that good." Now Sam wearily raises himself, and it reminds Steve of his grandfather, the way that in the last years of his life he would groan when crossing the room, opening up a jar of pickles or just generally being. The man, it seemed, was always groaning about something. Sam shuffles to the other room to show Steve his works in progress, even though Steve now just wants to get the hell out of there. "Come here, have a look."

Steve trails behind Sam until they get to the two canvases in the kitchen. Each is about four feet by three feet, and it's obvious to Steve the way that Sam would have had to kneel and bend over to fill the centers of each canvas with some degree of control. The one closest to the living room looks like a portrait of a man, his chin tucked into his chest, and he even seems to be wearing an open-collared shirt, even though his face is blank and the only surface features discernible are a chin and ear, noticeable from the curvy outline. The painting hugging the lip of the refrigerator (some dark blue slashed against the baseboard) actually looks to be of a woman, as seen from the back, a set of shoulders and a neck, hair up in a bun (another outline with a circle within), while two dress or maybe even bra straps, painted black, drip off the canvas and onto the floor.

"I painted her from a picture in the J. Crew catalog." Sam points to the girl, and motions toward the other painting. "And *him,* well, he used to be a drummer in my band."

Underneath the wide expanses of skin in each portrait (Steve sees a shampoo-sized container of Dresden Flesh paint sitting on its side) he can see where Sam had earlier drafted eyes, noses, and mouths on each figure, only to wash over these features later. It seemed to Steve that Sam was at least trying.

"God, I can't stand looking at these pieces of crap."

Steve looks from the paintings to Sam.

"Why not?"

"Because they suck, that's why!" Suddenly Sam feels a sharp, warm pain shoot down his back. He rubs his hands above his waist to soothe the sensation. His neck begins to tense up, as if begging him to stretch his muscles, only that's what he's been doing all morning. He imagines his tired muscles are a group of old rubber bands (and colored that way, too, eraser pink) that have already been stretched too far and will now live life perennially in slack. "I just can't do anything right."

"What are you talking about?"

"Well, look at this!" He motions to the canvases even though it hurts him to do so. "I can't paint. I can't hold down a job *or* a relationship, and I'm still not sure which is more important. It's like in *Barfly* when Rambo's brother says to Chinaski, 'You can't work, you can't fuck, and you can't fight.' That's how I feel."

"Uh, yeah, look, the reason I—"

"I guess what also aggravates me is that I wasn't always like this. I mean, I had a girl who cared for me, and I fucked it up. I had a decent job, but I quit it because I thought it was beneath me. I deliberately ruined so many things in my life on a whim, or because I felt affronted in some way. Stupid, huh?" Sam takes his hands from his coiled back for a second and places them across his chest. "I guess I fucked all those things up because I didn't know what the chance of my life looked like. I guess you never know."

"Trust me, I know. Now, the reason I came over . . ."

"Let me guess." Sam grins, looking cocky, the real him. "Some special Yuletide cheer?"

Steve quickly nods his head in the affirmative. Sam goes into the bedroom to retrieve the stuff, the way Steve's seen him do half a dozen times now, from a drawer in his nightstand that locks shut with a miniature golden key.

"How much do you want?"

"Just an eighth," Steve shouts out as he heads for the bathroom between the dining room and bedroom, "and *just* pot."

Steve takes his piss, more a nervous reaction than anything else, and it reminds him of the first couple of times Bottlecap played live, how he was so nervous he was in the bathroom for half an hour trying to urinate even though, after the third or fourth time, nothing would come out. As he shakes off he hears someone at the door, someone who lets himself in and who startles Sam in the hallway.

"Well, it worked!" The voice, recognizable to Steve, says excitedly, "It worked!"

"Really?" Sam says, his own voice hushed, trying to show interest in a whisper.

"Yeah, Mark is out and *I'm* in."

Steve envisions various faces and bodies, the brain of his computer rapidly scanning for a match. Finally it comes to him: Hanes.

"No shit?"

"Yeah, Henry James just called me."

"That's great but . . . one of them's *here*."

Steve hears Hanes laugh.

"Which one?"

"Sucker number two, Steve."

"Then I guess I'd better not stay, right? I just wanted to say thanks."

Steve hears some sort of coarse shuffling sound and then childish giggles. Sam scampers to his room and Steve hears the drawer croak shut and then the unmistakable *click-clack* of the key being turned in the lock.

The voices lead out of the living room onto the porch, the slamming of the door punctuated by laughter. Steve flushes the toilet and exits the bathroom.

Sam greets him in the hallway, a clear baggy in his hand filled with an inch of dull green bud.

"Since it's Christmas I'm giving you this on the house."

As Steve approaches him his right arm rises slowly, gaining momentum, and by the time it is halfway to Sam's face it is as if a catapult has been released, and his fist strikes Sam with alarming velocity. Sam stumbles backward, into the kitchen, his heels catching on the paintings laid out on the ground, and he falls upon them with all his weight. The wooden support cracks and the canvas splits, sounding like a pair of jeans ripping in half. Sam tries to get to his feet, only his hands can't get a grip on the slick surface of the paintings. Steve, somewhat amazed at his reaction and also at the fact that his hand is now on fire with pain, more so perhaps than Sam's already-turning-red jaw, walks into the kitchen and pushes Sam down just as he gains a grip, having to poke his motorcycle-booted foot through the bottom edge of the picture frame. Steve leans over and punches Sam two more times, sending his head jerking to the right with one blow and then back in the other direction, Steve using his left hand now because the right is already too sore, and he is impressed that the left was so effective. Sam falls back on his own meager creations, now ruined, the skin-colored paint on his own skin, only it looks more like calamine lotion than real flesh.

Steve turns to leave, but then turns back around, slightly out of breath.

"You know what? You're right, you *can't* fight."

Mark stops walking only when his feet become sore and his hand, curled around the cheap plastic handle of the guitar case, falls numbly asleep.

He bends over, blood rushing into his feet where for the past half hour (or has it been an hour?) the blood has been sloshed upward by every angry step he made in whatever direction it was he took upon leaving the stoop of Corinne's apartment building. Rage had blinded him the way that lethargy had earlier, but his emotions had since given way to a queer sort of detachment, as if the view from out his eyes were looking onto a movie screen and he was just sitting back and watching the drama of scripted actors and could not bother to get involved. The effect was oddly liberating in the same way that Steve felt the week before, sharing a needle with Sam in his living room.

Gary, ingesting the love and musky scent from between Whitney's legs on Saturday, was also high.

Mark unclasps the brass latches on the guitar case, feeling as if anchoring a suitcase in a hotel room he's going to be staying in for a while, as if the strange Hollywood street corner where he now finds himself will be his home for some time. He looks at the shiny guitar, the moonlight glinting off the polished black pick guard and a yellow Fender Thin pick pinned underneath the first four strings at the top of the worn neck.

Before Mark has a chance to extricate the guitar from the case, a large truck takes a right too sharply, gargantuan knobby tires riding up on the curb and over the shiny black case, squashing the contents in seconds. The guitar breaks like a balsa-wood airplane, as if in a single breath, and a sound of laughter hangs in the air as the truck, unscathed, continues on its way.